D1067629

SPI
EGE
L&G
RAU

# THE DEVIL IN SILVER

# THE DEVIL
# IN SILVER

—

A NOVEL

*Victor LaValle*

SPIEGEL & GRAU

NEW YORK

Published in the United States by Spiegel & Grau, an imprint of The Random House Publishing Group, a division of Random House, Inc., New York.

SPIEGEL & GRAU and Design is a registered trademark of Random House, Inc.

LIBRARY OF CONGRESS CATALOGING-IN-PUBLICATION DATA

LaValle, Victor D.
The devil in silver: a novel / Victor LaValle.
p. cm.
ISBN 978-1-4000-6986-6
eISBN 978-0-679-60486-0
1. Psychological fiction. I. Title.
PS3562.A8458D48 2012 813'.54—dc23 2011034970

Printed in the United States of America on acid-free paper

www.spiegelandgrau.com

2 4 6 8 9 7 5 3 1

First Edition

Book design by Christopher M. Zucker

*For Gloria Loomis,*
*who I love like family*

*The fear, the horror, that I had of madness before is already greatly softened. And although one continually hears shouts and terrible howls as though of the animals in a menagerie, despite this the people here know each other very well, and help each other when they suffer crises.*

—VINCENT VAN GOGH

# VOLUME 1

—

# INTAKE

# 1

THEY BROUGHT THE big man in on a winter night when the moon looked as hazy as the heart of an ice cube. It took three cops to wrestle and handcuff him. They threw him in their undercover cruiser and drove him to the New Hyde mental hospital. This was a mistake. They shouldn't have brought him there. But that wasn't going to save him.

When they reached the hospital, everyone got out. The big man refused to walk. The three cops mobbed around him, trying to intimidate, but to the big man they just looked like Donald Duck's nephews: Huey, Dewey, and Louie. A bunch of cartoons. It didn't help that they were dressed in street clothes instead of blue uniforms.

Dewey and Louie walked behind the big man and Huey stayed up front. The big man's hands were cuffed behind his back. Dewey and Louie pushed him like tugboats guiding a barge, one good shove and he floated toward the double doors of the building. The lobby was so empty, so quiet, that their footsteps echoed.

New Hyde looked like a low-rent motel. Bland floral-print cushions on the couches and chairs, the walls a lackluster lavender. There were no patients waiting around, no staff members on hand, not even an information desk. But Huey, the lead cop, knew where he was going. The big man frowned at the décor and the empty seats. He'd thought they were taking him to a lockup. What the hell kind of place was this? He got so confused, his feet stopped moving, so Dewey and Louie gave him another shove.

They reached the far end of the lobby and found a hallway. The cops turned right but the big man went left. It might've looked like an escape attempt except that the big man stopped himself after two paces. So confused he actually turned back to look for *them*. Huey, Dewey, and Louie were watching him now, to see what he would do. They were relaxed because they knew he could do nothing.

Huey raised his right hand. He wore a chunky silver diver's watch that looked expensive even under the hospital's terrible fluorescent lights. He beckoned and the big man stepped closer to them. It was quiet enough that the cops could hear him lick his dry lips.

Now this guy was big but let's put it in perspective. He wasn't Greek mythology–sized; wasn't tossing boulders at passing ships. He wasn't even *Green Mile*–sized; one of those human-giant types. He stood six foot three and weighed two hundred seventy-one pounds, and if that doesn't sound big to you, then you must be a professional wrestler. The dude was big but still recognizably human. Beatable. Three smaller men, like these cops, could take him down together. Just to get that straight.

The big man returned to his captors, without a word, and once again they all moved in the same direction.

The hallway was clear and empty, just lavender walls boxing in a thin runway of industrial carpet. But the big man could see that the runway ended at a big old door, heavy like you'd find on a bank vault. Unmovable. This was no Motel Six. His footsteps faltered. But this time the cops weren't going to let him wander off. Dewey yanked that big boy backward, by the handcuffs. His shoulders popped in their sockets and his face went hot with pain.

"*Now* he's scared," the lead cop said.

They reached the door. A small white button sat in the wall. Huey pressed it and kept his finger on the button. The buzzer played on the other side of the door and sounded like a duck's quack, as if Huey was throwing his cartoon voice.

The secure door featured a window the size of a cereal box. With his finger still steady on the buzzer, Huey peeked through it.

"Just break the glass," Dewey said.

He seemed to be joking, but he hadn't smiled.

Huey clonked the sturdy silver face of his diver's watch against the window. "You couldn't shatter this shit with a bullet."

The big man opened his mouth. He had plans to speak but found no words. He couldn't stop staring at that door. Not wood, not faux wood, fucking *iron*. Maybe. The damn thing had rivets in it, like it had been torn off a battleship. Bombproof; fireproof; probably airtight, too.

He finally found the words. "This place is locked up tighter than your Uncle Scrooge's vault."

Huey turned away from the door. His eyes brightened with joyful cruelty. "You think these jokes are going to save you, but they're only making things worse."

Louie said, "He's just trying to get one of us to hit him. So he'll have a lawsuit."

Dewey said, "We didn't hit him before, why would we start now?"

Huey said, "You're applying logic to a man who's not thinking logically."

"What the hell does that mean?" the big man asked.

"We think you might be a danger to yourself because of your mental condition," Louie added sarcastically.

The big man's body went rigid. "What mental condition?"

Dewey said, "You attacked three officers of the law."

"How was I supposed to know you were cops?!"

To be fair, the big man had a point. The three men wore plain clothes. Their shields, hanging around their necks on silver chains, were tucked under their different colored sweatshirts. But who cared? Here was one rule you could count on: You were never allowed to punch a cop. So forget about punching two of them, repeatedly, and trying hard to connect with the third. It didn't matter if they were in uniform, wearing plain clothes, or rocking a pair of pajamas.

But before he could get into a debate about the finer points of an entrapment defense, an eye appeared on the other side of the un-breakable window.

Well, a head at least, with a mess of grayish white hair, but the only part they could make out clearly was that eye. The outer ring of the pupil was blue but closer to the iris the color turned a light gray. Cataracts. The other eye was shut because the person squinted. Man or woman? Hard to say, the face was smooshed so tight against the pane. The clouded pupil swam left then right, as alien as a single-cell organism caught under the objective lens of a microscope. It surveyed the big man, and the three cops. It blinked.

The big man frowned at the person in the window. Dewey and Louie unconsciously stepped backward. Only Huey, still pressing the white button, didn't seem startled by the watchful eye. He smiled at the big man, more broadly than he had all night. Relishing what he would say next: "Welcome to New Hyde." He pointed to a plaque embedded in the wall right above the door: NEW HYDE HOSPITAL. FOUNDED IN 1953.

Dewey said, "When can we leave?"

Just then the eye seemed to slip away from the window and another face replaced it. This new person stood farther from the glass so they could make out more of him. A man. Brown-skinned. With puffy cheeks, a soft chin, and a nose as round as an old lightbulb. He wore glasses. A bushy mustache. And a scowl.

They could see his chest, the tie and jacket he wore. An ID card, sheathed in plastic, hung around his neck on a plastic cord.

The big man said, "He wears his ID on the *outside*, see? That's how people know what his job is."

The three cops sighed with exhaustion. Nine-twenty at night and all three were tired. They just had to hand the big man off and file their reports, then each could finally go home. (To their mother, Della Duck?)

The brown man looked out at Huey, and his gaze followed the cop's arm down as far as it could go, toward that finger, *still* mashing the white buzzer. The brown man then stared up at Huey again and brought one finger to his lips in a shushing motion. Huey pulled his hand away so quickly, you would've thought the buzzer had just burnt him.

The bolt lock in the door turned, clacking like the opening of a manual cash register's drawer. Then the door opened with surprising ease for its apparent weight. The doorway exhaled a stale, musty smell.

They could now see the brown man fully. His big round face fused right onto his round body. Imagine a wine cask, upright, wearing glasses. Not tall and not fat, just one solid oval.

And yet he must be someone with authority, if he had the keys to open this mighty door. Which was good enough for the big man, who said, "I'm innocent."

The brown man looked up at the big man. "I'm not a judge," he said. "I'm a doctor."

The doctor narrowed his eyes at Huey, who suddenly seemed bashful.

The doctor said, "I didn't expect to be seeing you again."

Huey nodded, looking away from the doctor. But then he seemed to feel the gaze of his partners, and he snapped out of his shame.

"This is legit. He jumped two of my guys."

The big man appealed to the doctor. "I thought they were meat-heads, not cops."

The doctor looked at the two cops on either side of the big man. He smiled, which made his bushy mustache rise slightly like a cater-pillar on the move. He stepped aside and invited them in. "My team is waiting down the hall," he said, locking the door behind them. "Second room."

The cops led the big man forward. Dewey and Louie holding his arms tighter than before. They didn't like the meathead line. Huey, with the watch, rested one hand on the big man's shoulder and to-gether the quartet followed the doctor.

The room looked like nearly any medium-sized conference room you'll ever find. The walls were an eggshell white, a dry-erase board hung on one of them with the faintest red squiggles half erased in an upper corner. A pull-down screen hung on another wall. In the middle of the room sat a faux-wood table, large enough to seat fifteen, but ringed by only fourteen faux-wood chairs with plastic padded backs. Another ring of cheaper, foldout chairs was placed against the walls. The working class of meeting spaces. All the people already in the room looked as tired as the décor.

Tonight the full intake team was in attendance: a social worker, an activity therapist, a registered nurse, three trainees, an orderly, a psychologist, and a psychiatrist (that was the brown man). These poor folks had been ready to leave at the end of their shift, but then the cops called ahead and said they were bringing in a new admission, so the doctor demanded that everyone stay. The team had been waiting on the big man for two hours. This was not a cheerful group. Ten people, plus three cops, plus the big man. It would be a crowded, grumpy room.

Before the guest of honor arrived, the men and women on staff had sat at the table with notepads and files spread out in front of them, doing busywork for other patients while they waited. Some used cell phones to make notes, or to text, or answer email. The orderly, at the far end of the table, watched a YouTube video on his phone and sagged in his chair.

When the cops brought the big man into the conference room, the staff members leaned backward, as if a strong wind had just burst in. The doctor pointed to a faux-wood chair that had been pulled back from the table about three feet.

"He can sit there."

Huey brought the big man to the chair and unlocked his handcuffs. He then took the big man's right wrist and handcuffed it to the arm of his chair. The staff watched quietly and without surprise. Only the orderly looked away from the scene, replaying the video on his phone.

Once the big man settled, the doctor walked to the open door of the conference room. Somewhere outside the room, farther down the hall, deeper into the unit, buzzing voices could be heard. A television playing too loudly. The doctor pushed the door shut, and the room became so quiet that everyone in it could hear, very faintly, the *bump-bump-bump* coming from the orderly's cell phone. The tinny thump of music playing over small speakers.

The doctor walked the length of the room and chucked the orderly on the shoulder as he passed to collect a folding chair for himself.

He set his plastic chair in front of the big man and sat down. He smiled and the bushy mustache rose.

"I'm Dr. Anand," he said. "And I want to welcome you to New Hyde Hospital. This building, this unit, is called *Northwest*."

The big man looked at the other staff members. A few of them managed a New York smile, which is to say a tight-lipped half-frown. The others watched him dispassionately.

Dr. Anand—like the big man, like most of the people in this room— had been raised in Queens, New York. The most ethnically diverse region not just in the United States, but on the entire planet; a distinction it's held for more than four decades. In Queens, you will find Korean kids who sound like black kids. Italians who sound like Puerto Ricans. Puerto Ricans who sound like Italians. Third-generation Irish who sound like old Jews. That's Queens. Not a melting pot, not even a tossed salad, but an all-you-can-eat, mix-and-match buffet.

Dr. Anand was no stranger to the buffet table, a man of Indian descent who sounded a little like a working-class guy from an Irish neighborhood. He dropped those r's when he wasn't being careful. He sounded like he was talking through his nose, not nasal but surprisingly high-pitched.

The big man wasn't concerned with ethnography just then. He hadn't said anything since crossing the threshold of the big doorway. That's because he wasn't actually there. Only his body filled his chair. The rest of him lagged a little behind. It was still back in the lobby.

The big man knew he should be listening to this doctor. If anyone could explain how soon he'd be released, it must be the barrel-chested Indian dude squatting on the dinky chair right in front of him. But he just couldn't do it. His ears felt stuffed up and his mind fuzzy. He wanted to turn and look over his shoulder, try to find that lagging part of him that would make sense of this moment. He didn't actually move, for fear the cops might pummel him.

"So why do you think you're here?" Dr. Anand asked.

The whole room waited for his answer.

Except for the orderly, who pulled out his cell phone again, muted the device, and tilted his head down toward the screen. He wore the glazed-eyed grin of a man watching something that showed skin.

In some strange way it was deeply reassuring for the big man to see this familiar incompetence. He asked, "If this is a hospital, how come you're not checking my blood pressure or something?"

Three of the staff members at the table recorded this question in their notes. The patient's responses during the intake meeting were vitally important. Not only what he said, but how he said it. Did he seem agitated? Morose? Distant? Combative?

(Combative.)

Dr. Anand nodded slowly. "This is a *psychiatric unit.* We'll take your vitals and all the rest, but first we want to get to know you."

Psychiatric unit.

Two words the big man could honestly say he'd never imagined hearing in a sentence pertaining to him. Open container in public, public urination, twice he'd been in fights where the police had been called. He'd never had trouble that caused him more than an overnight stay in a lockup. Most of the time they were just ticketable troubles. One time he hopped a turnstile—in a rush to get to Madison Square Garden for Mötley Crüe's Girls, Girls, Girls tour; the one where Tommy Lee did his drum solo in a rotating metal cage suspended over the crowd—the cops scolded him, gave him a ticket, but he still made the show. (And it was great.) That's the kind of trouble the big man had been in. But this?

Dr. Anand leaned forward. "Is this your first time?"

Huey answered for him. "As far as our records indicate."

Staff members noted this in their paperwork as well. All those pens writing on the tabletop at the same time sounded like a skateboard's wheels on pavement.

"I want my lawyer," the big man said. Wasn't that what he should tell them?

Huey squeezed the big man's shoulder. The silver diver's watch appeared in his eye line. The big man blinked rapidly, as if the cop was about to conk him. Instead the cop explained, "It don't work that way. You haven't been charged with a crime yet so an attorney isn't your right."

The big man pulled at the handcuff attached to his right wrist. The metal thunked against the armrest. Even the orderly looked up now. Inside New Hyde this orderly counted as the muscle, the one to hold a thrashing patient down, separate two patients fighting over a kid-sized carton of milk. (Nurses did the same, but that was not what they'd been hired to do.) Now the orderly sized up the big man, tried to figure if he could handle the new admit once the cops, and their handcuffs, were gone. The big guy wore cheap khaki slacks and a button-down light blue long-sleeved shirt. Both in sizes you only find in Big & Tall stores. The new guy had size to him, no doubt, but it was the kind of bulk you find on bouncers at shitty bars; the kind of guys who wear overcoats to hide the fact that their bellies are bigger than their chests. A big man but not a hard man. He'd probably do more damage falling on you than punching you. The orderly came in a smaller package, but was made of denser material. He'd been a wrestler in high school and stayed in good shape. He felt sure he could maintain control later on. Threat assessed, he looked back down to his screen.

The big man pleaded, "If I'm not charged with anything, then you can let me go."

Dr. Anand shook his head faintly. "Unfortunately, no. You're categorized as a 'temporary admit.' Which means the police leave you in our custody for seventy-two hours."

"Three days? I'm not staying here three more minutes!" He bucked in his chair. Dewey and Louie had their hands firm on his shoulders in an instant, keeping him seated.

Nearly the whole room scribbled notes after that. And instantly the big man saw that his usual headfirst routine wasn't going far. *Can't bulldoze through this.* He knew what he had to do then. Stay calm enough to convince them of the truth.

Dr. Anand leaned forward in his chair. "You'll be with us for three days. That's the law. It's Thursday night. You'll be with us until Monday morning. And in that time we'll evaluate your mental state."

"I can tell you my mental state."

Dr. Anand nodded. "Let's hear it."

"I'm pissed." Being mellow had never been one of his talents.

From the back of the room the orderly rose as high as he could in the chair. "Language, my man."

The big man took him in. "You watching music videos or porn on your phone?" he asked.

Dr. Anand looked at the orderly.

"It's off!" he said, as he fumbled with the device.

The big man grinned and said, "I'm going to call you Scotch Tape. 'Cause I see right through you."

The orderly said, "Look here. . . ."

But Dr. Anand caught the orderly's eye. If this was a contest of power, you can guess who won. The other staff members studied their laps, and silence choked the room. The orderly pulled his chair forward and set the cell phone on the tabletop, facedown.

A moment after that, the big man heard a snorting noise from the back of the room. It sounded like the radiators in his apartment. They would snort and hiss, too, at odd hours. Sometimes they produced heat, other times they just made a racket. The snorting stopped. The room didn't get any warmer.

Dr. Anand returned his attention to the big man. He didn't look angry, more like exhausted. "Why don't we just start with a *name*. What should we call you?"

Huey had the big man's wallet. He handed it to the doctor.

"You've got my name," the big man said. His brown pleather wallet, old and overstuffed, carrying more ATM receipts than currency, sat in the doctor's hand.

Dr. Anand shook the wallet. "I'm not asking what it says on your license. I'm asking what you like to be called."

Why was this doctor talking to him like that? Like he was a dunsky? He spoke so slow it seemed like another language. Being treated like a newborn only riled the reptile in the big man's brain.

He said, "You can call me 'Ed the Head.'"

Two staff members actually wrote this down, the others just looked confused.

Scotch Tape couldn't control himself. From the back of the room he shouted, "I am *not* calling you no 'Ed the Head!'"

The big man nodded. "Then call me . . . 'Blackie Lawless.'"

Scotch Tape leaned forward and snatched up his phone as if it was the big man's neck. "Watch it, white boy!"

Blackie Lawless was the lead singer of an eighties band called W.A.S.P., but the big man didn't have time to give Scotch Tape a history lesson in heavy metal.

The cops shifted in their stances. They wanted to be done. Dr. Anand seemed the least exasperated by all this. He opened the wallet, pulled out the driver's license, and read the name to himself.

"Your name's not Edward. And it sure isn't Blackie!"

The big man felt foolish. What was he really doing here? Giving a little shit to an orderly? Confusing a doctor? But to what end? He couldn't think past the anger caught in his throat. In other places, his taste for pointless conflict made him seem a bit wild, lippy, a guy who wouldn't back down. He liked that. But that's not how they'd see it in a psychiatric unit. These people at New Hyde were *evaluating* him. He had to remember that.

*Just breathe. Be calm. Speak to the doctor for real.*

"Pepper," the big man said in a subdued voice. "Everyone calls me Pepper."

"Why do they call you Pepper?" Dr. Anand asked.

"Because I'm spicy." He couldn't help it, the words just came out. Now he looked at the doctor to see if this would earn a demerit, too. But Dr. Anand didn't seem bothered.

The snorting began again. This time it seemed closer, no longer playing in the back of the room. It came from under the conference table. And it no longer sounded like a radiator. More like a living thing, but not human. A bull. The snorting grew louder. Pepper watched the table. He felt confused but refused to show it. What could he say that wouldn't make him look like a grade-A lunatic? Then, once again, the sound abruptly cut out.

Dr. Anand put the license back into the wallet and balanced it on Pepper's thigh. "Thank you for telling me."

"I get to keep that?"

"This isn't prison," Dr. Anand said. "You have rights."

"Except the right to walk out of here tonight," Pepper said.

Dr. Anand nodded. "Except that one."

The doctor turned in his chair again and spoke to the staff, but stared directly at the orderly. "Let's all remember Pepper's name."

Scotch Tape wanted to howl but he also wanted to avoid getting written up again. Dr. Anand would probably already make a little note about the business with the phone. And it was 2011. If there was ever a year to be cavalier about employment, well, this sure wasn't it. So Scotch Tape nodded and said, "Pepper."

The snort came for a third time. It was even closer now. Immediately to his right. As if the animal had crept right up to his ear. Even worse, there was a smell. Musky and warm, like old blood. It made his throat close, and he wanted to wretch. The hospital's staff members sat around the conference table taking notes, or watching him. Not one of them seemed to notice anything. How could they not smell that stink?

Pepper cut his gaze to the right, but was almost afraid to do it. What would be worse? Seeing a snorting, stinking beast there or nothing at all? All he found was one of the cops. Dewey. There was something strange about the cop's face, though. His face was flushed. His nostrils flared. His stance was tense. Surreptitiously he, too, was peeking to his right. The snort came again. Dewey heard it! Had to be. Pepper almost cheered with relief. Then Dewey caught Pepper looking at him. Instantly he lost his fearful expression. He looked straight ahead, doing his best impression of tranquility. The snorting faded, along with the smell.

Dr. Anand said, "I think we're ready to transfer him, officially."

The cops undid Pepper's handcuff, and Dr. Anand filled out some forms right there in front of everyone. Pepper tried to catch Dewey's eye.

"You . . ." Pepper began.

"I didn't hear *nothing*," Dewey said, cutting him off.

But when Dr. Anand opened the door, Dewey practically stampeded to get out first. The other two cops and some of the staff watched him with quizzical expressions. Then the doctor escorted

Huey and Louie out the door. When they'd all left the room, the staff didn't even look at Pepper. They pulled out their cell phones and clicked or tapped or viewed or listened to messages.

Then Dr. Anand returned and the phones were set facedown on the table, while the nurse walked over to take Pepper's belt and the laces from his work boots. Pepper let her have all three items because he couldn't quite believe the police had actually left him here.

Dr. Anand took the same plastic seat in front of Pepper. "Now what we want you to do is tell us a little about your family. Treat this like a celebrity interview. We're the paparazzi and we want to know all about you."

Scotch Tape chided him. "Act like you're on *TMZ!*"

Pepper wondered if that paparazzi pitch worked on other people. Maybe younger ones. It sure didn't mean much to him. But he talked about himself anyway. He talked so he wouldn't hear the snorting. His shoulders remained so tense they would be a little sore in the morning.

He told them about his parents, Maureen and Raymond, who ran a video store in Elmhurst. Raymond died not long after VHS tapes did, and Maureen sold the business and lived alone for eight years. She stayed in Maryland with Pepper's brother, Ralph, now. Ralph had a wife and son, and Maureen took care of the kid so the parents could work. Pepper couldn't remember his nephew's name just then and felt bad about that. Pepper graduated from John Bowne High School in Flushing and spent one semester at Queens College. His brother, Ralph, had the business sense of their father and owned a Wendy's in Gaithersburg. Pepper had inherited his mother's work ethic, a facility for the regular grind; she was the one who'd actually kept the family's video store running day to day. Pepper figured that if he told them as much as he could they might realize the truth: He didn't belong in here. He only didn't tell them where he worked, figuring they might actually call. He couldn't afford to be fired again.

"And what about relationships?" Dr. Anand asked. "Not with your family. Personal ones."

"There's a woman in my building," Pepper admitted.

"And what's her name?" the doctor asked.

"Mari."

"And where is Mari now?"

"She's probably in her apartment, with her daughter. Isabelle."

"Is Mari your girlfriend?"

The word sounded so silly in Dr. Anand's mouth. And even sillier applied to Pepper, a man of forty-two. "It's early still," he said.

What he didn't add was that Mari was actually the reason he was in here. It sounds a little old-fashioned, but he'd been trying to protect her honor when it all went so badly so fast. She didn't even know where the cops had taken him. He wanted to let her know where he was and even more, he wanted to hear that she was okay. And how was he supposed to be of any good to her trapped in here? Pepper didn't say all this out loud. They'd ask him what he did, and why it all went badly, and the story would only make him seem even rowdier.

Never mind, though. Dr. Anand had plenty of other questions.

But the more Pepper told them the less he seemed to matter. He might've been relating the inventory of the truck from yesterday's job. Dr. Anand and his staff weren't listening, only gathering the necessary information to refine his classification. After forty-five minutes he was a case history; a new admit awaiting diagnosis; a subject.

After an hour Pepper was, officially at least, a mental patient.

# 2

WITH PEPPER'S INTAKE meeting finished, Dr. Anand walked him out of the conference room and back into the hall. Pepper expected some ceremonious next step, but the doctor just pressed him back against the hallway wall, as if he was about to use a pencil to mark Pepper's height.

"Stay here," Dr. Anand said, already turning away. "A nurse will be by quickly. She'll take you to your room."

And just like that, the doctor returned to the conference room and shut the door. Pepper felt like a fridge left out on the sidewalk.

The walls in this hallway were eggshell white like those in the conference room. The floors were cheap beige linoleum tiles. On the wall, right beside him, at shoulder level, hung a framed landscape painting. There was another across the hall. An empty beach by his shoulder; a path through empty woods across the way. Soothing images, by reputation. In truth, Pepper felt more comfortable around apartment buildings and even on subway platforms—maybe not beautiful, but his natural habitat. Not just his, but likely that of nearly every damn person associated with this hospital, from the staff to the patients to the cops who'd brought him in. So why decorate the walls with someone else's dream of peace? Maybe they were just feeding that most natural human appetite, the hunger for *somewhere else*. A yearning Pepper could relate to just then.

No nurse appeared, and for fifteen minutes Pepper just repeated the same words to himself: *seventy-two hours. Seventy-two hours. You can stand anything for seventy-two hours.*

The loud voices playing from a TV somewhere down the hall, deeper inside the unit, had changed to loud explosions. Maybe someone had switched the channel, or the show had come to a moment when the world starts blowing up. Pepper knew it was just a television show, but the sounds seemed to grow as they traveled from wherever the TV sat to where Pepper still stood in the long, empty hall of closed doors. The howl of human beings, the victims of those crashing sounds, played louder and louder. Like the people themselves were about to come flooding into view. Maybe not even people, but people's parts. A wave of blood. Dismembered limbs breaking the surface of that wave like sharks' fins.

Pepper knew this couldn't happen, but his chest felt tight.

He looked to his right and focused on that secure ward door. What if Dr. Anand hadn't locked it behind the cops? What if all Pepper had to do was give a little push?

*Seventy-two hours. Seventy-two hours.*

He couldn't stand this for that long. He couldn't even make it twenty minutes before he tried to escape. Pepper lurched toward the big door.

He grabbed the handle and pushed lightly. But of course the door didn't open. He pushed harder. He tried to turn the knob. It didn't shimmy. He let go of the handle now and pressed both his meaty hands against the door and leaned into it. He set his broad, laceless boots down flatly, repositioned his large hands, and now he powered against that door, straining like a bull. But the damn door stayed secure.

Finally he pressed his face to the shatterproof window. There were little lines embedded in the plastic, like chicken wire. He'd been on the other side less than two hours ago. Two hours before that, he'd been on the other side of Queens! He'd been trying to help Mari by having words with her ex-husband, a man who wouldn't leave Mari be. And yet here Pepper was, locked away. He pressed his face to the window, fucking confused. There was nobody on the other side. He closed his eyes.

"Better not let them see you doing that."

Pepper opened his eyes, expecting—not hoping, but expecting—to find himself on the E train, having fallen asleep and only now waking to learn he'd dreamed up New Hyde Hospital. Instead he found himself still staring through the plastic window.

"If you understand English, then step away from the door," the voice continued.

But Pepper didn't move fast enough. Before he could stand up, stand back, and turn around, he felt fingers grip his wrist.

After having three cops wrestle him to the ground in a high-school parking lot, then being handcuffed to a chair, Pepper really wasn't in the mood to get hemmed up one more time. No more hands on him tonight. He turned and *yoked* the person grabbing him. He actually pulled off a pretty sophisticated move, mostly through momentum and a great weight advantage. He yanked his wrist free from the person's grip, turned and enveloped the body behind him, and lifted it into the air.

When it was over, Pepper had a seventy-six-year-old woman in a bear hug.

And before he could apologize, or loosen his grip, or set her back down on her feet, what did the old woman do?

She kissed him right on the mouth.

He dropped her and she landed harder on one foot than the other, yipping like a dog whose tail has been caught.

Now Pepper bent to cradle her on instinct, in case she'd been badly injured. But the old woman threw her arms out to stop him.

"You like it a little too rough for me," she said.

The door of the conference room finally opened and Dr. Anand's round head peeked out. He watched them both for a moment. Pepper and the old woman turned their attention to him.

"I see you've met Dorry," the doctor said. "She's our unofficial ambassador."

"Hello, Captain." She saluted him, any hint of leg pain hidden.

Dr. Anand tipped his head toward her slightly, then looked back down the hall, deeper into the unit, toward the TV sounds.

"Miss Chris is late again," Dr. Anand said.

Dorry patted her chest. "She deputized me."

She looked up at Pepper. "I can take him to his room."

She jabbed Pepper in the belly. The new admit looked comically large next to Dorry, like a sheepdog beside a shih tzu.

Dr. Anand looked down the hallway once more, but Miss Chris made no appearance. He said, "Take him to his room, Dorry, but don't go *in* his room."

Dorry poked Pepper's belly again.

"Dr. Anand thinks I'm a raging *slut*," she said.

Dr. Anand stepped all the way into the hallway and waved his arms as if clearing smoke. "I never said that, Dorry! Now come on."

Pepper couldn't help it, he laughed. The old woman made him feel at ease. The blush burning across Dr. Anand's brown face also helped. Pepper decided to join in the banter. He set one hand on Dorry's shoulder and said, "Maybe me and her will just run away together."

Dorry quickly slipped away from Pepper's hand as Dr. Anand stepped toward them with surprising quickness. "There is *no* intimacy allowed between patients on the unit. Do you understand?"

Pepper wanted to point out how ridiculous the warning was. What they were just doing counted as intimacy, too. But he knew, from past experience, no one likes a nitpicker. Especially not one who looked like him. Such a small act as begging to differ, from such a large man, tended to make people particularly angry. In general, people thought he took up too much room on the subway and often sighed or grunted to let him know. The only benefit to his great mass was that he could lift heavy things. He'd been a professional mover for eleven years.

As Dr. Anand continued to glare, Pepper stepped back an arm's length from the old woman. Then he stuck his arm out and wiggled his fingers to show the distance. The playful moment over, Pepper again felt the gravity of this night—*I'm locked in a mental hospital*—as dead weight in his legs.

Dr. Anand nodded at Dorry. "He's in five." The doctor reentered the conference room and shut the door behind him with a click.

The old woman was right beside Pepper, pinching the back of his left hand. "I thought you were going to tell him about how you kissed me next."

"*Me?*"

"Don't insult a lady."

Dorry's hunched back only made her look smaller than she already was. She had wiry white hair that clearly hadn't been combed in days. It shot from her scalp in fifteen unflattering directions, like a feral child's. Her faded blue nightdress came down to her shins. On her dry, bony feet were faded blue slipper-socks. She wore gigantic glasses, big plastic Medicare frames. Their lenses so thick they looked slathered with Vaseline. Even if you didn't know this woman was crazy, you'd think she was crazy.

Pepper said, "I'm sorry for grabbing you. I didn't know you were a woman."

Dorry frowned. "What the hell kind of apology is that?"

Pepper gripped his hands together. "I didn't mean it like that! I'm sorry, that's all. All right?"

"Let's put the past behind us," she said. "I always greet the new admits. You should see a friendly face first."

Then Pepper pointed one finger at her eye, though not too close.

"That was you!" he said. He realized she really *had* been the first person he'd seen.

Dorry took off her glasses and the resemblance became exact. She winked at him.

"I'm always getting recognized by my fans."

Pepper pantomimed applause. He didn't actually clap because he didn't want to give Dr. Anand another reason to step into the hall.

Dorry reached out and wrapped her left arm around Pepper's right elbow. She looked up at him over the tops of her glasses. From here he could see the off-color band around her iris. She clearly wasn't blind, but maybe blindness wasn't too far off.

He was surprised to feel grateful for the tenderness in the touch.

"Let me give you the tour," she said.

———

"They call this building Northwest," Dorry began. "That's just because it's located in the northwest corner of New Hyde Hospital's grounds. So much for creativity, right? Anyway, there's three buildings at the center of the hospital campus and that's the heart of the operation. Emergency room, surgery, children's unit, geriatrics, ICU, almost everything is in those three buildings. Everything but us, really. You've got those three buildings, then the main parking lot. A couple hundred parking spaces. Then, you've got us crazybirds, tucked into the northwest corner. Some people say we've been *exiled* out here, but I prefer to think our building is *exclusive*. You've got to have a special invite to enter Northwest. They're called commitment papers! I'm just kidding.

"So Northwest is the psychiatric unit. No other kinds of patients. It used to be an ophthalmology ward but that was over fifty years ago. Before *I* even got here, and that's saying something. Fifty years ago they made Northwest a psychiatric unit and moved all the old ophthalmology equipment up to the second floor. It's just a big attic. The layout of the second floor is exactly the same as the first, but none of us has any business up there.

"Think of the unit as a wagon wheel. That's the easiest way to picture it in your mind. There's one roundish room in the middle of Northwest and that's where you'll find the staff. There's a big old desk unit in there called the nurses' station. All roads lead there. It's the hub of this wagon wheel.

"Then you've got five hallways. They're like the spokes, going to and from the nurses' station. Like this hallway here, it's the first one any new patient enters, so it's called Northwest One. Northwest One has all the conference rooms." She slapped one of the closed doors. "This is where you'll have group sessions, mornings and afternoons. But don't think of these as classrooms because then you'll start thinking of Northwest like it's a school, with schedules and activities and lots of structured time. But it doesn't work like that! You can wander, watch television, or lie down in your room. That's how people spend most of their day, every day, on the unit."

Pepper grabbed the handle of a closed door and tested it.

"Come on. Stop jiggling that. The only way to open these conference-room doors is with a set of keys. And only staff members carry those. Keep moving."

She yanked on Pepper's arm and he followed her.

"Now here we are. The hub. And that's the nurses' station. Right in the center. Ugly isn't it? And it's not even real wood. Or at least it's not *good* wood. It looks kind of like a Chinese food–restaurant counter, doesn't it? I've seen enough of those!

"I guess the biggest difference between those Chinese-food places and the nurses' station is that this one doesn't have those bulletproof windows separating the workers and customers. And there's no Chinese people working back there, either. Mostly it's blacks. Usually the blacks are on the *customer* side, am I right? Chicken wings and French fries! They love that chicken-wings-and-French-fries combo. And extra hot sauce, please! I'm just kidding. They never say 'please.'

"So you can see the five hallways from here. That's Northwest. And while you're in here, that's pretty much the whole world. You'll see. Northwest One, Two, Three, Five."

"What about Four?"

Dorry stopped moving. Almost seemed to stop breathing. "Forget about Northwest Four, you understand me? You don't go *near* Northwest Four."

"You going to tell me what's over there, or can I guess?" He couldn't take her seriously.

"That's where the buffalo roam," she said absently. Dorry's eyes lost focus, a thousand-yard stare.

Pepper stifled a grin. "Ooooooh-kay."

"Do I look like I'm joking with you?" she asked.

*You look bonkers*, is what Pepper wanted to tell her. Instead he said, "No, ma'am."

Just as suddenly, Dorry's glare disappeared. She smiled as if they hadn't just had this little confrontation. She continued the tour.

"Each hall has its own purpose. Northwest Two is for the men. All male patients sleep in rooms on Northwest Two. All female patients are in Northwest Three. They're *serious* about that. No slipping past them. I'm the only exception. I've been here long enough so they trust me. And I'm so old they can't imagine I'm going to screw anybody. Boy, are they wrong. Kidding!

"Now here you are. Northwest Two, room five. I can open the door for you but I can't step in. Look! They've put fresh sheets and a pillowcase at the foot of your bed. And one of their finest pillows. Hah! The damn things are thinner than a throat lozenge, but don't bother asking for a second one. They'll write that you're a 'narcissist' in your file. I remember the patient who was in that bed before you. He was discharged two weeks ago. Or is he dead? I forget.

"Anyway, that's the tour. Gratuities aren't mandatory, but they are appreciated!"

# 3

HE DID NOT give her a tip.

Dorry didn't actually wait around to see if he would. She wrapped up her talk and left Pepper standing in the threshold of his new room. He watched her waddle off, hunched and surprisingly quick, and even when he turned away he could hear her padding down the hall-way. From a distance—Northwest 4? Northwest 5?—Pepper still heard the television. Someone must've switched to another station, no more explosions or human howls, just the electronic snap of some teenage R&B number. Pepper didn't recognize the song, but he knew the style because at least one or two of the guys on his moving crews were kids. At some point during a six- or seven-hour job, you could count on one of them to start playing loud music out of his phone. Pepper wished he had his phone now, but they'd confiscated it with his belt and laces.

He stepped backward into the room and shut the door. The sounds of the television, Dorry's footsteps, the general buzz of the hospital unit, were muted and now he was alone. He flipped on the light.

This room had the same eggshell-white walls as in the hallways. It was about the size of the living room in his Jackson Heights apart-ment. There were two beds in here. The bed frames, industrial metal, twin-sized, were both unmade. But where Pepper's had the sheets folded neatly at the foot of his mattress, the other's sheets were tossed like a wind-ravaged sea.

Pepper had a roommate.

Besides the beds, there wasn't much furniture. A pair of cheap, narrow dressers backed up against two opposing walls. They came up as high as Pepper's shoulders. One looked unused, the dresser top bare, while the other, next to the messy bed, had eight soda cans sitting on it, stacks of newspapers, and a dozen old pens in a plastic cup, each pen cap chewed until it was warped.

Pepper reached down to the handle of the closed door, looking for a lock he could turn. But the only way this room would lock was with a key.

Pepper walked to the bare dresser, crossing the linoleum tiles. He opened each dresser drawer but found nothing inside. He sat on his bed. The mattress was long enough to accommodate him if he didn't stretch out. If he did, his ankles and feet would hang over the end. A metal bed in a mental hospital. Now that's some reality few folks are prepared to face. Pepper let go of the frame.

*Do something. Do something.*

He picked up the sheets at the foot of the bed and, to his own surprise, made the bed. It was something to do. The only thing he could think of. The sheets were whiter than the walls, crisp but far from plush. He snapped the fitted sheet on, pulling each corner tight. He slipped his thin pillow into its case. As he worked he heard Dorry's patter in his head, but kept trying to forget it. He didn't want to remember the layout of Northwest. Didn't want to remember where Northwest was situated on New Hyde Hospital's grounds. He didn't want to wonder if the last patient in this room—in this bed!—was discharged or . . . not.

Eventually he finished making his bed. What could he do to distract himself next? His bed sat flush against one of the long walls in the rectangular room. Above his bed were two tall windows. A pair of thin, yellowed curtains, were drawn back.

*Windows.*

Pepper immediately flashed back to the only thing he knew about mental institutions: the film version of *One Flew Over the Cuckoo's*

*Nest.* After Jack Nicholson got lobotomized then smothered by the Indian, hadn't Big Chief used a piece of machinery to bash open one of the windows and go running off into the gray dawn? Couldn't Pepper do the same?

He climbed onto the bed he'd just made, and left some big old boot prints right on that white top sheet, but so what? He was inspired. When he stepped on the bed the springs yelped. He took a second step and the frame itself groaned. He leaned against the windows and wondered if he could use this bed frame as a battering ram.

But then he saw the same white chicken wire woven into the window, and he recognized it as the same unbreakable plastic outfitting that small window in the ward door. He rapped on the surface, as if it was a door that might creak open. But that didn't happen, of course. He would've bashed at the windows with his fists, his elbows, but what would be the point? That cop had been right; you couldn't get through this shit with a bullet. Jack Nicholson and the Big Chief had lived in more breakable times.

When Pepper pulled his face back from the window the chicken wire fell out of focus and the outside world became clearer. Nighttime in New Hyde. A lawn ran just below Pepper's window, cut so low it was almost bald. It ran about fifty yards until it reached a chain-link fence that surrounded the whole New Hyde campus. The fence was topped with two rows of barbed wire. Pepper could see it from here, like unpolished silver in the moonlight. How bad would that stuff cut him, if he got out and tried to climb?

With the door shut, the television silenced, Pepper could hear the sounds of traffic running along Union Turnpike, the largest roadway nearby. From this distance, the engines rumbled as one, sounding like a rushing river. Only some bleating car horns reminded him he was listening to a street. That people were in their cars, going elsewhere.

Pepper stepped back from the window, still on the bed. The reflection he now saw wasn't his face, just a blurred circle. It looked like an enormous thumb had been pressed to the window from the other side. His blurry head the thumb pad.

He stepped down off the bed and one of his boots slipped off his foot. Without laces they weren't too secure. He kicked off the other one. It tumbled across the floor and stopped by the door. One tan steel-toed Belleville boot, size 14.5.

Pepper noticed another door. He opened it and found the tight, windowless bathroom. He stepped inside and shut the door behind him, standing in the dark without bothering to turn on the light. Eventually his eyes adjusted. He took in the stand-up shower stall to his right and sink to his left. A soap dispenser hung next to the sink, attached to the wall, like the kind you'd find in any fast-food restaurant's bathroom. He fumbled for the cold-water knob at the sink and then listened to the water flow. The hiss of the water leaving the tap sounded like steam leaking out of those radiators in his apartment on Northern Boulevard. His home.

He looked at what he thought was the mirror above the sink, but couldn't find his reflection there. Just another blurry shape.

He slapped at the walls, searching for the light switch now. He needed to see himself. To prove he was still there. But when he found the light, he saw the problem. No mirror above the sink, just a buffed metal pane. He stood before the semi-reflective surface with dismay. That was him? An elongated pink *smudge*? Vaguely humanoid. Hardly him. But when he tilted his head, that thing tilted its head, too.

He smiled and the thing sprouted fangs.

He finally turned off the tap but still thought he heard rushing water in his ears.

Pepper moved to the toilet seat and closed the lid. He sat down and slumped to his right, resting his face against the cool wall. That felt nice. Even comforting. Maybe he'd stay here for a while, until he could figure out a plan.

But soon enough he'd slid off the toilet and went down on his knees to pray. He'd been a churchgoing boy once, long ago, though he couldn't even remember more than a few words of the Lord's Prayer. He did remember shutting his eyes at prayer time and that always made the world slow down. He closed them now. Eyes closed, head slightly bowed, he breathed. His mind slowed.

He'd fucked up tonight. The cops had brought him here without warning. He hadn't expected that, nor being reduced to this. Two hours in New Hyde Hospital, 120 minutes inside Northwest, and he'd become a guy who prays on the floor, in the dark. As close to panicking as he'd come as a grown man. Two hours was all it took to capsize him.

But that was okay. Happened to nearly everyone sometimes. The fear just gets you. And in a place like this? A mental hospital? Anyone would feel thrown upside down. Even someone who belonged here. No need to feel crushed. He'd been scared, confused, but the feeling was passing. He just needed to control himself. He'd made the bed, and it was late enough, probably right around eleven o'clock.

He got off his knees, returned to the bedroom, and turned off the lights. Only moonlight lit the room, coming in through the shatter-proof plastic windows. He pulled the thin curtains shut. He was out of ideas, but only for tonight. He could get a little self-control going tomorrow. Stay so calm and gentle they'd release him by Saturday. A little rest was what he needed. He lay flat on his back and let his feet dangle off the edge.

Did they give you one free phone call in mental hospitals, like in jail? That was all he needed to start correcting things.

Tomorrow he'd call Mari.


Around a quarter to four in the morning, Pepper opened his eyes.

He might've been a workingman but he wasn't this early a riser. Not naturally. But there he found himself, back to the room, facing the two large windows above his head, seeing the deep night fade into a faint purple dawn through the thin curtains.

Awake. Why?

Because somebody was jabbing him in the small of his back.

As groggy as Pepper was, he remembered the incident from seven hours earlier, when he'd yoked that old woman. He couldn't afford to risk something like that again. He wouldn't be completely surprised if Dorry had a way of sneaking in here. Maybe she was after that tip.

Maybe she had more tour-guide information to give. He turned his head slowly, expecting to see the old woman.

Instead he found a man's face. So close to his own that Pepper could smell the man's turkey dinner. A broad, round face. Smooth skin, and practically bald. Brown complexion, darker than Dr. Anand's. Not an Indian guy, but a black guy. There was no other way to put this: the guy's head looked like a malt ball.

Poking Pepper again, the guy said, "Let me get a quarter."

He had a wide, flat face and a wide, flat nose and tiny little eyes set deep into his head. He was a grown-up but you could imagine what he'd looked like as a child. Almost exactly like now.

Pepper could feel this guy's *nail* digging into him. He was more than aggravated by this. He was mildly disgusted.

"Come on, Joe," the guy said. He spoke with an accent, the English slightly clipped, which didn't really tell Pepper much. He might be from another country, but in this borough there were probably five hundred countries to choose from.

"You're my fucking roommate." Pepper didn't state this as a question. More like someone who's just realized he'd stepped in dog shit. He shut his eyes, turned his head back toward the windows, and pretended to fall back asleep. Maybe his roommate would give up. But this malt ball–headed bastard just moved his finger higher. Poking Pepper in the shoulder. Harder. Pepper turned to look at him.

"Let me get a quarter," the man repeated.

This guy's round face looked wet with desperation. His cheeks, his chin were shiny and moist, as if he'd been sweating. Or crying. Or both. He began stabbing at the back of Pepper's exposed neck with a nail as thick as the edge of a flathead screwdriver.

It was all too much, finally.

Pepper rolled onto his back, to protect his neck, and so he could move on this man. But when he tried to pull an arm free from beneath the covers he found he couldn't quite do it. Pepper had wrapped himself up in his own sheets, his head sticking out one end of the wrap, his feet dangling from the other.

The guy hunched over him with a puzzled look. He scanned the length of the bed, saw the trap Pepper had sprung on himself, and dropped his poking finger. He crab-walked backward two steps just to take this ridiculous sight in.

"You look like an enchilada," he said quietly. "How you going to give me a quarter now?"

Pepper said, "I wasn't going to give you any damn money. I was going to smack you in the head."

The man nodded, the top of his round head catching the dawn light.

"Well, you won't be doing that, either."

Pepper shimmied in the tight sheet.

"Just give me a minute," Pepper said.

And the man did. He crouched and watched Pepper move. When the minute was up, very little had changed. "Now what?" asked Pepper's roommate.

Pepper lay there, still tangled, but refused to ask this guy for help. Then he'd have to give the man a quarter. He'd rather lie here and starve himself loose.

The roommate leaned forward. "There's an important person I'm trying to reach." He looked over his shoulder, at the door to their room. "A man in the *government*."

Pepper let out a long, slow sigh. Of course. Weren't crazy people always trying to contact someone important? A man in the government. The Queen of Mars. The Knights Templar.

Pepper laughed to himself and relaxed and the sheets seemed to slip right off him.

"Patients are allowed to make phone calls?" Pepper asked.

"But it's not free, Joe. You have to pay for the call."

"That's why you want a quarter."

"Yes."

"In the middle of the night."

The man shook his head. "I want a quarter all the time."

Okay then. Bonkers or not, the man had helped Pepper a little bit. Patients could make phone calls. Pepper had money—bills in his wallet and coins in his pocket. He wouldn't call Mari this early, but it was good knowing that he could. He reached down into his pocket and felt the handful of coins waiting there, jingling a little.

"That's it," the man whispered. "Yes, yes, I hear the good news."

Pepper found the coin he wanted to give, held out his hand, his fingers closed around the quarter. The man grinned.

As soon as Pepper released his fingers, his roommate snatched the quarter out of the air and ran from the room without shutting the door.

Pepper yelled, "And stop calling me Joe!"

But the guy was already gone. The lights in the hall filled the room like the headlights of a double-decker bus.

Pepper had to get up. He shivered in the slight chill of the air-conditioned room, cursed as he walked to the door and shut it, and bumped his shin on the metal frame of his bed when he reached it again. He flopped into his bed and, looking across the room at his roommate's, wondered if the guy ever even slept there. Maybe he collected his alms around Northwest all night. Dorry had warned him that life in Northwest would be unstructured, but he would've thought the staff at least discouraged panhandling.

As the sun began rising on Friday morning, Pepper tried to fall back to sleep.

No luck. The door to his room blew open. Louder than an explosive charge. His roommate turned on the overhead lights, soaking their room with queasy yellow light.

"It's a *Canadian* quarter!" he shouted.

Pepper lay still, faking the steady breathing of deep sleep. But underneath the covers he nearly laughed as he listened to his roommate pacing. Would the man escalate things? Would Pepper have to fight? That sure wouldn't help to get him out of this place any sooner. Just that quickly, Pepper worried about what his roommate might do.

But the poking never resumed. The roommate finally turned out the light and went to bed.

From beneath his blanket, the guy whispered, "That's cold, *Joe*. Real cold."

Pepper slept until seven a.m.

# 4

PEPPER WOKE UP with the sun. He hadn't forgotten where he was, but even in here, with an ache in his neck from the thin pillow, having slept in his street clothes, and even through sheets of shatterproof plastic, the sunlight sure felt pleasant. He practically purred in his bed, a great cat rousing.

But who the hell had drawn the curtains? Pepper thought of his roommate. He pictured himself sleeping deep and that guy standing over him long enough to tug the curtains. It just made him feel so vulnerable.

"Wake up! Wake up!" a woman's voice sang. It wasn't his roommate looming at his bedside, and not Dorry, either. A different older woman moved to the head of his bed and snatched his top sheet off. Didn't even pause to check if Pepper had his pants on or off. (Thankfully, for all involved, they were still on.)

"I don't plan to run a bath for you," she explained tersely. She had a Caribbean accent. "It's seven in the morning. Wake up! And get out of your bed."

The woman's actions screamed "Staff Member" but her wardrobe cooed "Casual Grandma." A beige blanket sweater and shapeless jeans, comfortable black sneakers, and hair cut short. She had a batch of keys hanging from a plastic cord around her wrist. They jangled as she tugged the top sheet one more time, all the way off him.

"You'll make your bed when I leave, hear?"

Those keys, that tone, the direct but disinterested stare, that's how Pepper knew she was an employee and not a patient.

And Pepper nodded at her as he sat up. He almost said, *Yes, ma'am.*

"Now you take this," the woman said. She opened a clenched hand. Two pills sat in her palm: a light green pill and a little white gelcap.

He looked at them with horror. As if she'd offered him poisoned Flavor Aid.

*Remember who you are!* he thought.

Pepper unfurled himself and stood, knowing he was a big old banner of a man. People tended to crane their necks and read the sign: STEP BACK.

But not this time.

The woman didn't move. The pills in her palm didn't even tremble as his body took up so much space. She simply tilted her head back and cut her eyes at him. She was old but her face still remarkably smooth. She had that power. You could see it in the way her lips drew down now, her lower jaw jutting out like the Don Corleone of the West Indies. Her eyes went from mildly cloudy to suddenly, strikingly clear.

"You going to give Miss Chris the business, heh? Trust me, you a big man but a small potato! And if I have to leave here and get a doctor, I promise you I coming back to make *mash* potato."

What was it about that accent and that set of the chin? That aura of threat and premonition? Miss Chris had struck fear into badder men than Pepper, he felt sure of that.

What was Pepper going to do anyway? He'd had a grandmother of his own. Different color, different country of origin, different personality, but just as fearsome. Nearly everyone could be undone by an old woman's displeasure.

Miss Chris held her hand above her head, so the pills hovered just below Pepper's chin. "I won't make another request."

Pepper plucked both pills and Miss Chris dropped her arm.

"At least tell me what these are," he said.

"I'm your psychiatrist or your nurse? Because if I'm you're psychiatrist I'm due a better paycheck."

The light green pill was Haldol. The white gelcap was lithium. Miss Chris actually knew this, but was too vexed by the big man's attitude to explain.

Pepper said, "I need to make a phone call."

Miss Chris raised her eyebrows. "That's a phone in your hand or two pills? Deal with what's in front of you first. Then if you want to make a phone call, you go make your phone call. I'm here to dial the numbers for you? No! No!"

Miss Chris continued talking but she wasn't actually addressing Pepper, so he stopped listening. He brought his lips down to his hand and slurped up both pills. They sat on his tongue. His mouth hung open as if the pills were scalding hot.

"I'm a Verizon employee?" Miss Chris continued. "Put your eyes to my ID and it will tell you different."

He wasn't getting past Miss Chris, out of this room, toward that phone call, if he didn't swallow the pills.

Pepper finally closed his mouth and gulped. He felt the dry taste of the pills at the back of his tongue as Miss Chris wound down her rant.


Once Miss Chris had seen him swallow the meds, her job was done. She turned and left the room without even a wave.

Pepper didn't want to run out right after her. He didn't want to follow behind her down the hall. So he went into the bathroom where he found two sets of towels and washcloths on a rack by the shower. One set looked used, the other set clean. Pepper undressed and took a warm shower. There was a soap dispenser on the wall here, just like the one by the sink. Pepper squeezed out a few dollops of Pepto-Bismol-pink soap. He tried to wash off the moment with Miss Chris. He stood under the showerhead with his eyes closed and wondered what effect those two little pills would have. They'd been so small.

He dried off, dressed again, and left his room.

The hallway gave the feeling of a community college. Institutional.

Low-budget. But now he noticed the wooden railing running along-side either wall. It ran about waist height. Unbalanced patients could cling to these wooden rails and pull themselves down any hall.

Parallel to the railing hung a strip of wallpaper, like trim just be-neath the ceiling. A series of five repeating images. Lighthouses. A lighthouse at night, under a full sun, at dawn, in the evening, over-looking the sea during a storm. The painted lighthouses ran all the way down Northwest 2.

Pepper followed their lights.


He reached the nurses' station, the room at the hub of the unit. Four staff members worked at the station, all seated. Pepper noticed Miss Chris moving down Northwest 1. She stomped toward the secure door in her practical shoes, still speaking out loud. But to whom?

The nurses' station was a rectangular desk area, with two tiers. The outer tier stood as tall as a bar top. Behind that top tier was a second one, lower, where staff members could sit and work at desk height. Pepper saw the tops of four heads. He didn't recognize any of these people from the intake team last night. Two nurses, an orderly, and a social worker were all in there, hunched over, heads down, filling out forms in the natural posture of the public-hospital worker.

Pepper wanted to walk over and ask about that phone call. But first he had to make his mind understand what his eyes were seeing. The image wasn't blurry—four staff members worked inside the nurses' station—but the meaning of that image made less sense. He could've been looking at a giant terra-cotta pot, the tops of the four heads like four plants just breaking the surface of the soil. He was swaying and didn't even realize Dorry had grabbed his hand until she yanked on his pinky.

She looked up at him, unsmiling. "You better hurry if you want breakfast. They're about to shut down. Are you hungry?"

Pepper was hungry. In fact, ravenous. Huey, Dewey, and Louie sure hadn't taken him out to dinner before they dropped him at New Hyde last night. He hadn't eaten since yesterday's lunch.

"I have to make a call first," he said.

But whose voice was that who said it? His, but not his. Distant. Slow.

"It's eight twenty-five," Dorry told him, and to Pepper her voice sounded faster, a bit daffier, than it had the night before. "They shut breakfast down at eight thirty and don't serve food again until lunch. You want to wait that long?"

He didn't. He couldn't. His naturally big appetite had been enhanced.

"Wait," Pepper said. "How can it be past half past *eight*?"

Dorry pointed at a wall where no clock hung. She kept her finger pointed there as if he just couldn't see it. Miss Chris had given Pepper those pills at seven a.m. He'd lost almost an hour and a half since then? Those two little pills had *walloped* his ass.

Now Dorry pulled at his pinky again. "You can eat or you can talk, but you can't do both in five minutes. The phones will be there when you're done. I promise."

Pepper nodded at her, or at least he hoped he did. He had a hard time feeling his body. For instance, he was already walking now and he'd hardly noticed. Dorry led Pepper around the nurses' station and held on to him. Not one staff member looked up at them. All he heard when passing them was the skritching of their pens.

Dorry pulled Pepper down another hallway. One she hadn't showed him the night before. "This is Northwest Five," she said. "You remember the wagon wheel?"

Pepper did but he couldn't say yes and nod his head and walk simultaneously. So he just looked down at his feet in their gray thermal socks. He hadn't even put on his boots. *Left, right. Left, right. Left, right.*

Much like Northwest 1 and 2 the hall here was lined with closed doors. They barely registered in Pepper's periphery. *Left then right.* So when they reached the end of Northwest 5, Pepper didn't expect the room to be so big and bright. It was filled with chairs and tables and surprisingly natural light. It was twice the size of the room at the hub of the ward.

"This," Dorry said, sweeping her free hand and speaking in a theatrical whisper, "is the television lounge."

There were six round wooden tables. Each could fit four or five people. They were spread out in a crescent shape, running along two adjacent walls that were entirely made up of ceiling-to-floor windows. These windows even looked like glass without chicken-wire veins.

Dorry seemed to read his thoughts. "Pretty, aren't they? But don't get too excited. They're glass *coated* with shatterproof plastic. They're actually even tougher than the windows in our rooms, they just don't look as industrial. It's expensive stuff! Which is why New Hyde only paid for it here, in the lounge."

This lounge was the closest the psych unit had to a showroom. A place where photos were taken on the rare occasions when the psych unit made it into the hospital's brochures. (Four times in forty years.) More important, the lounge was where families sat with patients during visiting hours. It had to offer a better view than the bedrooms.

And what could Pepper see through those floor-to-ceiling shatterproof glass windows? A decrepit old basketball court. Half-court, actually. With one tired-ass basket. The rim oxidized from orange to a sickly brown. The once-white backboard had gone gray. Even the pole tilted forward about ten degrees. It wouldn't be hard to dunk on a hoop like that, but then patients weren't ever taken out there to play basketball.

Dorry said, "There's five smoke breaks a day. They let patients stand out there to puff."

Dorry brought Pepper to a tall wheeled cart, like the kind used in school cafeterias. Gray as a gunship, with large black wheels at the base. An orderly stood there, but didn't seem like he wanted to linger. It wasn't Scotch Tape, but a different black guy, tall and skinny and disinterested. The orderly removed the last full tray and almost handed it to Pepper, but Pepper couldn't get his hands raised. His arms just stayed there at his sides even though the fingers did wiggle. Dorry took the tray for him. And with that, the orderly checked his watch—8:32—and pushed the cafeteria cart out of the television lounge and down Northwest 5.

Dorry moved toward an empty table, farthest from the other patients. The tables and chairs were the kind of dining sets you might buy from a defense contractor. They lacked any beauty and weren't even comfortable. But neither the people who sold it—in bulk—nor the people who purchased it—in bulk—were ever going to sit at these tables, so what the hell did they care?

Dorry settled down at the far end of the crescent. Pepper took fifteen minutes to catch up. No joke. A walk of no more than ten feet took him a quarter of an hour. He regretted waiting to make the phone call more and more. Having breakfast in this place only seemed like he meant to stay.

Sitting down gave Pepper trouble, too. He had to coordinate pulling the chair out without being in its way. He had to aim his butt at the chair cushion and not smack into the armrest instead. And he had to scoot forward in his chair, which meant working up some traction between his thermal socks and the tiled floor. The man had sweat on his forehead when he finally picked up his fork.

Dorry smiled widely. "Those meds are *murder*, aren't they?"

There were other patients gathered at the tables on the other end, by the TV mounted to the wall. Some sat with their breakfast trays in their laps and their heads cocked back so they could see the thirty-two-inch flat screen.

Eight patients stared at it, men and women, pawing blindly at their breakfast trays. Their mouths hung open and their eyes looked heavy in post-dosage stupor. What else could they do to ride the dosage out but watch television? Pepper couldn't even manage that.

The news played, though what was on hardly seemed to matter. The patients watched commercials and weather reports as intently as "breaking news" when they were in this state. Pepper heard the anchor's voice. "Thousands packed Cairo's Tahrir Square for a 'Day of Victory' to celebrate the one-week anniversary of the ouster of Egyptian President Hosni Mubarak."

Pepper tried to focus on his breakfast tray. A small box of cereal, a green apple, an eight-ounce carton of milk, a four-ounce juice cup, two pieces of white toast, and a set of plastic utensils. Very little of this stuff actually qualified as food. Food*like*, maybe. Pepper looked away from his tray, slowly raising his eyes, if not his entire head, to peek at the half-court out there. But what he saw, just beyond the court, was that same chain-link fence topped by barbed wire. The door to the half-court had three locks.

*How am I here?* Pepper wanted to ask.

But he couldn't form the words. Not only was his body still working at sludge speeds, but now his mouth was so dry he could feel the bumps of his tongue against the roof of his mouth. He needed a sip of that juice. The most appetizing item on the tray. He meant to move his arms, to grab the tiny cup, but couldn't. His fingers didn't work, either.

Dorry watched him struggle without offering help. It wasn't that she was being cruel. It was that she was on meds, too. Pepper recognized it on her face. She smiled widely again. Had he said something funny or was she reacting on delay to something she'd heard minutes ago?

He stared into her mouth. Dorry had tombstone teeth, bent at all angles and going gray. Her giant glasses showed streaks, like a window that's been wet but not wiped clean. She wore the same blue nightdress from the night before. She was the kind of person Pepper might've given change to on a subway and never thought about again. Not a good thing to admit, but it was true. And now here he was, looking to her for help with his meager breakfast. His thirst overwhelmed him.

"Dorry," he whispered.

Speaking, just that one word, and barely a whisper, made his parched throat burn. He puckered his lips, he opened and closed them. He stared down at the breakfast tray, at the juice carton, and hoped she understood.

Dorry said, "Do you know much about the American buffalo?"

It took Pepper a moment to register how mind-bogglingly random Dorry's question was. If he'd been in control of himself, he might've chucked his table at her out of frustration. But he couldn't do much of anything. He watched the little juice cup with an almost romantic longing.

Dorry rose from her chair.

She shuffled around the table.

"Two hundred years ago, or something like that, the American buffalo dominated the West. There were millions of the great beasts, running in herds so big it sounded like thunder rolling toward you. A population of five million. Ten million. Maybe more."

Pepper couldn't quite focus on her words. By now his mind seemed to be floating. Or sinking. Either way, his brain was an untethered balloon. If he hadn't been able to see the tabletop right in front of him, see his arms balanced on the chair's armrests, he would've thought he'd been let loose to float into the sky.

His throat felt so *dry.*

"When the settlers started crossing the country in droves, the American buffalo met its match. People wanted the skins for warmth, they ate the meat, they used the horns and the bones and all the rest. Those Native Americans used even more of the animal, but they hunted it all out of proportion, too. Used it for themselves and sold it to the settlers. The American buffalo became big business. Nothing stands in the way of *that.* In no time, maybe three years, those beautiful beasts were almost extinct."

Dorry stood by his side now. She reached across his tray for the four-ounce juice cup. But she couldn't pull the foil top off the thing. Even though she'd been on the unit for much, much, *much* longer than Pepper, she, too, had been walloped by her morning dose. What she took would've put Pepper into a coma.

"People used to go out and hunt them with rifles. Hell, they even leaned out of moving trains and picked the buffalo off with potshots. They also call the American buffalo a bison. Same animal, two names. Don't know why that happened."

Dorry finally opened the juice. Like Pepper used to do when he was a kid enjoying a quarter water after school. She popped two holes with her teeth then jabbed one finger inside to make a kind of spout. She tilted back Pepper's head and opened his mouth.

"But the worst way to kill them, in mass numbers, was to drive a herd toward the edge of a cliff and just make all those big dumb things jump right off. It was messy. Some people think the men did it just for fun. Or maybe it was more efficient. Didn't use any bullets and you had all of them right there at the bottom of the cliff. The sight, from above, must have been something truly hellish. Just thousands of bison, broken into pieces. Heads and hooves and tails and guts. Blood everywhere. Some of them didn't die right away. They might be down there snorting and wheezing and slowly drifting off toward death. But it hardly counted as a loss for anyone but the buffalo. Even though it sounds wasteful, the profits were so big it didn't matter."

Dorry finished by slowly pouring the apple juice into Pepper's mouth.

Pepper's arms shivered and his tongue expanded in his mouth like a sponge. His eyes focused on the old woman standing over him. He smiled at her: a mama bird feeding its chick.

After drinking two ounces, he regained some control of his body. He raised one hand and took the juice from Dorry, sat up straighter, and slurped the rest himself.

And Dorry returned to her chair, snatched both pieces of toast off his tray, and winked. The price of partnership.

Pepper grabbed the green apple and bit it once. A chomp so huge it exposed the core. *Smaller bites, Pepper.* After he finished chewing he asked, "Dorry, why did you tell me that story about the buffalo? It's horrible."

They laughed and the mood seemed to lighten.

Then Dorry said, "I want you to understand where you've found yourself, big boy. In here we're the buffalo. And New Hyde is the cliff."

Pepper wasn't any goddamn buffalo, or bison, or whatever. He was a *man* and he'd be leaving soon after he made his phone call. Of course, Pepper couldn't say those things to Dorry. Instead he spent forty-five minutes finishing his apple while she calmly watched him, as if she knew exactly what he was thinking.

"We'll have to go back to the nurses' station if you want to make that phone call," she said. "You remember where it is?"

How could Pepper be expected to forget? What kind of dimwits was Dorry used to dealing with? But then Pepper remembered he'd been unable to walk half an hour ago, so maybe he shouldn't be too smug.

"Down that hall." Pepper gestured with his head.

Dorry grabbed the cereal box off his tray and held it up. She raised her eyebrows and Pepper consented to let her take it. Dorry marched over to the gaggle of patients by the television. She skirted around one table, closer to the windows, and stopped beside an old black woman wearing a purple pantsuit and matching little church hat. Dorry leaned close and spoke into the woman's ear, then set the cereal box in her lap.

Pepper and Dorry turned their walk back to the nurses' station into a funny kind of race. Dorry held on to the wooden railing running along the right wall, and Pepper held on to the one on the left. They used the railings for balance, and to drag themselves forward. Eating breakfast had spiked Pepper's blood sugar enough to put a dent in his paralysis, but he still needed a little help. And Dorry did, too. Clinging to their respective rails, they lumbered in harmony.

When they reached the nurses' station again, the same tops of the same four heads were still bent over the same paperwork. The staff members hadn't shifted. Just as Dorry and Pepper reached the oval room, a phone rang behind the nurses' station and one of the staff, a woman, picked up.

"Northwest," she answered, as if this was her name. She listened for a moment. "The doctor is not on the unit just now. Let me put you through to his voice mail. All right?" She asked without waiting for a reply. A faint click could be heard as the nurse pressed the transfer button. Then a clunk as the plastic phone went back into its cradle. The woman went back to paperwork. At New Hyde the term for this was *charting*.

Pepper found he could best move through the room if he focused on its discrete little details. If he spent too much time planning his phone call to Mari, everything he needed to explain and to ask of her, then he got tripped up. *Stick to the basic motor functions, Pepper!* Footsteps, and hands held tight to the railing, and keeping pace with Dorry as she led him forward.

But then he lost himself by counting hallways. They'd just left Northwest 5 and as they veered to the left, making a circuit around the nurses' station, holding to the curved railing, they reached Northwest 1. As they crossed the mouth of that hallway, Pepper turned and recognized the secure door. Miss Chris stood in the open doorway. A delivery man held a white bag, food from a place nearby called Sal's. Miss Chris counted out her money. Pepper couldn't even consider escaping just then, he could barely stay upright. Then they passed Northwest 1 and Pepper clung to the railing again. Up ahead was Northwest 2, the men's hallway, where his room lay. He looked over and saw Northwest 3, the women's. There he saw a pair of middle-aged women walking together, dressed nearly identically, and laughing over some impossibly funny joke. Really happy, at least in that moment. Were they patients? How could they be smiling if they were in here? He couldn't stop watching the women as he moved.

And that's how he bumped right into Dorry, nearly knocking her over. But he caught himself and her. The wooden railing groaned as the two of them held to it.

"Sorry," Pepper said.

Dorry said, "My son was the same way. Never looked where he was going."

Two of the staff members at the nurses' station rose from their seats, just high enough to peek over the desktop at Dorry and Pepper. One of them was Scotch Tape, who recognized Pepper from last night and didn't feel like being bothered this early. No one being hurt, no one attempting to escape, no one refusing treatment. As far as the staff's checklist went, there were no problems then. He returned to his charting.

Dorry and Pepper had stopped midway on the wheel, between Northwest 2 and Northwest 3. Between the two halls there was a little alcove.

"Pay phones," Dorry said.

"I can make as many calls as I want?" Pepper asked. Surprised that prisoners were limited to just one, but mental patients had unlimited access.

"As long as you've got the money," she said.

He had the change right in the pocket of the slacks he'd slept in. Pepper reached into the pocket and pulled out the coins. Only then did he realize the act of balance he'd just achieved. A minor feat for anyone over two years old, agreed, but you'd be surprised how that medication makes you feel like a wobbly infant. It had been two hours since he'd swallowed the meds and he still didn't feel clear-headed, but maybe they had lost their worst effects.

The change in his palm looked like shiny communion wafers.

The alcove wasn't terribly big. There were two pay phones. Both were in use. By the same guy.

Pepper's roommate.

Mr. Malt Ball held one receiver to his right ear. The other was balanced on his left shoulder. He looked like an old-time receptionist, putting through calls. He didn't notice Pepper, even in that cramped space. This guy had admirable powers of concentration. Either that or he was just ignoring the big man.

The roommate spoke into the phone by his right ear. "Yes, I will hold."

Then he set that phone onto his right shoulder and lifted the other one to his left ear and said, "Hello? Hello? Come on!" But he'd already been put on hold on that phone, too.

Dorry peeked in. She said, "That's Coffee."

At least Pepper had a name for his enemy.

"I should warn you," she said. "I wouldn't go around flashing my change like that." She pointed at Pepper's open hand and he closed his fingers. "Coffee's going to ask for money if he sees that."

"He already did. He's my roommate."

Dorry winced like someone who's just touched an open flame. "For the first time since we've met, I actually feel *sorry* for you."

Dorry meant this as a joke, but why did it make Pepper flinch?

He walked right up to the still oblivious Coffee, who had returned to the phone at his right ear. His eyes were tilted upward as he listened to the hold message play for the fifth time in a row. That's why he didn't understand what was happening when Pepper snatched the other receiver out of his left hand to hang up the line.

"*I'm* using this phone now," Pepper said.

Pepper stood half a foot taller than Coffee but, more important, Pepper outweighed Coffee by at least eighty pounds. And Pepper's face, with its high, flared nostrils and bared teeth, looked about as pleasant as an etching of a Chinese demon. The sensible reaction for Coffee would have been to make peace. Or even to get his ass out of the alcove. But let's say this for Coffee: the man was out of his mind.

Coffee squared right up to Pepper, chest to belly.

Then he spat in Pepper's face.

The saliva struck the big man's chin, slid down, and hung there like a chrysalis for a full three seconds before Pepper hit the man.

Actually he *crushed* him. The alcove didn't have enough room for real blows to get thrown, so instead Pepper threw himself. The smaller man got caught between a wall and two hundred seventy-one pounds of medicated murderousness. Coffee might as well have been ground into a fine powder. Ready for the French press. (Sorry!)

Coffee howled and went down to the floor. The other receiver slipped out of his right hand, striking against one wall like a gavel. A recorded announcement played from the receiver, repeating what it had already been saying for many minutes:

"Thank you for calling 311 in New York City. We're here to help. . . ."

Coffee was curled on the ground, hands over his face. Pepper stooped over him. Pepper wanted to thump this guy for spitting on him. Really one of the most cowardly and disgusting moves a person can pull in a fight. But before he could do more, Pepper felt that saliva dripping down onto his neck and he panicked. What if this dude's spit had passed through his lips, even just a little bit, and gone down his throat? AIDS? Hepatitis C? Who knew what could happen? The moment the thought came up, it was impossible to put down. He stuck his tongue out and pressed it to the sleeve of his shirt. Licking his arm to clean his tongue. Coughing loudly.

Try to imagine what Scotch Tape and the other staff members saw when they entered the alcove, drawn in by Coffee's screams and Pepper's wretching. The staff found a very large man standing over a smaller one, menacing the smaller man who was, even now, scrambling to get hold of the dangling pay-phone receiver to try his call again. And the big man was—what the hell else could you say?— *licking himself.*

Crazy-balls. The scene was absolutely crazy-balls.

Scotch Tape sucked his teeth. He stared up at Pepper with distaste. "Damn, my man."

Pepper stopped applying his tongue to the fabric of his shirt and turned toward Scotch Tape. Below them both, Coffee spoke urgently into the phone.

"Hello?" he whimpered. "*Please.* I've seen it. I know where it lives."

"Thank you for calling 311. . . ."

Two nurses poked their heads into the alcove, but with Coffee, Pepper, and Scotch Tape already inside, there was no more room. From farther outside the alcove Miss Chris shouted, "What's this foolishness?!"

Scotch Tape called out, "New admit attacked Coffee."

Hearing it like that, from a staff member, made Pepper understand what he'd just done. Hadn't he resolved to control himself? To make the best impression possible? But getting spat on had to count as a mitigating circumstance. Pepper wanted to explain.

"I needed to make a phone call," he began.

Scotch Tape waved the words away. "I'm taking you back to your room now, and you're going to stay in there for the rest of the day. You hear?"

Coffee rose to his feet now, pushing himself up with his back against the wall. He shook the receiver of the phone Pepper had hung up. "Now you owe me a quarter, Joe! An American quarter!"

Pepper said, "This guy was using both phones and I just . . ."

Scotch Tape stepped closer to Pepper. They were squared up just like Pepper and Coffee had been, but Scotch Tape wouldn't have to spit on anyone to make his point. That was clear.

"Save that shit," Scotch Tape said. "You can explain all this to Dr. Anand."

The way Scotch Tape said it, the name sounded like "AndAnd."

From outside the alcove Miss Chris added, "Oh-ho, it's Charlie Big Potato causing the fuss? I already told him to be easy."

In defiance, desperation, and drugged-out confusion, Pepper grabbed the phone on the left, lifting the receiver out of its cradle. He'd make his phone call.

But Scotch Tape wouldn't let that happen. He pressed two fingers down on the cradle, and the dial tone choked before Pepper even got the phone to his ear.

Then, another quick flash of temper, Pepper half-raised the receiver like he'd bring it down on Scotch Tape's head. But he stopped himself from making a bad day terrible and put the phone back in the cradle.

Scotch Tape grinned.

"That's smart, big boy. First smart move you've made since you got here."

Oh, how Pepper would've loved to pick up Coffee and use him to bludgeon Scotch Tape to death. Would that count as black-on-black crime?

Scotch Tape misread Pepper's contemplative look. He spoke with a mix of compassion and condescension. "You calm now? All right, then. Let's go. You and me. Back to your room."

As Pepper followed Scotch Tape out of the alcove, Coffee still clung to the pay phone like a man adrift, trying to stay afloat. The receiver was tucked against his ear.

The automated voice on the other end thanked him, once again, for calling.

"It's *here*," Coffee said quietly.

# 5

SCOTCH TAPE MOVED alongside Pepper, shaking his head as if he'd just seen a kid do something that would earn a powerfully strict punishment.

"I believe you," Scotch Tape said as they walked.

A pair of old men, one small and one medium-sized, walked past Pepper and Scotch Tape, going in the opposite direction. They wore sport coats and walked in synchronicity. Scotch Tape nodded at them but they ignored him. The smaller one peeped Pepper.

"You believe me about what?" Pepper asked.

"What you said last night," Scotch Tape continued. "That you don't belong here. I believe you."

Pepper stopped to reach for the handrail, put off balance by the residual effects of the medication or what Scotch Tape just said.

"Why do you believe me?" Pepper asked.

"You seen Dorry? Or Coffee? Most of the patients in here? Shit, I've seen crazy. And you're not that. You can be an asshole, though."

"Why don't you unlock that big door for me then, so I can just go home."

Scotch Tape shook his right arm and the red plastic cord slipped down below his wrist. It looked like a miniature Slinky. His keys dropped and he caught them with practiced cool.

"Today's February 18. You got a seventy-two-hour watch and you're not getting out any sooner than February 21. But if you keep acting stupid, you're going to be staying a whole lot longer."

Pepper didn't say anything smart because even he'd known that rolling on Coffee had been really dumb.

Scotch Tape said, "Let's keep going."

Scotch Tape entered room 5 with Pepper and shut the door behind him. He moved to Pepper's dresser and rested an elbow on it.

"You know how you got here?"

Pepper couldn't get a handle on what this moment really was: surprising camaraderie, or just a staff member messing with a patient. So he said nothing.

"That cop who brought you in, the one who did the talking, his name is Detective Saurez. He brought you here because him and his boys aren't getting no more overtime from the NYPD right now. Processing you at the precinct would have taken hours. Without that overtime they'd basically be working for free. But they know if they drop you off with us you're our problem and their workday is *done*. Half of them got second jobs to get to. Like we don't."

Pepper shook his head. "That's why I'm here? Because Huey, Dewey, and Louie got lazy?"

Scotch Tape looked confused for a moment, but he let it pass. He tapped the top of Pepper's dresser with two fingers, for emphasis.

"That Saurez dude has pulled this same shit with Dr. Anand before. Plenty times. I'm telling you. And we have to process you. But I'll bet you Dr. A is making some phone calls today."

Pepper noticed one of his laceless boots standing by the door. The other was most likely under his bed. Yes. He fished beneath the frame and there it was. Pepper collected his shoes and set them both down, together, neatly by the foot of his bed. A little bit of order.

Pepper said, "They can't just *do* something like that."

Scotch Tape shook his head as if Pepper were a silly child.

"And yet here you are," Scotch Tape said as he left the room and locked the door from the other side.

Pepper sat on his bed.

He wasn't actually surprised to be locked in his room as punishment. Even if this was a hospital, they'd fallen back on some old-school discipline. His mom and dad might've done the same, thirty years ago, when Pepper got into a fight with his kid brother, Ralph.

Locked door, still no phone call made, Scotch Tape's revelation about why he'd been brought in here, and even Dorry's little story about the American buffalo. The whole mess swirled in Pepper's head until he imagined a cliff with a mound of bodies at the bottom. But his vision was far worse than what Dorry had described. He saw buffalo heads and human arms, bison's legs and human torsos, a mess of discarded flesh and fur. And the three cops were at the top of the cliff. Huey, Dewey, and Louie, not even wearing their plain clothes but the brightly colored sweatshirts those duck kids wore in the cartoons. One red, one blue, one green. They were pushing something big to the edge of the cliff, and he knew who it was.

What to do with all that?

Pepper put on his boots to get rid of the dark thoughts.

The boots were three years old now. Bought from a military shoe-maker. The soles were flexible, the toes durable, and lots of ankle support. Perfect for furniture movers, as well as soldiers. Even without the laces it felt good to have his work shoes back on. He worked exclusively for Farooz Brothers Movers. He was very good at his job.

Pepper was thinking maybe he should call the Farooz brothers himself, risk asking them for help, when he heard a patter against his shatterproof windows.

It was rain. A sun shower. The best kind of storm. They always made Pepper feel drowsy. Rain against the windows. The faint tapping got stronger, but only slightly. A sun shower on a Friday morning. Pepper slid his butt backward and lay flat on his bed, the boots still on his feet.

Pepper liked to watch that painter on television, Bob Ross. His voice was as pleasant as this morning rain. His voice as soft as his white-guy afro. If Pepper was ever switching through channels and happened across an episode of Bob Ross's painting program, he would lie down (if he could), lower his eyelids, and just *lull*.

And that's what happened to him there, in his bed at New Hyde. A sun shower and memories of Bob Ross blissed him right out. Until someone unlocked that room's door, there was nothing else he could do anyway. He listened as the rain seemed to creep up the side of his windows instead of down, until the patter seemed to dance against the roof of the building. Pepper had forgotten what Dorry told him, about Northwest having a second floor, so he thought the noise above his head was just rain hitting the roof. That's why Pepper listened to it calmly. It lulled him. Up there the noise changed slightly. It sounded more like creaking. Like wood stretching. A faint, fast rhythm to it as the sun shower became a little more forceful.

The rain grew even stronger and the sun got crowded out, but by then Pepper had nearly fallen asleep. As more clouds burst outside, the creaking in the ceiling only got faster and the tapping against the windows turned into slaps. There was so much to worry about, so many mistakes to sort out when he got out of bed again. He almost worked himself back into a frenzy when he thought about Mari and what her ex-husband might be doing to her right now. But he couldn't do much about any of it right then, so he just listened to the sounds of the wild world. Slapping and creaking and carrying on. Drowning out everything, even Pepper's rising fear that he might not get out of Northwest. Not in seventy-two hours. Not for far longer than that.

Forget all that right now.

As Pepper's eyes fluttered closed, he could almost hear the alizarin-crimson voice of Bob Ross, whispering, "And until next time, I'd like to wish you happy painting, God bless, and I'll see you again."


When Pepper's eyes opened again, who did he find stooping over him? Not kindly, sweet, semi-burnt-out Bob Ross. No, it was Coffee.

Fucking Coffee.

And Pepper had a feeling about where this would head next. He'd fallen asleep flat on his back, above the covers. Instinctively, he shoved his hands into his pockets just in case Coffee had been planning to rob his ass in his sleep. Coffee noticed Pepper doing this and sneered as he backed away.

"I don't need your money that badly, Joe."

Pepper lifted his head off his pillow. "Stop calling me Joe."

Coffee pointed at the tray on top of Pepper's dresser. "I brought you lunch."

Pepper sat up now, starving. The change in his right pocket shook as it settled. He got up and walked toward the tray. As he moved, his clothes felt stiff and his feet, still in the boots, felt wet and sweaty. His wool socks had been in need of a wash when he put them on Thursday. So by now they might be getting a bit ripe. Then he felt self-conscious. Even though he'd showered that morning, he already wanted to wash himself again. But not in that tight, windowless bathroom. Not in that stand-up shower stall. At home. In his tub. He probably hadn't taken a *bath* in eight or nine years, but he'd earned such an indulgence. He'd even throw in some Epsom salt for the sciatica that had the left side of his lower back hurting. Wait. How had a luxurious indulgence turned into an old man's nerve therapy? And so quickly?

Pepper looked down at the lunch tray: a small orange, a plastic carton of apple juice, a tuna-fish sandwich on white bread (the bread looked like dry wall and the tuna, grout), a small cookie prepackaged in plastic. The cookie was just dough with a mysterious small red ruby in the center. It looked like a wedge of beet, to be honest. A *beet* cookie for dessert? Who would do that to people? Even crazy people deserved better.

Pepper knew he should thank Coffee for bringing him the food, especially considering what had happened in that alcove. Yet this meal had all the hallmarks of a punishment. Pepper said nothing.

Coffee sat in bed, where he'd brought his own lunch tray and a can of soda. He tapped the top of the can with the same bony nail he'd used to poke Pepper the night before.

Pepper looked at the wealth of bad options on his tray. Which should he start with? It was like deciding between torture and torture. While Pepper pitied himself, Coffee kept rapping on that soda-can lid. Must've been at it a whole minute. The kind of rap-tap-tapping that made Poe flip his lid. Exactly as Pepper almost did. But then he looked at the man making the noise. Late twenties maybe, slumped forward on his messy bed, the can between his thighs, banging away. Pepper thought of one of those little toy monkeys clanging a pair of cymbals. (Pepper did *not* mean that in a racist way.) Coffee had been at it so long that it seemed maniacal, but here was a lunch tray right in Pepper's lap. A kindness that deserved a little respect. So instead of going off on Coffee, Pepper tried to think of why someone might tap the top of the can like that. And keep going. Like a person clearing his throat, again and again, until you finally realize he has something to say. Something to share. Maybe he just wanted to be asked the right question.

"Where are you from?" Pepper asked. Usually an easy way to start a conversation in Queens. But Coffee didn't respond. Just kept drilling that soda can.

"How long have you been in New Hyde?"

That caused Coffee to miss the top of the can and poke at the air, but just as quickly he went back to his routine.

Pepper had to think about what other subjects there might be, the ones that really mattered to Coffee. It didn't take much longer to guess. He sighed.

"Who were you trying to reach? On the phones."

Coffee smiled into his lap. He stopped tapping. "You really want to know?"

Based on that grin, the width and brightness of it, now Pepper wasn't so sure. If this guy ended up saying he'd been trying to ring up the Illuminati or Reverend Al Sharpton (Okay, Pepper, now that one *was* a little racist), Pepper wouldn't want to hear it. It would just be too sad.

Coffee said, "I was trying to reach the mayor's office."

Was that sane? Pepper couldn't quite say. Ambitious, but not necessarily nuts. Lots of people called the mayor with problems. Pepper picked up the small orange, the size of a handball. He closed his fingers around it and it disappeared.

"The mayor of . . . *where*?" he asked.

Coffee finally snapped the tab of his Sprite can. When the top opened, it sounded like a sizzling pan.

"The mayor of New York City. Who else?"

(Mayor McCheese?)

Pepper opened his hand and bit into the top of the orange skin. He spat the chunk onto his tray and peeled the rest. "And why were you trying to reach him?"

Coffee drank half his can of soda in slow gulps. When he finished, he looked at Pepper directly. Each man sat on his own bed, with his lunch tray on his lap. They looked like kids bunking at sleepaway camp.

Coffee said, "I had to let him know this place is dangerous. I've seen its true face."

Pepper dropped the rest of the orange skin on the tray and tore the fruit in half.

Pepper held up the orange and said, "I'll trade you for a can of soda."

Coffee set his tray on his pillow, rose from the bed, grabbed another Sprite from his dresser and exchanged it for half the orange. He wobbled slightly as he moved across the room. Coffee leaned down so he could be close to Pepper's face. So close that Pepper leaned backward. There had been the faint accent, and now this complete ease with closeness. Pepper felt sure this guy hadn't been born in the United States. While the rest of the world seems happy with only a membrane of personal space, Americans need a bubble.

Coffee said, "The mayor ought to know it's killing us."

"And you think Bloomberg can do anything about that?"

Coffee tore off a slice of the orange and slipped it into his mouth. He hardly chewed before he spoke. "The man got three terms in a city where two terms are the law! He changed the law to help himself, so why can't he do it to help others?"

"But why would he want to?" Pepper asked. "What would he get?"

Coffee laughed quietly as he went back to his bed. He pulled the lunch tray onto his lap and lifted the tuna sandwich. He sniffed at it, then set it down again without tasting.

Pepper ate his sandwich in two bites, damn the funny smell. And if Coffee didn't eat his soon, Pepper would offer to eat it for him. As bad as it tasted, all this would help get his strength up. The morning pills weren't making his mind drag anymore. They had worn off. His body no longer drifted. A little fuel, any fuel, would fill his tank.

The rain had stopped and the clouds parted. The sun reappeared.

Bright out. The windows were still slick with drops but they dried fast in the daylight.

"You ask why the mayor should care." Coffee pointed at Pepper. "You're an American. That's right?"

"That's right."

"I am not. That is why I *know* what you cannot *believe*. This country might look like it's about to break down for good."

"That's the truth," Pepper said, as he choked down the tuna. Just then, even a bad job was a good job in this woefully unemployed country.

Coffee raised his Sprite as if he was giving a toast.

"But listen to me because I'm serious. America is not broken yet."

Pepper wanted to argue. To educate this outsider. He knew the way systems ran in this country. For instance, he wondered how long it would take for Coffee to reach the mayor. A week? No chance. How about a thousand years? And then to be heard? To have something done about New Hyde? Count that shit in eons.

He wanted to say all that, but maybe he should've been more concerned about the sound of Miss Chris's shoes coming down the hallway. In one hand she carried a small white plastic cup. In that cup were two small pills for Pepper. His midday meds.

Miss Chris plus Haldol plus lithium. A recipe for bed rest. He'd lost the morning and now it seemed he was going to lose the afternoon. She entered the room, ignored Coffee (because he'd already gotten his dose), and practically tossed the two meds down Pepper's throat. As he drifted away, it occurred to him that he might end up spending the entire seventy-two-hour observation period with his eyes shut. Practically comatose. Then it occurred to him that this might be intentional.

So he slept through the afternoon, and in the evening Coffee did Pepper the kindness of bringing the dinner tray. A scoop of macaroni and cheese, a spoonful of green beans, two slices of plain white bread, a plastic container of apple juice. (Again with the apple juice?) And another sugar cookie with a beet-looking blob stuck in the middle. This dessert, like the afternoon's, would remain in its plastic.

Pepper ate the food, and a nurse, one he hadn't seen before, came in to bring his nighttime meds. New nurse, same pills. He was knocked out even before the nurse had returned to the nurses' station.

And that, friends, was almost all of Pepper's first full day on the psychiatric unit.

The last thing to happen was this:

He opened his eyes at 2:45 a.m. He was on his side, facing the door. He saw Coffee under the covers of his own bed. The room's lights were out, the door shut; behind Pepper the moon was up. Pepper got up to use the bathroom and this took a little while. He had to roll himself off his mattress, and then he spent a few minutes on his hands and knees on the floor. The tiles felt cold against his palms and even through his slacks. He planned to stand up and walk to the toilet, but he just couldn't coordinate his muscles. So he crawled to the bathroom on his hands and knees while Coffee watched in silence.

In the bathroom Pepper clutched on to the sink to pull himself up. Who was that in the bathroom, grunting and groaning? It was him, but the sound seemed so far away.

He splashed water on his hands and face. He peed. He washed his hands again. He returned to bed. This time he lay down facing the windows.

The view wasn't so bad at this hour. Pepper could see the tops of the trees outside and the starless dark sky and the moon, nearly full. He couldn't see the chain-link fence or the barbed wire at the top or make out the headlights of cars in the distance. It felt good.

Which is why the intrusion bothered him so much.

Pepper heard a muted *thump*. It could've been something dropping from above, but Pepper couldn't figure out what that might be. Then he thought of a set of bedcovers being tossed to the floor, and Pepper assumed that Coffee had climbed out of bed.

Next there was a shuffling back and forth on the tile floor, and Pepper remembered Coffee's routine from the night before. He imagined Coffee was getting up the courage to ask Pepper for the coins in his pocket. Maybe he'd only been bringing the food so he could ask for even more money. No kindness without a cost.

Finally a shadow moved across Pepper's top sheet.

He smelled an unclean body. Something sour. Like the ammonia-haunted corner of a subway platform that has never been truly cleaned.

Pepper kept his back to the room. Hadn't he and Coffee made a sort of truce? Talking, eating together, sharing soda and oranges—didn't that earn Pepper a night without panhandling? The more Pepper thought this way the angrier he felt. The more Pepper anticipated that tap he was about to feel against his shoulder, the more he wanted to finish the fight they'd begun in the phone alcove.

But then someone just leaned close to Pepper's ear and *breathed* into it. Fuck! Pepper's ear felt so hot that he instinctively pulled the covers up to hide his face. But the breathing stayed steady on the other side. Still right by Pepper's ear. So hot it soaked the fabric, and the covers turned damp at the spot. The breath felt so hot that it actually began to burn.

Pepper pulled the covers back down now, trying to inch away, toward the windows, but able to move only so quickly in his addled state. And when the covers came down from his head, he felt the touch of rough hair against his neck. Rough like gnarled wool, matted. And the burning breath kept coming as though pumped from a bellows, until Pepper's skin felt like it was puckering.

Pepper opened his mouth to call out to a nurse or an orderly—even Scotch Tape—anyone who might come in here and separate the two of them. But when Pepper opened his mouth he couldn't speak. The only sound coming out of Pepper was a wet cough, a choking sound.

Because someone had three fingers in Pepper's mouth.

And it wasn't Coffee.

The fingers reached all the way to the back of Pepper's tongue, one nail jabbing his uvula.

Pepper was so shocked, so disgusted, working so hard to keep from vomiting that he couldn't bring his teeth down on those fingers hard enough. He was too dazed.

The thing pulled Pepper's head back, away from the windows, with enough force to move the rest of Pepper's body. Until the two finally made eye contact.

The eyes Pepper met were white and empty. They had no pupils. Just the white meat of the eye, faint red veins running just below the surface like the chicken wire running through the shatterproof windows.

Was this person having a seizure?

Once Pepper was on his back, the fingers drew out of his mouth, the nails raking his tongue. His jaw ached from being yanked. In the dark, Pepper couldn't see much more than those white eyes. Matted hair dangled down across his attacker's face. The hair scratched at Pepper's nose and lips. It felt like fur.

Pepper was looking up into a face he couldn't understand.

The hair against his skin *was* fur, after all. And resting in that thick pelt he now saw a wide, wet nose, black and quivering.

Was this a hallucination? Something brought on by the pills? Like Ebenezer Scrooge's old bit of undigested beef? An apparition? This had to be an error. This was only his roommate, *Coffee,* standing over him. *Coffee,* who had woken him up. *Coffee,* who wanted a quarter. Pepper was just too tired, too drugged out, too confused to see clearly. He had to slow down, breathe in, he was just caught somewhere between wakefulness and sleep. That place where monsters really exist.

Pepper looked at his roommate's bed.

There was Coffee, wide-eyed and shivering.

Watching.

The figure above Pepper's bed leaned closer now. Its hot breath burned the tip of Pepper's nose like direct sunlight. And its own wet, black nose wriggled as it sniffed him.

*Stop this,* he thought. *Just leave me be.*

But Pepper wasn't addressing the thing standing over his bed. Because he knew it couldn't really be there. He was pleading with his own pill-addled mind.

Then the door to their room rattled and shook. Pepper's eyes blinked and fluttered. The thing by his bed moved away so quickly, it seemed to fly.

"Who locked this?" a nurse's voice called out.

She unlocked the door and snapped on the overhead light. It was the night nurse, who'd given him his nighttime dose earlier, along with an orderly.

"You two stop all that screaming!" the orderly shouted, stomping into the room.

Had they been screaming? Both of them?

The nurse shook two white plastic cups, one in each hand. The tranquilizers inside rattled like backgammon dice.

Coffee and Pepper sat straight up in bed.

Pepper scanned the room, he even peeked under his bed frame. The animal was gone. The only thing different about the room was a ceiling panel on the floor by Pepper's dresser.

"Now this is just sad," the orderly said. He picked the panel up. "This place is just coming apart."

The orderly had to leave the room and return with a folding chair so he could slide the panel back into place.

Now the nurse shook the little white cups again. "Y'all know what's coming."

*Please knock us out!* That's what they were both thinking. Right then Pepper only wanted to disconnect. He didn't want to see what he'd just seen. *If* he'd seen it. Felt it. Bad dream. Bad dream. (Shared dream?) Bad dream. Better to be knocked out than to lie awake till dawn.

# 6

PEPPER WOKE UP thinking of butts.

And nothing else.

Ladies' butts.

Skinny butts, big butts, saddlebag butts, flabby and firm butts, the kind that sit so high they seem like part of the woman's back, the kind that ride low and form a UU just above the thighs like in the old television commercials for Hanes Underalls, butts that wiggle and butts that jiggle, sagging butts and robust butts, butts that hardly make an impression under a pair of jeans; sidewinder butts and trumpet butts—the ones so meaty they actually spread out until they appear to be a woman's thighs (ass so fat you can see it from the front), butts as knotty as acorns, butts as smooth as a slice of Gouda, butts with pimples and butts with cellulite, the kind that have pockmarks or red splotches, butts with tattoos and butts with bullet scars. Butts you can cup in your warm hands. Butts and butts and butts.

In other words, Pepper woke up horny.

Let's take a moment to be impressed. Three doses of Haldol and lithium topped off with a Vicodin nightcap and the *urge* still arose, like a flower growing through concrete. And he sure hadn't been staring at any butts while in here. He just hadn't had the itch. All those butts, and more, were stored in Pepper's memory chip. It was as if his

mind had known the surest way to rouse him from the pit of seda-
tion. Asses would work.

Pepper's mind woke him up. He found himself in his bed yet again.
No butts in sight.

*Now Pepper, get your big ass out of bed.*

Outside his windows Pepper heard the muted rumbles of traffic
moving down Union Turnpike. Ambulances whining as they sped
toward the hospital. Car horns composing a fugue of frustration.
From where the sun sat he guessed it was midday. He'd probably slept
through breakfast.

In fact, it was four thirty on Saturday afternoon.

Coffee's bed sat empty. The sheets tussled but the body gone. The
door to the room was open. Pepper walked to the corner where the
ceiling panel had fallen down. He stood under it but couldn't make
himself raise his hand and touch. It felt like standing under a cold
shower, being right there. Pepper's big body tensed so hard he shivered. He half-expected someone, something, to come crashing down
on him. But that didn't happen. So finally he backed out of the room,
keeping an eye on that ceiling tile until he'd left.

He stepped into the hallway gingerly. Would one of the staff members appear, tackle him, and hold his mouth open? Why hadn't Miss
Chris or Scotch Tape or whoever was on duty done that to him this
morning like they did the day before? Maybe they preferred to let a
sleeping patient lie.

Northwest 2 was empty. Quiet. Yes, the fluorescent lights in the
ceiling made noise, the low drone of an electric insect. But other than
that? Not much. Pepper didn't even hear his own footfall. He had
only his Smartwool socks on his feet. He went back for his boots.

He still wore the clothes he'd had on when the cops brought him
in. Now the fabric looked a bit ragged, more wrinkled than an old
man's balls.

He reached the nurses' station and found just one orderly back
there, charting.

The orderly looked up from his seat, over the tall shelf of the
nurses' station, and nodded at Pepper. A thick folder of paperwork
sat in front of him. The orderly had stopped writing to flex his aching

fingers. Like the other staff members, he wore his keys on a short, red plastic cord around his wrist. When the orderly looked up at Pepper again and stretched his aching hand this time, his keys tinkled.

"Last night . . ." Pepper said, but he couldn't finish the sentence, didn't want to say it out loud.

The baby-faced orderly kept watching Pepper, but his hand dropped back on the papers and the fingers searched blindly for the pen, working nearly autonomously.

"You need something?" the orderly asked.

How old was this guy? Twenty? And in this place he had almost total authority over Pepper, a forty-two-year-old man.

"Where is everyone?" Pepper asked.

The orderly jerked his head once, behind him, toward Northwest 5, the television lounge.

"It's visiting hours."

Finally the kid looked down and found his pen. He snatched it, then looked up and frowned, clearly unhappy to find Pepper still standing there.

Now the orderly leaned over and lifted a clipboard.

"You had your lunchtime meds?" He scanned the list but wasn't sure of this patient's name.

Pepper saw an opportunity. "Oh, yes," he said. "I had those. *Definitely.*"

"What's your name again?" the orderly asked, torn between the clipboard and the charting.

"Thanks!" Pepper shouted as he walked to Northwest 5, and the orderly just set the clipboard back down with a shrug. He clicked his pen and returned to work.

Even from halfway down Northwest 5 the lounge looked like it was jumping. Every table was occupied, handfuls of folks were forced to stand. The natural afternoon light flushed against every face. And most of the people in there weren't even looking up at the television, though the television stayed on.

Pepper didn't make it all the way to the lounge. Part of the problem was that he saw Dorry in there, at a table with a slightly tired-looking woman in her forties, and two enthusiastic kids under ten. The kids were in their chairs, on their knees, holding playing cards close to their faces. Dorry, too, though she kept dropping her hand theatrically and one or the other child would shout for Grandma to *be careful!* The woman in her forties had a hand of cards, too, but hers were facedown on the table. She looked out the window and seemed to wish she was anywhere else.

And Coffee sat at another table with a pudgy man in a tight white button-down shirt and wide tie. His suit jacket hung on the back of his chair. He and Coffee were hunched over documents spread out on the table. Filling the entire table. Reams of data of some kind. And the man in the shirt and tie looked exasperated. He'd take one form and hold it up and read it, then place it facedown on a growing pile. Then lift another, read through, shake his head, and place it facedown with the others. Meanwhile, Coffee merely slid yet another sheet of paper toward the man. Pepper wasn't sure which of them he should feel sorry for.

There were meetings of various kinds at every table. Some folks had even brought in food. Chinese, or pizza from Sal's, bottles of soda or juice, chips or cookies. Like they were having picnics on the psychiatric unit.

How could this place be so active, so lively, when last night he saw . . . ?

Pepper chose to focus on one table with three people sitting around it. An older woman, in her fifties, a heavyset man in his thirties, and a teenage girl who looked to be about sixteen. He couldn't figure out which of them was the patient. Why did that bother him just then? It was like he suddenly wanted to *know.* Like he should just be able to tell. He assumed it was the guy in his thirties but, if he was being honest, that was only because the man was kind of chunky. He assumed the woman in her fifties was the mother, but mostly because she kept handing out egg rolls and cartons of Chinese noodles to the other two. She pulled a board game from a shopping bag. Pepper realized that these "clues" also proved nothing. Only the teenager seemed the unlikely choice. She wore baby-blue Nikes and a matching light blue knit cap pulled over her head. The cap had two small light blue pom-poms that dangled from the top. Pepper imagined some celebrity, one he couldn't name, had worn much the same outfit recently. The kid just looked so put together in that high-school high-fashion kind of way, where a fifteen-year-old tries to look like a twenty-year-old and ends up making herself seem like she's twelve. He wished he could excuse her from this room, so she could just go out and enjoy the prickly fruits of childhood. At least until the next time she and her mother visited the chubby guy.

But this sleuthing didn't really matter. From his place at the lip of the television lounge, Pepper could be sure of only one thing: No one was there to see him. He pitied himself.

But instead of indulging this emotion too long, Pepper went back to the pay phones. If most of the patients were here in the lounge, then maybe, finally, the pay phones would be free. He could make that call. The person he most hoped would visit didn't even know where the cops had taken him. Time to call her.

"Mari."

"Who's this?"

"You can't guess?"

"There's a number but the caller ID just says 'New York City.'"

"It's your favorite neighbor."

"Gloria?"

"That's funny. It's Pepper."

She paused.

"Hi, Pepper."

"You sound as tired as I feel."

She paused again.

"Were you worried about me?"

"I was worried about what you did to Griff."

"Is he all right?"

"He's okay. I guess. I don't talk to him if I don't have to, but since the police haven't come here and arrested me for conspiracy, I figure he's not dead."

"You want to know where I am?"

"Why did you have to do that, Pepper?"

"What? You told me he was threatening you, so I figured you wanted some help."

"I was just *talking* about it with you, Pepper. You know? I thought you were being my friend. I wasn't asking you to fix anything."

"You don't tell a gentleman about a problem and expect him not to help."

"So I guess it's my fault, right? You went to my *job*."

"*His* job."

"It's the same place! God! You know how it looks now? Like I hired a man to come to my job and beat up my ex-husband. What does that say about me? I teach seventh-grade Spanish!"

"I went to Van Wyck to tell him to keep his distance. That's *all*."

"I can handle myself! *I'll* call the cops if he really tries to hurt me. But that's *my* business anyway. I was just talking! But now you make me look like . . . My students saw you hitting him in the parking lot. How do you think they're going to look at me at school on Monday?"

"Why would they know it has anything to do with you?"

"Teenagers *know*. I'm telling you. I'm trying to act like a grown-up and you make me look like a fool. How am I supposed to teach them how to act if I can't keep my own life in order? This is my job, Pepper. It's like you're trying to get me fired."

"I meant to do something good. For you."

"Look, Pepper. I don't know how else to say this. I'm sorry to say this. But it's not going to happen like that. Between *you* and *me*. I'm not trying to be mean, but you have to hear me."

"Do you know where I am now? Your ex-husband . . . who the hell is named *Griff* anyway? Your ex-husband was the one who tried to get tough with *me* when I asked him nicely to stop threatening the mother of his child! He threatened to sue me. For *menacing*. Is that a crime? Okay, I admit, I lost my temper at that point. I smacked him one. So then we both got into it. Then three guys drive up in a Dodge Charger and I'm supposed to know they're cops? In a Dodge Charger? I *assumed* they were meatheads. But they were fucking cops. Patrolling a school zone. Now I'm in a *hospital* behind this shit. And last night I was *attacked*! I don't know what's going to happen to me, so I'm sorry but I called thinking that if anyone might give me a little understanding it would be the woman I was trying to look out for!"

"I'm sorry about all that, Pepper. I *really* am. But I don't know what you want me to do. You wanted to help me, but you never asked me what kind of help I needed. All I wanted was to talk about it. It was nice to do that with you down in the laundry room all those times. You were already helping. I don't think that mess with Griff was about me at all. It was about *you*."

"Marisol."

"You have a brother, right? Your family is who you should be calling if you're in a hospital."

"You mean Ralph? I haven't spoken to him in six years. Maybe more."

"But he's your brother."

"It's not going to happen, Mari. I'm not calling him. And he'd probably hang up as soon as he heard it was me."

Mari sighed into the phone. Pepper was going to make even coming to his aid into a hassle. She said, "Hold on and I'll find a pen. . . ."


Well that was depressing.

But also just *confusing*. How could she and Pepper see the same actions so differently? It made him wonder if the cops, or that dickhead Griff, had spoken to Mari and explained the fight in a way that made him seem as terrible as possible. Speaking to her about it forced him to see the same afternoon from a new angle. A big guy stomps into a parking lot and beats up a teacher. Then he beats up three cops. Good God. He'd begun seeing this version of himself—a thug, a marauder, a monster—when Mari mentioned calling his brother, when she asked him to hold on while she found a pen.

He had no choice. He told her Ralph's name. And that he lived in Maryland now. But when she asked him for the actual number, he couldn't give it to her. His cell phone knew the digits, not him. She said she'd go online and find Ralph's number and give him this one and explain as much as she could. She wished him sincere good luck.

And that was it.

Pepper left the phone alcove, despondent. In part because he knew, even if Mari actually did track down his brother, Ralph wouldn't call. He probably wouldn't even tell their mother Pepper was in the hospital. Pepper had entered the alcove thinking he had at least one ally. He left knowing he had none.

He left the alcove and looked toward Northwest 2 and the room waiting there. Another day and a half. How many more chances would that give last night's visitor to drop in?

He looked to his right and saw that unclassifiable trio—woman in her fifties, man in his thirties, teenage girl—walking from the television lounge and down Northwest 5. He watched as they entered the room at the hub of Northwest and circled around the nurses' station. They barely spoke to one another but didn't look angry, really. Maybe just a little worn out. The time spent getting ready for the visit, traveling to the hospital, sitting around with your loved one inside a sealed (if sunny) room. That's going to get you tired. Now they spoke to one of the staff. A nurse led the family to Northwest 1, toward the secure ward door. She moved ahead of the family, already picking through her ring of keys for the right one. The one that would let them leave. Pepper watched all this carefully.

He felt so low just then, at a complete loss. Dogged out. Abandoned. Without the willpower to be prudent, to check himself. A feeling known, generally, as *fuck it*.

Pepper trailed behind the family who trailed the nurse. No alarms went off as Pepper moved closer. No one even noticed him.

The nurse had her back to the hallway and the proper key in hand. She pulled it forward, moving it toward the lock, and the red plastic cord squeaked faintly with the stretch.

It was then that Pepper realized he was really going to try to escape. He worried about the dude in his thirties, but not that much. The guy was doughy, not very tall; the kind of man who made a living but rarely worked. And, for all Pepper knew, heavily medicated. Pepper could get past him. His slow walk turned into a trot.

The nurse slipped the key into the secure ward door and this is the moment when she got a bit lazy. She should have looked over her shoulder to be sure there were no other patients crowding close. In fact, the orderly should actually have accompanied her and the family to the door. All this was basic training. But there was only the one young orderly on shift, and he'd gone to the television lounge to let people know visiting hours were about over.

The nurse stood at the door alone. She'd offered to go open the door for this family just to avoid the damn charting for a few minutes. The most pleasant part of her job for the next few hours would be these moments when she got to usher visitors out. She took some pride in smiling at them as they left, like a good hostess. She was new, on the job for only two months. She unlocked the secure ward door and pulled it open.

A moment later Pepper rear-ended her.

The big man was *fast* when he had the proper motivation. Like getting out of the nut hut. Like stepping outside and breathing fresh air.

Pepper moved toward the door. He reached that family and mushed them out of the way. First the man: it was like brushing past a sack of dirty laundry, that's how soft the man's body felt. The guy slipped and went down. Then Pepper made his harshest decision. He chose to vault over the woman in her fifties. He thought this was better than barreling through her. But the man was no kind of athlete. Pepper had no ups. If he went three inches off the ground it would be an all-time best. He bum-rushed that poor woman and she went stumbling forward, plowing into the nurse's back. The two smashed into the wall just to their left.

No time for apologies. The door was completely open. Look at that lavender wall paint in the hallway right outside! Pepper could've maneuvered a Zamboni machine through the doorway. He was free. He was free. Even if it was the worst idea he'd had, in a week of *lousy* ideas, the man could still escape. He made it past everyone.

Except the teenage girl.

She didn't have Pepper's size or weight, obviously, but what she did have in her favor was rage. She had the Crazy Strength. (Retarded folks are rumored to have powerful—nearly mythic—strength but don't shortchange the mentally ill. In the proper state they can bring the ruckus.)

This teenage girl was the patient. The woman in her fifties, the mother. The soft-bodied man in his thirties, her brother. Pepper had guessed wrong, and he would pay for it.

The kid mounted him from behind. She grabbed his shirt right by the waist and planted her feet on the backs of his shins. Even though she didn't weigh that much, Pepper couldn't stay upright with that pressure on his calves. With that surprisingly simple move she toppled the big man.

As he fell, time slowed, giving Pepper a moment to once again take in the painted trees in the framed pictures on one wall. The images seemed to move away from him now. Before his face hit the floor, he had one clear thought.

*I'm a fucking idiot.*

When Pepper's face connected with the linoleum tiles, his mouth opened and his front teeth connected with them and he heard one of his teeth crack, and small bits of enamel skitter through the doorway, to the other side.

The young woman ran *up* his back, clawing forward, until she grabbed the back of his head and pulled at his hair. Brown strands in her hands. And this whole time those two blue pom-poms on the top of her blue knit cap were bouncing and bobbing playfully.

"Put your hands on my mother again!" the teenager howled. "Put your hands on *my fucking mother!*"

The girl brought her right elbow down on the back of Pepper's neck; her elbow stabbing right into the ball at the top of his spine. Pepper couldn't even yell, he coughed violently and foamy spit covered his lip and chin. He dropped the side of his face against the floor and he huffed and heaved and snorted.

The woman in her fifties had found her footing by now. She grabbed her daughter and pulled her away. "That's enough, Loochie! Come on now! Get off him! Loochie!"

The nurse and the girl's brother got up, too. The orderly on duty and two other nurses stampeded down the hall and surrounded Pepper's prone body.

"He hit my mother!" the girl shouted. "It's not my fault!"

The orderly grabbed Pepper's shins. Pepper kicked but there wasn't much power in him. The orderly then dragged Pepper backward, away from the open door and farther into the unit, like a roped steer. It took a great strain to move Pepper's body just three feet. Then the nurse who'd opened the door shut it again. She locked it.

Pepper looked up at the wild child, to see her staring down at him, one arm hooked around her mother's shoulder protectively. The girl's brother shivered as he leaned against a wall.

A nurse arrived with Pepper's punishment. When a patient fucked up this fully he wasn't just given another pill. This time they brought the high-dose solution. It came in liquid form, inside of a needle.

# 7

THEY HAVE TO keep patients medicated on a psychiatric unit. Staff are trying to get the patient's illness back in control. If a person is in the hospital, it's probably because his or her levels are off. Some meds are tried, a few work and others don't but staff are always trying to find the exact right combination for each patient.

But the other reason they have to keep patients medicated, even sedated, is because life on the unit will scramble anyone's brains.

What is there to do in a mental hospital? Watch television, sit in your room, wander the hallways, step out for a smoke break, attend group meetings. Every day, that's all you get. It's why visiting hours mean so much. Even patients who didn't get along with their families on the outside are pleased to welcome them here.

Being stuck inside and doped up to the gills can make the place feel like a time machine, as Loochie knew, even by age nineteen. The distinction between the days, the weeks, the months, the *years* fade. It all seems like one long day. You just lose track. It's shocking how quickly that can happen.

So if Pepper lost the next day or two because of the injection (plus the Haldol and lithium) well, it shouldn't be all that surprising. It took him hours to swim back to the shores of consciousness. And who was waiting for him right there on the beach? A nurse carrying a small white cup. Casting him out to sea again.

It takes time for a body to adjust to the meds. Really not all that different from building up one's tolerance to alcohol. Once, one beer had your head wobbling loose on your neck, but in time, it might take five or six. You learn to hold your liquor. In the ward, you learn to hold your pills.

But it takes time.

Pepper's seventy-two-hour observation period came and went, and he hardly realized its passing. Not that he forgot, he was just so busy swimming. Who petitions for his legal rights while trying desperately not to drown?

When he came to New Hyde, it was the third week of February.

When he finally shook off his medical haze, it was the middle of March.

# 8

PEPPER DIDN'T UNDERSTAND how much time he'd lost until he wandered out of his room and down Northwest 2 and shuffled up to the nurses' station. He put both elbows on the top tier like a man sidling up for a drink. He even smiled as he looked down at Scotch Tape, Miss Chris, and another nurse charting. He meant to ask how he could sign himself out of his padded cell. Seventy-two hours had surely come and gone.

Then he saw a copy of the *New York Post* up there on the nurses' station. It lay flat, facedown, the back cover showing the lead story of the sports section. Unofficial policy saw staff often leaving their old newspapers out for patients to read. A minor kindness. And at the top of the page, Pepper saw, almost in passing, a mention of March Madness, the NCAA Division 1 Men's Basketball Championship. *March.*

How could the *Post* already be talking about fans bracket picks? In February?

Pepper might've been impulsive, a little quick to throw hands, but he wasn't stupid. And as he came to understand the *real* news the paper was delivering to him—it's March 17!—Pepper had to clutch at the nurses' station desktop just to keep from keeling over.

He grabbed at the desktop and leaned forward. He looked like a man halfway in a lake, trying to climb back into the boat. He flailed out with one hand and sent the newspaper flying from the station like a gray bird.

Scotch Tape rose up and Miss Chris rolled her seat backward, out of the nurses' station, and around the side to get closer to Pepper, without lifting her butt from the chair. The other nurse already had her keys in hand and was fiddling with the drawer where they kept the tranquilizers.

Pepper looked at Scotch Tape directly and said quietly. "It's March. Why am I still here?"

Scotch Tape looked into Pepper's eyes. He realized the big man wasn't trying to come over the desk, wasn't attacking the staff, so he spoke as calmly as he could. "That was the doctor's decision, not mine."

"I want to see him," Pepper said.

Miss Chris clapped a hand against her thigh. "You and me both!"

She put one hand on the nurses' station and pulled herself up from the chair.

"That man makes the rules, but we the ones who enforce them. And we get all your scorn in the bargain."

Pepper let go of the desktop and stood tall again. "But he can't just decide to keep me here like that. Without telling me."

The other nurse, whom Pepper now recognized as the one he had knocked down during his escape attempt weeks before, stopped jimmying the desk drawer and grabbed a three-ring binder. She opened the cover and flipped pages and finally found the one she wanted. She stood up and stepped closer to Scotch Tape, then set the open binder on the desktop so Pepper could see.

A form with four paragraphs of single-spaced legalese. It looked like a warranty.

"So what's this?" Pepper asked. He barely glanced at it. He didn't want to *read,* he wanted to be *heard.*

Scotch Tape said, "Consent form, big man. Agreeing to be admitted as a patient. Everyone has to sign one if the seventy-two-hour period ends but the doctor thinks you still need to be with us."

The nurse reached down and tapped the bottom of the page with one finger. Her wrist was still sprained from the fall she'd taken thanks to Pepper.

"You signed it. You agreed," she said with some satisfaction.

Now Pepper actually looked at the page. That scrawl at the bottom was his signature? It looked more like someone had drooled blue ink on the page.

"I've been in half a *coma* for the last four weeks."

Miss Chris moved closer, right next to his left arm. She looked at the consent form. "Looks like your hand was working."

Pepper understood that this was a joke, but not for him. Not even really on him. It was the gallows humor of people who've seen this kind of mess happen before. And will again. What can you do? That was the unspoken phrase at the end of every sentence. *What can you do?* Just go along.

Pepper felt his rage just then like a series of small explosions. In his gut. His chest. His throat. His hands. The rational part of him was howling, *Don't do anything! Don't do anything! Calm down!* But it was like holding a conversation right below a rumbling jet engine. Whatever Pepper did next was going to fuck him, long term. But he felt incapable of stopping himself.

Then Pepper felt the small, bony fingers wrap around his wrist. A touch he knew, even in this state. The only person who'd put her hands on him with any tenderness in this wasteland.

Dorry was there, at his right side, pulling at his wrist, looking up at him serenely.

"You've been down there, Pepper. You already know that road. You know exactly where it ends."

Pepper started to pull back, despite himself.

She said, "More punishment. More drugs. That's what they'll give you."

The nurse next to Scotch Tape said, "That's not *fair,* Dorry."

Dorry sighed. "But it's still true."

Pepper's hands relaxed and his shoulders did, too. That rage in his gut, his chest, his throat—it left him like a bad spirit being cast out. Dorry still held his wrist.

He exhaled. He felt like a lost child who has wandered into the wrong house.

"What should I do instead?" he asked her weakly.

"For now?" Dorry grinned. "Let's go to Group."

Then Dorry quietly led Pepper to one of the conference rooms on Northwest 1.

There were already a few people inside the meeting room, on their feet, and when Pepper entered the room, an older man called out to him.

"Grab the end of that table, please."

But Pepper couldn't follow the order. Had he even heard it? No. He was repeating the date in his head.

*March 17. March 17. March 17. March 17. March 17. March 17.*

The older man clapped his hands loudly and Pepper finally snapped back. The guy looked to be in his fifties, red-faced, bald. The way he grit his teeth, he looked like Bob Hope; the chin like a shovel, the broad forehead and high cheekbones.

He looked at Pepper and said, "The others already know me. I'm Dr. Barger."

Dr. Barger was broad and short. He seemed unlike any doctor Pepper had ever seen. He wore a sport coat, but the top two buttons of his shirt were undone, the reddish flesh of his chest visible. Thick gray chest hairs ran all the way up to his Adam's apple. And he wore a thin gold chain that lay in the hair like an extension cord in a shag carpet. Dr. Barger looked like a swinger.

"Let's go," he said sternly, pointing at one end of the conference table again.

What did Pepper know better than this? Moving furniture. It was almost comforting to do the work. He grabbed one end. He'd lifted it a foot off the ground before he even asked where he was supposed to take it.

Dr. Barger couldn't heft the other end. He gave it two tugs and a vein on his forehead throbbed perilously. He stopped trying and looked around the room, at the other patients. "A little help," the doctor said.

And who came to the rescue? The teenage girl who'd chopped Pepper down. Loochie. The kid didn't get her end as high as Pepper's—how could she, she stood a foot shorter—but the weight of the table didn't seem to bother her any more than it did Pepper. She still wore that light blue knit cap. The pom-poms sat on either side of her head like mouse's ears.

Pepper and Loochie frowned at each other.

*This little thing took me out?* Pepper thought. He felt a dose of grudging respect.

Dr. Barger, oblivious to any tension, waved toward the far end of the room. "Put the table over there. Line it up against the back wall."

As Pepper and Loochie moved the table to the back of the room, the four other patients rearranged chairs. There were only seven people in the room, including the doctor, so they'd only need one table for their group session.

Pepper recognized a few of the patients. Dorry, of course. And Loochie. Coffee, too. A pair of white women who looked like each other—identical short haircuts, similar light blue mom jeans and Old Navy T-shirts showing the American flag. Even their bodies looked alike, bottom-heavy like butternut squash. Not twins, not siblings, but *alike*.

As everyone sat at the conference table, Dr. Barger smiled. "And now I'd like to welcome you all to our weekly Book Group."

One of the two short-haired women said, "How can you call it a weekly *Book* Group when we never have any *books*?"

The other said, "Don't be too hard on the doc. Have you looked at this bunch? I'm not too sure all of us can read!"

The first woman pointed across the table at Pepper, and said, "Hey, Frankenstein. You hate books as much as you hate fire?"

"Sammy!" Dr. Barger barked.

Both women laughed together. It didn't matter to them if anyone else enjoyed the joke.

But Pepper felt too angry about the four weeks he'd lost to be insulted. Instead he pointed at the doctor. "I was supposed to be here for a seventy-two-hour observation, but now . . ."

Dr. Barger wagged one short red finger.

"I'm at New Hyde as your therapist. Dr. Anand is the staff psychiatrist."

"So?"

Dorry said, "Dr. Barger doesn't have the *power* to release you."

Dr. Barger's mouth narrowed into a frown. "I wouldn't put it that way, Dorry."

"Well, what would you say then?" Dorry smiled pleasantly.

"Dr. Anand's authority *supersedes* my own."

Loochie crossed her arms and leaned forward in her seat aggressively. "How's that different from what she said?"

Dr. Barger looked at the teenager, his red face reddening even more. "I have authority here. It's just not the kind that can . . ."

Then the doctor stopped himself. He shut his eyes and rested a hand on the top of his head. He breathed quietly for a moment, and when he opened his eyes, all the patients were watching him in silence.

Dr. Barger spoke with overdone civility. "I want to welcome you all to our weekly Book Group. I'm happy to see so many of you back." He nodded at Pepper. "And to welcome our newest member."

Pepper and Dorry sat on one long end of the conference table. Loochie, Coffee, and the two jokers sat opposite them. Dr. Barger sat at the head. As they settled, the nurse from Pepper's escape attempt entered the room, pushing a three-tiered cart full of books. She wheeled it around the table and stopped behind Dr. Barger. Pepper could see that the nurse was young. Probably not much older than Loochie. She stood next to the book cart and smiled. Her cheeks were as plump and smooth as the Gerber baby's.

Dr. Barger sat back in his chair. He rested his hands on his belly proudly.

"So you see, Sammy? This time we *do* have books," he gloated, looking around the table as if awaiting applause.

But only Coffee reacted, raising one hand like a pupil with a question for the teacher.

Dr. Barger ignored him. "As you can see, I've been able to acquire these."

Coffee continued chopping the air with his raised hand. He huffed now, too, and looked even more like that kid in the front row.

Finally, Dr. Barger acknowledged him. "Okay, Coffee, do you have something to say? About *Book Group*?"

Coffee revealed a thin blue binder. He set it on the table and opened it and flourished a pen. Everyone but Pepper and the new nurse sighed loudly.

"The phone number of New York City Comptroller John Liu," Coffee said. "Can you please provide it for me?"

Dr. Barger dropped his voice an octave. "What does that have to do with Book Group?"

Coffee ignored that. He said, "Attempts to reach the mayor have failed. I was recently visited by a representative of his office who threatened to have me arrested and to sue me if I don't stop calling. So I accept that. Mr. Liu seems like a serious alternative. I believe he will help."

Sammy leaned forward and said, "What does a comptroller do, anyway?" She turned to her best friend, her doubles partner, setting the woman up for a match point. "Sam?"

Sam said, "I don't know, but if you hum a few bars I can fake it!"

This made the two of them crash backward with laughter. Their chairs buckling. They laughed so loudly that Loochie, right beside them, pulled her knit cap down over her ears. That only made the two women laugh more.

"You're giving that poor girl *brain* damage," said Sammy.

"Well, we're in the right place for it!" shouted Sam.

Coffee tapped his pen against the table. "Dr. Barger," he said. "The number?"

Now the doctor knocked on the table with force and the women's laughter quieted. Even Coffee stopped tapping the pen.

Then the nurse spoke up. "These books won't be useful anyway."

Dr. Barger looked over his shoulder. "Excuse me, *nurse*?"

"Have you looked at the collection lately?"

Everyone in the room scanned the shelves. This Bookmobile

was hardly a fine library. It looked like the dumping grounds for vocational-training manuals. (*ISP—Industrial Security Professional Exam Manual; Automotive Technician Certification: Test Preparation Manual; Medium/Heavy Duty Truck Technician Certification: Test Preparation Manual,* and so on.) There were a few spy novels, a few mysteries, the Book of Common Prayer (it had curse words written in the margins of many pages). Not great reading material maybe, but also only one or two copies of each. Not enough for everyone. The nurse was right. Not only poor quality, but also poor quantity.

Dr. Barger couldn't pretend to miss the problem. But he could refuse to admit the fault was his. He looked up at the nurse and said, "I told *you* to bring all the books from the trunk of my car."

Before the nurse could argue, explain, or apologize, Dorry proposed, "Why don't we vote on one book we want to read together. Then maybe New Hyde could get us all copies of that."

Pepper pointed at the book cart. Why did it bring him a childish pleasure to see the choices were so bad?

"What do you mean?" he joked. "Don't we all want to read the *Medium/Heavy Duty Truck Technician Certification: Test Preparation Manual*?"

Dorry tapped Pepper's forearm, another subtle but effective correction. "I can speak to Dr. Anand. I'll get him to buy us the books."

Dr. Barger strained forward at the table. "*You'll* talk to Dr. Anand?"

Sammy and Sam clapped. Sammy said, "We like this idea. A title to vote for."

Dr. Barger just shook his head. "Fine then. I'll buy us the books if I have to."

Dorry grinned at the other patients, ignoring Dr. Barger's glare. "Isn't that generous?"

"Georgina, will you go get us some tape, and a legal pad?" Dr. Barger asked the nurse.

She nodded, but just as she left the room she said, "My name is Josephine."

"Better bring a black marker, too," Dr. Barger said.

Something in Josephine wanted to argue the point—*Say my name, say my name!*—but realized Dr. Barger was one of a dwindling population: old mutts who were never trained to find others terribly worthwhile. Have an hour's conversation and these men might be charming, funny, captivating, and kind. But they wouldn't ask *you* a single question about yourself. Not one. They simply wouldn't be interested. They were never trained to be curious about others, and they sure weren't going to start now. At twenty-four, Josephine already knew she could spend the next minute trying and failing to make Dr. Barger hear her, or she could do something to help these patients. Only one choice was worth it. She left the room to fetch the man his pad and pen and tape.

Dr. Barger said, "Okay, so let's have some suggestions for books."

One of the two jokers raised her hand.

"Thank you, Sammy."

"I'm Sam," the woman said. "*She's* Sammy."

Dr. Barger said, "What's your choice then, *Sam.*"

But it was Sammy who answered. "*Ask Click and Clack,*" she said.

Dr. Barger's nostrils flared. "I have no idea what that is."

Pepper leaned across the table, toward Sammy and Sam. "The Tappet brothers, right?" He looked at the doctor. "It's a radio show called *Car Talk.* I love that show."

Sam pointed at Pepper enthusiastically. "See that, Frankenstein knows what we're talking about."

Despite himself, Pepper laughed.

Sammy applauded him. "Hey, that's nice. Frankenstein's got a sense of humor."

Sam and Sammy whistled and cheered.

Dr. Barger knocked on the table again. "We're *not* reading a car book."

Then Loochie spoke, no hand raised, no permission requested. She said, "Magazines."

"What does that mean?" the doctor asked.

Loochie shrugged. "*Magazines.* That's what I like to read in here. *Vibe. XXL. Black Hair.*"

Pepper said, "You want us all to read *Black Hair* in Book Group?"

Sammy opened her mouth, she had a joke, but thought better of sharing it.

Dorry spoke calmly. "No offense, Loochie, but I think the rest of us are too old for *XXVibe* or whatever it's called."

Loochie laughed like a native speaker at a foreigner attempting to master her tongue.

Josephine returned with the materials.

"How about Ken Kesey?" Josephine suggested. "*One Flew Over the Cuckoo's Nest*? That book meant a lot to me in high school. I think *you* all might really like it."

Sammy frowned. "Well, why don't you read *Slaughterhouse Five* to a roomful of cattle."

Sam shook her head. "You'll have to excuse my best friend. She only reads the covers of great books."

Sammy grinned. "That's usually the best part!"

Josephine didn't give up.

"I just thought you all might like it because it's about a mental hospital."

Dorry took off her glasses, which instantly made her look less nuts. Her eyes were smaller, and she seemed younger by ten years. She blew on the lenses, and small specks of dust, flakes of skin, and dandruff fell like flurries toward the tabletop. She put the glasses back on and, nutty again, looked at the nurse.

"Here's what you have to understand about that book, *Josephine*. As good as it is, it *isn't* about mentally ill people. It takes places in a mental hospital, yes. But that book is about the way a certain young generation felt that society was designed to destroy them. Make them into thoughtless parts of a machine. To lobotomize them. That book is about *them*, not about people like *us*."

Josephine stammered, trying to respond, but Dorry didn't stop talking.

"If you remember the patients who really mattered in that story, most of them were *voluntary*. Do you remember what the main characters called the other ones? The ones who would never leave because they could never be cured?"

"No," Josephine admitted quietly.

"The Chronics. Most of them were vegetables. Brain-deads. Maybe violent. Chronically sick. Diagnosed as everlastingly damaged. All of us here at Northwest? That's who *we* are. Northwest is nothing but Chronics. We've all been committed, and most of us are not voluntary. So why would we want to read a book that barely mentions us except to tell us we're *fucked in the anus*?"

Dr. Barger shouted, "Dorry!"

Josephine could withstand Dr. Barger's callousness, but to get torn down by Dorry actually hurt.

"I was only trying to . . ."

Her eyes reddened, and she quickly walked out of the conference room without looking back.

*How could Dorry know all this?* Josephine thought. *How does some daffy old lady mental patient in a New Hyde psych unit understand that book better than me?* Josephine didn't mean to be so dismissive, but it came surprisingly easily. Then, almost as quickly, she questioned many of the judgments she'd made in her life. Mental patients can't be intelligent. Junkies can't be articulate. And so on. But really, honestly, how many did she actually know? Josephine left the room feeling embarrassed and shallow, but also determined to do better, to know these people, with time.

Back in the conference room, Pepper realized there was only one thing he wanted to discuss.

"I want to read about a monster," he said.

This quieted everyone.

Dr. Barger finally said, "Why?"

Pepper said, "Because I've seen one."

Why did everyone in the room suddenly sit up straight? All except Dr. Barger. The doctor lifted a black marker and pulled off the cap. He watched Pepper coolly. "That's a *belief* we'll have to discuss more in Group next week. But, okay. We can read a horror story. Nothing too gory, though. I can't stand things like that."

"Let's read *Jaws*," Pepper said. It was like he could only look at the monster obliquely, to avoid being stricken blind by the horror of direct sight.

Loochie raised her eyebrows at him. "About the shark?"

"Yes."

Loochie, to her own great surprise, felt interested. She raised her hand to vote yes. So did Sam and Sammy and Coffee and Dorry.

Dr. Barger, underwhelmed, said, "*Jaws*. All right then. I'll order it."

Every hand went down except one.

Dr. Barger sighed. "What is it, Coffee?"

"The comptroller's number, please. You can find it for me on your phone."

# 9

BOOK GROUP ENDED with a silent march. The patients left the conference room quietly. Sam and Sammy went together. The others, one by one. Only Pepper remained at the table. Dr. Barger and Josephine waited for him to leave so they could lock the door behind him.

What had Pepper been expecting? To declare he'd been trapped here through deceit and have the others, who'd been trapped even longer, gnash their teeth and weep for him? To confess he'd seen a monster and have everyone melt and hold him close? Maybe so. But that's not what he'd gotten. He'd admitted to being frightened. The reaction of his peers? They wanted lunch.

Pepper finally left the room.

Josephine moved behind him, keeping the Bookmobile between them.

Dr. Barger locked the door.

Lunchtime.

When Pepper reached the nurses' station, he found half the patients in an orderly line. Scotch Tape stood inside the station, holding a clipboard. He caught Pepper's eye.

"No more room service for you, my man. Before every meal, you come here first to get your meds, like everyone else."

Pepper didn't see any point in refusing. He went to the back of the line. Where Loochie and Coffee and Dorry and Sammy and Sam were. They didn't speak to him. They didn't even look at him. Had he said something wrong in there?

Miss Chris was beside Scotch Tape, holding a tray of small white cups. As each patient stepped up to the desktop, Scotch Tape read off a series of medicines: Risperdal. Topomax. Depakote. Celexa. Luvox. Nardil. Dalmane. Haldol. Lithium. (Just to name about a third of Scotch Tape's list.) Miss Chris checked the cup to be sure the right pills were in each. Then she handed the cup to the patient and both staff members carefully watched each one swallow.

That was the system. Meds at breakfast, lunch, and dinner.

Pepper swallowed his Haldol and lithium. He was strangely grateful for the pills. They shaved down the sharp edges of his emotions. Until he felt smooth and round. Easier to roll along, no matter the bumps and curves. He walked down Northwest 5, toward the television lounge, alone. No doubt he'd lost his job with Farooz Brothers by now. Those guys would fire someone if he missed more than two days. Forget about four weeks. But Pepper just kept rolling.

His rent was paid automatically from his checking account. A system that his landlord (an agency rather than a person) had demanded of all tenants back in 2009 when layoffs first began in big numbers. Electricity, gas, even the cable was probably still working. His life had been disrupted, but not his billing cycles. His cell phone was paid automatically, too. Which meant he might still have service. Where had they put his phone? In a baggie with his boot laces and belt. (That baggie then went into a cubby, like in kindergarten, kept with all the others in a locked room on Northwest 1.) How long could he keep current on his bills? How long would his life outside wait for him? He had about four thousand dollars in his checking account. Which would last longer—his savings or his captivity? Keep rolling.

He reached the television lounge and the orderly handed him a lunch tray. The gray tray, with its little segmented sections, reminded Pepper of the ones they used to hand out in grade school.

Pepper moved to an empty table, as far away from the television as possible. The flat screen showed the local news. There was a remote control for the TV, an old man held it like a scepter. He lifted it high and increased the volume so he could hear over the chatter of the growing lunch crowd.

The orderly said, "Not too loud, Mr. Mack."

The old man turned and glowered at the orderly, a kid. "It's my half hour to control the remote," he said. "That *includes* the volume."

Mr. Mack looked to his best friend, who sat beside him. "Is this youngblood giving *me* orders?"

His friend shrugged noncommittally.

Both men wore threadbare sport coats. Under these were their patient-issue blue pajamas; theirs were bright and stain-free. Both had on worn-down loafers, too. They looked sharp, especially in here. Compared with everyone else, they looked like Duke Ellington and Cab Calloway.

The orderly raised his voice now. "You've got to think of everyone in the room."

"Fuck everyone in the room," Mr. Mack muttered.

"Language!"

Mr. Mack put up a hand in a gesture of peace. "I *mean* I'm trying to help these people learn about current events." Mr. Mack looked back at the orderly. "And Frank Waverly doesn't think I need to listen to you anyway."

The orderly said, "Frank Waverly is no fool. It's you who's being defiant."

Mr. Mack grinned at this as if he'd just been complimented. He raised the remote again and lowered the volume. But just one bar.

Pepper, meanwhile, had settled himself at his table, ignoring the skirmish. Instead of the staff and patient, he watched the sunlight as it lit up the half-court outside the lounge.

He didn't notice he had company until they sat.

Loochie, Coffee, and Dorry.

At the other end of the lounge, Mr. Mack's hand rose again, the remote aimed at the screen, and the little green volume bars appeared again. The sound went up.

"Mr. Mack!" the orderly shouted.

Dorry reached over and put her hand on top of Pepper's.

"So," she said, when he looked at her.

She leaned toward him without smiling. She squinted, as if trying to see deeper inside. Loochie spoke next, though.

"It's been around *long* before any of us. I mean any human beings. They found it living here and built Northwest just to hold it. You understand? Northwest is a cage."

Coffee leaned forward to add, "But every living thing needs to eat, Pepper. You can keep something in a cage, but then you have to feed it. Now look at us here. The food makes us fat. The drugs make us slow. We're cattle. Food. For it. And best of all, for New Hyde, no one notices when people like us end up dead."

Behind the group, a new skirmish unfolded. Mr. Mack's half hour of television privileges had passed. This was as much of a rule on the unit as the medication schedule. The only way to keep so many different patients occupied. It was Sammy's turn to hold the remote. But Mr. Mack wouldn't let it go. He and Sammy were now tugging at either end of it like it was the key to New Hyde's front door.

The orderly intervened. "Your time is *up*, Mr. Mack."

"I got one minute left! I got one minute!"

"You got milk breath!" Sammy yelled back at him. "And your teeth are yellow!"

Behind Sammy, Sam added, "And those are his good qualities!"

Frank Waverly, Mr. Mack's friend, nodded at this. Even though Mr. Mack was his best friend, he couldn't disagree with Sam's point.

Now the orderly clomped over to the tables to break up their nonsense.

Dorry, Loochie, and Coffee paid this chaos no mind. They were on another plane. Dorry leaned in to speak, snatching that wretched cookie off Pepper's tray and dropping it into her lap before opening her mouth. "I'm going to tell you the *truth* about what you saw last night." She glared at the others. "Not stories."

She stole the cookies off Coffee's tray, then Loochie's with surprising quickness and dropped them into her lap.

"I've been here longer than Coffee and Loochie combined. I have the distinction of being the second patient ever committed to Northwest. And that thing you saw the other night? He was the first. Let me tell you this, with no ambiguity. He's a man. Deformed. Very troubled. Very angry. But just a man."

Pepper could feel that breath burning his ear again. Could see those white eyes, missing their pupils. Felt the fur. "I've never seen a man like that," he argued.

Loochie and Coffee nodded solemnly.

Dorry shook her head. "I'm telling you what I *know*."

The orderly stood over Mr. Mack now and put his hand out in a gesture common to any parent. Exasperated authority. Mr. Mack looked at his wristwatch and counted out loud. "Nine . . . eight . . . seven . . . six . . ."

When he reached zero, he opened his hand and held the remote out to Sammy, but the orderly snatched it first to turn the volume down. When Sammy got her turn, she chose an episode of *American Chopper*.

She and Sam pulled their chairs right up under the screen. Even the patients who didn't like the show remained in their seats and watched to pass some time. On the screen a burly guy with a graying mustache slapped the side of a silver motorcycle, grinned at the camera, and said, "This beast looks like it was forged in *hell*!"

Coffee rose from his chair. "Why don't we just show him?"

Dorry shook her head. "Not yet."

Pepper said, "Show me what?"

Loochie picked the green apple off her tray. She bit into it and chewed.

"Show you where it lives," she said.


The four of them walked down Northwest 5 as a pack. Loochie and Coffee in the lead, Dorry and Pepper behind.

Dorry said, "What's on Northwest One?"

Pepper said, "The exit."

Loochie said, "That's no exit."

Coffee said, "It's just an entrance, for us."

Dorry asked, "What's on Northwest Two?"

Pepper said, "Male patients."

Dorry asked, "What's on Northwest Three?"

Pepper said, "Female patients."

As they entered the room at the hub of the unit, Dorry said, "And what's on Northwest Five?"

Pepper said, "Television lounge."

Loochie turned back to him and the pom-poms on her knit cap bounced. "We would've accepted smoker's area, too."

They ignored the staff members sitting inside the nurses' station just as the staff members ignored them. They were in two overlapping realities.

Dorry touched Pepper's shoulder to stop him. "So what's left?"

"Northwest Four," Pepper said. "You told me not to go anywhere near it."

Loochie and Coffee and Dorry and Pepper gathered at the threshold of that hallway. Northwest 4 looked like all the others. Eggshell-white walls, beige tiled floors, fluorescent lights buzzing overhead. There were doors running down either side, but here was the first difference: None of the doors had knobs. Even from the lip of Northwest 4, Pepper could see door after door with the handle removed and the lock sealed. A whole hallway of rooms that were never used.

At the far end of Northwest 4 sat a large stainless-steel door.

It looked like the little cousin of the secure door in Northwest 1. Stainless steel instead of cast iron, sleek where that other one was rough. But it, too, had a shatterproof window. The lights of the room behind that door were out. Totally dark.

"There," Dorry said quietly.

Loochie lifted one foot. "Watch this."

Her baby-blue Nike crossed the threshold of the hallway, and instantly Miss Chris called out from the nurses' station.

"Off-limits."

Loochie winked at Pepper and planted her foot over the line. She lifted her back foot and brought that one over, too. There she stood, just barely, in Northwest 4.

Scotch Tape stood up and leaned his elbows on the desktop of the nurses' station.

"Loochie," he growled. "You heard what Miss Chris said?"

Loochie stepped back.

"They protect it," Coffee whispered.

Pepper couldn't look away from the stainless-steel door one hundred feet down Northwest 4. It bent the light cast down from the ceiling so that something seemed to move behind the plastic window. A figure on the other side, or just a reflection of something on this side? Pepper stared at the small window. His legs stiffened. His face turned warm.

He felt watched.

Then he heard his own voice in his head. It was saying, *No, no, no, no, no.* Not disbelief but refusal.

"I don't belong here," he told the other three. "This isn't my fight."

His spoken voice sounded so small. He watched Dorry and Loochie and Coffee deflate with disappointment. A story came to him, an explanation.

"In 1969," he told them, "the Doors performed at the Dinner Key Auditorium in Miami. About twelve thousand fans showed up to hear them play. Jim Morrison was drunk."

"You were there?" Loochie asked. "You been to Miami?" She sounded jealous.

"No," Pepper admitted. "I was *born* in '69. I read about this. In an interview with Ray Manzarek, their keyboardist."

Pepper looked to Coffee and Dorry and Loochie, but none of them seemed to recognize the name. Pepper decided not to be disappointed in them for this.

"Morrison performed, but he didn't sing much. Mostly he yelled at the crowd. And at a certain point he told the crowd he knew why they'd really come to the show that night. 'You want to see my cock, don't you?!' "

Dorry snorted, a little laugh.

"That's what he said," Pepper continued. "Then Morrison waved his shirt in front of his crotch and pulled it away and said, 'See it? Did you see it?' "

Coffee looked confused.

Loochie said, "This doesn't sound like a very good band."

"Listen to me. Four days later, the city of Miami issued a warrant for Morrison's arrest. After a trial, Morrison was convicted of two misdemeanors. Open profanity, I think. And indecent exposure. And yet, Ray Manzarek swears Morrison never exposed himself. No pictures were ever developed, from a crowd of twelve thousand. And no one ever showed real evidence that the . . . exposure ever happened. Manzarek called it a mass delusion."

Pepper stopped for a moment, to let the phrase sink in.

"But even years later, there were hundreds, thousands, who swore they'd seen Morrison's penis. It didn't happen, but to them it was still real."

Loochie and Coffee and Dorry backed away from Pepper. Pepper looked at his feet.

"You understand what I'm saying?"

Dorry nodded and shrugged.

"You're not one of *us*," she said. "Sure. We understand."

Loochie said, "If I had paid to see that concert, I would've got my money back."

Just that fast, they departed. Coffee slipped into the phone alcove. Dorry returned to her room on Northwest 3, where she slipped those cookies into a plastic bag, a kind of care package she was putting together for another patient, one of the many she took care of at New Hyde. And Loochie wandered back down Northwest 5. Her half hour of TV control would be coming soon and she wanted to watch something stupid and fun, music videos maybe; something to make her forget the story about Jim Morrison's penis. And how Pepper meant it to say she was seeing something that wasn't really there. *Fuck you, Frankenstein.* That's what Loochie wanted to tell him.

And Pepper? He returned to his room alone.

# 10

THAT NIGHT, THE big man couldn't fall asleep. He had the room to himself. Coffee stayed away, in the phone alcove trying the number for Comptroller John Liu. Dorry and Loochie ignored Pepper on line for nighttime meds, and at dinner in the lounge. The other patients seemed to be avoiding him, too. So he went to bed early. Pepper lay in bed for hours, but he couldn't sleep.

When Dorry, Loochie, and Coffee offered him membership in their conspiracy, he'd looked at those three mental patients and re-coiled. The shame made it impossible to doze off. He finally rolled out of bed at one a.m. Didn't know where he was headed, but he couldn't lie there anymore.

Pepper reached the nurses' station and found two staff members behind the desk. A man and a woman, neither he recognized. He walked around the station. He didn't look down Northwest 4, but as he passed that hallway he felt a pinch in his side, as if he'd been grabbed, but kept walking and slipped free from the phantom touch.

Four patients sat in the television lounge. Even at this late hour the room wasn't empty. The flat screen was on but with the sound set surprisingly low. One young guy had his chair pulled right up under the screen. He had a pockmarked face and stringy brown hair that almost looked like a toupee. The television's closed-captioning had been turned on, white letters on a black background filled the bottom half of the screen. The guy in the chair scanned the text. Every fourth word was misspelled or mistaken. Protesters around the Middle East were apparently causing Arab governments to "triple."

The guy in the chair said, "Topple."

The other three patients in the lounge were women. Three women at three different tables, leafing through stacks of magazines and newspapers. Their lips moved as they scanned the pages.

"Study hall?" Pepper asked.

One of the women, with long reddish hair pulled up into a bun, looked at Pepper, then back down at her copy of *Outside* magazine.

Pepper swayed there a moment. The vibe of the lounge, of New Hyde, seemed so much more peaceful at night. Not just lower volume, but also more thoughtful. Look at all these people reading. The lounge seemed like a library now.

Pepper hovered another minute before the redhead looked at him and said, "You don't belong here."

Pepper looked over his shoulder, as if she must've been addressing someone else.

The women at the other tables—one Chinese, the other Jewish—finally looked at Pepper. The guy sitting under the television even turned around in his chair.

The redhead said, "We hear you're not like us."

Pepper felt completely exposed and he crossed his arms.

"I didn't say that," he pleaded.

But just as quickly they ignored him again. The point had been made. Pepper shuffled out of the television lounge as quickly as he could, wondering if he looked as red as his face felt. He was a pariah on a psych unit. He couldn't imagine a lower state.

He reached the nurses' station again, staff members working inside. He heard one of them yawn in there. They were tired and preoccupied. Without another thought, Pepper turned right. He crossed the threshold of Northwest 4 without losing a step.

He marched toward the stainless-steel door.

The window in the silver door remained as dark as it had been that afternoon. He wanted to what? Touch it? Open it? He didn't know yet. As Pepper moved closer to it, the air itself felt warmer.

Pepper moved even closer. In lieu of a plan, he focused on the tangible details ahead. The silver door had a handle. The silver door had two locks. Now his face felt as if he'd walked through a cloud of steam. Moist. Sweaty. He smelled something new. Like the dirt of a freshly dug grave. At this point Pepper couldn't stop himself. He felt that pinch again, a grip closed around him. Was he walking toward the silver door, or being pulled?

"What the fuck!"

Pepper only registered those words *after* he'd been grabbed. The orderly on duty yoked Pepper from behind. Pepper reached out and, because his arms were so long, his fingertips grasped the door handle, just for a moment. The metal was so hot it burned his fingers.

The orderly, a big man, too, dragged Pepper backward down Northwest 4. Away from the stainless-steel door. "We got rules!" the orderly shouted in Pepper's ear. "You got no business in this hallway! You leave *that* door be!"

The farther they moved from the silver door, the less heat Pepper felt against his skin. The scent of fresh dirt dissipated and was replaced by that stale, hospitalized anti-smell again.

And the farther Pepper moved backward down Northwest 4, the greater his *relief*. His heart thrummed in his rib cage. Deep breaths expanded his lungs. He felt like he'd just missed being hit by a car, like the orderly had saved him. Without quite meaning to, Pepper laughed with gratitude.

The nurse appeared and she had the needle.

She remained silent, assessing Pepper, the wild affect on his face. His laughter didn't help his case. She watched him with displeasure.

The nurse, the orderly, and Pepper moved past the nurses' station and down Northwest 2. The doors of other patients' rooms creaked open. The trio of nurse, orderly, and unruly patient blasted into Pepper's room.

The orderly shook Pepper as if they were fighting, but Pepper wasn't resisting. *Au contraire, mon* minimum-wage *frère*. Pepper felt a relief that he didn't fully understand, and gratitude. He'd been about to do something very stupid. He felt sure of that now. And this orderly had saved him. *Thank you!* That's what he was trying to say. But Pepper couldn't explain. The only sounds coming out of his mouth were laughter and deep gulping coughs as he tried to take in air and talk. He seemed like a maniac.

But it was all still salvageable. Pepper would accept the needle. He'd been through that once before. He'd lose more time, but if that was the worst, he could bounce back. After this, he could avoid, all together, the games patients played on the unit. Whatever was on the other side of that door had nothing to do with Pepper and the world he planned on returning to as soon as he could. Let the patients tell all the spooky stories they liked, he would snub them just like they'd snubbed him tonight. Who gave a shit? He could weather it. He could ride out this time at New Hyde if he'd stop getting overwhelmed, emotional, and stick to the larger point. He'd tried and failed before, but he'd really do it now. All systems had their glitches, and Pepper's mistaken commitment to New Hyde was just one of them. It would work itself out, and he'd be released. He believed this. He knew this. He just had to keep the bigger picture in mind. Like now, stop fighting. Step one in getting on the staff's good side. Accept the needle—that was step two. After all, things couldn't get any worse than that.

But then Pepper noticed the orderly had *straps* with him.

*Who were those for?*

The orderly pushed Pepper onto his bed and pulled Pepper's arms down to his sides. He tied Pepper's wrists to the bed frame with the straps. First the right. Then the left.

The orderly tied up each of Pepper's ankles next.

Wait.

*Wait.*

They didn't need to do this. He was going to be compliant from now on. Didn't they understand?

The orderly shouted, "We been nice to you, my man! But you ain't been nice to us."

"No," Pepper muttered. "Please."

His arms and legs pulled at the straps. He wasn't resisting. It was a reaction beyond his control. These people were tying him down. What else were his limbs going to do but buckle?

The staff members didn't see it that way.

The nurse needed three tries to hit the vein in his forearm. The first two times she was just stabbing him. When she finally injected a big dose of Diazepam into Pepper's bloodstream, the doorway of his room was crowded with male patients, watching.

As Pepper faded, he scanned the faces in the doorway. Was Dorry really there? Had she snuck down Northwest 2 so she could see?

The nurse and orderly watched Pepper. Both were huffing from the scuffle. They scowled at him. Pepper pulled at the restraints, but they held.

Now the nurse and orderly shooed the patients from the doorway. They flicked off the lights, left the room, and locked the door behind them.

"*Please*," Pepper whimpered in the empty room.

# 11

PEPPER WOKE UP the next day. His ankles and wrists still bound. This was illegal. According to official guidelines, this should never be allowed. Restraints were acceptable for up to four consecutive hours, then the staff *must* release the patient. That's the law. Absolutely. But where were the regulators? A question worth asking in so many fields.

When Pepper had to go to the bathroom he called out for a nurse until Miss Chris heard him and appeared with a bedpan; a plastic bowl with a top shaped like a toilet seat. In her other hand she had a hard plastic pillow the shape and color of a wedge of cheddar cheese. She entered the room and undid one of Pepper's wrist straps then slid the wedge pillow behind Pepper's back so he could sit upright. Then she pointed at his butt and said, "Lift."

He raised his butt as high as it would go and Miss Chris slid his wrinkled pants down. She slipped the bedpan underneath him. She pulled the top sheet over him and as she left the room she said, "I'll give you some time."

The back of the bedpan rose higher than the front so it aimed his pelvis at an angle. This allowed all waste to remain in the bowl. Pepper had to shit so that's what he did. Miss Chris didn't return to the room for half an hour.

Pepper balanced on the bedpan while one wrist and both ankles were still attached to the bed frame. His body wracked into a bit of a corkscrew. The bedpan dug into his skin and the small of his back closed like a fist. The smell of his own shit rose to his nose. He breathed through his mouth.

Miss Chris wasn't even the first one back in the room. It was Coffee, blue three-ring binder in hand. He walked in and saw Pepper's forehead beading with sweat. Pepper waved Coffee closer with his free hand. For a moment Coffee looked stricken, concerned, but then his face dropped all expression. He entered the room and pulled a fresh pen from the plastic cup on his dresser. Then Coffee left.

"That's cold, Joe!" Pepper shouted.

But a minute after that, Miss Chris returned to the room. "I hear you're ready for me."

Pepper said, "I was ready for you twenty minutes ago."

Miss Chris said nothing, only reached into her pocket and brought out a packet of wet naps. She wiped Pepper's privates clean and did it thoroughly.

When she was done, she slipped the bedpan from beneath him and set it on the floor. She pulled his pants back up, slipped the pillow from behind his back and, without asking permission, grabbed his free wrist and slipped it back into its restraint. He didn't even try to stop her. She slid the wedge pillow under Pepper's bed. This is when Pepper realized they meant to keep him tied up for a while longer. Why leave the pillow in the room, otherwise? He didn't have any reaction to this. The stiff pain in his back took his attention.


At lunchtime Miss Chris returned with his food. She undid the strap on his wrist, slipped the pillow behind his back, held out his two pills and watched him swallow them. Then she set the tray down on his thighs, and from this position, Pepper had his meal. He ate everything. Even the cookie. It took a while because he only had one free hand.

Miss Chris returned and set his tray on the floor. Slipped the pillow from behind his back and under the bed. Without asking, she grabbed his wrist and pulled it back into its restraint. Pepper knew this step was coming this time, but that didn't seem to help him. His arm was attached to his body, but it no longer seemed like his property.

Pepper remained in restraints for a second night and learned how to sleep in this position. The meds could still knock him out quickly, if he let them. If he didn't fight the effects by being active. He complied with the general will of the psychiatric hospital: Shut up and don't cause trouble.

Only once did he wake up. Around two in the morning.

A woman screamed on Northwest 3. Two women, actually.

Pepper looked to Coffee, to corroborate that the sound was real, but Coffee's messy bed remained empty.

The women on Northwest 3 screamed until the staff huffed down their hallway, burst into their room. That must've been what Pepper and Coffee sounded like, weeks ago, when they were visited.

*Better them than me*, Pepper thought.

He was too demoralized to even feel ashamed of the sentiment.

# 12

BY THE THIRD morning, the restraints no longer seemed like a punishment. Pepper had just been forgotten. When a shift ended, the staff were supposed to chart any changes in the patients' health or behavior, but no one was going to note that they'd kept Pepper tied to his bed for the whole eight-hour stint. (And they sure as hell weren't going to note that he'd been pinned down for over forty-eight hours by now.) To avoid making notes about Pepper, the staff avoided him. They brought his meds and meals, and if he called for a bedpan, they obliged. But the rest of the time it was as if Pepper had disappeared. Lost in a fog. When staff members passed room 5, they averted their eyes. None of this was conscious. The staff didn't know they were doing it. Besides, there was so much else to handle at New Hyde every day. Every hour. Like charting. Plus fifteen other patients with needs. Pepper didn't slip through the cracks; he was stuffed behind a couch cushion.

And for the third night, Coffee seemed to be sleeping elsewhere, too. Where had Pepper's roommate gone? Were patients allowed to change rooms? Or was Coffee so stubborn, he'd rather sleep in the television lounge than bunk with Pepper anymore? Pepper tilted his head backward and peeked at Coffee's messy bed. He really missed that malt ball–headed bastard. Forget giving the guy a quarter; if Coffee had come in and just talked with Pepper for a while, Pepper would've given Coffee the credit card in his wallet. Coffee could even burn out the card's five-hundred-dollar limit (secured) if he wanted! Just come in here. Pepper watched the room's door and willed it to open.

His body had stopped communicating with him in the usual ways. Sometimes it sent an angry throb from the middle of the shoulders or the hips or the ankles. These felt like bursts of static. The small of his back had stopped feeling like a curled fist a day ago and now was just a pocket of cold fire burning through his waist.

He ignored all this and willed the room's door to open.

*Just come in. Just come in. Come in and talk with me.*

Pepper was so preoccupied with this silent petition that he didn't notice the ceiling tile in the far corner of the room when it buckled. The same tile that had fallen so many weeks ago. Pepper didn't notice when it bent. When it cracked.

Only when the two halves of the tile smacked on the floor did Pepper look from the doorway to the corner. From the ceiling, a pair of feet dangled out. They were long and wide. They kicked faintly and slid down.

Now a pair of legs came into view. Draped in the hospital-issue blue pajama pants. The cotton billowed loose around the thin legs as the figure continued to descend.

Pepper heard this hoarse *wheezing*, a congested person's breathing.

The upper body appeared next. An old man's naked torso, the skin sallow and mottled, a little paunch that jiggled as it moved. The hands clung to the ceiling frame, a pull-up in reverse. This thing wasn't falling. It was lowering itself.

Its wheezing continued, grew more forced, louder, with each move.

Its arms looked thinner than kindling, the shoulders soft. Pepper could even make out the fingers on its hands as it let go of the ceiling frame. Each finger was twiglike, gnarled at the knuckles and curled.

Then it landed.

And when its heels touched the tiles, they *clopped* like horseshoes on cobblestones. It huffed and tilted forward, stumbling, but righted itself.

An old man's frail body, but its head was massive, covered in matted fur that hung down to those small shoulders. In the moonlight its fur looked as gray as shale. It had a bison's head. Pepper saw this and couldn't deny it. But its body, from the shoulders down, remained gangly and feeble. Hairless. Human.

Somebody else's myth, somebody else's nightmare, had plunged into Pepper's room.

It watched Pepper. It huffed again and its wide, wet nose wriggled. Just below the nose, the fur parted and Pepper saw its mouth as a deep, wet pit. The hoarse wheeze sounded even louder now. It breathed and it watched Pepper. He couldn't hold its gaze. He looked away, in a panic, to the door. He willed Coffee into the room. Or Dr. Anand. Even those three cops—Huey, Dewey, and Louie—would be welcome.

But the only one who'd come to see him was this monster.

Pepper only looked back at it when he heard that *clopping* sound again.

Its feet lifted and fell. It stalked toward him.

Pepper would've liked to struggle against his restraints, but his limbs had stopped listening. He felt trapped inside his own body, the numbed vessel holding a panicked mind.

As the thing moved toward him, its body slumped forward again, stumbling. That massive head seemed too heavy for its body. The shoulders shrank, the small paunch quivered, the head dipped down until the thing seemed to bow.

But then it huffed again and righted itself. And Pepper saw its face again: those dead white eyes, the nose sniffing the air like a predator tracking prey. The mouth opened again and from this close, Pepper could finally see its teeth. They looked like stone arrowheads.

It wheezed again but this time, when it exhaled, he thought he heard his name.

"*Peter,*" it whispered, or was that just its breath playing through those jagged teeth?

It shambled closer and again the *clopping* of its heels echoed.

At that moment Pepper's body shivered. It mirrored the fear in his mind. Finally! It was such a strange relief to have his body and his mind coordinating again. His fingers dug into the sides of his mattress. His feet kicked at the bottom of his bed. They hit the metal frame so hard it sounded like a temple bell.

*Gong.*

*Gong.*

*Gong.*

Someone would hear that, right? Hear that and come to him.

Then it was there. Right by his bed. Over him.

Pepper looked out the window, at the moon. He would've prayed to it, if he thought that would help.

The thing grabbed the restraint on his right wrist and yanked at it. Pepper's whole body shook. The bed creaked under him. Three tugs and the rubberized restraint snapped off the frame.

The thing moved down to his right ankle and did the same again. Grabbed on to the strap and pulled. This time, it took only one great effort and the restraint shredded, as simple as pulling apart a rubber band.

Now the thing stopped and heaved and wheezed there at the foot of the bed. Out of breath. Pepper's right arm and right leg, finally free, just lay there limp. He tried to shake them, get the blood moving, but before he could, the attacker grabbed Pepper's left ankle, lifted the leg, and brought its nose close, like a cook inspecting a cut of meat. It grabbed the restraint and with two pulls the leg was free.

It wheezed as it moved back around the bed, heels striking the floor in uneven tempo. It grabbed the top of Pepper's head and *yanked*. Pepper's left shoulder howled in the socket because his wrist was still in a restraint.

The thing pulled at his hair even harder. For a moment Pepper's upper body actually rose off the mattress, the restraint and this monster battling for him.

Finally the restraint tore and Pepper's body crashed to the floor. He couldn't see for a moment. Everything went gray. A loud blast seemed to play in his ears. Cold rose up through the floor, into Pepper's clothes. His skin puckered all over. His upper body shot up at the waist, like he was doing a sit-up. But he was pushed flat against the floor again. A foot on his chest.

Pepper looked up at his attacker, but from here he could only focus on its foot. The one pressing against his sternum. Its heel gray and hard as a hoof.

The thing's thin leg trembled as it stomped down and Pepper swore he heard his sternum *creak*. In his ears it sounded like a Styrofoam cup being squeezed.

Pepper had a mouth, but he couldn't scream. He had no air in his lungs. His lips parted and his tongue stuck straight out. His feet rose and slapped against the cold floor.

Pepper looked up and saw the beast's great head pitch forward, the weak body out of balance again. Its white eyes seemed to be looking at him and through him, both at once. What could he call this creature? He wasn't a religious man, but only one name came to him.

The Devil.

The Devil stomped down on his chest again and snorted.

You don't want to be awake, aware, when your rib cage breaks. When your rib cage breaks you want to be passed out.

But somehow, Pepper hadn't.

It didn't hurt. He'd already gone into shock, which is the human body's last line of defense. Your body loves you too much to let you really feel trauma like that. So it wasn't pain that made the breaking rib cage such a terror for Pepper. It was a sound.

He'd heard the creaking of his sternum, so he almost felt prepared for the final crack, the tune of grinding bones, but he absolutely was not prepared to hear the ocean. That thing smashed his rib cage and suddenly Pepper heard the sea.

His gasping breaths, the snorts and wheezing of the Devil above him, even the thumps as the back of his head rose and fell, rose and fell while he thrashed on the floor. All of that was drowned out.

His ears filled with the splash of an ocean rolling toward the shore and breaking. If he shut his eyes, he would've sworn he was at Jones Beach. Or the dirty curl of Coney Island. Maybe it was just the sound of liquid filling his brain cavity, Pepper didn't know and he didn't care anymore.

*Let the sea roll over me,* he thought.

See the sea?

So when the room's lights snapped on, Pepper wasn't prepared.

Not just because of the brightness, or because the pressure on his chest suddenly stopped, but because he'd forgotten about psych units and shatterproof windows and meds three times a day; all the tortures of New Hyde. He'd inhabited a different world. He'd been on that shoreline.

So by the time he returned, drawn back into the hospital and his room and his own body on the floor, by then Pepper's life had already been saved.

Not by a nurse or orderly.

Not by his roommate, Coffee.

It was Dorry.

*Dorry!*

She stood over Pepper's body.

Wielding her bath towel as a weapon.

She had it rolled tight and snapped it like a whip. She aimed it at the corner where the ceiling tile had fallen in, but Pepper couldn't see around her. Couldn't focus well enough to see much of anything except that beautiful, badass old woman standing between him and his end.

"Hyah!" Dorry shouted.

She snapped her towel at the corner as if facing a lion in a cage.

"Bad boy!"

Somehow the staff on duty hadn't heard Pepper kicking his bed frame, but they sure couldn't ignore that old lady.

"Hyah!"

The towel's snap echoed in the room again.

"Dorry!"

The night nurse stood in Pepper's doorway. She looked at the big man, flat on the floor, and her mouth fell open in horror.

"What in the *hell* did you do to him, Dorry?"

Pepper shook his head, or at least he thought he did. He wanted to clear Dorry's name, but to everyone else it looked like he was having a seizure.

Dorry said, "*I* didn't do that and *you* know it!"

Scotch Tape, on night duty, stood behind the nurse, as stunned as his coworker.

"Don't back talk," he said.

Dorry snapped the towel at the corner again. This time, instead of snorting and wheezing, the thing only whimpered softly, like a whipped dog. A sound that everyone in the room seemed to hear, not just Pepper.

The nurse put one foot into the room. "This is a male hall, Dorry. How you even get here? You been sneaking?"

Dorry dropped the big towel and it landed across Pepper's legs. He felt its weight on his thighs. Scotch Tape and the nurse surrounded Dorry. Pepper curled up as best he could, afraid one of them would kick him in the head by mistake. This movement made his rib cage stab sharply and he gasped.

But before the nurse gave Dorry any tranquilizers, before Scotch Tape checked on Pepper there on the ground, before all other concerns, came the thing in the corner. It was practically mewling over there.

Scotch Tape stooped over Pepper and pulled the big body towel off him. Scotch Tape unfurled the towel and walked over to the corner where Dorry had been aiming her attack. A moment later Pepper watched Scotch Tape escort that thing out of the room.

Pepper couldn't see the head, or much of the body, because Scotch Tape had draped the towel over it. Only the pajama bottoms and those calloused heels. The soles slapped the floor tiles loudly as Scotch Tape led it out of the room. The Devil leaned against Scotch Tape for balance. Scotch Tape whispered soft assurances to it.

The Devil was there.

Even once the lights came on.

Even with the staff in the room.

No delusion. No dream. It was *real.* Pepper almost howled at the terrible truth of it, but he couldn't muster the sound.

"Okay now," Scotch Tape whispered to it. "We'll get you back. Come on."

Dorry looked down at Pepper.

"Maybe you feel like they've pushed you off the cliff already," she said.

The nurse peeked at Pepper, too. She saw him watching Scotch Tape and the thing under the towel. And the nurse shifted her body to block Pepper's view! In the same movement, she put an open hand to Dorry's mouth. Pepper knew what the nurse had in her palm. And Dorry didn't argue, she took the pills and swallowed them.

Dorry looked at Pepper once more, lips pursed in a sympathetic frown.

"You have to climb back up," she said.

The nurse sucked her teeth and squeezed Dorry's upper arm.

"Enough foolishness, Dorry. Why you come to this boy's room anyway? You forgot you're an old woman? He too young for you!"

The nurse laughed loudly, as if she could make everyone (herself included) forget what had just happened in this room. She pulled Dorry out.

The pair stepped into the hallway, and the nurse looked back at Pepper, who was still on the floor, on his back. His breathing stayed weak but at least it came steady.

"I'll be back to help you, soon come," the nurse promised.

Who would ever doubt her return? It just wasn't possible that Pepper would be left after such an attack.

But forty minutes later, no one had returned to check on him so he finally had to pull himself off the floor.

VOLUME 2

—

# COFFIN INDUSTRIES

# 13

NO WAY AROUND it, a doctor had to be called in.

Maybe Pepper's sternum hadn't actually splintered (since he had pulled himself, painfully, back into bed), but even if his chest plate hadn't cracked, the man's pain sure wasn't a delusion. The morning after his attack, Josephine came with morning meds. When she stood over Pepper, she saw the blood that had seeped through the front of his shirt. A hundred little red dots in the fabric, all bunched around his chest. Pepper opened his eyes and looked at her, but just opening his eyes was an exertion. He spat out a dozen shallow breaths but couldn't say a word.

Josephine sat on the side of his mattress. There wasn't much space, but she wasn't very big. One of the reasons people treated her like a kid, even though she was twenty-four, was because of how her body hid the years.

She set the small white cup with Pepper's meds down on the floor, and leaned over Pepper. His eyes shut, then opened again. She wasn't sure he could see her. His eyes wouldn't focus on her face. She wondered at the pain he was in, and if she wanted to keep doing this job, but then told herself to stop. Even if she quit tomorrow, she was here now.

"I'm going to open your shirt," she said.

She undid the buttons gingerly. The fabric had stuck to his skin, blood like an adhesive. Finally she got the top two buttons loose and peeked inside and smelled the stale punch of Pepper's dried blood.

Now she noticed one of the torn restraints, dangling from the side of the bed. She pulled at it and let it swing loose again. She looked at Pepper.

"What did you do to yourself?"

He shook his head so faintly that it looked like a tremor.

"I guess you'll need to see a doctor," she said.

When Josephine padded out of the room, Pepper figured that might be the end of it. She might say he needed to see a doctor, but that didn't mean she'd actually call one. It was just a way to get out of the room. Like last night's nurse. When he breathed too deeply, his ribs hurt; he was surviving on shallow breaths.

The morning meds remained in their cup, on the floor. Josephine had left without making him take them. He felt grateful for this. His throat felt so tight he couldn't even imagine ingesting something as small as a pill.

Ten minutes later, Dr. Anand walked in.

The man appeared at the doorway, just as slightly comical as he had been on that first night. Jacket and tie and ID on a plastic cord around his neck. Bushy mustache; cheeks as healthy and round as a brown Santa Claus. But he seemed a bit more rushed this time, maybe the intake meeting was the only time a patient earned the doctor's complete attention. Now he offered a new performance: the over-taxed physician.

Dr. Anand walked in quickly. Eyes down in concentration, not meekness. He wiggled a clipboard in his left hand. He reached into his pants pocket with the other and jiggled his set of keys. Dr. Anand pulled his hand out of his pocket and scratched his scalp. He patted his chin then the pocket of his coat, looking for a pen. Pantomiming harriedness.

He hadn't looked at Pepper yet.

"Okay, Mr. . . ."

When the doctor finally looked up, he grinned genuinely.

"Pepper! Right?" He moved toward Pepper's bed, reading the chart on the clipboard. When he reached the bed, he kicked the little white cup carrying Pepper's morning meds. They rolled under the bed but Dr. Anand didn't notice.

"Sounds like you hurt yourself."

"It wasn't me," Pepper said.

Dr. Anand giggled. "My daughter loved that song. I don't think she understood what it meant."

Pepper looked at the doctor directly. "The Devil did this."

Dr. Anand didn't respond to that. (Would you?) He finally sat next to Pepper on the bed and undid the rest of the buttons on Pepper's shirt. He moved more quickly than Josephine. Dr. Anand opened the shirt and looked at Pepper's bruises. The skin was reddish and purple all over. There were small cuts across Pepper's chest where the foot (hoof?) had crushed down on him.

Dr. Anand leaned back, his eyebrows raised. "Jiminy . . ."

The doctor set the clipboard on the floor and used both hands to press against Pepper's rib cage. He started light and then a little harder. It didn't take much force to make Pepper wince.

"Can you roll on your side?" the doctor asked. "Your back to me?"

It took a moment, but Pepper pulled it off. Pepper felt the doctor's hand pressing against his skin.

"Breathe as deeply as you can," the doctor said. Pepper felt the chilly rim of a stethoscope just below one of his shoulder blades. He always liked that feeling, and he liked it now. When Pepper inhaled, it hurt, and when he exhaled, it hurt more. He concentrated on the comfort of the stethoscope just to keep from crying.

Dr. Anand rolled Pepper onto his back again and pressed the stethoscope to his chest now. Pepper breathed in and out. Dr. Anand looked at his watch. He pulled the stethoscope off and stuffed it back into a pocket of his jacket. He reached down, grunting slightly, and grabbed the clipboard off the floor, wrote on Pepper's chart.

"Did your roommate do this to you?" Dr. Anand asked.

Pepper shook his head.

"One of the *other* patients, then?"

Pepper breathed in and spoke as he exhaled. "I already told you who."

Dr. Anand frowned. "No jokes here, Pepper. I want you to tell me the truth. Did a member of the *staff* do this to you?"

Right away, Pepper wanted to say yes just because that would be a manageable, rational, realistic problem. The staff had abused him. It wasn't untrue, was it? Maybe Dr. Anand would transfer him?

"Can you just get me off this unit?" Pepper asked quietly. He imagined being taken to the ICU, or for surgery—who cared what?—and being kept there. Away from whoever, whatever, had nearly killed him.

Dr. Anand held the bottom of the clipboard and tapped the top lightly against his own knees. "Transfer. Well, that's a problem, Pepper."

"Why?" Pepper's voice cracked.

"Because you were admitted here by *the police,* and you're being held here pending *criminal* charges. You understand? So, technically, this unit is your detention center. If you weren't in here, you'd probably be at Rikers awaiting a hearing. And believe me, this is a lot better place to be."

Pepper almost laughed, but that would've caused too much pain.

Dr. Anand looked down at Pepper's chest and sighed.

"*Generally,* this is a lot better place to be."

"You told me I'd be released in seventy-two hours," Pepper said. "That was over a month ago."

Dr. Anand nodded and winced, as if he was a salesman about to explain the unfair return policy of his store. "We did keep you for a seventy-two-hour observation. But what we observed is that you needed more time with us. So we readmitted you, as an involuntary admit."

"What does that mean?" Pepper asked.

Dr. Anand touched Pepper's arm lightly, consoling. "It means you stay with us until *we* feel you're ready to go. In your case, we might not feel comfortable releasing you until your arraignment date."

Pepper stared out the windows. "The only way I get out of the hospital is if I'm going to jail."

Dr. Anand stood up. "Let me be completely honest with you, Pepper. You came to us under a bit of a technicality, that's true. But while you've been here, you've been impulsive, quick to anger, in a potentially manic state at *least* three times according to the records my staff have made. Have you ever been diagnosed with a mental illness before?"

Pepper tried to sit up, but he could only raise his head. "I know I get heated up, okay? But there's got to be a line, right? I mean *everything* can't be a sign of mental illness."

"No. Of course not. And despite what you might think, I don't want to diagnose you with an illness. But you're here, however it happened, and I wouldn't be any kind of doctor if I didn't take a little time to try and see if you need help. And if you do, then I want to help you. That's the truth."

Pepper marveled at Dr. Anand's sincere tone. He knew Dr. Anand meant what he'd said, and yet it didn't comfort him.

Dr. Anand got up. Pepper watched him leave the room.

"I'll send one of the nurses to bandage you up. I'll prescribe a painkiller, too. Did you get your morning meds?"

Pepper rolled, with some difficulty, onto his right side, so he faced Dr. Anand. "I already took them," Pepper said. "Josephine gave them to me."

Dr. Anand watched Pepper a moment. Pepper wondered if the doctor would see the white cup, the two pills, under the bed. But finally Dr. Anand nodded. He said, "You'll meet your demons everywhere, Pepper. Let us help you face them here."


Josephine did return with a painkiller (Vicodin) and she dressed the cuts on his chest. She wrapped him with bandages. The whole time he kept on with that tight, shallow breathing, seeming impossibly weak. Josephine maintained a professional air but she felt bad for him. Hard to believe this was the same man who'd knocked down three people, herself included, with such ease. When she attached the clips to hold the bandage, Josephine patted him tenderly and, silently, said a prayer.

"I left your meds," she said, looking down at the floor. "I just realized."

Pepper reacted quickly. "Dr. Anand saw them. He gave them to me."

She nodded. Still new enough at the job that she accepted a patient's word.

"I brought you some clothes," Josephine said. She had the blue hospital-issue top and bottom, the blue no-skid socks, and set them on his mattress. She left because, sympathetic or not, she wasn't going to undress him.

Pepper got himself up and peeled off his shirt, but hesitated before slipping on the pajama top. Even if he was trapped, did that mean he had to wear the prisoner's uniform? But wearing a torn and bloody shirt would only look madder. What choice? No choice. He put the pajama top on. Then he slid off his wrinkled pants, and his whiffy Smartwool socks. Pepper folded the slacks and balled up his socks and left them in the top drawer of his dresser. It had taken a month, but now he even looked like he belonged.

He wanted to throw some cold water on his face, but that would mean standing in front of the makeshift bathroom mirror. Seeing some version of himself looking this way. He wanted to avoid that for a while longer.

Northwest 2 sounded livelier today. A room's door opened and shut and out walked that mumbly kid who'd been up in the lounge late at night, mouthing the close-captioned words at the bottom of the flat screen. The kid had the kind of pockmarked face that made him look fifty. He walked with his eyes focused on the tops of his feet. He wore faded jeans and a T-shirt with a cartoon figure on it. One word in big beige letters: HEATMISER.

Heatmiser passed Pepper in the hallway. He weaved around the big man without even looking. He hummed to himself and his voice wasn't half bad. Faint and mournful. Pepper watched Heatmiser until Heatmiser stopped walking and looked back.

Heatmiser said, "Heard you last night."

He watched Pepper quietly, wore no expression Pepper could read. Pepper touched his bruised ribs instinctively, but before he might say anything, Heatmiser spoke again.

"Better hurry if you want breakfast."

Then the guy walked on. He didn't slow down and Pepper couldn't catch up, with his wounded gait. He shuffled down Northwest 2.

Pepper stopped at the nurses' station because he needed to rest. His ribs seemed like they wanted to tear through his skin. He burned on the inside, and the heat ran up into his jawline. He might not have wanted the meds, but the painkiller would be nice just then. Pepper dropped one meaty forearm on the nurses' station and looked down to the desktop. There he could see what had captured the attention of three nurses and two orderlies: a computer.

A desktop device that looked forty years old. It had a big gray monitor with a screen that emitted faint green light. That thing had been out of date in 1982. The rest of the desk space back there showed stacks of paperwork, each a foot high.

The staff had been tasked with digitizing all the information in all those charts. The computer had been installed that morning. The files on the desk space surrounding the machine, files that would total eleven feet three inches if placed in a single stack, was just the paperwork that had been filled out in the last *three months*. The nurses and orderlies looked at the computer as if it had betrayed them. They looked at one another to see which of them might volunteer for the task of inputting the information. Frankly, you'd have a better chance of getting a Korean to marry a black person.

In an act of bravery or stupidity (both), Josephine parted her colleagues so she could sit at the chair in front of the computer. She opened the software the hospital had purchased to sync up record keeping throughout their system. As soon as she did this, the other nurses patted her gently with approval. The orderlies looked up at Pepper.

One said, "Go eat."

A pleasant morning to you, too!


Dorry said, "So you understand now?"

She sat across from Pepper. He'd come to join her and thanked her for helping him the night before.

Heatmiser sat with two other men at another table. All three looked up at the screen and didn't speak with one another. Pepper hadn't seen the other two men before, maybe he just hadn't been looking. One Japanese, one East Indian. But the two men seemed, somehow, like family. It took a moment for Pepper to realize it was because they both had some of the most awful teeth he'd seen on this side of the nineteenth century. Wow. Crowded, off-color, some bent in and others bent out. No wonder they'd found each other, brothers of the busted grills. He nicknamed them quick, in his own mind, Japanese Freddie Mercury and Yuckmouth. (It might seem to make more sense to nickname the Indian guy Freddie Mercury, since Freddie Mercury was an Indian—birth name Farrokh Bulsara—but that's kind of racist. Sorry. The Japanese guy actually looked like Freddie Mercury. The Indian guy just had a yuckmouth.)

Dorry sat with her back to the raggedy basketball court outside. It was the kind of day where you can see the sun behind a thin fog of clouds, like a lightbulb glowing inside a pillowcase. Dorry leaned forward in her chair so Pepper would stop gazing at the skies and pay attention.

"Do you *understand* now?" she asked.

It was PB&J for breakfast today. He separated the two halves of the sandwich and set them back down. The vein of dry brown peanut butter, the artery of gummy blueish jam. The sandwich looked as appetizing as an autopsy.

"I understand this meal is criminal," he said.

He was a bit surprised he'd been able to come up with the line, weak joke that it was. He felt surprised by the way his hands moved, too. They lifted and lowered quickly. When he thought of opening his hands and wiggling his fingers that's exactly what they did. Why?

He hadn't taken his medicine.

Dorry said, "You've heard of drug trials, right? They test out some new pharmaceutical on a set of people. Some get the real thing, others get a placebo. If the trial is a success, they sell the drug to the intended market. You understand?"

Pepper poked at the top of his sandwich. "What happened to me last night?"

Dorry said, "I'm trying to tell you." She picked up the pint of milk on her tray. Pepper had one, too. She lifted it and shook it and the milk inside sloshed. Somehow even the PB&J on his tray appeared more appetizing when he imagined washing it down with a nice swallow of milk.

Dorry said, "I can see you smacking your lips already."

Dorry brought the carton to her face, like right up against the left lens of her big glasses. She tore open the carton at one end. She pulled until she made a little spout. She sniffed it. Then she leaned even farther across the table so Pepper could do the same. He inhaled. He frowned.

"I think that milk is off," he said.

Dorry nodded, then lifted the carton to her lips and drank. Forget drank, she *chugged* that pint of questionable milk. The sight made Pepper's own throat close up. Little beads of milk trickled out the sides of the spout and ran along her cheeks. The stuff looked more yellow than white. When she finished, she set the carton back down and looked at Pepper with high seriousness.

"The milk *was* bad," she said. "But you can get used to it."

Pepper looked at the carton of milk on his tray now and couldn't imagine doing what she'd just done. Now the sandwich looked even worse than it had. He wondered if everything on this tray was past its sell-by date. Hard to keep from getting paranoid in a place like this. Bad food, constant doses of medication, human beings penned in and observed. He began to understand what Dorry might be telling him.

"You're saying the staff is experimenting on us?" Pepper asked.

Dorry pointed at him, frowning with disappointment. "You think this is about patients versus the staff. I understand why, but you have to think bigger. This isn't us." She pointed at the other patients. "Versus them." She pointed toward the nurses' station.

"*They* aren't even here," she said. "*Everyone* in New Hyde is trapped, in some way. Patients and staff. You think *they* ever set foot in a place like this unit? No, no. Our lives are a clinical trial, Pepper. We're all being tested."

Pepper leaned across the table, as far as he could. "By who?"

"The biggest corporation of all," she said. "Coffin Industries. They don't stop exploiting you until you're dead."

But what did all this have to with what happened to him last night? What he'd seen wasn't a man. He felt sure of that, at least. He wanted to grab Dorry's shoulders and shake her until she understood it, too. Then maybe they could actually talk about the damn thing clearly and not this nonsense about Coffin Industries.

Dorry reached across the table and snatched his carton of quite possibly putrid milk. She lifted it and said, "May I?"

You won't be too surprised that Pepper left the table before Dorry got to glugging. He hadn't wanted to watch it once, so why would he want to see it a second time?

His chance to escape witnessing Dorry's encore performance had come when one of the nurses entered the television lounge, flicking through the keys on her chain. She found one long four-sided key. As she moved through the lounge, half a dozen other patients appeared behind her, matter pulled in her wake. They followed her, and Heatmiser slid back from his place at the table to join them. The nurse stopped at the glass doorway in the lounge. She slid the key into the door's bottom lock and called out, "Smoke break!"

Pepper found himself excited by those two words. Even if it was only to stand around on a busted old basketball court. This would be the first fresh air he'd known in almost thirty days. He left Dorry, took his PB&J, and got in line to go out.

The *breeze*. It touched his neck and made him shiver. He opened his mouth and smacked his lips like a child conditioned to feed at the feel of his mother's nipple. He inhaled the oxygen and swore it even had a taste. His tongue quivered in the cage of his mouth. He had to clamp his teeth closed to be sure it wouldn't slip free.

Heatmiser and Pepper and a Puerto Rican kid in his twenties marched outside. (When asked, at his intake meeting four months ago, what he wanted to be called, the Puerto Rican kid told Dr. Anand he wanted everyone to use his "professional name," *Wally Gambino*, and Anand only blinked and said, "Wally it is!")

The nurse didn't walk outside with the patients. She didn't have to.

At the far end of the court stood that chain-link fence with barbed-wire icing. A less addle-minded person might be able to scale it and use a blanket to cover the razor wire, slip himself over to freedom, but that was sort of the point of New Hyde, no? These folks, by and large, couldn't even coordinate their outfits. Just about every patient wore a pajama top with jeans on the bottom, or pajama bottoms and a stained blouse on top. Some had showered recently, while others (Heatmiser) hadn't. Not a jailbreak population.

None of the patients wore coats, it was March but still a little chilly. They were all just so happy to feel the real climate that they didn't register the cold at all.

New Hyde didn't supply the smokes. Those were brought by family on visiting days. A (semi)cheap gift, but much appreciated. Once outside, each patient pulled out a loosie and sparked it. All Pepper had was his inedible PB&J. But who cared? He stood outside. He walked the length of the half-court. On one end, that raggedy basketball rim hung at an angle, and at the opposite end stood a tall maple tree. The tree threw shade over half the court. That's where nearly everyone went. Everyone but Pepper, eyes closed and face up toward the sun, and Loochie, who'd been one of the last ones out. She walked right up to the fence line and picked up a handful of rocks and pebbles. Pepper only opened his eyes when he heard Loochie stop in front of him. He heard this regular breathing and looked down to see her staring up at him, left hand heavy with stones. It was hard, for a moment, not to think of David and Goliath.

She squinted from the sunlight. "I want you to apologize."

He felt so surprised by what she said that he dropped his damn sandwich on the ground. Both he and Loochie looked at it there. What seemed less edible? The PB&J or the pebbles?

She picked up the sandwich and turned it over and brushed off the small bits of dirt and leaves that had stuck to the bread. Once it was mostly clean she brought it to her lips, gave it a faint kiss then held it over her head, toward the sky.

"Kissed it to God," she said. "Now you can eat it."

She handed it back up to Pepper and to Pepper's surprise he took it.

"Thank you?" he said.

She had on that same blue knit cap. She reached underneath and scratched at her scalp with one finger. The movement was so delicate that the pom-poms didn't even quiver as she did it.

"How come you're always wearing that hat?" he asked. He thought he was being playful but Loochie ignored him.

"To my mother," she said. "I want you to apologize for knocking her down."

"I didn't mean to hit her," Pepper said.

"You know that's not an apology, right?"

Pepper saw that someday this girl was going to be pretty, but for now she was such a teenage girl. Smallish, but stooped forward to hide her chest, which only made her seem even shorter. Her feet were big and only seemed bigger because of the snug jeans she wore over her thin legs. Her long-sleeved top didn't quite reach her jeans, so a band of her stomach showed and bulged out slightly, and she tugged at the bottom of her shirt to cover it. But the moment she let go, it slipped up again, showing skin. She yearned to be seen but felt awkward each time it happened.

In another context Pepper would've sighed when seeing someone like Loochie. Like if he was on the E train coming home from work and she got on with her friends. He'd expect her to be loud (and she would be), he'd expect her to obnoxiously barrel through the crowded car bumping anyone she pleased (and she'd do that, too). He'd hate her, honestly, as he did most teenagers. But taken out of that context, dropped in New Hyde alone, it didn't matter how tough she might be. Here he saw a kid.

"I'll apologize," he said.

She nodded and tossed one of her pebbles at the fence.

"I heard you last night."

Pepper wiggled the sandwich in his hand and then—why not—he took two bites. "Was I loud?" he asked.

Loochie threw another pebble. "Screaming usually is."

Now he bit into the sandwich again. "Why doesn't your mother get you out of here?" Pepper asked.

Loochie dropped all the pebbles. She wiped her hands clean. "She's the one who committed me."

"So why would you want me to apologize to her?"

She turned and took a step toward Pepper. Instantly ready to throw down. This seemed so young, too. That thoughtlessness, the rage that just has to become action. But he also understood it. He waved one hand in front of her face.

"Calm down," he said quietly. "Come on."

Her lips quivered. She looked away from Pepper and back into the television lounge. She said, "She's still my mother."

Pepper finished his sandwich. It had almost no taste at all. The smokers under the maple tree were down to the end of their butts.

"It's been in my room, too," she said. "You probably heard me."

He remembered the night when the women were screaming. When he felt lucky for being passed over. "That was you?"

She shrugged. "Could've been. Depends on the night."

How old was this girl? He wanted to ask but he wasn't sure how the question would sound. Like a criticism? Like he was about to turn all fatherly? It wasn't meant as either one. More like he was marveling at what he was up to when he was just eighteen or nineteen. For all the trouble he got into, he wasn't ever in a place like this.

"Do you really know what it is?" he asked.

The nurse returned to the lounge and unlocked the door that led outside.

Loochie said, "It's the Devil." She looked up at him, squinting because of the sun. "I think you know that."

So she'd confirmed his most delirious idea, unlike Dorry, and it actually felt *good* to hear the thing named out loud. By someone other than him. But what was supposed to happen right after that? Now what?

# 14

DR. BARGER SHUT the door to conference room 2 and smiled at the Book Group members. Loochie and Dorry and Coffee and Pepper. Sam and Sammy were not in attendance. Neither was Josephine or the book cart. Just four patients and Dr. Barger.

"Let's rearrange the tables," he said.

They did the same work again. One table over by the windows. The other table moved to the center of the room. Five chairs slid close for those in attendance, the others pushed back against the walls. Even Dr. Barger helped. With the chairs.

Then someone knocked on the door, and he said, "I've got a little surprise for all of you."

Dr. Barger opened the door and a woman stood in the doorway, carrying two canisters, one white and one silver. An old woman, black, quite slim, wearing a purple pantsuit and a tidy hat that matched. When Pepper had first arrived, he'd seen Dorry give this woman his box of breakfast cereal in the television lounge. The woman didn't even look at the doctor, only shuffled into the room in her slightly worn black Easy Spirit shoes. She entered carrying the two canisters close to her chest, as tender as a member of the congregation carrying the body and blood of Christ.

Dr. Barger waved his hand as if he'd conjured the old woman. "*I* bring you coffee and hot water for tea!" he said.

And against all better judgment, Dorry and Pepper and Coffee actually applauded weakly.

The old woman made it to the free table at the back of the room and set down the canisters. Under one arm she carried a short stack of white disposable coffee cups. She set those down next. Then she turned and left the room and Dr. Barger stayed at the door, held it open, as proud as a pharaoh. He grinned at the group. "See? There are rewards for your attendance."

Dorry raised her hand. Dr. Barger pointed at her to speak, as if they were in grade school.

"How come you're only bringing us gifts after four weeks of Group? We had three times as many people at the first meeting." Dorry leaned toward Pepper and poked at his sleeve. "That was before you joined the cast!"

Dr. Barger shrugged. "I had to ask Dr. Anand for money to buy you all some supplies, and he had to file the request with the board of Northwest who then passed it on to the governing body of New Hyde Hospital. From there, it had to be approved by the president of the hospital, or at least rubber-stamped by his secretary. And I'm guessing that request is still on someone's desk. Finally, I said forget it and just bought the stuff at Key Food."

Coffee wagged his finger at Dr. Barger. "You didn't have faith in the system."

Pepper looked at Dr. Barger. "Coffee's not an American. He doesn't know it's every man for himself around here."

Dr. Barger jutted out his lower lip, as if a specimen had finally done something worth noting. "Is that how all of you feel? Dorry? Loochie?"

Dorry waved her hand at Pepper dismissively. "Even Pepper doesn't *believe* that. He figures that's what he's got to *say*. You look stupid if you're sincere these days."

Dr. Barger pushed the conference-room door closed without thinking. He'd become engaged in this conversation and didn't want it to end. Because he wasn't paying attention he bonked the old woman in the purple pantsuit as she walked into the room. The tray in her hands flew; the tea bags, and packets of sugar, and a plastic cup of plastic spoons all tumbled to the floor.

The old woman wasn't hurt. She hardly stopped moving. She held on to the tray and stumbled into the room. Dr. Barger pulled the door back quickly and sputtered apologies. The old woman set the tray down on their table, lifted one arm and dropped a rectangular box of lemon cookies. She turned toward the mess, which Dr. Barger now stooped forward to clean up, and she pulled at the doctor's coat to move him. With the doctor out of the way, she bent and gathered up all the fallen items in two quick swipes. She used the plastic cup like a scoop. She set all the items back on the tray. Then she shuffled out of the room. She hadn't spoken, hardly acknowledged anyone the whole time.

Dorry punched Pepper in the arm lightly. "She's been here almost as long as me. I don't think the doctors even know her name anymore. They give her little jobs like that. You would almost think she worked here. We call her the Haint. *Haint* quite a patient. *Haint* quite the staff."

Coffee studied his open blue binder, as if he hadn't noticed any of this. Loochie snatched the box of lemon cookies.

Pepper said, "I need coffee."

As he poured it, Pepper realized it was the first cup he'd had in over a month. He used to buy two or three each day before. *Before.* The word made him feel slightly dizzy. He dipped one finger into the hot coffee and held it there, burning the tip of his finger until he came back to himself.

As he blew on his finger, Josephine arrived at the door pushing that same three-tiered book cart. It entered the room and gathered all attention, the ark of a cut-rate covenant.

The same bevy of professional manuals were on the shelves but now there were seven copies of one book, all in unblemished condition, across the top row. Hardcovers. Jackets in "near fine" condition (a used-booksellers' term). The background of the jacket was black and on each spine, the title in large red letters: *JAWS. JAWS. JAWS. JAWS. JAWS. JAWS. JAWS.*

Dr. Barger peeked outside theatrically, finally shutting the door. He sat down at the head of the table. Dr. Barger stretched out his hand and Josephine handed one of the books to him. They could all see the back cover. It showed the author's photo in black and white. The dude wore a black jacket and white turtleneck, stood in a slightly turned pose, and grinned faintly at all of them in the room. He cut a Hugh Hefner figure. And on the front cover that iconic image, an enormous gray shark's head moving up from the bottom of the black page and a small gray woman swimming at the top. The woman meant to get a little exercise, but the shark had other plans.

It was an old book-club version of the original. The shipping cost more than the books. Dr. Barger opened the dust jacket and scanned the flap. He read out loud.

" 'It's out there in the water . . . waiting. Nature's most fearsome predator. It *fears* nothing. It *attacks* anything. It *devours* everything.' "

He closed the flap and sighed.

"Oh, my," he said.

He dropped the book on the table as if it had dirtied his fingers. Then he looked up at the group, and smiled and said, "I'm *really* looking forward to discussing this book!"

Loochie ate a lemon cookie, spoke with her mouth full. "Liar."

Before Dr. Barger could argue, the door opened and in walked Sam. All eyes in the room scanned the doorway for Sammy. But Sam just shut the door.

She looked down at the floor.

Last time, she'd been dressed for the day; now, she wore her pajamas.

She moved behind Pepper and Dorry and took a seat at the far end of the table, directly across from Dr. Barger. Her face looked red, as if she'd been scalded, and they couldn't see her eyes because she wouldn't look up. The depth of her silence quieted the others.

Finally, Dorry spoke up. "No jokes today, Sammy?"

She lifted her head. Her eyes were red and veiny. She hadn't been burnt, she'd been crying. "I'm Sam," she said quietly.

Dr. Barger said, "You've been crying."

Loochie rolled her eyes. "Is that your professional diagnosis?"

Coffee said, "If you want to add a complaint to my own petition, I can include your name when I reach"—Coffee cleared his throat—"when I reach someone."

"Sammy's *gone*," Sam said.

Coffee looked down at a page and made a note.

"Dead?" Dorry asked.

Dr. Barger barked, "Dorry!"

Sam pointed at Dr. Barger and Josephine.

"*They* say they discharged her. But she didn't even say good-bye? To me? They said I slept through her release, but she didn't even leave me a note? She just disappears?"

Pepper surprised himself when he spoke. As he'd been listening to Sam, he'd been clenching his teeth. Not consciously, just a tightening in his chest, his neck, his jawline. And the two words found their way out.

"The Devil," Pepper said.

Sam narrowed her eyes at Pepper. "Maybe it didn't get who it wanted. So it came after her instead."

Pepper leaned so far back in his chair, it tilted.

Loochie raised her arm, making a fist. Was she about to hit Sam? Or fly across the table and throttle Pepper? Unclear, but Dr. Barger could see she was about to do something aggressive. Sam's sadness, her suspicion, her accusation ran through the room like a current. The newest admit had to use those words. *The Devil.* Dr. Barger thought, *Not this again.*

Dr. Barger said, "I'm sure Samantha will call you as soon as she's back home and settled in. You all know it can take a few days to readjust."

Every patient in here (except Pepper) knew this was true. Coming out of the hospital could feel like emerging from the amniotic sac, or from a tomb.

Dr. Barger added, "So why don't we give Samantha a few days before we decide that she's been sacrificed to *Beelzebub*."

A bit gruesome, that, but it did work. So much of the job in North-west was simply about management. The ugly truth was that these patients weren't here to be cured. There were no cures for them. They had illnesses that had to be managed, by them and by those who treated them. They were like ships that would never find a shore. The most you could do was bring them supplies; the most they could do was get used to the rocking, the unpredictability, of the vast, impenetrable ocean below them.

"Now," Dr. Barger said, smiling, seemingly relieved to have staved off a storm. He knocked on the front cover of the book. "Let's get back to this shark."

Book Group ended and they all fled. They were running from Sam, even if they wouldn't put it that way. She stank of desperation and loss. Dr. Barger couldn't stay because he had another job, late-afternoon patients at his private practice, a half hour drive from New Hyde Hospital. (You didn't think Dr. Barger was living solely on the salary he earned serving the practically destitute population of Northwest, did you?)

Last out of the room was Josephine, whose heart felt sore as she wheeled the book cart. She'd had to evict Sam before locking up. Sam didn't even argue as she walked out, head down again. Josephine watched her leave and wanted to grab Sam's hand. Just hold it. But she wanted to be a professional. Best to get back to work or Josephine would soon feel overwhelmed. The cart had to be returned to the supply closet in Northwest 1. Then back to the nurses' station to log on to the computer, continue transferring information from the charts. Who else would do it? Most of the staff couldn't handle an automatic transmission.

Pepper and Coffee walked together. Coffee had his binder and his copy of *Jaws* tucked under one arm. Pepper held his copy of the novel in one hand. They looked like schoolboys just then, walking home from class.

"You think she's right?" Pepper asked. And he had to repeat himself because Coffee didn't answer him. He realized he must've whispered.

"You think she's right? It took Sammy when it couldn't get me?"

They reached the nurses' station and Coffee said, "I wish I could tell you yes or no. But I can only say I'm happy you're all right."

Pepper touched his own chest lightly. "Not that good."

Coffee waved away any self-pity. "Better than Sammy, I bet."

It was almost dinnertime and all the staff, besides Josephine, were busy dropping pills into little white plastic cups. Preparing for the dinner rush. Coffee eyed the phone alcove.

Then Pepper reached over and slipped the blue three-ring binder from under Coffee's arm. The copy of *Jaws* fell to the floor with a smack, but Coffee didn't pay it any attention.

"What's in here?" Pepper asked.

But he didn't even have time to playfully flip through the pages. Coffee reached up and *thumped* Pepper directly against his wounded sternum, and Pepper hopped on one foot and his hands flew out and he huffed out one big breath. And Coffee's binder fell from Pepper's hands and Coffee caught it. Then he stooped and picked up his copy of *Jaws*. By the time one of the orderlies looked up from the tray of pills, Coffee was walking toward Northwest 2 and Pepper seemed to be doing some kind of interpretative dance.

The orderly said, "Go get ready for dinner."

Pepper steadied himself and breathed deeply as he walked. Trying to catch up to Coffee, who was already halfway down Northwest 2, almost at their room. First Loochie, then the staff, the Devil and now even Coffee. What was the point of being as big as he was if no one respected it? He didn't realize how much it would rattle his confidence to lose the power of his size. Besides that, what did he have? Other things, surely. But what?

He caught up to Coffee, standing in the doorway of their room.

Pepper stopped right behind Coffee and said, "What's the holdup?"

Coffee pointed. Up.

Pepper said, "Ah, shit."

The ceiling had sprung a leak.

Right over Pepper's mattress.

A rust-colored stain, about the diameter of a coffee mug, could be seen in the ceiling tile above his bed.

They watched as a drop fell from the ceiling and landed directly on Pepper's pillow. It wasn't the first. There was a reddish blot about as big as a half-dollar.

Pepper put one hand on Coffee's shoulder, for balance. His chest throbbed, his throat tightened. He whispered, "Should I report this?"

Coffee looked up at the ceiling and down at the pillow. Sadly, he knew this place much better than Pepper. He'd been at New Hyde a year.

Coffee said, "You should just move your bed."

The spot in the ceiling seemed to darken for a moment, then a bead of moisture gathered and dangled and descended. They watched it fall. As if they hadn't already seen what would happen. They watched it hit Pepper's pillow. The reddish blot grew.

"That's disgusting," Coffee said.

True. But how disgusting? What was it? Pepper took his hand off Coffee's shoulder. He looked down at Coffee with a look of pleading. Would Coffee go in first? But Coffee just shook his head. Coffee sure wasn't going in to investigate on Pepper's behalf. He wasn't about to be *that* black guy. (You know, the one who scouts ahead and gets his ass sliced in two. Somewhere near the first ten minutes of the horror movie. Although, to be fair, moviemakers have largely stopped that practice. Now there's usually one amiable but forgettable white person who dies first, *and then* they kill off all the nonwhite cast members.)

The ceiling dripped again. The drop fell. The pillow caught it. The reddish blot bloomed.

Coffee stepped aside and Pepper cautiously moved toward his bed, his eyes on the stain. He reached the pillow and pulled it away from the bed. He looked back at Coffee, who hadn't stepped any farther into the room. His roommate looked poised to book back down the hall.

Pepper lifted the pillow to his face. Up close the stain looked almost the color of a sunset, reddish brown. He thought of Sammy. Was her body right there on the other side of the ceiling tiles? Had that thing dragged her body into the darkness and done to her what it had meant for him? And brought her husk back to Pepper, like a cat presenting a dead bird?

Pepper brought the pillow to his nose.

He sniffed the fabric.

"Rainwater," Pepper said. "I think it's rainwater."

He wasn't just saying this. That's really how the pillow smelled. Musty, with a faint whiff of corroded metal. A backed-up rain gutter maybe. This was a worthless old building that hadn't been well maintained even when it was an ophthalmology ward. Standing water and poor construction and a rusty metal rain guard equals orangish musty water backing up, leaking through the ceiling. Onto his pillow. Obviously he didn't *know* that this was true, but it did make sense. Also, it was the preferable explanation. It wasn't blood.

Rainwater.

Pepper dropped his pillow on the floor. At the very least, they'd have to give him a new one, right? Then he moved to the foot of his bed, clamped one paw around the bed frame and pulled. It hardly moved. He tried again and his rib cage filed a protest. It sent shock waves of pain up into his skull. He actually saw small flashes of light in his eyes. Pepper let go of the bed and breathed and patted his chest and let the pain subside. Then he looked to his roommate—his friend?—Coffee.

"Will you help me?"

Pepper grabbed the bottom end of the bed again and waited there. Coffee watched Pepper for a moment and finally tossed his copy of *Jaws* onto his mattress. Coffee walked to the head of Pepper's bed and grabbed the frame with his *one* free hand.

Pepper gestured at the three-ring binder and said, "I won't swipe that from you again."

Coffee nodded. "Okay." But he didn't put the binder down.

And Pepper, still aching, decided not to push it. He and Coffee lifted and together they got the bed off the ground. Pepper nodded toward the opposite wall and they moved together, kind of crab-walking.

Picture it: Pepper's end of the bed tilted up about six inches higher than Coffee's, and he's popping a sweat because, even with the help, his injuries have made him weaker. And at the other end, you've got Coffee, concentrating more on the book in his right hand than the bed in his left. As a result, the frame wobbles and the legs at his end occasionally bump against the floor. Pepper wanted to give the man a few moving tips. (Paramount being: Use two damn hands!) But no one ever listens to a know-it-all so he tried a different tack.

"You ever reach that guy? The controller?"

"Comptroller," Coffee corrected. "I spoke to a guy who worked for the man. A 'fund-raiser.'"

"And what did this guy say?"

"He thought I was calling *for* New Hyde Hospital. Like maybe I was someone high up. He said I could probably talk to the comptroller if . . ."

"If?" Pepper couldn't suppress a grin. Though with the trouble he was having holding up the bed it looked more like a grimace.

"If I was interested in donating to the campaign fund. I laughed when he said that and explained that I was a patient."

The bed bonked the floor again, then screeched as the legs scratched the floor. Pepper wondered if the staff heard, but then he wondered if they would even care. Were patients allowed to rearrange?

"What did this guy do when you said you were a patient?" Pepper asked.

"He hung up."

They reached the opposite wall and Pepper lowered his end. Coffee just dropped his. The whole frame twanged. Pepper's chest heaved a bit from the labor. A month without work was like a month without exercise. He felt a little ashamed to have lost so much strength so quickly. But his mind wasn't quite as weak. He'd taken his midday dose with lunch when he came in from the smoker's court, but missing the morning dose still had made a difference. His mind felt more vigorous than it had in weeks.

"Where are you from, anyway?" Pepper asked.

Coffee seemed to stiffen, a conversation coming that he didn't enjoy. "I'm from Uganda," he said.

The glaze on Pepper's eyeballs could've been used to coat a turkey.
"Uganda," Pepper said. "Of course. I see."

Coffee sighed. "It's in East Africa."

Pepper nodded as if he'd known all along. "Where else would
it be?"

(Pepper had actually thought it was an island in the Caribbean.)
But then Pepper snapped a finger and said, "Idi Amin!"

At this Coffee seemed to deflate. "Still our most famous export."

Coffee looked at the front door, and Pepper could tell this guy was
about to run away. Maybe Idi Amin, the murderous dictator, wasn't
the best way to talk about Coffee's homeland. Or maybe that just
wasn't what Coffee cared about most now. Pepper needed to bring
the talk back to their situation *here*. They could talk about the glorious history of Samoa (Uganda!) later on.

"The mayor," Pepper said. "The *comp*troller. Who are you going to
try next? Department of Sanitation?"

"At least I'm trying something!" Coffee yelled back.

Pepper and Coffee pushed the bed up against the wall here. Coffee
and Pepper's beds were in the same position, lining the same wall, on
either side of the room's door.

Only problem now was that Pepper's bed sat right below the ceiling tile that had cracked and fallen in the night before. Thankfully,
someone on staff had come through and removed the pieces of tile
(though they hadn't swept up the dust) but the hole remained. Instead of sleeping under the stain, he'd be sleeping here? Pepper
climbed on his bed slowly and rose to his toes. Slipping his head into
the crawl space felt like he was slipping it into a tiger's mouth. The top
of his head felt hot. He remembered those two feet dangling down
from the darkness. He tried to see to the other end of the room,
where his bed had just been. Trying to make out the silhouette of
Sammy's body. But he couldn't tell. Soon enough the dust floating in
the air up there coated his forehead, his eyelids, his lips. He couldn't
stay up there any longer and he hopped down off his bed. He winced
and clutched his chest.

"This isn't going to work," Pepper said. And he wasn't just talking about where he'd rest his head. He meant maintaining. He meant facing whatever came next.

Then Coffee walked over to Pepper's dresser and said, "Help me move this."

The dresser looked like wood but wasn't. Didn't even seem to be some kind of plastic. It might almost have been made of cardboard, that's how cheap it felt. If they'd painted fake drawers on the back of a refrigerator box, it wouldn't have been much worse than this.

Pepper pushed the dresser and it slid so easily the move almost seemed graceful. He slid it until it was at the far end of this wall. Now it sat adjacent to the two windows in the room.

"You'll make fun of me if I tell you who I'm really hoping to reach," Coffee said.

Pepper tapped the top of the dresser. "Yes," he said. "I probably will."

When Coffee said the name it was unintelligible.

"Try again, my friend."

Coffee set his three-ring binder down on Pepper's dresser. He opened the cover and flipped through the pages. Columns had been drawn on every page, by Coffee's own hand. It looked like a ledger. Page after page filled with surprisingly readable script. Coffee had the most elegant handwriting Pepper had ever seen.

"These are my notes," Coffee began. " Every person I've reached in the last year. Their names and numbers, the offices they represent. What they said they would do. What they said they wouldn't do. What was actually done. You'll see there's nothing in that column. Council members. Lawyers. Reporters. Clerks. Secretaries. Everything goes in here. So I can prove my story."

"Prove that you've been ignored?"

Coffee flipped through a series of blank pages until he reached the very last page in the book. This one had two words written at the top.

"Prove that I tried everything. So when I finally reach *him*, he'll know I'm a serious man."

The two words at the top of the page were "Big Boss."

Pepper touched the letters. "You mean God?"

Coffee laughed, it was a soft sound, and his eyes narrowed when he smiled. "I don't appeal to God for man's mistakes. I just have to reach the man who will make things right down here. I don't write his name because when people see his name, hear his name, they go *crazy*. They get so angry. They get scared. Or disappointed. But it doesn't matter. His name means more to them than it does to me. His name could be anything, it's his power that counts."

Pepper stepped back and looked at Coffee's serious round brown face.

"Don't tell me. . . ."

Coffee raised his hand, palm open. "Don't say it. I *never* use his name. By now it has become like a superstition to me. I am trying to reach the *Black President*. I mean to tell him of our conditions, and ask him for help."

Pepper touched his belly lightly. He shook his head and said, "Let me tell you something and you need to believe it. I don't care who the Big Boss is. I don't care if someday it's a Big Lady! The whole game is fixed. Top to bottom. Left to Right. The Black President is just like the White President. 'Meet the new boss, same as the old boss.'"

Pepper heard what he just said in his own head. Was that racist? (Meh.)

Coffee closed his binder. "Dorry was right. You think all those things you say make you sound smarter, but I think you sound like a fool."

There might've been room for more argument but Pepper stepped away from the dresser, and now he noticed something remarkable about the wall space behind his dresser. It wasn't a wall.

It was a door.

It had been painted over. The door handle had been removed, but he could still make out the small indent in the paint where a handle would've fit. And the lock bulged through the paint as well, like a nipple under a tight shirt. Pepper wondered if the lock still worked. Forget schooling Coffee about his political naiveté, what the hell was this?

Coffee touched the bulge of the painted lock and anticipated Pepper's question. "All the bedrooms on the unit used to be offices. All the conference rooms used to be exam rooms. The television lounge was a 'recovery room.' They don't tear down and rebuild anything at New Hyde. Too expensive. They just seal off one door and create another one. They call it 'repurposing.'"

Pepper tapped at the sealed door. "So if we could get this open, we could just walk into the next room? We wouldn't have to step out into the hall?'

Coffee pressed one hand against the door. "I guess not."

"And if we kept opening the doors, where would the last one lead?"

"Where would you want it to lead?" Coffee asked.

Pepper didn't want to say the word outside out loud. Speaking the word might jinx it. He'd made fun of Coffee about the "Black President," but now look at him indulging his own superstition. So he said it to himself.

Outside.

# 15

PEPPER FELT CHARGED. He went into the bathroom and found his bath towel, folded and placed it on the floor in his room, right under the dripping ceiling. At the nurses' station the other patients were waiting in line for their nighttime meds.

Some might doubt the mentally ill could pull off an orderly queue. Aren't they raving lunatics? Shouldn't they be wandering off or howling at the moon? That's more dramatic, admittedly, but inaccurate. If most of these people weren't wearing blue pajamas, you'd have thought you were in a bank line, waiting to talk to the only available teller.

Pepper and Coffee were behind Mr. Mack and Frank Waverly. Mr. Mack had a well-maintained mustache. Frank Waverly had actually turned a paper napkin into a pocket square for his sport coat. Of all the patients Pepper had seen so far, these two seemed least likely. They were the kind of older folks you see less and less anymore. The ones who cultivate their dignity long after anyone's checking for it. The ones who don't think it takes an *occasion* to wear trousers. Even in here, even considering how long they'd been on the ward (six years for Mr. Mack; seven for Frank Waverly), the gentlemen still made an effort. A fantastic act of will. They were like a pair of leopards, held too long in a zoo. Remarkable, but a little ruined.

Pepper and Coffee got in line behind the pair. The smaller man, Mr. Mack, peeped them, top to bottom, then sighed with boredom and turned forward again. Frank Waverly didn't bother.

"That was a *door!*" Pepper whispered.

But Coffee's eyes were on the phone alcove. He couldn't move through this room without looking at it. Pepper had to grab Coffee's elbow to get his attention. When he did this, Coffee's arm squeezed tight against the binder tucked into his armpit.

Coffee said, "Do you want the staff to hear you talking about that?"

Mr. Mack looked over his shoulder again. Interested.

The line moved forward.

Pepper's two favorite people were administering the meds at the nurses' station. Scotch Tape and Miss Chris. She held the clipboard and Scotch Tape handed out the white cups of pills.

The sight of that tray gave Pepper a punch in the gums. His mouth hurt already, thinking of swallowing them. The lunchtime meds had worn off and he felt clearheaded again, like this morning. He felt good. Did he really have to give that up?

"I'm going to refuse my pills," Pepper said.

Frank Waverly turned his head so hard, the move seemed positively chiropractic. Then he looked ahead again, just as quickly.

Pepper grabbed Coffee's elbow again. "Do it with me. Say no."

Coffee didn't even answer him. The line moved forward.

Pepper said, "Strength in numbers."

Coffee patted the binder with his free hand. "These are the numbers that give me strength."

A fair point. Not about the numbers (that was kooky talk), but what Coffee really meant was that he had no history with Pepper. They weren't partners in crime just because they'd moved a bed. And maybe Pepper hoped to refuse the pills along with someone else. So much harder to do difficult things alone. That's why so few people try.

The line moved forward. Mr. Mack and Frank Waverly were up. Miss Chris read out each man's name (even she called Mr. Mack "Mr. Mack"), then Scotch Tape slid their doses over to them.

Pepper leaned close to Coffee. "I've got a credit card in my wallet. You can use it like a calling card. Call whoever you want. Even O—"

Coffee cut Pepper off with a glare.

"Even the Black President," Pepper said. "You can have the card if you do this with me."

Mr. Mack and Frank Waverly walked around the nurses' station and toward dinner in the television lounge. Pepper and Coffee were up.

Another nurse sat behind the station. She slapped at the "new" computer, inputting chart info. It wasn't Josephine. The nurse didn't seem to be doing well. She had a stack of old files, and she hadn't logged in one page of the stuff in over an hour. That poor woman was just tapping the Tab key over and over. She planned to do this for six more hours, until her shift ended.

Miss Chris looked at Pepper's chest very quickly. He saw her do it, though she tried not to be obvious. Dr. Anand, or maybe the nurse, Josephine, had spread the word of his injuries. But if Miss Chris felt any sympathy, she hid it well. She looked at his chest, then back at her chart and scanned for Pepper's name.

But before she could read it aloud, before Scotch Tape could track down Pepper's white plastic cup, Pepper said, "I don't want my medication."

Miss Chris stopped scanning her clipboard and Scotch Tape looked up from his tray. Coffee, too, nearly dropped his binder. He hadn't believed Pepper was going to say it. The handful of patients behind Pepper even stopped breathing.

Miss Chris held a pen in one hand and she tapped it on the clipboard once. "You're *refusing* medication, heh? Against the wishes of your doctor?"

Funny how she made that sound like a breakdown in military discipline. Like refusing the order of your commanding officer.

"Yes," Pepper said slowly, his voice catching. "I'm refusing."

The nurse at the computer had been listening on delay, so she didn't react to Pepper's words until just then. They surprised her, too. Instead of clicking the Tab key she hit Shift and suddenly her whole screen went blank, and she said, "Shit!" Which echoed the thoughts of her coworkers precisely.

Scotch Tape put both his hands on the nurses' station desktop and leaned toward Pepper. "You have the right to refuse," he said. "But refusal is taken as a sign that your illness is in control of you."

"What if I'm refusing because I'm *not* ill?"

Miss Chris almost barked. "If you was healthy, you wouldn't refuse!"

"There's no way I can win this argument," Pepper said, more to himself than to them.

"It's a guilty heart that refuses," said Miss Chris. "If you had nothing to hide, you wouldn't say no."

Her last line was the one that jolted Pepper. He'd had arguments like this with black friends, about the police. A couple of the younger men on some crew at Farooz Brothers would be talking about all the stop-and-frisk beefs they'd been getting into with the NYPD. The numbers had been just obscene, according to them, starting in maybe 2009. Even worse by 2011. And Pepper used to ask them why they cared about getting searched if they had nothing to hide. *If you had nothing to hide, you wouldn't say no.* That's exactly what he'd said to them. More than once. And they'd shake their heads like he was just some middle-aged white dude who didn't know anything worth knowing about such an experience. But in this moment, with Miss Chris and Scotch Tape, with their logic that not taking medication was a sign that a person was deeply ill, well, he wanted to laugh a little and explain—not to Scotch Tape or Miss Chris, but to a couple of young guys on his old crews—that maybe he had an inkling of what he'd sounded like. He suddenly understood this back-and-forth as a kind of conditioning. It wasn't about whether or not he took his pills, and it wasn't about whether or not some kids had a little weed in their pockets. This wasn't about an infraction, but dictating a philosophy of life: certain types of people must be overseen. Pepper hadn't considered this a problem before, he realized, because he hadn't been one of those *types.* Until now.

"I will be informing the doctor about this," Miss Chris said. "You can be sure."

Scotch Tape waved one arm, treating Pepper like a winged pest. "Well, go *on,* then!" he said.

Scotch Tape knew that most of an orderly's job on a psych unit was a simple matter of herding. Herd the patients toward their meals and meds, herd the patients toward their group sessions and family visits, herd the patients away from anything that might agitate them. Because an agitated patient was a troublesome patient. And these people could be enough trouble even when calm. So Scotch Tape had to send Pepper away before he and Miss Chris paid attention to the others in line. Let the match flame of that little rebellion burn out. Once it did, you wouldn't smell the shit.

Pepper looked at Coffee. Maybe he wanted to see his little act bear fruit immediately. (Not maybe.)

But Miss Chris sucked her teeth. "Don't look so frighten about Coffee. We know him a lot longer than *you*, heh? You can meet Coffee in the lounge when *I* done with him. You think we going to eat him?" Then she laughed with that special Caribbean venom. It comes from the back of the throat, like a chest-clearing spit.

And what could Pepper do? As he moved away from the station, Scotch Tape picked up the hospital phone on the desk and dialed a number. He glared at Pepper the whole time. Pepper skedaddled down Northwest 5, toward the television lounge. Looking back over his shoulder only once. Seeing Coffee at the nurses' station. Miss Chris speaking to him with such gusto that her body shook. And Coffee shrinking under the force of her wind.

He wasn't sure if Coffee would follow his lead, but as Pepper had moved away from the nurses' station, he felt something else, too. Pride? Power? Peace?

All of the above. He said no and they backed down.

When Pepper reached the lounge, he found half the tables occupied. Dinner trays and television, a pretty typical American evening.

Dorry sat at one table, alone, and waved for Pepper to join her.

Pepper considered one of the empty tables instead. He wasn't trying to be cruel, but he wanted to sit alone and see what was going to happen. He'd refused his medication and they'd been a bit pissed, but otherwise? He'd been expecting them to hang him upside down by his ankles. Or maybe just throw him a quick lobotomy. But nothing of the sort happened.

Pepper approached the orderly manning the dinner cart. He didn't ask for a tray, he just extended his two hands wide enough for a tray to be balanced between them. This wasn't considered especially rude for the unit. At New Hyde there was less goodwill between server and customer than at a ghetto Burger King.

But the orderly was on his cell phone. A device Pepper found himself eyeing with great envy. (Cell phones weren't supposed to be used on the unit, not by patients or staff.) Pepper waited until the orderly finished his call. The guy looked directly at Pepper the whole time, nodding and grinning until he hung up. Then the orderly, a big bohunk type, grinned and said, "We're all out of meals, man."

Pepper counted the six trays still on the rack.

"I guess my mind's playing tricks on me."

The orderly didn't even look back at the cart. He crossed his arms to make his beefy biceps look even fuller. "I hear you're not really hungry anyway," he said. "I hear you're actually *turning down* the things staff members offer you."

Aha.

Pepper nodded. "It's going to be like that."

The orderly shrugged. "Let's see if your appetite comes back by breakfast."

And why did this guy take such *pleasure* in this little act? It was cruel, but the cruelty wasn't really the charge for him. It was the rules. The order. Outside the unit (and even inside, mostly) this orderly, Terry, was a pretty decent dude. He volunteered at an animal shelter in Forest Hills and found it easier to care for animals than people. With people, you start getting into choice. To put it another way: Terry worked on a psychiatric unit but he didn't really believe in mental illness. A series of bad (or stupid) choices led folks to New Hyde's nut hut, that's what Terry believed. Like this guy, Pepper. The doctor says you need to take your meds, so why not take them? You can't leave until the doctors believe you're improving. They won't believe that if you're not dosed up. And maybe the damn things are even helping you act like less of a wackadoo. So why not do it? Why not? Why not? Why not? In this way, *not* evil, even understandable,

Terry justified denying Pepper his dinner. And Pepper could see Terry wasn't going to become some fifth column among the staff, so he walked away and finally decided to sit with Dorry.

Maybe she would share.

"Hello, Dorry," Pepper said. Even to himself, he sounded artificial. He wondered how broad a smile he might be showing.

But then he appreciated, enjoyed, that he could feel his lips move. That he could coordinate the thought of sitting at Dorry's table with the action. That the meds had been beaten back enough that he could feel himself smiling, even if it was just to try to trick an old woman out of a desiccated-looking orange on her dinner tray. (It was either that or, you guessed it, a beet cookie.)

But even as Pepper pulled the chair out, Dorry slapped one hand on that orange and closed her mottled fingers around it. And with that she got to peeling.

Three hunks—bing, bang, boom—right into her mouth. Hardly enough time to chew. It was as if she ate the orange just to spite Pepper. As if this woman, both a mother and grandmother, had learned how to recognize when someone was just being nice in order to get something from her.

When Dorry had finished, a line of juice running down her chin, she said, "You look hungry."

Pepper pouted. "I am."

"Well, that's what happens when you won't do what they tell you."

"News travels that fast?"

Dorry nodded toward the next table where Mr. Mack and Frank Waverly sat over their dinner trays. Mr. Mack lifted his head from his carton of juice as if he'd been monitoring Pepper and Dorry's conversation. He set down his juice, looked directly at Pepper and said, "I am a *grown* man. I do not gossip."

Then he returned to his previously scheduled apple juice. Once he did, Dorry raised her right hand and curled it into the shape of a duckbill. She nodded toward Mr. Mack again.

Quack, quack, quack!

The moment Mr. Mack looked up from his meal, Dorry dropped the pantomime.

And, of course, none of this had any bearing on Pepper's hunger. And, for that matter, on his recent stance. Hadn't he just gone all Spartacus? Where were his legions of gladiators rallying behind him?

Dorry just wiped her chin.

Mr. Mack looked at his wrist. "It's just about six thirty. I've got the slot."

The other patients hardly seemed to hear him. They either remained focused on their meals or on the game show playing on the screen.

"No whammies, no whammies, no whammies . . . !" shouted the man on the television, who hadn't been well dressed even when this show first aired twenty-six years ago.

"Come on," Mr. Mack said. "Who's got the remote? It's six thirty and I want the news."

Loochie sat at the table closest to the screen. She raised one hand, holding the remote. "*Almost* six thirty," she said.

Mr. Mack glared at her. "That's fine," he said. "But as soon as it's my time I want my show."

And finally here came Coffee.

Pepper watched as Terry, the orderly, received no follow-up phone call. Coffee just shuffled down Northwest 5, looking slightly *dulled,* and he reached the orderly. He was given a dinner tray.

Pepper watched as Coffee scanned the lounge. Looking over, through, past Pepper. Pepper didn't bother waving him over. Instead Pepper became improbably interested in the woman on the screen now and the question of whether or not some little red animated demon would destroy her dreams.

"Come on, no whammies," she chanted. "Come on, no whammies."

It was as if Coffee had been a reel of film that hadn't quite caught on the grooves of a projector wheel. Finally he *saw* Pepper (meaning his medicated vision and his consciousness synced). Coffee registered Pepper there at the table with Dorry and shambled over.

Coffee sat, and removed the orange, the cookie, and the juice carton from the tray. He slid the cookie to Dorry. He slid the tray, which held franks and beans for the main course, toward Pepper. Baked beans from a can, hot dog from a package, a bun that felt (and tasted) like a soft foam microphone cover. Pepper ate it all gratefully.

While Pepper chomped, Coffee said, "Give me your credit card first. Then I'll join you."

Pepper sneaked a look at Dorry.

"That's certainly one way to destroy your credit," Dorry said. She slipped the cookie into her lap.

"Stop!"

On television the woman risking five thousand dollars and a vacation to Fiji winced as an animated demon chortled and clawed back all her winnings. The game-show host offered his practiced sympathies, then said good night to the viewers with a vacant grin.

"She lost the trip to Fiji!" Loochie shouted. The kid looked despondent.

Mr. Mack shouted. "That's six thirty even!" He pointed at his naked wrist. And, sure enough, he was right. "Now stop daydreaming about places you are never going to visit and turn on channel 148."

But Loochie wasn't about to do his bidding. She dropped the remote on his table where its plastic casing thunked.

Pepper finished the last of his meal as Mr. Mack pushed his chair back and stood. He aimed the remote at the television. It took a few dozen presses on the controller before the machine did as it was told.

Dorry pointed at Pepper. "You like symbolic victories, I guess. You want to get Coffee here to refuse his medication just like you did and then *both* of you get written up, *both* of you get punished, and *neither* does anything to face the real problem on this unit. That's a brilliant plan."

The television roared now. A guy in his fifties who was modular-furniture attractive, sat in front of a nondescript news desk, wearing an expensive but unstylish jacket and tie.

"Good evening," he said. "I'm Steve Sands. Welcome to *News Roll.*"

Behind Steve Sands, a large flat screen showed images of Coffee's idealized leader, the Black President. And after him, a series of men and women in their fifties and sixties, all of them white except one black guy with glasses and a big smile.

"With presidential elections only a year away . . ."

Not even the local news, it was a "news program."

Cue the exodus!

Two-thirds of the patients scrambled. The Air Force's finest fighter squadrons don't move as fast. Patients skedaddled to avoid the yapping trap of Steve Sands.

Even the orderly, Terry, gathered the empty meal trays fast. Dorry, Coffee, Pepper, Mr. Mack, and Frank Waverly. They were the only ones who stayed.

Dorry reached out and grabbed Pepper's forearm. She said, "The real problem here is *fear*."

Pepper wanted to say, *Fear? Really? I thought the problem was the Devil coming into my room and stomping me out.* Fear hadn't nearly crushed him to death. And she should've known, since she'd been there.

On-screen, Steve Sands said, "As we gear up for the blood sport of politics in 2012, I thought we should look back to 2008, just to remember where we were then. And to help us think about where we might be going."

Mr. Mack tapped Frank Waverly and pointed at the screen, as giddy as a child watching "Elmo's World."

Steve Sands said, "Now my producers and writers, even my wife, had a lot of suggestions for the clip that should start us off this evening. But I knew exactly which one has stayed with me the longest. And it's not a major event. In fact, it's the kind of thing that might never have been noted in the pre-YouTube age. Remember this one?"

Now the screen showed an auditorium during a town-hall meeting. An older man in a black suit stood at a lectern. A microphone on a stand before him. He said, "Okay. Let's go. . . . This lady in red has had her hand up for some time."

The fingers of a right hand could be seen at the bottom of the screen, waving with great energy. When the woman was called on, the hand dropped and the camera pulled back to reveal seven other people up on the stage with the man in the black suit, all seated behind tables. Below those folks on the stage, people's heads and shoulders could be seen in the rows. The auditorium looked pretty full. The woman in red, her hair pulled up and held with a clip, said, "Thank you, Congressman, um, Castle. . . ."

The lady, in a red T-shirt, carried a plastic bag with a yellow sheet of paper inside and a tiny American flag. Her other hand gripped the microphone.

She said, "I wanna know . . . I have a birth certificate here from the United States of America saying I am an American citizen. With a seal on it. Signed by a doctor, with a hospital administrator's name, my parents, my date of birth, the time, the date . . . I wanna go back to January 20, and I wanna know why are you people ignoring his birth certificate. He is not an American citizen. He is a citizen of Kenya. I am an American. My father fought in World War Two, with the Greatest Generation, in the Pacific theater, for this country, and I don't want this flag to change. I want my country back!"

The audience went wild with cheers and that's when the video stopped. Steve Sands returned to the screen. He shuffled some papers on his desk and raised one eyebrow and leaned forward. It seemed as if he was about to really *say* something. Risk an opinion about what the woman had just said, or about the audience's reaction, or even about the President himself.

But instead, Steve Sands only said, "That was *definitely* a moment of 2008."

A blander pronouncement has rarely been made, and yet Steve Sands sighed deeply, nodded profoundly, as if he'd just signed the Declaration of Independence.

But back in the lounge, Dorry didn't have to worry about holding on to a job, or advertisers. She pointed at the screen as Steve Sands moved on to another "moment of 2008."

Dorry said, "You know what that woman sounds like?"

Mr. Mack turned in his chair and sneered. "I know exactly what she sounds like."

To this, Dorry merely nodded and grinned without commitment. Satisfied that he'd made his point, Mr. Mack looked back at the screen.

Then Dorry turned to Pepper and Coffee. She spoke in a quieter voice.

"That woman just sounds *scared*."


Mr. Mack's half hour passed and the silent pair—Japanese Freddie Mercury and Yuckmouth—came in to wordlessly request the remote. They switched to QVC and watched, rapt, as a vaguely familiar celebrity from the eighties talked up a line of skin products. Dorry, Pepper, Coffee, Mr. Mack, and Frank Waverly exited the lounge posthaste.

Coffee moved fastest because Pepper had handed over his credit card. An act of faith, he called it. (Mr. Mack, when he'd seen Pepper do it, called it "being an ass.")

Halfway down Northwest 5, Scotch Tape appeared, grinning like a villain. He pointed at Pepper. "You've got a curfew now, my man. In your room after dinner. Doctor's orders."

Pepper said, "But that other orderly wouldn't even give me dinner. You know that. You told him not to."

Scotch Tape said, "Don't make accusations like that unless you have proof."

Dorry trailed behind Pepper and Scotch Tape, all the way to the nurses' station. As she broke for the women's hall, Dorry called out to Pepper, "Solidarity!"

"Bitch, please," Scotch Tape muttered.

When Pepper returned to his room, he found that his mattress had been stripped of its sheets and his pillow was missing. A bare mattress lay on the bed frame. And the towel he'd set down on the floor, to catch the leak from the ceiling, had been taken away. In its place someone had stacked his slacks and socks. They were soaked orange.

Pepper had to admit these guys were good. He'd asserted his rights and they'd attacked his quality of living. How many more small cuts like this before he'd just give up? This was a method of control in many arenas. The indignities of an insurance claim come to mind.

Pepper wasn't sure what he should do about the clothes. The drip from the ceiling seemed to have stopped. Now there was just a dried orange blob on the ceiling tile, like a dollop of apricot jam. But the slacks and socks were still wet. He'd be wearing these pajamas for a lot longer.

Scotch Tape said, "I told you how to get out of this place, but you just couldn't be cool." He seemed disappointed in Pepper.

Pepper didn't feel the need to respond. Anything he said would probably only count against him sometime later. Right now he only wanted to show Scotch Tape that these little degradations hadn't bothered him. He couldn't think of a better way to assert his own strength. So he went to his bed where it now rested, against the wall with the painted-over door. He got in bed (*on* the bed, since there were no sheets). He reached over and pulled his book from the dresser. He held it up as a barrier between him and Scotch Tape.

*Jaws.*

Scotch Tape said, "Hope it don't get too cold in here tonight!" Then walked back down the hall.

Pepper stayed focused on the novel. He read in a whisper, a habit since he was little and trying to drown out the sounds of road traffic coming from Kissena Boulevard.

"A hundred yards offshore, the fish sensed a change in the sea's rhythm. It did not see the woman, nor yet did it smell her. Running within the length of its body were a series of thin canals, filled with mucus and dotted with nerve endings, and these nerves detected vibration and signaled the brain. The fish turned toward shore."

Pepper lost time. As he continued reading, he lost even more. The late evening passed and, except for getting up to use the bathroom twice, he forgot himself. He wasn't transported from New Hyde to the beaches of Amity, he didn't feel the New England sun on his skin or the salty breeze on his tongue, but he was reminded of the life beyond this bare bed, and distracted from all the hard questions he'd face once he put the book down. The reading became a muscle relaxant, a sedative, a salve, and there was nothing wrong with that.

Which is why Pepper wasn't stressed when Coffee got press-ganged into the room. Terry practically tossed Coffee through the open doorway. Coffee stumbled into the room, and Pepper, at ease from the enjoyable reading, looked up casually. Coffee's blue binder flapped into the room next. Then Terry slammed the door shut. A second after that, the door was locked.

Even this didn't cause Pepper much alarm. He grinned at Coffee conspiratorially and said, "We're the bad boys of this unit!"

Coffee remained serious. He pointed at the door and said, "Listen."

Terry's sneakers squeaked as he padded down Northwest 2. Pepper heard the clank of another door being locked. And another. Again, and again. Every room in the men's hall. The whole unit going on lockdown.

Pepper sat up. "Did everybody but you refuse their meds?"

Pepper's shoulders tightened as he imagined the glory of such a thing. It had taken a few hours, but they *had* followed his example!

Coffee rolled his eyes. "You're not Jesus Christ. You do know that, right?"

Pepper frowned and set the book down, got up from the bed and crept to the door. Since there was no window to look through, he pressed his ear to the metal. "So what is it, then?"

Coffee came to Pepper's side. "The EMTs are here."

"Someone's hurt?" Pepper asked.

"Someone's dead," Coffee said.

# 16

PEPPER AND COFFEE checked the door when they woke at dawn. Still locked. They had to lie down again, try to force themselves to sleep. Coffee managed, but Pepper couldn't. He showered and returned to bed where he read a little more of *Jaws*. Now the book was about a marriage, and adultery. Of course, the shark still lived out in the waters off Amity, but the police chief, Martin Brody, had another predator to watch out for. This one walked onshore. The oceanographer Brody brought in to investigate the great white must've had his own thin canals of mucus and nerve endings, because he could sense that Mrs. Brody, the chief's wife, was drifting alone in the sea of her marriage. And that dude smelled blood!

The lock sounded and Pepper and Coffee got up. Pepper peeked outside. Josephine continued down Northwest 2, unlocking all the other doors. Pepper and Coffee walked out of their room, moved down the hall, and found a line at the nurses' station, like any other morning.

The women had been let out first. There were still five waiting to get their meds. Pepper and Coffee joined the queue without thinking. They were like conscientious objectors who'd mistakenly wandered onto the front line. Sneaking off again, unnoticed, hardly seemed possible in a room that size. Pepper stepped one foot out of the line, and a staff member at the nurses' station cut her eyes at him. He stepped back in. He didn't see how he'd have the nerve to refuse his meds this morning if he couldn't even muster the courage to walk away.

Loochie stood two places ahead. She'd looked back at him as he'd put one foot out and pulled it back again. Her eyes were red, the pouches under them so dark they looked black. The pom-poms on her blue knit cap drooped down to her ears. The kid looked wrecked. Not beat up, worn out. She let the woman between them go ahead so she and Pepper could talk.

Pepper said, "I heard someone got hurt."

Loochie said, "Sam."

Pepper looked down Northwest 1, toward the conference room where they'd had Book Group the afternoon before. Almost as if he were watching Sam now, walking out of that room the day before, distraught because of Sammy's disappearance.

Loochie pointed toward the nurses' station, the staff members. "They said she killed herself."

"They told you that?" Coffee asked.

Loochie shook her head. "I heard them say it. My room was right next to hers."

"But did anybody *see* her do it?" Pepper asked.

Loochie shrugged. "With Sammy gone, Sam had the room alone."

Coffee and Pepper and Loochie took a step forward on the line together.

Loochie said, "The Chinese lady saw Sam's body before they took her out. Right before they put us on lockdown."

"What Chinese lady?"

Loochie sniffed at Pepper, ignoring his question. She looked at her hands and pooched out her lips. Forget about crying, the kid looked like she was going to melt.

Loochie said, "Sam took Sammy's bedsheet and drowned herself with it."

"*Hung* herself," Pepper corrected. "That what you mean?"

Loochie clenched her hands. "If I meant 'hang' I would have said 'hang.' The Chinese lady said Sam got the sheet down her throat. She swallowed it."

Coffee and Pepper couldn't respond. They only breathed quietly, focused on the feeling of air in their tracheas. Each one imagining the feeling of a bedsheet clogging the pathway.

Loochie said, "The Chinese lady said one of the nurses pulled the sheet out of Sam's throat and the end of it was bright yellow. It was yellow because it was down in Sam's *stomach*."

"Who kills themselves like that?" Pepper said.

Coffee huffed. "Nobody does."

Then the trio reached the nurses' station. The nurse read off Loochie's name—Lucretia Gardner—it was the first time Pepper had ever heard it. He felt compelled to share his real name with her, right then, to be fair. But the nurse handed over Loochie's meds and moved on to Pepper quickly, and that feeling passed. The orderly placed Pepper's little white cup on the desktop like a bartender setting down a shot. Before the nurse could read his name out, Pepper placed his hands behind his back and said, "I refuse."

The orderly laughed. "You *refuse*? You sound real dumb right now."

Then Pepper looked directly at the orderly and said, "I'm not taking that shit." He gestured at the white cup with his chin. "Smart enough?"

These two took the news with a lot less shock than the staff from the night before. The nurse just wrote something on the clipboard and began to say Coffee's name.

But before she could finish, Coffee said, "I refuse."


When they reached the lounge, most of the tables were full. Pepper hadn't seen a turnout like this, outside of visitors' hours, in all his weeks on Northwest. There were some patients who woke up only long enough to snack on their morning pills, then slept through the breakfast hours; others who snuck their food back to their rooms and ate alone, or with their roommates. (Sam and Sammy had been like that.) And others who were usually up all night and only went to bed when dawn light crept through the grand windows of the television lounge.

But this morning, all the patients were up and out of their rooms. Maybe it was a reaction to having been locked in overnight. Maybe none of them wanted to feel isolated, all by themselves, alone in their rooms. Whatever the reason, the lounge stayed *packed*.

"That was real stupid," Loochie said as they moved toward the orderly handing out breakfast trays.

Before they reached him, his cell phone rang.

Pepper said, "They can't make you take those pills. If you say no, they have to respect that."

Loochie snorted. "Think you have to tell me? I've been on psych units since I was thirteen. I know the laws."

Pepper stopped short and reached out for Loochie's arm. "You've been at Northwest for *six years*?"

Loochie laughed with genuine glee. "Not here. They have juvenile psychiatric units, and adult ones. I was in the juvenile ones, on and off, since I was—"

Pepper cut her off. "Thirteen."

He looked at Coffee, who seemed just as stunned. Both men were struck by the idea of being in a place like this—whether juvenile or adult—since that age. How could anyone stand it? Right then, Loochie looked like some battle-hardened centurion to both men.

But Loochie didn't linger in their surprise. She knew what usually came soon after. Pity. And she sure wasn't interested in something like that. Especially not from Pepper and Coffee; she would've called them Abbott and Costello, but she was decades too young for a reference like that.

"You accept the pills so they don't punish you," Loochie said. "Simple."

They reached the orderly and he gave Loochie her breakfast. The other two he waved off and they knew why.

Pepper said, "But then you end up taking the medicine and getting all . . ." Pepper rolled his eyes back in his head and let his mouth go slack.

Loochie slipped her tongue into the pouch of her cheek and dug out all three of her meds, still intact. She had her back to the orderly so he wouldn't see this. Then she slipped the pills back into the side of her mouth with an expert's ease.

She said, "You think I could've brought you down so hard if I took all the pills they give me? I skip at least one round a day."

Pepper muttered, "I didn't go down that bad."

Loochie ignored him, still focused on the trick of tucking away her pills. "Didn't you ever hide your vegetables as a kid?"

Pepper shook his head, almost proudly. "My parents never made me eat them."

"The all-American diet," Coffee said disdainfully.

Only one table had three seats free. It was the table closest to the garbage bin. Also, Dorry sat in the fourth chair. She caught Pepper's eye, but this time she didn't have to wave him over. Pepper came to her right away. Coffee and Loochie in tow.

When they sat, Dorry handed out portions from her tray. The apple for Coffee, the dry toast for Pepper. She liked giving it out when she wasn't being manipulated. Loochie looked down at her own tray and, not to be outdone, gave her dry toast to Pepper. Coffee got her small box of Froot Loops. The four of them broke bread.

Dorry took off her glasses and pulled at the right sleeve of her nightdress. She buffed the lenses while they watched her. When she put them back on, the damn things looked even cloudier than before.

"You may be wondering why I summoned you all here tonight," Dorry said.

Loochie said, "It's morning."

"And you didn't summon us. We showed up," Pepper said.

Dorry raised one hand, the pointer finger standing straight. "I'm going for a little atmosphere here."

Coffee, less prone to bursting bubbles, said, "We're here to talk about Sam. And Sammy."

Dorry closed her eyes for a moment. "And about Marcus, and Bernadette, and Gustavo, and on and on."

They sat quietly, even as the rest of the lounge filled with conversation.

"We're here to talk about what's to be done. And the *best* way to do it," Dorry said.

Loochie bit into her apple, and to the other three, the crunch sounded louder than the television nearby.

Dorry said, "Making phone calls hasn't brought in the cavalry." She looked at Coffee and tilted her head slightly. "I'm sorry, Coffee, that's no reflection on you."

Coffee shook his head. "I just haven't reached *him* yet. But thanks to Pepper I've been able to make a lot more calls. And I finally got the number for the White House switchboard."

Pepper and Dorry and Loochie watched Coffee quietly. He leaned forward in his seat; he grinned at them with such enthusiasm that no one wanted to be snide.

Pepper said, "What if we made a plan for what we might do just in case the Big Boss is . . . delayed in helping us? Just to have a backup."

Coffee nodded. "I guess that would be smart."

Dorry said, "So what's the first big problem we face?"

"The Devil is trying to kill us," Loochie said.

"That's our final problem," Dorry said. "We can't face that *man* until we're ready."

Pepper opened his mouth and closed it. Opened and closed it. On the third try he actually produced sound, words. "We all have to get off these medications. That's first. You can't fight if you can't think straight."

Loochie said, "If we did that I might stop . . ." She didn't finish the sentence, but one hand rose and touched the side of her knit cap.

". . . I might stop doing harm to myself," she finished.

Dorry rapped the tabletop, right in front of Coffee. "And you might do better with the people you reach if you sounded a little more . . ."

Coffee stiffened. "I'm always polite and direct."

Loochie said, "Really? 'Cause a lot of the times it sounds like you're just yelling into those phones. Maybe you think you're really saying something, but a lot of times it just sounds like noise."

Dorry lowered her eyes. "I'd have to agree."

Coffee brought one hand to his throat. "Really? That's what I sound like?" He looked to Pepper but what could Pepper say? He hadn't actually heard any of Coffee's calls. But from Loochie's description they sounded bonkers.

Coffee dropped his head. "Maybe that's why they never call me back."

He sounded so despondent that Pepper wanted to give the small bald dude a hug.

"And I . . ." Dorry began. "I'd just like to get one night of true *rest*. I don't think I've had a natural sleep in"—she pointed at Loochie— "since before this girl was even alive."

To sleep, to be less self-destructive, to communicate clearly with the world. Those all sounded like reasonable dreams to Pepper. But what came after that? Once they all cleared their minds of the pharmaceutical junk and found themselves, in a word, *potent* again. Then what?

"I almost made it to the silver door," Pepper told them.

The others looked at him patiently. It seemed as though all the other people in the room, and even the sunlight warming the lounge, moved at a different speed than the four people at this table now. With the mere mention of the silver door, time left them behind.

Coffee shook his head. "No, you did not."

"You didn't see me. I touched the door handle. That's why they put me in restraints."

Coffee sighed. "It does not matter. You'll never get inside its room. They'd never let you."

"Well, then," Loochie said. "What if we let it out?"


But, as Dorry pointed out, first things first. The problem of the pills and how to avoid the punishments Pepper had already experienced. The staff had worse than that at their disposal, too. There were so many ways to punish patients! No more bath soap, not for weeks, until even the patients on the other end of New Hyde's grounds would complain about your odor. You could be exiled to your room, no television privileges. Denied family visitation. And, of course, the date of your release could be pushed back indefinitely.

All these methods came into play if staff merely *suspected* you weren't doing as told. A hint of cognition aroused suspicion. The lack of slurred speech raised doubts. The staff were trying to stave off more than just hard work. A psychiatric patient without meds was like having a cyclone in your living room. That's the fear, anyway. On the meds that same patient becomes a passing breeze. You can't really blame the staff if they want to avoid storms. But what does the weather want?

When Pepper and Dorry and Loochie and Coffee got in line for their lunchtime meds, they all understood the pills weren't their arena for insurrection. The point wasn't to spit the pills into some staff member's face. The four of them had to stop taking the antipsychotics and the antidepressants and the tranquilizers, all the various "stabilizers," *in order* to mutiny. The rebellion required a little subterfuge first. So at lunch they got in line and plopped the pills into their mouths, tucked them under the tongue or by the gums and then discreetly spit them out later. No real challenge there. That wasn't actually the hard part.

The trick was to *seem* medicated even as their bodies kicked. Because staff wouldn't actually prod open their mouths and swish a finger over their gums. As long as the pills went in the staff assumed the pills went down. They were actually supposed to take every patient's blood each week and test it to be sure the dosages weren't too high or low, but this, like so many sensible hospital practices, went undone. Instead, the staff just tracked behavior. They noticed if the patient was being a little more *aggressive* recently. If the patient questioned staff commands more often. Even if he or she moved with new grace. These were all tip-offs. (And they didn't generate lab costs.) So Pepper and Dorry and Loochie and Coffee had to enroll in acting class. To slouch like always; to let drool drip past their lips and onto their clothes at indiscreet times; to waver and wobble as they walked the halls; to never break character.

And the nominees for best actor in the role of reduced capacity are . . .

# 17

THREE DAYS OF practice and Pepper thought he'd mastered a thoroughly convincing slur. At this point he could make his lower lip dip down so far, make himself so damn unintelligible, that even Mushmouth from the Cosby Kids would be like, whatbee da fuckbee is dis guy talking abeebout?

He'd also learned to drag his left leg slightly when he walked. Step lively with the right but throw a little hitch into the left. The stride of the medically polluted.

This is why it took Pepper about fifteen minutes to get from his room to conference room 2 for Book Group. Truthfully, he wasn't even sure if he should attend the meeting. What was the point? He was ready to get to the next stage of their uncertain project: figuring out how to open the silver door.

But he had finished *Jaws*, read it even more quickly with his mind cleared, and actually wanted to discuss it. Though he wasn't sure how he should handle slipping intelligent conversation between his fake droopy lip. He thought on this as he moved down Northwest 2 and into the oval room that held the nurses' station. He pretended not to notice the three staff members all hunched in front of the computer, each one squinting at the screen in exasperated bafflement.

"What kind of program is this?"

"I booted it up three times. You can't read what it says?"

"'Equator. Equator. Equator.' I *see* it, but that's not the same as understanding it!"

Pepper passed them quietly, which was for the best. Those three were so angry at the computer and its almost willfully impenetrable program that they might've stuck him with a needle just to release their frustrations.

He reached Northwest 1 and looked at the ceiling, the tiled floors, the closed doors of the other conference rooms, the insipid nature paintings, looked at anything but the front door because he couldn't be sure that he wouldn't break character and go running for it again. The dream of freedom is a hard one to forget. But he managed to ignore it until he'd reached conference room 2.

To find that he was the first patient in attendance. Dr. Barger was clicking on the keypad of his Smartphone. His copy of the Benchley book facedown on the table. Next to that, a notepad and one pen.

"Pepper," he said evenly, without seeming to even look up.

Pepper sat quietly. He felt like a student who's made the mortal error of being the first kid to walk in the classroom, and he squirmed awkwardly.

In just another second, Dr. Barger set his phone down and said, "You look well."

"I do?"

Pepper felt worried. Maybe his speech had been a little too clear when he responded just now? His face flushed. He did an internal check on his features: mouth slack? Check. Shoulders slumped? Check. Eyes vacant? Check. But then Pepper realized that to Dr. Barger all this counted as *well,* and Pepper felt the pride of accomplishment.

Dr. Barger said, "I was just in Aruba."

"Yuh?" (That's a slurred "Oh, yes? Do go on!")

The doctor smiled warmly and leaned back in his chair. He rested one hand on his large hard belly. "I go down and do work with locals who don't have any other access to treatment." He wiggled his head side to side. "And I slip in a day or two of relaxation."

Dr. Barger laughed and Pepper didn't begrudge him. He actually kind of liked that this guy didn't pretend life wasn't happening out-side the unit. Liked, even, that the doctor talked about things like vacation, relaxation, joy. He would've preferred to hear about the days on the beach more than the days at some clinic for locals. Some-times, when you're in bad straits, it's actually nice to hear about plea-sure and not more gloom. Pepper almost asked Dr. Barger about the good days down in Aruba but the next member of Book Group ar-rived. It was Dorry. And she was *not* acting well.

Dr. Barger said, "Dorry?"

The woman wore a purple cardigan and pink blouse underneath. The lapels of the blouse flared out over the lapels of the cardigan and the top two buttons of the blouse sat open. Exposing a string of *fake pearls*! Dorry still rocked her gigantic glasses, but they were so clean, it was as if they'd been sandblasted. And she'd washed her hair; it now sat in a blunt bob that made her look fifteen years younger. She used to look like Angela Lansbury in *Sweeney Todd*. Now she looked like Angela Lansbury on *Murder, She Wrote*.

Pepper might actually have started hyperventilating at the sight of her. What happened to their pact? There were supposed to be no obvious signs they'd stopped taking their meds.

But if Pepper experienced a mild panic, Dorry didn't seem to no-tice or care. She swayed as she entered the room, looking serene. "I woke up this morning and just *had* to spruce up," she said.

Dr. Barger nodded and lifted his pen and wrote something down on his pad. Pepper craned his neck to try to read the words upside down. But he was too far away and Dr. Barger caught him trying to peek, so Pepper returned to his routine, making his face as soft as a bowl of porridge. Any words he might have for Dorry would have to be saved for after Book Group.

Then Loochie arrived.

Her transformation was less of an overhaul. She'd already been the type to wash up and change clothes pretty regularly. And she re-mained the same stylish teenager. But she wasn't wearing the blue knit cap. What could have been more jarring to Pepper? Maybe it was finally seeing what lay underneath. Half Loochie's scalp was hairless. She had dark brown hair that came down to the bottom of her ears, but there were irregularly shaped bald spots in five different places. The largest was the size of a softball. But when Loochie entered the room, she strode as gracefully as Dorry.

Dr. Barger couldn't hide his surprise. "This is the first time I've seen you . . . so confident," he said, trying to be kind.

Loochie nodded as if he'd meant the line as a compliment. She touched her head, one of the hairless patches, as she sat. "I think the Geodon was making me pull my hair out at night. I didn't even know I was doing it."

"Was?" Dr. Barger asked.

Loochie shrugged, dramatic nonchalance. "I don't know why, but I just haven't felt the compulsion recently."

"That's wonderful," Dr. Barger said dispassionately. He wrote something else down on his pad.

Loochie said, "I talked to my mother, and she told me I needed to let my scalp breathe so the hair could start growing again." She shook her head from side to side as if it had already all come in. "So that's what I'm doing."

Pepper glared at Loochie. He would've expected a teenage girl to be existentially mortified by exposing her patchy scalp this way, but she wasn't acting that way at all. She seemed almost proud of her audacity.

Dr. Barger said, "There's a different air to the room today. Have you noticed?"

Pepper wondered why he bothered to maintain his pretense. A different *air* in the room? There might as well be a whole new atmosphere.

"Hello, my friends," Coffee said when he entered.

Pepper did the quick up and down. The man hadn't suddenly grown some enormous glorious afro. He hadn't walked into the room wearing an African suit. (Pepper didn't know what he meant by that exactly. A bright draping cloth? A Western suit made out of that bright draping cloth? Better to not dwell on it.)

Coffee looked like the same man as always. He still wore his pajamas, still wore the blue slipper-socks, and his face maintained the look of concentrated dissatisfaction it had always worn. In fact, if

Pepper hadn't watched Coffee dropping his meds into the bathroom sink in their room these last few days, he would've sworn Coffee remained medicated. So okay, at least he and Coffee would carry the torch for subterfuge.

But when Coffee sat down, he looked at Dr. Barger and said, "I liked seeing the sun through my windows this morning."

And Dr. Barger stared back, baffled.

As did Pepper.

Coffee said, "Doctor?"

Finally, Dr. Barger coughed and squeezed his lips in a tight smile. "I don't think I've ever heard you mention *anything* but the phone numbers of governmental employees. Not in even *one* of our interactions over the past year."

Coffee looked at Pepper quickly, then down at the table. "I'm sorry. . . ."

Dr. Barger laughed. "Don't say 'sorry.' It's nice. Makes me feel like, well, maybe *I've* been of some help."

Coffee looked up again and offered the doctor a generous smile. "Oh, of course you have."

Dr. Barger rubbed his belly proudly.

Pepper watched Coffee for another moment and realized he had missed something. There was one glaring difference to Coffee that should've been obvious from the moment the man arrived.

No binder.

"I was sorry to hear about Sam," Dr. Barger said.

No reaction from anyone in the room. None of them knew what to say or do. They were sorry, too. Maybe there was nothing more.

Dr. Barger recovered by smiling. He hoped to return to the elation in the room just before he'd mentioned the death. He said, "All this good cheer only makes my bad news more difficult to share."

Pepper looked at Dr. Barger. He'd wondered how the man couldn't have noticed all the signs of reversion; the slip back into attentiveness, empathy, self-control. In other words, normalcy. How could this trained professional miss all that?

Dr. Barger said, "Unfortunately, this is going to be our last Book

Group session together. The board of New Hyde Hospital has informed me that my services aren't *affordable*."

The doctor paused there, as if the patients were going to cry out in horror. When they didn't, he said, "And keep in mind, my work here is subsidized by both the city and the state, since New Hyde is a public hospital. So that means the board has decided that I'm not worth even the pittance they have to pay out of their own account in order for me to work with all of you. They've basically told me I'm worth nothing and I just . . ."

The man had been looking at his own hands as he spoke, the volume of his voice increasing. But now he stopped speaking all together. He looked at Coffee and Loochie and Dorry and Pepper, and though he smiled, his eyes were small and wet.

"It's silly of me to complain. Especially to you. Each of us has a burden and I shouldn't share mine. I guess I just hoped for time. With a little more of it I thought we might really do some good."

God bless her, Loochie responded fastest. Veering away from the maudlin, changing the subject. "So what do we do instead? Watch TV?"

"Book Group isn't ending," Dr. Barger said. "My contract is ending."

Dr. Barger got up and walked around the table and stepped outside the room. He called out, "You can come along now!"

Josephine arrived, pushing the Bookmobile.

Now don't worry, this wasn't about to turn all *Dangerous Minds*. Josephine entered the room and rolled the cart around until it sat right beside Dr. Barger's chair.

He said, "New Hyde Hospital has enough in its budget for keeping this room heated while you use it for Book Group. And for this Bookmobile to be made available to you. So that's what you're going to get. And, as a part of the salary she already receives, Muriel will stay in the room and supervise."

Pepper looked at Josephine. "So she's going to lead our discussions?"

"*No*." Dr. Barger leaned forward in his seat and lifted his pen and tapped the tip against the table. "There is no money for a facilitator. And she isn't trained as one. She can only bring the cart and take the cart."

"Well, then, what's the point of being in this room?" Loochie asked.

Dr. Barger sighed. "Truthfully? It's so that New Hyde Hospital can tell the city and the state that it provides group sessions to its patients. Not *therapy*, but *sessions*. That way, they comply with the letter of the law, if not the spirit. That way, they'll continue to receive state and federal grants for the sessions, but cut out the cost of a professional like me."

Dr. Barger looked toward the door, as if he expected the board of the hospital, or at least Dr. Anand, to rush into the room and charge him with excess honesty.

Josephine tapped the side of the cart. All three tiers were full of new books. "I listened to what you all said last time," she began.

The doctor seemed surprised to hear her voice. He'd been expecting to milk the pained silence for another minute or five. But he also didn't interrupt her. What would be the point? When he left this room, this unit, he'd never be back. Too much paperwork to fill out for compensation anyway. And too many different agencies spitting up some small portion of the total bill. He looked at the four patients, two men and two women, and felt a stabbing kind of sympathy. This was the new American Austerity. The reality of our lives in the aftermath of economic disaster. The tighter belts, the slashed spending, the death of compromise. The twenty-first century threatened to look a bit like the nineteenth. The Century of Sharp Elbows was upon us. This economic prudence was supposed to affect everyone, but you could bet it was going to whip some people much worse. Dr. Barger felt the pain of these realizations but with a little time, and distance, his discomfort would pass.

"My library was having a book sale," Josephine said. "Getting rid of a lot of things. My mother and I went there on Saturday and Sunday. I found a bunch of stuff that I thought you might like. I had fifty dollars to spend and they were selling titles cheap."

Dr. Barger snorted. "At least New Hyde spit up the cash for that!"

Josephine shook her head. "Actually, the money came from me."

Dr. Barger looked back at her again and nodded. He didn't offer anything more.

Josephine said, "You don't have to wait for Book Group to pick something. If you come find me, I'll let you borrow a title."

Dr. Barger turned back to the table and looked at his copy of *Jaws*. He said, "How many of you actually read it?"

Every hand, including Josephine's, went up.

Dorry said, "We're ready."

And Dr. Barger nodded, opened his copy of the book.

"We're ready," Dorry repeated, and the doctor waved to let her know he'd heard.

He heard but didn't understand.

Dorry wasn't speaking to *him*.

She watched Pepper who finally looked up from his book. The old woman stared at him.

"We're ready," she said.


But ready for what, exactly? The spirit was willing, but the flesh was a little . . . disorganized. They'd stopped taking their medications with the hopes that it would allow some clarity. So they could make their next decision—how to confront the Devil? And what to do when they released it?

That wasn't a conversation for Book Group, though.

So they talked about *Jaws* and passed an hour. Dr. Barger shook each person's hand before he had Josephine walk him to the secure door and let him out for good. She looked over her shoulder before sliding the key in the door this time. When Josephine returned to conference room 2, the four patients had left for the television lounge where they waited on the next smoke break. Miss Chris was the one who opened the way this time. She unlocked the shatterproof glass door and did a head count as the patients shuffled past.

"Eight out!" she shouted, for no one's benefit. It's not like one of the orderlies, or another nurse, or any of the higher-paid staff, was standing around with a clipboard, taking count. No. Miss Chris called out the number only to alert the other staff members back at the nurses' station that *she* had monitored this break and she better not be bothered to cover another soon.

Four of the eight patients spent their time smoking. Japanese Freddy Mercury and Yuckmouth, Wally Gambino and, of all people, the Haint. They stood around the tilted basketball rim and lit up. The other four gathered under the maple tree. The ground showed dozens of maple seeds, gone brown because they'd fallen and found only concrete. Nowhere to grow so they died. Dorry reached down and picked one up and twirled the stem between her thumb and forefinger.

"My son used to like playing helicopters with these."

"He never visits you?" Coffee asked. He didn't realize the line might sound harsh.

Dorry let the husk go and it fell without whirling. "I like to think he's always near me. But my daughter visits." She seemed glum but smiled after a moment. "And she brings my grandsons."

Out here, away from the watchful eye of a moderately vigilant staff, Pepper dropped the droopy lip and straightened his left leg.

Loochie said, "Why are you acting like that?"

"I'm trying to make them think I'm still on my medication. We were all supposed to do that. Remember?"

Loochie said, "I *was!*"

Dorry and Coffee nodded, too. As if their chicanery had been clear. And Pepper understood that this, right now, was how they *thought* they appeared all the time, even when the medication had been wrecking them. Even Dorry, who'd been at New Hyde for decades, had never seen herself as she'd been seen by others.

And what about Pepper? Before he got all incredulous about the distance between the reality and the perception of Dorry, Coffee, and Loochie, maybe he'd better consider the difference between the man he believed he was and the man so many others encountered. His brother and sister-in-law. His mom and dad. The super of his building, once or twice when his apartment had no heat in the depths of winter. And, of course, Mari. He'd hoped she thought of him as a valiant knight, but from that phone call, she seemed to think of him as, at best, a bother. He wondered if she'd ever found his brother's number. So far Ralph sure hadn't called or come by. Maybe nobody ever saw themselves completely objectively. Every self-image needs a flattering mirror or two.

Pepper said, "Well, let's talk about *now*. Let's talk about what's next."

Loochie, without thinking, crouched and found a half dozen pebbles there on the ground and as she gathered them up she said, "We let it out. Then we light it up."

She stood again and shook the handful of small stones in her palm.

Pepper said, "That's one vote for fighting."

Coffee said, "I just want to get the right people in here so *they* can make this place work the way it's supposed to."

Pepper said, "That's one vote for insane faith."

Coffee cut his eyes at Pepper and Pepper corrected himself.

"That's one vote for optimism. How about that?"

Coffee said, "Accurate."

"I want to talk with him," Dorry said. "He needs to hear us. We need to make him understand that he's hurting us. Maybe he doesn't even realize what he's doing. Have you considered that? Once you know someone, it's a lot harder to remain enemies."

Loochie shook her closed fist at Dorry. "So you want to make friends with the Devil? That's your plan?"

"He's a man!" Dorry shouted. The patients by the rim looked over quickly but soon returned their attention to their cigarettes.

"And I would think that if anyone should be able to feel a little sympathy for a person with troubles," Dorry added, "it's people like us."

Loochie said, "People like you, maybe. People like me? We don't shake hands with monsters."

Dorry laughed. "What does that mean? 'People like me.' Teenagers? I've got *bras* that are older than you."

Loochie scrunched her nose. "That's nasty."

Coffee poked Pepper in the arm. "What about you, then? What do you want to do?"

"I want to get out of here," Pepper admitted. "I don't want to open that door or fight or have peace talks with that thing. I want us to *leave*. It's like you people forgot what it's like to live anywhere but here!"

Loochie and Coffee and Dorry flinched at that.

Dorry squinted at Pepper. "And where will we go once you open the big door? Will I stay with my daughter in Greenpoint? Where she'll treat me like a burden every single day? Until eventually she calls an ambulance for me, because I just don't fit into her life there, and I'm escorted back to New Hyde Hospital by the EMTs. That's your plan?"

Pepper tried to speak, but Dorry reached across and touched Loochie lightly on the side of her head.

"And Loochie will go back with her mother and her brother, yes? At least until they call the police to come get her after one too many fights. And then she'll be right back at New Hyde, you can bet."

Dorry pointed at Coffee next. "And he'll be free for as long as he doesn't attract anyone's notice. But as soon as he does, they'll come talk to him about his *status* in this country. And when they find out that he's overstayed his original visa? They'll send him right back to Tora Bora."

"Uganda," Coffee said.

Dorry nodded. "You're welcome."

She stepped right up to Pepper, one shoulder bumping him in the gut.

"So when you say you want us to leave, who are you really thinking of? *We* can't run from what's coming. But if you want to go, you can go. Why don't you climb that fence right now?"

Pepper looked at the chain link, the kind he'd been climbing since he was a kid, all around Queens. Even with the lingering ache in his rib cage, even with the barbed wire bundled along the top edge, he thought he could do it. Strip off his pajama top and toss it over the barbs to protect his skin. He'd get cut, but he could manage. With the meds out of his system for three days, he felt in so much more command of his body. He felt sure even his wounds had healed faster. He watched the fence line and the other three watched him. Until

Miss Chris opened the door to the lounge again and called the patients back in.

Miss Chris shouted, "Eight in!"

"If you're going to stay with us," Dorry said, calmer now, "I think we should wait until Saturday night."

"Overnight weekend shift," Coffee added.

Loochie said, "Only two staff on duty then. That's smart."

Saturday night.

Two days from then. Forty-eight more hours of dumping their meds down bathroom sinks; 2,880 minutes of gaining strength; 172,800 seconds before Pepper had to decide if he would fight alongside them, or flee.

# 18

SATURDAY MORNING, PEPPER woke up to find himself alone in the room and its door halfway open. Since his bed sat right beside the hidden door in the wall, he'd taken to touching it at the bulge where the handle used to be. In the last two days, he'd probably rubbed the spot two dozen times. The motion had become reassuring, soothing, as he tried to decide what he'd do tonight. Pepper touched it now but, in a flash, saw this behavior as if watching himself from across the room. He thought of Coffee at the phones, dialing and dialing. Or Loochie, pulling out her own hair on so many nights. Obsessive ticks. Maybe he was developing one, too. Pepper pulled his hand away. He jumped out of bed. He needed to do something else, to focus on anything else.

Pepper closed the door. He went across the room to Coffee's dresser, and slid it away from the wall. He wanted to see if there was a door outlined under the paint here, too. But when Pepper moved the dresser, he found all these small black droppings on the floor. Rat turds. Wonderful.

Pepper rested one arm on Coffee's dresser, which made the flimsy thing slide toward Coffee's bed. When it connected, he heard a rattling sound. Pepper stooped and pulled open the bottom drawer and found pills. Handfuls of them. He'd seen Coffee dump some of his meds down the bathroom sink for the past few days, but who knew how many were assigned to the man each day? Pepper had been kept on a steady diet of two pills, three times a day, so he'd assumed that was about normal. In fact, there were patients on the unit who took six, seven, nine pills *per meal.* Imagine that. Twenty-seven doses a day. Coffee was one of those. This drawer full of pills represented just five days of abstaining.

The sight made Pepper downright nostalgic for the days of Coffee pestering him for coins. It was a wonder Coffee had been able to do that much with this many pharmaceuticals in his blood. Nickels, dimes, and quarters. For a moment Pepper was reminded of the simple—stupid!—pleasure he used to take in gathering up his coins and going to a Coinstar machine at the Key Food near his apartment. Feeding the change into that swiss-cheese grill and listening to it all rattle as the machine counted up the currency. Sometimes he'd even forget to take the slip to the register and redeem it for cash right away. The joy had been in finding out how much he'd collected. That's the kind of thing that being inside the unit made a person miss.

As Pepper slid the drawer shut again, he wondered if, and when, the police would ever return for him. When they'd bring him before a judge. When he'd receive sentencing. Or was this the sentence? Not what they'd intended when they picked him up but just as good. He wondered where he might be in the NYPD's system. How long after the paperwork was filed before Huey, Dewey, and Louie would return for him? In books, movies, television, the justice system worked with a ruthless efficiency. Arrest, arraignment, trial, and verdict, all in forty-six minutes and forty-eight seconds.

Not here.

Since the conversation under the maple tree, Pepper had been evading the other members of his revolutionary cell. When Coffee went out to "take" his meds and get breakfast, Pepper pretended to still be sleeping. Yesterday, he didn't eat one meal with Coffee or Dorry or Loochie. If they'd noticed, they didn't stress him about it. All that mattered, for their purposes, was what he'd do tonight. But he still didn't know.

Before leaving the room, Pepper went to his dresser and took out his street clothes. The slacks and socks had dried. They were a little stale, but they didn't stink. They now showed large orange splotches where the dirty water had soaked through and stained. On the right butt cheek of his slacks, and in spots down both legs. The heels of both socks, too. And yet Pepper put them on. His shirt had been ruined so he still had to wear the pajama top.

With those spotted clothes on he almost looked like a man wearing desert camouflage pants. He even put on his boots again.

Pepper walked to the nurses' station after all the other patients had been there and gone. Miss Chris and Josephine had been on duty together, but only Miss Chris stood waiting for him now. Josephine sat in front of the computer again. The screen glowed slightly green, and she stared at it with an expression beyond confusion, beyond frustration. Josephine almost looked serene as she watched the screen. Her arms were crossed, as if waiting for the computer to address her. As if it might offer an ingot of wisdom if she sat there long enough.

Miss Chris, on the other hand, waggled the clipboard at Pepper when he entered the oval room. "This the one I waiting on." She took one look at his stained, spotty slacks but said nothing. At least he wasn't walking around without them.

Pepper reached the nurses' station and stretched out his right hand for his pills.

"Eh-heh, just like that? You come late-late and don't even *apologize*?"

She gave Pepper the sharp eyes. But he'd been on the unit for a month and a half and felt less intimidated by her now. It wasn't that he thought she was harmless, he just couldn't hide that he also found her to be a pain in the ass. Pepper kept his hand out and did not apologize. He looked her directly, defiantly, in the eye.

"You think *rudeness* is how you strike back at Miss Chris? Heh? When all I do for you around here?"

He still didn't respond.

Miss Chris read Pepper's medications aloud, practically shouting. She slammed the little white cup on the counter as best she could with an item that weighed all of an ounce.

"Put it in my hand," Pepper said.

What happened to keeping up the pretense of the compliant patient, Pep? He couldn't manage it just then. And not with Miss Chris. They entered a contest of wills. She wouldn't lift the cup and he wouldn't move his hand, and the whole scene was beneath the dignity of six-year-olds.

Josephine was the one who asserted adulthood. She left her place in front of the computer, even as she suspected—on some paranoid level available to us all in the face of willful technology—that the machine would flash the secret of its inner wisdom at the moment when she left her chair. Nevertheless, she stood up and she took the white cup and turned it over so the pills fell into Pepper's palm.

Miss Chris and Pepper looked at Josephine with scorn *and* relief, though neither of them would ever admit to the latter.

Miss Chris patted Josephine. "You too soft for this line of work, child."

Josephine nodded and thought, *You're welcome.*

Pepper brought his palm up to his mouth, slowly, showing the back of his hand to the two staff members. As he'd learned to do by now he slipped the two pills into the space between his lower lip and gums.

Miss Chris nodded at him, satisfied, then set down the clipboard with a clatter and left the nurses' station to go and double-check the rooms in the men's hall. Looking for lollygaggers. She knew there were none—all medications had been administered—but some part of her always suspected trickery and that life required vigilance.

Leaving Pepper and Josephine at the nurses' station. Josephine, hoping to avoid a return to the computer, to that program whose name she even dreaded thinking. (Equator!) And Pepper, who wanted to avoid thinking about what was to come that night. Pepper coughed once, bringing his hand to his mouth, and spat the Haldol and lithium into his palm.

With that done, Pepper said, "You didn't talk much during our last Book Group."

"I didn't want to hear the doctor give me another wrong name."

Josephine looked back at the desktop computer, as she'd feared the menu on the screen had changed; it had actually gone back a step, to the log-in page. Where a staff member was to input his or her employee ID number in order to process the mounds of intake forms for electronic collection. They had all figured out how to log in, but little more than that. Equator discouraged all attempts equally, whether by Josephine or Miss Chris or Scotch Tape or Terry. (Thus far, none of the doctors could be persuaded to try. And the social worker had been let go three weeks back.)

There was actually a very good reason for all the headaches this computer caused the staff: The hospital had acquired the wrong program for their system. Equator was a program used by banks, to help home owners who were trying to avoid foreclosure of their homes. People would call to speak to a representative but would only reach the voice-command operator instead. That operator would then walk the home owner through the Equator program, which helped to explain which forms were required, when and where to submit them, and how soon the home owner might expect to see their foreclosure issue processed. And Equator was a ripping success for the banks. It was less of a success for the troubled home owners. The number of successful foreclosures almost quadrupled once the banks started using the program. It regularly misfiled forms, misstated the dates when those forms were due, and most often it simply lost all records of the home owner ever having tried to negotiate adjustments to their mortgages. By the time a human representative from the bank (let's say, Bank of America, for instance) finally got in touch with the home owner, who'd been calling frantically for months, the case would've already been ruled in the bank's favor. So, really, that human representative was only calling to let the home owner know they were now home*less*. At least three major American banks would consistently claim these errors were aberrations, glitches in the software, but if you were caught in the loop of this program's machinations you'd start to believe it had actually been designed to *erase* people's traces of home ownership. You'd believe because it so often did just that.

So why on earth had New Hyde Hospital arranged to purchase and use this fantastically inappropriate software? Because most systems (particularly a public hospital's IT department) barely work. Which means that most systems regularly fail.

Like when New Hyde Hospital's psychiatric unit, generally known as Northwest, had been deemed in dire need of *modernization,* and in its zeal to get the work done, the hospital had saddled the unit with a computer program whose only real-world application was to mishandle struggling home owners. A program to take advantage of people who were being ground down. That's what the hospital bought. So while it was the wrong program for Northwest's specific needs, it did fit Northwest's overall theme.

And why would Josephine want to return to dealing with all of that?

Which is why she wanted to extend the conversation with Pepper. Better to linger with him than grapple with Equator again.

"I'll tell you something I did find out," Josephine said. "Peter Benchley felt guilty about *Jaws* for many years after it came out. He turned into an activist for sharks!"

She slapped the top of the nurses' station desktop.

"He said that, in one year, in the whole world, only *twelve* human beings are attacked by sharks, on average. But every year human beings kill *one hundred million* sharks. Isn't that crazy? He made us scared of them, but they're the ones who should be scared of us."

"Where'd you read that?" Pepper asked. He, too, appreciated the diversion this conversation provided.

"I watched a video of him on YouTube. But I didn't bring it up during Book Group because, I don't know. I was just listening mostly."

Pepper felt a pang similar to the one he'd had when he remembered the Coinstar. YouTube! How quickly that silly phrase sounded like a high point in human culture. To go online and witness someone's ugly kid doing something cute. To watch snippets of great movies that had been overdubbed with grating music by some moron who thought they were improving the film. To stumble across human beings with insipid thoughts, video cameras, and the utter lack of humility that made them use one to immortalize the other! Of course, Pepper should've registered Josephine's remark about the sharks. The horror of those numbers. The outsized power of fear and the way it reshapes reality. But instead, Pepper felt a throbbing nostalgia for YouTube, and it was, sad to say, the detail that made him decide what he was going to do tonight. Dorry was right, he could fit back into the outside world. And that's where he wanted to be. Tonight, when the other three ran toward the silver door, Pepper would be walking *out*.

Pepper said, "I'd like to take you up on that offer. The books you bought for us."

Josephine exhaled happily. Another chance to avoid that computer.

"Come with me," she said.

She led him to Northwest 1, but when they reached the door where the cart was kept, she waved Pepper backward until he stood against the opposite wall. "You wait there."

Josephine came out a moment later, pushing the three-tiered book cart. Pepper touched the side of the cart as they returned to the nurses' station, as if they were guiding the vessel together. Josephine popped inside the station to find her handbag, from which she pulled out a small spiral notebook with a plain green face.

On the front she'd written two words: "Washburn Library."

"What's that mean?" Pepper asked.

Josephine shrugged. "I paid for the books, so I figured the library should be named after me. Josephine Washburn."

Pepper looked at the books. "What did you pick?"

Josephine brushed her hands along the top tier of titles. Like many books bought at library sales, these were a bit battered. Mostly hardcovers, a few paperbacks.

"Believe it or not, I really did *listen* at the last Book Group. What Dorry said. I tried to pick books that were more about people like you."

*Like me?*

But rather than protest, Pepper let her comment pass. He looked at the books instead.

*Ariel, Darkness Visible, The Noonday Demon, The Yellow Wallpaper, The Golden Notebook, Wide Sargasso Sea, Hard Cash, He Knew He Was Right, Angelhead, The Three Christs of Ypsilanti.* And more.

"I don't know any of these," Pepper said, feeling embarrassed.

Finally, he found one book that at least carried a name he recognized. A paperback. He straightened and Josephine went onto her toes slightly, to see the cover.

"Is this a book of his paintings?" Pepper leafed through the pages but found only a handful of images, toward the center of the book. All in black and white.

"Letters," Josephine said. "He wrote lots of letters in his life."

Pepper weighed the book in his open hand. The cover showed a painting of the artist's face; at least this was in color. The man looked both dour and vibrant, somehow. Pepper thought, strangely, that he recognized the expression on the guy's grill. "I want this one," he said.

Josephine felt more gratified than she could say when Pepper tucked the book under his arm. It seemed to erase Dorry's dismissal from the week before, and the frustrations of the computer program and the always-curt Miss Chris. Josephine took this job because she needed the paycheck, but she chose this line of work—nursing— because she thought she was good at helping others. She'd had very little chance to prove it since she'd started at New Hyde. The job often felt like triage, not care. Under such circumstances, lending Pepper this paperback seemed like a small victory. Take them wherever you can, Josephine.

She opened her spiral notebook to the first page and wrote out the title in full: *The Letters of Vincent Van Gogh to his Brother and Others (1872–1890).*

"Just put your initials here next to the title," she said.

Pepper looked at the pen in her hand, the page of the spiral notebook, but hesitated.

"It's a *library*, right? You don't keep the books. You borrow them."

She didn't say this with an attitude. More like this was another part of the fun, the game. So Pepper wrote his real initials—"P.R."—and Josephine watched him do this with a grin.

"You can keep it as long as you like." She snapped her notebook shut. "No late fees!"

He appreciated Josephine's enthusiasm. She saw this book as a loan, but Pepper knew it was more of a parting gift. He'd be taking it with him tonight and he wouldn't be back to return it.

"Thanks," he said. "And good-bye."

She pushed the Bookmobile back toward Northwest 1. "I'll see you again on Monday," she said. "Don't be such a drama queen." She laughed.

Pepper nodded slightly and squeezed the book with two hands.

"Sure," he said. "What could happen between now and then?"

# 19

FIRST THING THAT happened after he said good-bye to Josephine was that Pepper ran into Mr. Mack and Frank Waverly. He was returning to his room, library book under his arm. The old men were out for their midmorning constitutional. As Pepper passed the pair, Mr. Mack pinched the sleeve of Pepper's shirt and tugged at it. *Pulled his coat,* as old heads used to say.

Pepper turned back and Mr. Mack spoke as if they'd already been conversing for a while. "Now the way I see it," Mr. Mack began. "And I do *see* it. The big problem you face is how to stay hid once you make it out the front door."

Pepper pulled his sleeve away, took two extra steps, before he realized what Mr. Mack had just said. The larger, watchful Frank Waverly remained silent.

Mr. Mack grinned and nodded at Pepper.

"You escape out of here and they just go into your file and find out where you live, where you worked, who your people are. You told them all that at the intake meeting, am I right? That's enough information for triangulation. They'll snatch you back up before the sun rises."

Pepper looked past these two men. He saw Josephine at the nurses' station. And at the far end of Northwest 1, Miss Chris, opening the front door, walking out and shutting it again. Neither one had heard Mr. Mack broadcasting Pepper's escape plan.

Mr. Mack slipped his hands into the pockets of his sport coat, which gave him a professorial air. "Now you could go on the run, leave the city or even the state. But here's something they don't tell you about being a fugitive. That mess is expensive. And you don't look independently wealthy to me. No offense." Then Mr. Mack snickered to show he certainly did mean to offend.

Pepper hardly registered the slight. *Who blabbed?* That's what he wanted to know. Not that Mr. Mack would've told him.

"The trick, for you, big boy, is going to be getting your records. That's where they'll have all the facts you related on your first night. You go to another hospital and the record here will eventually make its way there. I've had it happen to me. So the trick, *before* you run, is to leave no records behind. No file, and you could settle right down the block. They would never realize you were you. I promise you that."

Mr. Mack squared up close to Pepper's chest, like the two men were boxers meeting in the middle of a ring.

"But whatever you do, you need to remember you're taking the coward's way out, big boy. Sound harsh? It is harsh. But I'm trying to get through to you. There's only one thing that needs to be done with the motherfucker in that room. It won't stop until somebody stops it."

"Why don't you do it, then?" Pepper asked.

"I'm an idea man," Mr. Mack said. He poked Pepper's beefy arm. "And my idea is that you've got the strength. But not the resolve."

With that, Mr. Mack and Frank Waverly walked off.

Pepper returned to the room and posted himself at the two large windows and surveyed the land before him. It seemed even more urgent that he work out his route if, already, some of the others were talking to patients freely. How long before word made its way to the staff? Rather than panic, he planned.

The fence line around the basketball court had a barbed-wire buffer at the top, and the parking lot of New Hyde Hospital was (nominally) manned by an (underpaid) guard. So if he did get that secure door open, it would be smarter to slip around to this side of the building, pad through the grass in front of his windows, climb the sweet-gum tree right near the fence, inch out on a branch, and drop down to the sidewalk. Leave New Hyde Hospital and disappear into Queens. Maybe it would be smart to have his file tucked under his arm when he left. But how would he get it? Where to even look?

All this planning turned Pepper a bit distracted, so he didn't notice Coffee had entered the room until Coffee came to his side and set his precious blue binder down on the sill.

"You told those old guys a lot," Pepper said.

Coffee looked out the window, too.

"I've been making contacts, morning and night, on the pay phones. I haven't even had time to sleep. So I sure wasn't talking with anyone."

"Did you burn out my card?"

Coffee reached into the breast pocket of his pajama top. The "gold" card was really more of a muddy yellow. He dropped it on the windowsill.

"All done. But it was useful."

Outside, the sun shone brightly and Pepper wondered at how good the air must feel. He put his hand to the pane and enjoyed the chill.

Coffee said, "I tracked down his number."

Pepper nodded, not really listening, still imagining the fresh air.

"*His* number," Coffee said quietly.

That broke Pepper's spell. He looked at his roommate. "Come on."

"Well, not really his, but his social secretary's. The private line."

"You want to get invited to a party at the White House? I hear you can just crash if you look like you've got money."

Coffee rolled his eyes at Pepper. "Don't bring me gossip and tell me it's news. I have the number for a real *someone,* not just that stupid switchboard. I'm not going to yell. I'm going to be clear. I know I can do that now. Without all the meds. I'll explain our situation and then you'll see what *He* does for us."

"I already know what's going to happen," Pepper said.

Coffee looked up at Pepper wearily. His eyes narrowed. "You don't know," Coffee said. "But you will never admit that."

Pepper could see Coffee wouldn't be swayed by anything he had to say, so he knocked on the cover of Coffee's blue binder. "Why didn't you bring this to Book Group?"

"I don't need it anymore," Coffee said.

"Because you have that new number?"

Coffee shook his head. He placed his hand on the cover of the binder. "I have all these numbers. Memorized. I've called each one so many times. But until we stopped taking the pills, I couldn't remember even one. Now, they're all here."

Coffee pressed two fingers against his temple.

"The numbers come to me fast, fast, fast now. I wouldn't have had the courage to do it alone. I don't think Dorry and Loochie would have, either. So I have you to thank for that. And I mean it."

Pepper did feel good to hear it. To know the lucidity in Coffee's eyes was, at least in part, due to him. Vanity? Of course. But that's okay. No one here was a martyr or a saint.

Lunch and dinner passed without event. Pepper sat in the television lounge and read some of Van Gogh's letters. He found he could drown out the television if he concentrated on the page hard enough. He liked being in the lounge, around others, instead of alone in his room. He had nothing more to say to Coffee. Not to Dorry or Loochie, either. They were only waiting for the overnight shift to begin.

By eight thirty, all four members of the small conspiracy sat in the television lounge, though they weren't together. Dorry and Loochie and Coffee and Pepper, each at a different table.

Scotch Tape and Josephine were on the night shift. This was much to Josephine's surprise. She was meant to be relieved by Miss Chris, but Miss Chris had walked out that front door earlier and hadn't returned. When Josephine used her cell phone to call Miss Chris around dinnertime, the call went straight to voice mail. As did Josephine's next five tries. To put it plainly: The old lady had bounced. Leaving Josephine to work a double until the next shift change, around four a.m. Josephine sure didn't like this, but what could she do? Leave Scotch Tape alone?

(Yes!)

No.

At nine, Dorry rose from her seat and beckoned the other three toward her. When they were together, Dorry said, "I think it's time. Don't you?"

The words seemed to rest on each of their shoulders like a heavy cloak. They all stooped forward slightly from the weight. Dorry saw the burden and nodded. She was dressed just like she had been at Book Group. Well, *almost* the same. Pepper realized her sweater was on inside out.

He looked at Loochie, who wore a bright red scarf tied around her head. He hated to admit it, but he felt relieved by this. The site of her patchy scalp had been depressing. He knew it was selfish, but he was happy she'd covered it. Then her right hand floated up and two fingers slipped under the red scarf. Loochie hardly seemed aware of the action. Then, as if waking up from a bad dream, her eyes shifted and she caught herself and pulled her hand back down to her side again.

"Once we take care of the staff," Coffee began, "each of us has a choice to make. I'm using the staff phone to make my call. After that, I'll support whatever the group wants to do."

Dorry said, "Why don't we try working *together* on this. First, Coffee gets his phone call. Then, I have a talk with the man behind the silver door. Then, Loochie gets to . . . What do you want to do, Loochie?"

Loochie's eyes had trailed off to the lounge's windows.

"Loochie?" Dorry asked again. "What do you want to do?"

"I just want to be a girl," she said quietly.

Pepper almost laughed. "You *are* one!" he said.

Her eyes drooped. She looked soul-tired for a moment. "I haven't been a girl since I was thirteen. I'm just a diagnosis."

Dorry raised one hand for peace. "Loochie, I'm sorry, but that's probably not something we can fix tonight."

Coffee sensed that they might be about to spin off into some grand philosophical conversation that would derail any concrete action. And he was ready to act. "It's time," he reminded them. "We're ready enough."

He moved. Loochie got in step beside him. Dorry came around

the table and pinched Pepper out of a moment's paralysis. They hadn't asked him what he wanted to do. Maybe they didn't really want to know. *Find my file. Find my way out.* That's what he would've said.

Josephine sat at the nurses' station. With paper and pen she filled out a complaint against Miss Chris. She wasn't even looking up as Dorry, Loochie, Coffee, and Pepper entered the oval room. Scotch Tape was in Northwest 1, pushing the meal rack, and all those empty dinner trays, into the conference room that had long ago been repurposed as the storage room.

Coffee knocked on the nurses' station desktop and said, "I need to use the phone."

Josephine didn't even look up. She was in the middle of writing the word *negligence* and had lost herself in the pleasure of using it to describe Miss Chris.

While they waited on Josephine to look up, Pepper said, "Hey, Coffee. How did you get the social secretary's private number? You never said. I'm sure the White House switchboard didn't just give it out."

In the storage room, Scotch Tape slid the meal rack to its usual place near the back of the room. If he didn't keep it far from the hallway door, the rats (he believed it was actually only *one* enormous, graying rat; he'd seen it so often he felt familiar with it), the rat might be tempted to slip into the hall and then it would be sprinting down Northwest 1 openly, causing panic among patients. And who would be sent to try to kill it again? Him. Clarence Green. (He didn't refer to himself as Scotch Tape, obviously.) He'd been sent on that mission before, dropping poison pellets all over the abandoned second floor, and learned his lesson. That rat had the run of this building, more than any other living thing. (*But what about the freak on Northwest 4? What about the . . . ? Shut up with that, Clarence. Shut up with that, right now.*) Scotch Tape got the rack to the back of the storage room and switched off the light and pulled the door closed. He locked it and returned to the nurses' station.

Where he heard Coffee's answer to Pepper's question.

Coffee said, "I went online. That's how I got the social secretary's number."

Josephine looked up from her complaint form.

"Coffee, you know patients make all calls on the pay phones."

Coffee pouted. "But I don't have enough coins for a long-distance call, and Pepper's card is maxed out. I don't think he had very good credit."

Pepper said, "Hey!"

Scotch Tape entered the oval room, saw four patients crowding around the station and said, "What's going on over here?"

Dorry ignored the question, imploring Josephine. "It'll only take a minute, sweetheart."

But by this time of night, Josephine couldn't muster any more goodwill. "Pay phone, Dorry," she growled. *"Pay phone."*

Scotch Tape came around the station so he could see the group's faces and they could see his. "I asked you all a question."

Loochie brushed him away with one hand. "Go mind your own business."

Scotch Tape roared with laughter. "My business is *you*. Now you can make it pleasant business . . . or *un*pleasant business."

Pepper touched Coffee's shoulder. "Wait. How did you go online?"

Josephine pushed her chair back so she could stand as well. Feeling edgy because of what Loochie had said to Scotch Tape. Her move left the staff phone unguarded on the desk. Boldly, Coffee grabbed the receiver.

"Coffee!" Josephine shouted.

Pepper shouted now, too. Repeating himself. "How did you go online, Coffee?"

Coffee looked back at Pepper. "The mind was the first computer!"

A line that silenced everyone for a moment.

Finally Pepper said, "Well, what the fuck does that mean?"

"The mind is technology beyond anything human beings have invented so far," Coffee said. "Without all those meds in my bloodstream, I could access the Internet with my *will*. From anywhere. I only had to shut my eyes and concentrate. I have full use of my mind's power now. You see?"

And this is the moment when Pepper thought of Dorry's sweater, inside out; of Coffee discarding his binder; even Loochie's fingers slipping under her red scarf. Each person slightly different from the healthier picture presented only two days ago. Maybe these folks were on psychiatric medications because they actually needed them. Why hadn't Pepper seriously considered that before now?

Two words slipped out of his mouth. Pepper said, "Oh, shit. . . ."

But it was too late for turning back.

Scotch Tape grabbed Coffee's wrist. He looked like he'd tear Coffee's hand off just to get the receiver back.

Dorry shouted, "Wait! Wait! We can talk this out!"

"Talking is done," Scotch Tape growled.

Loochie said, "You got that right."

Then she punched Scotch Tape square in the throat.


Scotch Tape went down easier than Josephine. The guy straight-up *collapsed* after Loochie yapped him.

That isn't meant to clown Scotch Tape, or make him seem weak. Really. One punch from Loochie Gardner could topple small governments. The man simply found himself overmatched. As Pepper had been when he made the mistake of giving Loochie's mother (and brother) the bum rush.

By comparison, Josephine was much luckier than Scotch Tape; she only faced Pepper and Coffee and Dorry.

In light of what happened to Scotch Tape, Josephine didn't hesitate. She scrambled. Over the nurses' station. Climbing on the low desk and vaulting right over the higher counter. She fled. But when she landed on the other side she slipped and nearly fell. Pepper and Coffee caught her. To them, this looked like gallantry, but from Josephine's perspective, two *wild men* had just grabbed her arms.

And then Josephine just freaked.

She hollered, yes, but that was actually the least of it. Her arms went stiff and her hands balled into fists and her legs dropped out from under her so fast that Coffee and Pepper nearly went to the floor themselves. It was like her lower half fainted.

Meanwhile her mouth continued to wail.

Boy, did it.

Pepper became annoyed instantly. Maybe she thought they were going to rob her? Rape her? She acted like they were going to cut open her belly and feast on her organs. All this after he'd just borrowed a copy of Van Gogh's letters! Funny to say it, but Pepper's feelings were really hurt just then.

But here's the thing: Pepper had it wrong. Josephine wasn't thinking about them when she snapped. Not really. She didn't scream just out of fear for herself in that moment. It was also a deeper terror. When Loochie punched the orderly, Josephine felt a raw, cold shock, of course. But when the two men grabbed her, she felt *the fear*.

Because she thought of her mother. Lorraine Washburn.

Who lived with Josephine, the only child, in a two-family house out in Rego Park. Her mother hadn't been able to take good care of herself anymore and moved in with Josephine in 2009. And Josephine had welcomed her mother. Because, even though she was young, Josephine had spent the last few years cultivating little more than her own loneliness. Then here came her mother, Lorraine, a woman who'd been quite independent herself once, but couldn't manage it any longer. And Josephine received the woman as the wick welcomes the match. Josephine appreciated her mother's company, now that she was becoming a woman and no longer a girl. So when Pepper and Coffee grabbed Josephine, she screamed, and struggled, from a place beyond self-preservation. Josephine saw Lorraine waking up tomorrow morning to find her daughter hadn't returned home. Josephine saw Lorraine mystified by this sudden change in their soothing routine; saw her mother retreating to the living-room couch out of fear; sitting there, unable to imagine who else she might rely on. Unable to recall even a cousin's phone number. Paralyzed and puzzled. So scared she might not even eat, as was her way. Starving from *fright*. Dying on the second floor of the two-family house after days of confusion and despair. (The first floor reserved for the home owners, Mr. and Mrs. Martinez-Black.) Josephine was going to leave her mother to *that*? A woman who'd raised her so decently? No. No. No.

Josephine fought hard to make her mouth work, to talk these patients out of doing anything with lasting repercussions. But she couldn't master speech at the moment. Yelling seemed the best she could do. Josephine Washburn would not let herself die today. *No,* she would've begged if she could. *Please.* But the only sound that came out of her was this primal howl.

So Coffee and Pepper continued to restrain her.

Then Loochie raised her arm. Loochie made a fist. But Loochie didn't throw the punch.

Instead, Dorry spoke.

Calmly.

Dorry said, "All right now. All right. Everybody stop and think. Loochie, you don't want to hit her. And she doesn't want you to hit her."

Loochie lowered her arm. It was true. She didn't want to hit Josephine. She didn't like the nurse, but she didn't dislike her, either. She couldn't say that about Scotch Tape, which is why it had felt so satisfying when he crumbled. And even Scotch Tape wasn't someone she hated. There was only one person around here that she hated.

One *thing.*

Josephine looked everywhere but at the old woman. This wasn't on purpose, but an instinctive response. The reptile part of Josephine's brain, trying to figure how to save its tail.

Dorry said, "Look at me now. Look at *me.*"

Josephine's shoulders went looser at the soothing measure of Dorry's voice. She unclenched her fists. Pepper and Coffee didn't let go of her wrists.

"I'm a mother," Dorry said. "And a grandmother. So believe me, I know you're somebody's little girl, too. No one wants to hurt you. That's not what we're here to do."

Dorry touched the pearls around her neck. As if drawing Josephine's eyes to the pearls would prove these four patients weren't murderous, violent psychopath cannibals. Would such people wear jewelry? In fact, the pearls only made Dorry seem more peculiar in these circumstances. But what could Josephine do but trust the old ambassador? At least while she found herself trapped between the salt-and-pepper sentries.

"What do you want?" Josephine asked quietly.

"Keys," Pepper answered, and the nurse looked at him nervously.

"I can't let you all out of here. I'm sorry but I can't. You'll hurt . . . yourselves."

Dorry frowned at Pepper to shut him up. She tugged at Pepper's fingers until he let go of Josephine's wrist. Then she did the same with Coffee.

Dorry said, "We don't want to escape."

"What, then?"

Coffee blew out a deep breath. "The silver door."

Josephine looked up at Pepper and at Coffee. "I'm not going to let you hurt another patient."

"You got a lot of rules for a bitch that's outnumbered," Loochie said.

Josephine crossed her arms and both Pepper and Coffee winced, afraid of another eruption. They placed their hands over their crotches, just in case; they looked like two soccer players awaiting a direct free kick.

Dorry said, "Nobody's going to get hurt."

Josephine sucked her teeth. "Sure."

Dorry said, "Look at me. We want to speak with him. You give us the keys. We put you and Clarence into one of the rooms. As soon as we're done, we let you out. And we'll take any punishment that comes after that. Okay?"

This all could've been over much quicker. Just let Loochie start swinging. But it seemed important to Dorry that the nurse hand over the keys on her own. That the nurse trust Dorry. This didn't matter so much to the other three at first, but as they listened to Dorry, they, too, felt a change. They didn't want to batter and steal like criminals. They didn't want to rampage like frenzied animals. They were human. Dorry put out her hand to accept the nurse's keys and the others waited patiently.

Josephine looked at each of them, moving from one face to the next. Josephine made twelve dollars an hour at this job. That should put all cries for courageousness into context. Taking this job for that pay had already been an act of bravery.

Finally, Josephine opened her hand and the looped red plastic key chain dangled from her thumb. It swayed side to side. All five of them listened to the keys as they jangled like a wind chime.

Finally Josephine set the keys in Dorry's palm.

Dorry led Josephine toward Northwest 1. Conference room 2 awaited. Pepper and Coffee followed behind them like members of a broke-ass Praetorian Guard. And last was Loochie, dragging the unconscious orderly backward by the arms. She'd demanded that Pepper and Coffee let her do this alone. Like hauling what you've hunted. It was an effort, but she managed.

They brought Josephine and Scotch Tape to the room. Loochie laid the orderly flat on the floor with more tenderness than any of the others might've expected.

Dorry sat Josephine in one of the chairs. Pepper and Coffee and Loochie left the room. As Dorry pulled the door shut she said, "We won't be long. And thank you."

Josephine didn't respond. She watched her hands, gathered limply in her lap. After the door was closed and locked, she listened as the footsteps receded.

When Josephine couldn't hear them anymore, she reached into her pants pocket. They hadn't thought to pat her down before they locked her in. Josephine pulled out her cell phone.

# 20

WHEN ALL FOUR patients returned to the oval room, they found themselves stopped up. Like froze up. Shocked. They found a nurses' station without a staff member behind it. And they didn't quite know how to react. They weren't actually *free,* still stuck inside New Hyde, but even an unattended desk felt like liberation.

And not only for them.

Heatmiser, Mr. Mack and Frank Waverly, Japanese Freddie Mercury and Yuckmouth, Wally Gambino and the Haint, those three women Pepper had seen poring through magazines one night—the redhead and the mousy-looking woman and the Asian (this had to be Loochie's "Chinese Lady," right? The one who'd seen Sam's corpse?)—all these patients surrounded the vacant nurses' station now, and Pepper's crew joined them. Wally Gambino leaned over the top of the station and peeked under the desk space as if another nurse or orderly might be hiding there. This was a trick. Had to be.

The patients walked around the station in a circle. All of them, like a game. Inspecting the empty station closely. If only the Trojans had been this methodical! But even after everyone made the circuit, all fourteen patients, they still couldn't *believe* it. They kept a prudent distance from the nurses' station, as if it were a bull that had only been stunned.

Then Coffee broke the spell.

He stepped inside the nurses' station. A bit of a jolt, just to see that. Then he grabbed one of the wheeled chairs sitting under the desk, pulled it out, and rolled it to the lip of Northwest 5. The others watched him quietly. Then Coffee pushed the chair as hard as he could and it went spinning. It didn't stop rolling until it reached the television lounge.

"Look at that," Dorry said quietly.

The patients all turned to Coffee again. As if he should do another act of magic. There was a second chair under the table, but that little trick wouldn't work twice.

You might expect them to smash the computer next. It was still on, its fan rumbling louder than a dryer in a Laundromat. But these mental patients only gawked at the shoddy equipment, almost like they pitied the staff for having to do their jobs with it. Yes, even this population was well aware of laptops and Smartphones.

Dorry lifted her right hand.

All thirteen other patients looked up at her. What next?

Even Pepper and Loochie and Coffee wondered.

Dorry opened her hand and let the nurse's keys dangle. They clinked and all the patients looked over their shoulders, around the various bends, so used to having staff members appear seconds after that sound. Heatmiser's mouth even dripped slightly with saliva. But no one else appeared.

"Does anyone know which of these keys opens the desk drawers?" Dorry asked.

Pepper felt a hot flash of concern. What did that have to do with anything? He'd been choking back his anxieties, but they threatened to spill out now. Coffee with his *Internet brain;* Loochie whose strength and ferocity only seemed to have *increased* between the time she'd tangled with him and with Scotch Tape; and now Dorry wanted to do some drawer hopping. It wasn't just fear that he felt, but guilt. He'd urged Coffee to join him in turning down the meds. And then helped enlist Dorry and Loochie. He'd thought he was doing them a solid, freeing them from the shackles of their sedative servitude, but already it seemed likely he'd been wrong.

Dorry looked at Pepper and whispered, "Have a little faith in me."

None of the patients knew which key opened which drawers, so they waited as Dorry tried one, then the next. Finally, she found the right key for the right drawer and Dorry peeked inside. She smiled at all the patients who hadn't joined their Velvet Revolution. (Velvet*ish*, counting Loochie's punch.) Then Dorry made a big show of stepping back, sweeping her hands over the open drawer. The patients crowded closer. They peeked around and over one another. One voice cried out.

"Cigarettes!"

"This is the staff's stash." Dorry smiled. "Take as many as you like."

Half a dozen hands went into the drawer right away. The staff didn't stockpile packs, but cartons. (This job was stressful.) There was enough in the drawer for each patient to walk away with a pack of his or her own. Even the ones who weren't smokers figured, *Why not?*—and took some for themselves. It was the surprise of the moment, the fact that the stuff belonged to the staff. The idea made all of them a bit giddy. Even if it made them sick, they were going to puff.

Dorry opened her hand again and the keys jangled as they swung. She reached into the drawer and plucked out one cigarette for herself. She didn't smoke. It was a trophy. A memento. She tucked it into her bra.

She smiled at Pepper, and Pepper did feel relieved by the seeming sanity of this step. Distract the others. Dorry spoke to the patients still milling about. She said, "Now, how about a long smoke break outside?"


All this negotiation took only ten minutes.

Back in conference room 2, Josephine Washburn couldn't get her phone call through. She hadn't dialed the police directly because that wasn't hospital protocol. Instead, she was to first call the head of security on the grounds of New Hyde Hospital. That's the system that had been put in place, and no one making twelve dollars per hour was encouraged to improvise. The head of security's phone rang and rang and rang until finally the guy's voice mail picked up. But even then, Josephine recognized there was a problem. Namely, the voice on the hospital's security-greeting message was someone she didn't recognize. It was actually a guy who'd been fired almost a year before. The former head of hospital security. Eugene Klutch. A man who'd been caught stealing food from the hospital kitchens. Not a turkey sandwich, but *one hundred* frozen turkeys. He'd been behind a series of pantry thefts that had been going on for three years at New Hyde Hospital. At their most brazen, the Klutch crew had stolen two ovens (industrial ovens) from one of the kitchens over in the main building on the campus. Klutch hadn't gone to jail, just been forced to retire. And now, nearly a year later, that man's voice *still* hadn't been changed on the security center's answering machine. Josephine knew another man had been hired because he was the one who'd given the new employees the lecture about the hospital-security protocols. He'd growled at the new hires, but hadn't been savvy enough to record a new message? How much faith could Josephine have in hospital security? But she left a message because she was smart enough to know there needed to be evidence that she'd followed protocol.

Next, she called the head of hospital administration. Also as per guidelines. The one rule at New Hyde, above all others, was to avoid embarrassment. (*Embarrass,* meaning "leave vulnerable to lawsuits.")

While it was nearly ten p.m., the head of hospital administration could be reached. Or, if not him, then his answering service. (Yes, they do still exist.) So Josephine called those offices (all numbers she'd programmed into her phone at Orientation) and left a message with the woman who answered the line. Josephine explained what had happened, that she was a nurse over in Northwest, that the patients had overpowered her and the orderly (who still hadn't woken up), and now those patients were roaming the ward freely. "Doing what?" the woman on the line asked, though she sounded magnificently disinterested. Setting fires? Taking drugs? Who knew? The fact that Josephine was locked in a room made it impossible to say. At the end of all this, the woman only sighed, and said, "Please hold the line while I connect you directly."

Josephine said, "What was the point of asking me those questions if you're just—"

Then instead of connecting the call the lady hung up on her.

Quite a system.

At that moment, Josephine should've called the cops. She'd done all she could to protect New Hyde Hospital. She'd tried to follow protocol, but the protocol was ass.

But for a few seconds she could only stare at the cell phone. Going through all this nonsense to reach someone in charge, this was the first time she'd ever been treated like, well, a patient. With rules that defied all common logic; people employed to help you who are unable, really, to even hear you; the sense that the system's goal is only to keep trouble *contained*. It's not like Josephine had been so all-fired powerful when she was a nurse, but supervising the patients had at least allowed the illusion of some difference between her and them. But now it felt damn hard to pretend. In many ways, at this moment of crisis, she was just as powerless as they were. Josephine didn't make this connection consciously, but it tickled at her in a way that made her mind freeze. She looked at the phone and knew what she should do, but she couldn't make her hand act the way her mind wanted. (And even this was quite like the average patient's day.) Josephine wondered how anyone was supposed to live under such conditions and remain sane.

This is what was happening to Josephine while Dorry handed out cigarettes, walked to the television lounge, and unlocked the door to the basketball court. Pepper propped the door open with a heavy chair, which allowed a fresh breeze to blow into the unit. First time in a *long* while for that. You could almost see the walls inhaling.

Josephine stared at the keypad of her cell phone and willed herself to dial 911. Dorry and Loochie and Coffee and Pepper left the television lounge, marching down Northwest 5. The police hadn't been called yet. Whatever they were going to do could still get done.

They still had time.

Pepper, Dorry, Loochie, and Coffee returned to the nurses' station. They were much quieter than the patients in the lounge, whose voices played louder than the television. It seemed like a party was being thrown. There was an undertone of forced cheer, though. As if those patients were working hard to celebrate. Hoping to drown out the sounds of whatever was coming next.

Coffee walked into the nurses' station and touched the beige plastic phone. He seemed to forget the others. He whispered the phone number to himself now, ten digits: "5102821833. 5102821833. 5102821833."

Dorry and Pepper watched Coffee with concern. Even Dorry couldn't ignore what Coffee had said about accessing the Internet with his mind. Let him dial the number, if that made him feel better. The rest of them would do the real work.

"What now?" Dorry asked Pepper. "You want me to unlock the front door for you?"

Pepper took a step inside the nurses' station, too. There were so many files, multiple stacks. Was his there? He grabbed a handful of folders and looked at the names written on the tabs.

"I could make it," Pepper said as he scanned for his name. Those files were for one patient: Samantha Forrester. Was that Sam?

Dorry hesitated a moment, she hadn't expected him to leave. Finally she said, "Where would you go?"

"I've got an apartment. Rent's paid automatically."

Dorry looked bereft. She put her hand against the nurses' station desktop for balance. Coffee was clearly cuckoo. In a moment Pepper would walk away. Not much of a team.

Coffee mashed at the phone with an open palm. "It won't let me make the call."

Coffee tried again while Dorry and Pepper watched.

Dorry sighed. "You have to press the pound sign, then nine, then three. Then you can make an outside call."

Coffee did as she said. He looked up from the keypad. "It's ringing!"

Dorry looked at Pepper, who'd taken up another handful of files, hunting for his. She leaned her elbows on the desktop.

"As soon as the police brought you in, I *knew* why you'd ended up here."

Pepper set down the next handful of files and lifted another.

"I'm not talking about your crime," Dorry continued. "I'm talking about something bigger than that."

"Destiny?"

He didn't even look up. *Destiny. Fate.* Solace for losers. And a defense for the ones who'd hoarded success. By almost anyone's math, he hadn't made too much of his life. Not as much as he would've imagined by forty-two. Not referring to money here, or some kind of fame, but *worth.* He'd wanted—let's say, expected—to be valuable by this age. Somehow. But so far he'd done little worth treasuring. So if that was his fate, then fuck fate.

He dropped the folders to the floor. The papers scattered at his feet.

"I'm talking about a calling," Dorry said. "When they brought you in here, I saw you and knew you were here to meet your purpose."

That got Pepper's attention. Dorry looked into his face, and while it's true that her sweater was inside out and her hair maybe didn't look quite as well kept as it had been two days before, but her half-blind eyes didn't look wild just then. If the time off the meds had been just a little too long for Coffee, maybe Dorry had been off them just long enough to say something absolutely right. Maybe she could see something in him that even he couldn't right now. She believed in him. Who doesn't hope for something like that, at least once?

But before Pepper could ask what purpose Dorry saw for him, Coffee yelled into the phone. "Hello? Yes! Who am I speaking to?"

Coffee stood straighter, erect with pride.

"It's good to speak with you Ms. Hong. I am called Kofi Acholi, and I wish to speak with your superior. What? Yes, that's Kofi, K-O-F-I."

Dorry slapped the top of the nurses' station. "Your name is *Kofi*? Do you know we've been calling you *Coffee* all this time?"

Coffee covered the receiver with one hand. "I am aware," he said.

Then Pepper finally asked the question that should've come up minutes ago. "Where's Loochie?"

Coffee returned to the phone. "You *do* know who I mean, Ms.

Hong. Of course you do. Our President. The Big Boss. I don't need to say any more. Now, let him know I am calling about conditions in New Hyde."

Dorry and Pepper were less concerned about the phone call that wasn't apparently magically connecting to the fucking President's social secretary, and instead they moved around the nurses' station to seek out their fourth member.

"Maybe she went to smoke?" Dorry asked.

Pepper said, "No."

Dorry turned and saw Loochie walking calmly as you please. She was three-quarters of the way down Northwest 4.

"What are you doing?" Dorry shouted. "We haven't even figured out what we should say to him yet!"

Loochie looked over her shoulder. "You all were stalling! You weren't going to ever open this fucking door!"

Coffee's voice rose. He was screeching. "Washington, D.C.! The nation's *capital*. No, that's not where *I* am. That's where *you* are! What do you mean 'Oakland'? The President doesn't live in Oakland!"

Dorry called to Loochie. "Well, how are you going to open the damn door if I've got the keys?!"

Loochie didn't even look back, only extended her right arm, and there, dangling from *her* wrist was Scotch Tape's set. They hadn't searched Josephine for her cell phone, so it shouldn't be surprising that they'd forgotten to secure the extra set of keys, too. When Loochie dragged Scotch Tape to the conference room, she'd snatched them off his wrist. That's really why she'd volunteered to haul him.

Coffee pleaded with the person on the other end of the line. "Do not hang up on me! Please! Do *not* hang up!" His voice softened, it quieted. "You are my last resort."

Then the receiver fell out of Coffee's hand and bounced against the floor.

But there wasn't any time to comfort Coffee. *Kofi*. Not for Pepper, anyway. He sped toward Loochie. When she heard his boots clomping, she picked up the pace. She sprinted.

Running aggravated Pepper's still-tender ribs. He winced and hunched forward when he sped up. He almost tripped. The closer he came to Loochie, the closer he was to the silver door. The air became warmer, just like the last time he got this close.

There was that smell again. The one from the first night the Devil visited Pepper's room. The scent on an unclean body. So strong here that it tainted the walls, the floor, the silver door. An unclean place. The air so sour his throat closed up and his eyes burned.

Down the hall, Kofi howled. "Okay, then! *I tried!*"

Loochie slid the key into the lock. There were twenty keys to choose from, but she found the exact right one on the first try.

"Don't," Pepper pleaded.

But Loochie turned the key.

She let the Devil out.

# 21

THE SILVER DOOR didn't just open; it seemed to explode.

The stainless steel swung back so hard, its handle *clanged* against the wall and busted a small hole in the Sheetrock. It was as if the Devil had been inside the room, straining to get out, too.

Then: animal fur, *sour* and *matted*, passed between Loochie and Pepper.

The smell of waste, worse than from a public toilet, hit them, too. Sewer water, sewage, sweat, and saliva that have caked and dried. Loochie and Pepper's eyelids fluttered. Their eyes watered. From a distance, this looked like tears.

The Devil rushed into the hallway. Its enormous crown leading the charge. Animal fur, *sour* and *matted* and curled into *knots*.

There were two smallish ears on its long, enormous head. They were small compared to the skull's grand dimensions. The ears were the size of children's mittens and about the same shape; they flipped and shook, as if bitten by gnats.

Just above those ears were its *horns*. Not very long, but thick and gnarled. Points turned upward, toward the ceiling. They were grayish white, the color of exposed bone. Each tip seemed as sharp as a lance's. Animal fur, *sour* and *matted* and curled into *knots*, all of it brown as mud.

The head of a plains bison charged through the open door. The sight unmistakable under the hallway lights.

And somewhere, in all that hair, were the Devil's two small eyes. Glassy and white and without fear.

Pepper actually cackled at the sight of thing. Not laughter or bravado, but something crazed. He stood in Northwest 4 with a monster. Such things were impossible, he knew this, but there it was.

The Devil rushed right past Loochie and Pepper. Its head tilted down. It was charging. The horns aiming to gore.

Dorry stood at the lip of Northwest 4. She watched the Devil stampede.

"That's *fine!*" Kofi howled again, inside the nurses' station. He pulled at every drawer in there. Dorry had only unlocked the one that held the staff's cigarettes, so the others remained locked tight. "Dorry," he called. "Give me the keys!"

Loochie and Pepper watched the Devil bolt forward. It had passed between them without any resistance. In twenty paces it would smash into Dorry.

The old woman stood, paralyzed. She held the key chain in one hand and in the other a clipboard. It was the one the staff read from when handing out medication to patients. She looked as if she planned to read off the Devil's name and proper doses.

"I see you," she muttered, looking into the Devil's empty eyes.

Luckily, for all of them, the Devil looked different from behind. A fiend from the front but from the back, the Devil had the body of an old man. A skinny, half-naked old man running down the hall. Now who's going to be scared of that?

Not Loochie. Not Pepper.

The pair finally got their wits back. They ran down the hall now. The Devil had a head start, but they would catch up quickly.

Its body looked even thinner than Pepper remembered, saggier. The flesh jiggled and swayed. The skin looked reddish, like there was a heat rash all over it, the color of a stewed tomato. Splotchy and mottled. Weak.

But they could still see the back of that vast head, its weight driving the puny figure forward. And its feet, the bottoms hard and nearly gray, *clopped* like hooves.

Loochie caught up to the Devil first, halfway down Northwest 4. She came from behind and grasped its right horn with her right hand. She held the horn and *leaned* backward, her weight would do the rest. This was a variation on the way she'd taken Pepper out. Apply a little weight and momentum properly and nearly anybody will go down. Loochie was small but she knew how to tussle. She'd learned how to protect herself on the juvenile psychiatric ward.

The Devil's head jerked to the right, hard, and for the first time it looked back at her. It noticed her. And she saw more of it. The white eyes and the twitching ears and those two sharp horns. The long slope of its face, leading down to its wet nose, which sniffled and snuffed. And last its mouth, which fell open with surprise. Then its tongue shot out, almost a foot long and the color of uncooked dough.

Loochie Gardner had yoked the Devil.

It didn't speak, it grumbled like an old Johnny Popper tractor. The Devil snorted, once, and from its nose snot slapped against the floor. A gray puddle the size of Pepper's foot. The Devil shook its head twice and, just that fast, Loochie lost her grip. She was flipped forward. She went down to the floor, on her stomach, right in front of the thing.

The Devil raised its right foot to stomp her in the small of her back. But she wasn't alone. Pepper was there, too.

He didn't have the finesse to go grabbing horns like rodeo-riding Loochie, so instead, he just full-body tackled the beast. Well, that makes it sound a bit too graceful. Pepper threw his body at the Devil's left leg, which was supporting all its weight. This was a variation on the way Pepper had taken down Loochie's family. It didn't take much to topple the Devil just then, and Pepper gave it all the *not-much* he had.

The Devil and Pepper fell into a heap. Loochie scrambled off safely.

Right after they both fell, Pepper felt like he'd been dropped into a freezing pool. The pain in his chest, all along his rib cage, made him lose his breath. He gasped from it. He *shivered*. His vision went nearly black.

The Devil fell face-forward, onto its stomach. Its head slammed hard against the floor, a thump as loud as a couch being dropped. In that position it couldn't right itself. The thin arms, frail branches, pushed and strained but didn't have the strength to lift that enormous head. The Devil huffed on the ground, spraying more snot as it breathed, the mucus catching in the fur around its mouth and nose. Its legs scrambled, but they were pretty powerless, too. The Devil couldn't get up. Now it looked as vulnerable as any living thing.

So when Loochie climbed onto its back again, when she grabbed both horns from behind, when she *pulled* with all the strength her wiry shoulders could muster, it was difficult not to feel just a spark of sympathy, yes, for the Devil. Pepper experienced shivers of recognition: when the cops had him in handcuffs, or the orderly wrestled him to his bed, or the days stuck in restraints. Pepper didn't want to make that connection when looking upon the Devil, but he did.

That empathy wasn't lost on Loochie, either. She pulled the great head and it reared back. She smelled the fur, sour and unwashed, and she recognized the scent. If she shut her eyes, she might believe this was just another patient, trapped on the unit for so long that he'd stopped bathing, stopped caring. Heatmiser was like that. Hadn't she felt the same at more than one point?

But then the Devil bucked and kicked and Loochie lost her grip.

Her right hand slipped loose from one horn. The Devil thrust its head up in the next moment. Its horn stabbed Loochie's palm. It burst through her skin and dug in. Then the Devil yanked its head left and the horn *tore* out of Loochie's flesh. Right away, her blood ran fast, down her forearm.

The sound Loochie made, it wasn't a yell or a cry, it was more like a honk. And yet she wasn't actually in pain. She was saved by her acute-stress reaction. The trauma of this moment would hit her later, but right now she just had to stay alive. So she stayed where she was, on the beast's back. Her left hand gripped its left horn. And when she spoke, it was only to give instructions.

"Grab his legs," Loochie muttered. The blood from her wounded right hand had soaked her whole shirtsleeve already.

Pepper had only half-recovered from the pain of his tackle, but there wasn't any more time.

Loochie shouted, "Pepper! *Please!*"

Pepper moved on his hands and knees and dropped all his weight on the backs of the Devil's spindly legs while Loochie tried to regain control of the head. Her left hand stayed in place and despite the gash in her palm she squeezed her right hand around the right horn again. Loochie held on even tighter than before. She pulled the Devil's head so far backward that its nose pointed up at the ceiling. Like this, its throat was exposed.

"Now what?" Pepper shouted. "Now what?!"

Kofi had stopped calling for Dorry to give him the nurse's keys. He wasn't actually thinking at all in this moment. He was so confused. He'd been sure he had the solution to their collective dilemma, but with each second he felt stupider for having made that phone call. For having faith that someone else would fix everything. How silly he'd been. How naïve. How crazy. A new desperation filled him now. It made Kofi feel powerful in an ugly way. A fierceness fueled by disappointment. Which is why Kofi stopped asking Dorry for the keys to the locked drawers of the nurses' station. He didn't need them. In his desperation Kofi found access to that Crazy Strength. He tore each of those locked fucking drawers right out of the desk.

He dumped the contents of each drawer onto the ground as Pepper and Loochie wrestled the Devil. Finally he found the right drawer. Where the staff stored the syringes used on unruly patients. Kofi grabbed the largest ones he could find: 18-gauge Seldinger needles. Coffee tore two of them from their plastic wrapping and moved out of the nurses' station. It looked like he held a tiny fencing saber in each hand.

He reached Dorry at the lip of Northwest 4. The old woman remained impassive. Mumbling to herself. She'd dropped the keys and they'd landed on her right foot. The keys looked like a small brass spider, about to crawl up her leg. She still clutched the clipboard, but it wouldn't serve as much of a shield.

"Now what?!" Pepper shouted. "Now what?!"

Kofi raised his hands. Pepper saw the syringes and smiled.

Then there was a new sound, someone rattling the big door on Northwest 1.

"Police!" a man shouted. "We are entering the premises!"

"Hurry, Coffee!" Loochie grunted, straining to hold the Devil's head up.

Kofi moved past Dorry. Down the hall. "I'm going to stab out its eyes."

"Do it fast!" Pepper begged from the floor.

The police slammed at the front door, using a two-man Stinger battering ram. The sound like a series of small explosions.

"Hurry now," Loochie muttered. The blood from her wounded hand had soaked her shirtsleeve and half her back.

And the Devil?

It stopped bucking. It almost seemed to *wilt*. Its legs went limp and the head stopped twisting. The Devil actually whimpered. A quiet little bleat, like a sheep. Not even a sheep. Like a lamb.

Kofi spoke to himself as he approached it. "I came all this way. I came all this way." He looked at the Devil. "I can go a little farther."

The front door of the unit thumped even louder now. The strain on the lock could be heard. It *creaked,* almost in tune with the Devil's *bleating.* Both about to break.

Finally Dorry came out of her slumber. Just as the secure door flew open. She heard the cops—a tactical squad—clomping down Northwest 1. They'd be on the group soon. Dorry looked around, still slightly dazed. What to do? What to do? Dorry had the clipboard. No other weapon in hand.

"Hold them off!" Pepper shouted to her.

"Just another minute!" Loochie said.

The Devil kept bleating, a kind of pleading. Dorry lifted the clipboard over her head. Her best chance of delaying the cops was probably to cause pure confusion. No one was going to shoot an old woman, right?

She saw the black uniforms of the tactical force. They were carrying guns, though she could hardly discern them. They were just figures—phantoms—filling the oval room. The Devil's cries rose behind her, even louder, *desperate.* Dorry ran. Waving the clipboard. But she wasn't racing toward the cops.

She moved down Northwest 4. A dozen steps. Until she was behind Kofi. Then she slammed the clipboard against the back of Kofi's head.

Dorry hit him once. Twice.

Loochie shrieked.

And Kofi turned toward his attacker. Such confusion on his smooth round face. He held the syringes up but no longer seemed sure of how to use them. Or who to use them on.

"I can't let you kill him!" Dorry shouted. "I *can't!*"

Kofi opened his mouth to ask the question—*Why?*—but she bashed him with the clipboard for a third time.

"He's mine!" Dorry moaned, desperate and inconsolable.

The Devil bleated again, a babe calling out for protection.

"He's my *son.*"

By then the tactical force had reached Northwest 4.

And what did they find? Kofi waving two large gauge syringes at Dorry.

An old white woman fighting off an armed black attacker? That's not a difficult equation to solve. You can do it at home, without a calculator.

Kofi saw it happening. Time moved more slowly for him than for all the rest.

One of the officers ran forward and tackled the old woman out of the way. The rest fired on the crazed man. Him.

Kofi thought, *Why have you forsaken me?*

Then the cops fired forty-one shots.

The assailant was hit nineteen times.

Kofi Acholi died of his wounds later that night.

# 22

WELL, FUCK.

The black guy did die first after all.

(Excluding Sam and, possibly, Sammy, yes. Amiable white folks that they were.)

Coffee's death was reported in the *New York Post* and *Daily News*, only a day after it happened. Small items. Not even a quarter of a page. The day after that, the *Daily News* ran a longer feature that highlighted the poor supervision at New Hyde. There was mention of how the suspect (listed as *Kufi* Acholi) assaulted two staff members before menacing a fellow patient. This second, longer article included a photo of *Kufi* looking absolutely homicidal. Where had they found the picture, buried in an abattoir? It made Coffee (or Kofi or Kufi, poor guy) resemble, at least in spirit, that famous old woodcut of a wild man: on his knees and wearing rags, a baby in his mouth and a woman's severed head in the background. The woodcut is of a man who believes he's a werewolf. *That's* how the photo in the *Daily News* article made Coffee seem. Like something inhuman, too bizarre to be real. The kind of monster any sane person would *hope* to see killed in a thunderstorm of gunfire. Good riddance. Coffee's photo inspired only one emotion. *Horror.*

Not that Pepper and Loochie and Dorry had the luxury of pondering such an injustice to their friend's memory. The direct aftermath of the takeover was arrest. Once Josephine and Scotch Tape were freed, they fingered the other three as coconspirators. While Coffee was wheeled into the emergency room of NHH, the others were handcuffed and placed into three separate cruisers.

Though an NYPD tactical unit had been called in, Loochie, Dorry, and Pepper were held on the New Hyde Hospital campus. The hospital's security chief was completely ineffective when it came to preventing a mess, but he was better at sweeping up afterward. All he had to do was make sure the trio was driven from Northwest to New Hyde's main building. There, he handed them over to actual officers employed by the New York City Department of Health and Hospitals Police. (The main building was operated by the New York City Health and Hospitals Corporation, a city agency, so it was entitled to a security detail made up of NYPD officers. But Northwest—along with two other units—was operated by a private organization called the *New Hyde* Health and Hospital Corporation. Its security was contracted out to a low-budget security firm that would have trouble guarding a Waffle House.)

When Loochie, Dorry, and Pepper were taken to the main building's detention "center" (two conference rooms and an out-of-order bathroom), they were officially being handed over to police custody but without—here's the important part—without having to leave the New Hyde campus. How do you keep a family problem within the family? You don't let the children out. Only Loochie had a short detour when she was taken away to have her hand cleaned, stitched up, and bandaged. By the next day, all three patients would be returned to the custody of Northwest's security detail. They'd be driven four minutes across campus and returned to the psychiatric unit. Most systems barely work, but those same systems cover their asses much more successfully.

And Coffee? His body went to the emergency room. Then, briefly, to the Intensive Care Unit. Then, last, to the hospital's morgue, a place the staff called the "Rose Cottage."

Loochie and Dorry were originally supposed to spend the night together in one of the two detention rooms. But if they were in the same room, Loochie made a habit of trying to tear Dorry's head from her neck. Dorry didn't fight back, either. So the cops had to separate the pair. Loochie spent the night in one room and Dorry in the other. (Neither room had beds, so they slept in chairs.) Pepper had to spend the night in the out-of-service bathroom. Which actually wasn't as terrible as it sounds. It had been out of service so long that the place was cleaner than either detention room.

Once alone, Loochie and Dorry fell into fitful sleep.

Kofi was at rest in the Rose Cottage.

Pepper sat on the toilet in that bathroom. He couldn't get comfortable enough to drift off, so instead, all night, he remembered: Pepper and Loochie had gone flat on the floor when the cops started shooting. They were handcuffed only moments after Kofi fell.

The police left the Devil to itself. They didn't touch it. They moved around the body. Peeked at it and, just as fast, averted their eyes.

It lay on the floor, facedown. It didn't move, or even seem to breathe. Pepper and Loochie entertained the wish that it had died somehow. A stray bullet maybe. Could that happen? Could the Devil die? But when Josephine and Scotch Tape appeared, it moved again. It whimpered. Seeming to call out for their help.

The cops watched quietly as Josephine and Scotch Tape checked the Devil for injuries. Scotch Tape and Josephine helped the Devil to its feet and walked it back to its room. Josephine pulled the silver door open and all three shuffled inside. Soon Josephine and Scotch Tape returned to the police, who were grouped by the nurses' station. Pepper and Loochie sat on the floor, surrounded by them. Pepper's hands were bound behind him. Loochie held up her torn right hand as if signaling a waitress to bring the check. Dorry had been walked to the other side of the nurses' station where she'd collapsed. A young cop sat with her and held her hand tenderly because he thought she looked just like his great-aunt.

The cops and the staff milled around, still coming down from the chaos. A tall cop pointed toward the silver door and asked, *What's wrong with that one?* Scotch Tape frowned and shook his head regretfully. He said, *That's the sorriest case we got. Doctors don't know what to do for him.*

How could Scotch Tape talk about the Devil like that? Pepper wondered. As if it was just another patient and not the *thing* they'd seen. Could anyone work so hard to deny reality that he'd mistake the Devil for a man?

In a way it felt better to focus on such questions than to remember his friend, *Kofi,* being shot to death. A pair of syringes in his hands. What had he really planned to do with them? They weren't knives or swords. Was he going to poke the Devil into submission?

Pepper had seen Kofi's face just before the shooting began. A thought seemed to pass across his friend's eyes. Pepper wished he might know what that thought was. Had it been something ridiculous? Maybe wishing he had one last quarter, even after all that had proved so damn useless. What was that last thought? Sitting on the inoperable toilet, Pepper feared he might fall into a loop. One where he wondered about Coffee's last thoughts for hours and days and weeks. Until he might drive himself screwy trying to grasp at one last connection with the man he'd come to know. Better to think of anything else. Something concrete, tangible, real.

Kofi's blood traveled up to the <u>fluorescent lights</u> when he was shot.

Now Pepper couldn't get that image out of his head.

Kofi's blood, up there, on the ceiling.


The next the morning Loochie and Dorry and Pepper were returned to Northwest, much to the staff's unhappiness. When the security officers left, the staff put each patient into restraints. Dorry had been in her own room for years. Loochie was moved to a room of her own as well. Loochie's previous roommate, the Haint, hardly waved goodbye as Loochie took her stuff out. And Pepper was returned to his room.

Where Coffee's messy, empty bed looked like an open grave.

Though Pepper lay in restraints, he curled his head back as best he could because he kept wishing, praying, he'd catch sight of Coffee once again. When the pipes in the bathroom rattled, Pepper forgot and called out for Coffee, asked if he'd share a can of soda. But of course Coffee never answered.

The day after that, each member of the revolution had long meetings with Dr. Anand. Debriefings. Pepper was the last.

They sat him down in conference room 2. Dr. Anand was already at the table. Miss Chris sat in attendance. And a man whose gray flannel suit was more memorable than he was. He had an iPad propped up on the table. This guy didn't look at Pepper. He just tapped at the screen with one finger. (He was there to make notes for any potential legal actions that could be brought against the hospital at some future date.)

Dr. Anand placed both hands on the table and didn't bother with any introductory talk. "Pepper, we're looking for some kind of explanation for what happened." He put up one hand before Pepper could respond. "We've already met with Dorry and Loochie, so we're looking for a simple and clear explanation. Simple and clear, *please.*"

Pepper nodded, but what could he tell the man? Did he believe what Dorry had said? *He's my son.* Coffee thought he'd been searching the Internet telepathically. And look how that part turned out. He'd thought those digits would save his life, but they were just a wrong number in Oakland. Good work, Kofi! How's that for clear? Pepper saw no way of summarizing all this, so he said nothing.

Dr. Anand looked disappointed. He sat back in his chair. He said, "Miss Chris will need to take some blood and check your blood pressure."

Miss Chris rose. The blood-pressure strap in one hand. "Doctor says I to do it and you gone let me do it, hear?" She spoke as if Pepper was a dog, but there was something desperate in her voice. "You *hear?*" she repeated.

Miss Chris was scared of him. They probably all were. He didn't feel pressed to reassure them. He felt like seeing them squirm.

" 'In the mist dark figures move and twist,' " Pepper said to her. " 'Was all this for real or some kind of hell?' "

Dr. Anand took off his glasses and rubbed his eyes, exhausted. Even the uninvolved legal rep peeked up from his tablet screen.

Miss Chris put one hand on her hip. "That from the Bible?"

"That's Iron Maiden," Pepper said.

Miss Chris frowned, now more confused than fearful. Pepper decided to stop talking and let the woman do her job.

Dr. Anand leaned across the table, slid a few strips of newsprint toward Pepper. "This is how the incident has been reported so far."

As Miss Chris pulled up Pepper's pajama sleeve and slapped the blood-pressure strap around him, he focused on the terrible picture of Kofi.

"That's no glamour shot," Pepper said.

"That's how Coffee looked when he first came to us," Dr. Anand said. "We'd made a lot of progress."

Pepper wriggled his arm as it went slightly cold below the strap. Miss Chris stopped pumping and air hissed as it leaked out.

"You got him to cut his hair and take a bath."

Dr. Anand shook his head. "We got him off the street. We got him to *maintain* his hygiene. We taught him how to contact government agencies so he could get the benefits he was entitled to upon his release."

Miss Chris removed the strap and searched for a suitable vein in the crook of Pepper's elbow.

"And when was that going to be?" Pepper asked.

Dr. Anand spoke plainly. "Release depends on so many variables."

The doctor sighed. He looked as tired as Pepper had ever seen him.

"We do everything we can to find solutions," Dr. Anand said. "But we only discover greater mysteries."

Miss Chris slipped a needle into Pepper's vein. He hardly felt it go in. She pulled back the stopper on the needle and all of them—Pepper, Miss Chris, Dr. Anand, even the legal rep—watched Pepper's blood fill the vial.

After Miss Chris finished taking blood, Dr. Anand had a few more questions. None of them seemed concerned with understanding why the four of them had revolted, only to record the order of events should a timeline ever be needed for a legal proceeding. After all that, Dr. Anand said, "There's still time for you to get lunch."

Pepper felt surprised. "I thought you were going to put me back in restraints."

Dr. Anand's face turned red (reddish brown) and looked at the nearly catatonic representative. He said, "No one wants to use restraints on you at all." Then he looked at Miss Chris and said, "Do we?"

Miss Chris smiled at the legal rep. "*No*, doctor."

Which wasn't the same as saying they hadn't used them. Or wouldn't.

Now both staff members looked at Pepper cautiously. Maybe this was his moment to testify to the man with the iPad.

But the rep defused the situation. "I'm sure a staff as qualified as ours only uses restraints within the limits of existing laws. I have *no* doubts."

With that, the man returned to the screen. Tapped a few more times, then shut the black case that held the spiffy device. "We're all done," he said.


Pepper and Miss Chris walked down Northwest 1 until they reached the nurses' station. There were four staff members on duty besides Miss Chris and Dr. Anand. Two more nurses and two orderlies. Extra muscle. The uprising had been good for one thing: overtime pay for the underpaid staff.

Miss Chris brought Pepper to the counter, and the other nurse brought out his small white cup of pills. They hadn't changed the medications, not even the doses, but when he put the pills in his mouth all five staff members watched him closely.

"No cheating," Miss Chris taunted.

After he swallowed she said, "Pop your mouth."

Pepper opened his mouth. He *had* swallowed the pills. Nevertheless, Miss Chris pulled on a latex glove, rose to her toes, stuck one finger between his lips and gums and checked.

"Tongue," she said.

He lifted it and her finger felt around faintly, almost tenderly. It was the gentlest moment the two of them had ever shared. She slipped her finger out and pulled the glove off with a snap. She said, "Lunch then."

Miss Chris walked behind Pepper down Northwest 5 and he felt like she was leading him to his execution. A shot in the back of the head. Maybe he'd even find the bodies of Dorry and Loochie and Coffee already there. Four corpses left in an empty room. New Hyde's headache relieved that easily.

But slow down, Pepper. You ain't Lorca! You're not even Tommy from *GoodFellas*. The only punishment awaiting him was a lunch tray.

The other patients had been eating for a while. When Pepper entered the lounge, they watched him. He couldn't be sure if they seemed sympathetic or accusatory. As the pills began to numb him, he found he didn't much care. He sat alone at a table and looked down at his food. He felt both hungry and repulsed by the idea of eating.

Mr. Mack and Frank Waverly were at one table. Neither man looked at Pepper. At another table he saw another familiar couple. Sam and Sammy! But then he focused and realized they were two different women, new patients, similar but decades older than Sam and Sammy had been. Japanese Freddie Mercury sat at a table alone and it took Pepper a moment to wonder where his pal, Yuckmouth, might be. But really, who cared?

Who cared? Who cared? Who cared?

Pepper ate but tasted nothing. He blinked and breathed.

When Pepper finished lunch, Miss Chris and two orderlies appeared. They surrounded him. They walked Pepper back to his room. They looped the restraints around Pepper's ankles and wrists. They left him there.

# 23

NOW THAT THE legal rep had gone, Pepper's every meal was served in his room. His meds were brought to him. Loochie and Dorry were treated the same way.

There was a time when Dr. Anand knew of, but perhaps willfully ignored, his staff's overuse of restraints on patients. But after the *incident* with Coffee, he'd check in on Pepper or Loochie and Dorry and find them in wrist and ankle restraints but, to his own quiet surprise, he didn't care. When one of them complained about the aches (their backs, from lying prone for so long, especially) the doctor nodded his head and became engrossed in the charts in his hand. Soon enough, he got so used to seeing them tied down that he really didn't even see the restraints anymore.

For the first *two weeks* after Coffee's death, the trio didn't spend much time on their feet or out of bonds. During the third week, they were freed in shifts. Each got eight unstrapped hours a day. The other sixteen, they were flat on their backs or, for variety's sake, the restraints were rearranged so they could spend the sixteen hours on one side. Each time Pepper was lashed down, he asked the nurse or orderly if they'd leave one arm free so he could at least read during the hours he lay awake. And do you know who was the only staff member to indulge him? Miss Chris. Go figure that one. The times when Miss Chris left one arm unbound, Pepper read from the only book in his possession, the letters of Vincent Van Gogh. With his bed in its new position, he faced a wall instead of the windows and the sunlight streamed in over his back and illuminated the pages throughout the day.

Pepper was free from eight p.m. until four in the morning. Then back to bed.

The Devil didn't return. As if Coffee's murder had appeased it.

But for how long?

Six weeks later, on April 11, Miss Chris and a new orderly found Pepper asleep in his bed. They didn't wake him until they'd removed the restraints. The orderly kicked the side of his bed. Pepper opened his eyes.

When he sat up, Miss Chris stretched out her hand, a small plastic cup in her palm. He accepted the pills without a fuss.

Then the orderly handed Pepper a small plastic bag from T.J. Maxx. Inside, he found a pair of slacks, a shirt, underwear, new socks. One new outfit, the same size as the clothes he'd worn in.

"Dr. Anand bought those for you," Miss Chris said. "Since your other clothes got ruin."

"You can move around the unit freely now," the orderly said.

"But we're watching," Miss Chris added.

As Pepper washed his face in the bathroom sink, he found himself smiling in the mirror.

*Look at that,* he thought. His fuzzy reflection couldn't stop smiling, which meant *he* must've been smiling. Pepper brought his cheap towel to his face and dried off, but he couldn't feel that rough fabric against his cheeks. He dropped the towel, then traced the smile in the mirror with his fingertip. He tapped the metal with one long fingernail, and it sounded as if he was clicking the reflection's teeth.

He'd lost weight while in restraints. Sure, he hadn't been able to move much for six weeks, but he hadn't eaten hardly at all. When the nurses came to feed him, he sometimes refused. Not really a hunger strike, more like a hunger tantrum. But the staff didn't try to persuade him when he did this. You don't want to eat? I'll see you in the morning. Just like that. You're not Bobby Sands if no one's paying attention. You're just starving.

Pepper dressed in his new clothes. Good to get out of those pajamas. Then he went to breakfast.

He moved through the unit with his head down, ignoring the staff, and ignoring the phone alcove as well. He heard a patient in there, a woman, talking on the phone with pleasure, laughing to a loved one. And Coffee wasn't in there, on hold on the other phone, because Coffee was dead. So Pepper ignored the alcove and stumbled into the breakfast line. He picked up his tray of cereal and milk, a small green apple and two dry pieces of toast.

No one else in the television lounge paid attention to him. They had their own troubles and a television show to watch. Mr. Mack had control of the machine again and he'd picked his favorite.

On the screen, the same anchor, as well maintained as a pre-owned luxury car, scrabbled through a handful of papers on his desk and looked up at the camera as the show returned from a commercial break.

"Welcome back to *News Roll*, I'm your host Steve Sands. As you know, we focus on the big news, national *and* international, but we're even more committed to covering the big news that's *local*. That's right. Casting an eye on the stories that matter most to New Yorkers like you and me."

Pepper chose a table that looked out on the decrepit basketball court. In a couple hours, about noon, the staff would open the door here for a smoker's break. Would they let him go out there? Pepper wondered how many of the patients still had their staff schwag. At least he'd distributed free cigarettes to the masses! That's the best thing he could say about the incident: He'd helped a bunch of people flirt with cancer.

He took an empty table, his back to the rest of the lounge, and looked out on the court. He ignored Steve Sands. Halfway through the meal, he actually felt the sunlight on his face. Despite the meds, he sensed the warmth. Such a small thing, but so pleasant. He ate his toast quietly in his chair. He tasted the sweetness of the butter and almost laughed.

"You eating that?"

He knew the voice even before he saw the hand reach over his shoulder and take his apple.

Loochie.

"I *am* eating that," he said, and swiped at the fruit with his left hand.

Or, he meant to swipe at that fruit. By the time the signal left his brain, hacked through the underbrush of antipsychotics, and actually raised his hand, that girl had already taken it.

His reaction time still needed work.

She took the seat directly across from him. She wore the blue knit cap again, but the pom-poms were missing. Two sad blue strings lay limp. Pepper wondered if she'd even plucked the pom-poms off while suffering some involuntary spasm in the middle of the night.

Loochie finished the apple, down to the core. She wiped her fingers on her polo shirt. Loochie said, "Share your cereal with me?"

Pepper set the Frosted Flakes down and opened the back of the box. While he opened the plastic and poured the milk, Loochie went to the nurses' station and demanded a plastic spoon. When she returned, Pepper pushed the box toward her, it sat halfway between them. They took turns dipping their spoons in. It wasn't much, but it was something.

Loochie finished her last spoonful and said, "Thanks."

Pepper touched the plastic spoon to his forehead in a salute.

"So, we going to kill that old bitch or what?" Loochie asked.

Pepper actually ate one more spoonful of cereal. It wasn't until he'd finished chewing that he understood what Loochie had said.

"You with me?" she asked, smiling like she'd just asked him to go hang out at the mall.

No.

That was his answer. The only answer. Loochie looked at him, confused. "Pepper?"

On the television, Steve Sands looked into the camera and seemed to speak directly to Pepper. "My friends, the world gets more frightening every day. The news I report to you stays with me when I go home to my wife and children every night. As our politicians fail us, and our once-mighty institutions suffer from *rigor mortis,* it's become clear that we're kind of on our own out here. Am I right? That's just how it seems to me. It may sound harsh, but the new American reality is this: *every man for himself.* Make sure *your* butt is covered."

Mr. Mack actually applauded from his chair. "That man is speaking the *truth* right there! You can't save nobody but yourself."

At the same table Frank Waverly picked at his scrambled eggs. When Mr. Mack slapped his friend's shoulder, looking for a little corroboration, Frank Waverly leaned away from the touch.


Pepper returned to his room and read. At lunch, he came out to the nurses' station, took his pills, then ate. Though they were making sure he took his pills, his body was starting to react with slightly less *tilt.* The body adapts. At eleven p.m. he found himself awake instead of zonked into a narco-coma. His body had adapted in another way, too. Weeks spent walking the ward from eight in the evening to four a.m. meant that his clock had readjusted. He came to life during the haunted hours.

Pepper still hadn't been given a new roommate, though the staff had at least cleared Coffee's bedsheets. The only thing they'd left behind was his blue binder. It had been on the windowsill, and when one of the nurses went to grab it, Pepper said it was his. They'd cleaned out the bottom drawer full of pills without comment. Scotch Tape even moved Coffee's dresser away from the wall and swept up all the rat droppings. The room had been cleaned, cleared, but that didn't make it feel empty.

Eleven thirty, and Pepper put down Van Gogh's letters and left his room.

He passed the rooms of the other men in Northwest 2. Nearly all the doors were shut. He passed the nurses' station and didn't pay attention to the staff. Since he'd taken his evening meds, they had no reason to linger over him. They were making more stacks of paperwork for the electronic filing to come. They'd been promised a solution to the computer problem. The proper program would soon appear. So they prepared.

Pepper paced down Northwest 5, to the television lounge. He only realized he wasn't wearing shoes or socks when the chill in the floor leached into his soles. Since it was late, he found the late-shift patients on duty. The night birds.

There were still only four of them: Heatmiser, who still watched the silent television screen and read along with the closed captioning. He had a chair right under the television. Footage of a tornado-wracked territory showed on the screen. The closed-captioned text read: "Residents of Alabama are bracing for moors."

"More," Heatmiser corrected.

The other three patients were there, too. The redhead, the woman who never seemed to make eye contact with anyone, and the Chinese Lady. Each sat at a table by herself like a sovereign, newspapers spread out across her tabletop like scrolls.

Pepper repeated one sentence to himself as he walked toward them: *Do not call her the Chinese Lady. Do not call her the Chinese Lady.* But the more times he thought this phrase, the more afraid he became that he'd say it. He approached the redhead because that seemed safer. She was also the only one who'd spoken to him that night, long ago now, so she seemed like the leader. Make introductions to the Redhead Kingpin, and the others would follow.

"You reading all those papers?" he asked her, smiling lightly.

Redhead Kingpin didn't so much as sigh.

Pepper, feeling slighted, moved around Heatmiser, reached up to the television set, and turned the volume up. Now the news was being yelled at them. A childish act, no doubt.

He pulled a chair up beside Heatmiser. Heatmiser rose from his seat, mumbled something, and wandered from the television lounge, looking confused. On-screen, footage from the Kentucky Derby played. The hoofbeats on the track sounded louder than bombs at high volume.

Finally, Redhead Kingpin turned in her chair. She watched Pepper quietly for maybe one more minute. "You're just going to make noise until we invite you to play with us," she said.

Pepper's only response was to cross his arms. Was the man actually pouting?

The redhead cleared her throat. The other two women—the one who never made eye contact and *not* "the Chinese Lady"—stopped their reading and looked up for the first time. "Does anyone have a problem with . . ."

"Pepper."

"Does anyone have a problem with *Pepper* joining us?"

The one at the next table still didn't lift her head, but her hand did rise, as if she was in a classroom. Then she waved the hand side to side.

Redhead Kingpin said, "Say your piece."

The woman lowered her hand. She spoke into her clavicle. "He can stay, but he can't read any of my periodicals."

Pepper sniffed at her. "I don't even want to read any of your periodicals."

Just like that, the woman lifted her head. The woman had the coloring, and shape, of a sweet potato. Hardly the type to seem threatening. But what Pepper saw in her eyes actually made him tremble. She looked more rageful than Loochie just then. A scowl that would've made the Devil quake. He'd had thugged out guys (thugged out *black* guys) who hadn't stiffened his spine so quickly. (Was *that* racist?) (Probably.)

"It was just a joke," Pepper muttered.

The woman nodded once, like Pepper had apologized, and looked back down at her magazine.

Redhead Kingpin splayed her hands flat and wide apart on her table. Three or four newspapers were spread out there. She adjusted each, just slightly, the way you might straighten an off-center painting.

"Well, my table's all full," Redhead Kingpin said.

Finally, the third woman (*not* the . . . you know) said, "He can sit with me."

Pepper walked to her table. But before he sat, Redhead Kingpin cleared her throat again. She pointed at the television. "How about you lower that before you get all comfy?"

After he did, the redhead added, "And please don't start the same trouble you did with your other friends."

"I didn't—" he began to explain. He stopped when he realized these three women (and probably all the other patients) blamed him for what happened. Were they wrong?

Pepper sat at the Chinese woman's table. She had newspapers and a few magazines. She offered him a copy of *Backpacker* magazine, which he accepted. But he couldn't concentrate.

The woman was generous enough to let him sit, to offer the reading material, but she didn't make conversation. She wasn't interested. She scanned a copy of *The Washington Post*. When she found some article that snagged her interest, she pulled out a pen and underlined the text. Finally, she folded the page with great precision, until there were deeply creased lines around the piece. Carefully she tore it free. Didn't even need scissors. (She wasn't going to be given any in here.)

"What's that for?" Pepper asked. He spoke quietly.

"For the files," she answered, as she turned the page, scanning new articles.

Ah, yes, *the files*. Pepper kept making the mistake of confusing the appearance of sanity with the real thing. Did she mean *The X-Files*? *The Rockford Files*? *The Wackadoo Files*? Who knew? But Pepper wouldn't push. It didn't matter if she was saving these articles to use as toilet paper in her room. She'd let him sit for a while, right? Being quiet in her company was kind of nice, wasn't it? Just be happy with that.

Pepper looked out the windows of the lounge. He saw the disused basketball court. At the edge of the court stood the not-so-tall fence with barbed-wire curlicues at the top. He saw the empty parking lot of New Hyde Hospital. He decided, just now, to find peace in even this view. To sit quietly and let the sound of turning pages become like white noise. A lullaby. In a little while, he might want to move again.

But not yet.

# 24

ESMIN GREEN DIED at Kings County Hospital in Brooklyn, New York; she was only forty-nine. A patient on the hospital's psych unit, she'd been brought to the psychiatric emergency room for "agitation." After waiting to be seen for twenty-four hours, she collapsed on the dirty waiting-room floor. She lay there like salmon on a skillet, the heat rising below the pan and making the flesh jump. Her head slipped under one of the waiting-room chairs. Her legs splayed out straight. She lay there and *two* security guards looked into the room on *two separate* occasions. A doctor did, too. All three men watched her lying there on the floor. They didn't even step into the waiting room. At last, a nurse arrived to check on Esmin Green, who'd been on her back for an hour. To see if the woman was conscious, the nurse kicked Esmin Green's leg.

But the woman was already dead.

And the only thing that made the case against that doctor (fired), the nurse (suspended), and the two security guards (both suspended) was the hospital's surveillance tape. Someone on staff had doctored the medical records so they read that at 6:20 a.m. Ms. Green was "sitting quietly in waiting room." If not for the video footage, and its time stamp, Esmin would've been passed off as an unforeseeable accident, the kind of thing, as is said "that no one could've prevented."

Who would've challenged the official version? One cosigned by four staff members. Would anyone give credence to the other two patients, clearly seen in the video, also stuck in that waiting room—the ones who saw Ms. Green's death happen? How would they be treated as witnesses? How easy would it be to make wackos seem nuts? Were the good people of the jury supposed to take their word over a nurse's? Over a *doctor's*? It was just too horrible to believe that such a thing could happen. People don't get treated that way. A nurse wouldn't do that. A doctor takes an oath. Security guards . . . well, okay, maybe no one would be too surprised that some security guards fucked up.

The jury's verdict (at best) might've been: We really feel *terrible* for these people. (And here's the hard part, they really would.) We feel terrible, but we have doubts. We doubt the world works this way, because it has never worked this way against us.

Luckily for Esmin Green's family, cameras are considered legally sane. Their testimony above reproach. Kings County Hospital reached a settlement with the Green family. Turns out Esmin had blood clots in her leg; her complaints of pain were legitimate. The clots caused her heart to stop, and because she was left unaided, she expired.

This happened in 2008.

# 25

THE NEXT NIGHT, Pepper returned to the television lounge just before midnight. He found Heatmiser under the television screen, Redhead Kingpin at her table, and Still Waters sitting at the next. Pepper grabbed the back of a free chair at the third table, but before he pulled it out he asked, "May I join you?"

She shrugged. Good enough! Pepper sat across from her.

The Chinese woman flipped through a copy of the *New York Post*, the pages slightly spotty because she'd had to fish it out of the trash.

"Anything interesting?" he asked.

"Not yet." She looked up from the page. "You don't have anything to read?"

"I left my book in my room." Pepper pointed at her piles of newsprint and periodicals. "Maybe I could borrow one of yours?"

She smiled without opening her mouth; a tight grin. "You better think of something else," she said.

Pepper didn't see why she had to be hardheaded about it, but also didn't want to get booted out. He liked the lounge at this hour. No Loochie, no Dorry, and far from his empty room. But without anything to read, he wanted conversation. He said, "You want to hear about Vincent Van Gogh?"

She frowned, surprised. "The painter?"

"The *Dutch* painter," Pepper said, proud he could be more specific.

This seemed to please her. That he didn't back down or apologize. She smiled again, a little wider this time, but still showing no teeth.

Behind him, Pepper heard the Redhead Kingpin clear her throat. The Chinese woman looked over his shoulder and rolled her eyes.

"Tell me something interesting about his birth," she said, speaking loud enough that it seemed defiant.

"He was born on March 30," Pepper said, "in 1853."

"Everyone is born sometime."

Pepper considered this. "His father was a pastor."

She peeked at another magazine on the table. Pepper was losing her. Behind him, another bout of throat clearing. Which only made him speak a bit more loudly, too.

"But he wasn't a very good one," Pepper said. "People adored Van Gogh's dad, as a person, but as a pastor he was second-rate."

This made the Chinese woman look up again with some interest. "It's not a good scandal or anything. But I do like to hear about people who aren't very good at their jobs. Not terrible, not great, just okay. I like people who are just okay."

Pepper said, "So what's your name?"

She crossed her arms. "What does everyone around here call me?"

Pepper shrugged cartoonishly, raised his eyebrows. "How would *I* know?"

She twisted her lips and sighed. "My name is Xiu," she said. "But you won't be able to pronounce it."

"Xiu," Pepper repeated, but it came out sounding like "zoo." He knew that wasn't quite right because he'd just heard her say it. He tried to hold his mouth closed the way she had. It seemed like she clenched her jaw, pursed her lips, and (somehow) simultaneously parted her teeth to make the sound come out.

"Xiu," he tried. "Xiu." But it only sounded worse. It made his neck hurt.

Finally she tapped the tabletop with an open hand. "Just call me Sue."

Pepper said, "I'm going to keep practicing."

She nodded. "But until then . . ."

"Sue."

She looked to be about his age. In her early forties. She had a wide round face, and her smile never grew bigger than that grin. In all the lines she'd spoken just now he had yet to actually see her *teeth*. It didn't seem like they were missing, but like she consciously kept them covered with her lips. Such a self-conscious way of speaking. She had a broad, flat nose that seemed to float off her broad face. Thinning black eyebrows. Deeply black hair that fell limply on either side of her face and hid her ears. Her eyes were also black and, somehow, *remote*. They were like closed shutters. But he could see, even through those slats, her lights were on.

"I'm Pepper," he said.

"I know who you are."

"You've been asking about me?" He sat higher in his seat.

"You tried to escape," she said.

He slumped. "I don't know what we tried to do. But it didn't work."

She grabbed a copy of *Outside* magazine from her pile. "No. It really didn't."

Sue stopped on a page with a photo of a waterfall spraying down a mountain. She pressed a finger to the water as if her skin would come away wet. "So what will you do now?" she asked.

"I think I'll go into real estate."

"Commercial or residential?"

"I'm going to make a bid on the ball court over there."

"How much will you offer?"

"A dollar forty-nine."

She bugged her eyes wide. "Don't you know the bubble burst? A dollar forty-nine sounds like 2006 prices!"

They leaned toward each other, just slightly. They hardly noticed it. She reached into her stack of magazines and slid a different one to him: *National Geographic Traveler*. Pepper looked at her. Sue creased a picture of a desert oasis. She tore it out carefully.

"For the files," Pepper said.

She held the picture up. A series of date-palm trees surrounding a small pool of water. "This one isn't a *file*. It's a *dream*."

Sue reached below her chair where she had an old plastic Associated Supermarket bag. Inside there were two somewhat worn accordion folders. One manila, one blue. She opened the blue one, and Pepper saw dozens and dozens of clippings from glossy magazines. Each one a fantasy spot worth visiting. Sue slipped the image of the oasis in there. Then she pressed it shut with the Velcro tab. She touched the blue folder. "The dreams." She touched the manila folder. "The files."

Pepper watched her quietly. Was this crazy or was it cute? And did Pepper care? At least right now? He was with a woman whose company he already liked. And she seemed to like him. In a coffee shop, at a party, or in a psychiatric unit, some interactions always feel good.

"So will you come see me again tomorrow?" Sue asked.


On the third night, Pepper arrived *early*.

The three women (and Heatmiser) tended to hit the television lounge at about ten p.m. This allowed the dinner rush to pass and the food (and meds) to hit the other patients. By nine o'clock, most couldn't stay awake even if you set a limb on fire. By ten there was hardly anyone left. That's when the quartet hit the stage. They fought through the haze rather than fall asleep. Other patients did exactly the same during the day, after breakfast meds, or lunch. They chose to keep alert then because they liked being up with the sun. These four were just on a different schedule.

And now there were five.

Sue came in carrying her plastic bag with two accordion folders and the night's reading material clutched to her chest. She wore a thin white sweater over her faint blue nightdress and white Keds that had been through a hundred or more cycles in a washing machine, clean but eroding. To Pepper, she looked like a librarian. And in a way, that's what she was.

Before she'd even settled herself in her chair, Pepper pulled his hands out from under the table. He waved his book at her. "I brought something tonight!"

At the television Heatmiser shushed Pepper. Pepper looked back as if he'd like to mess with the kid, but that boy's face already looked five kinds of tired, weary in a way that had little to do with sleep. So Pepper only nodded and said, "Sorry."

Heatmiser turned back to the closed-captioned scroll on the TV. The words appeared on the bottom half of the screen. "Catherine Zeta-Jones is touted for bipolar II disorder," it read.

Heatmiser laughed to himself. "I think you mean 'treated,'" he whispered.

Sue laid her stuff out at their table. Not the magazines, but the newspapers this time. She had the manila accordion file on the table; the blue one, for dreams, stowed under her seat. Pepper saw two words written in black ink on the side of the manila folder.

"No Name."

This gave Pepper a chill, as if he were seeing that phrase etched into someone's tombstone. He didn't want to look at it. Pepper raised his book and showed her Van Gogh's self-portrait on the cover.

"That's him?" she asked. "He looks intense."

Sue leaned closer to the page. "Actually, I think he looks a little like Elliott." She pointed at Heatmiser.

Pepper looked back at the television. "That's his name?"

Sue said, "Let me see some more of his paintings."

Pepper flipped through the book's pages fast as a deck of cards. "These are his letters, mostly to his brother. There's only a few pictures in here and they're only in black and white. But I think his stuff was mostly in color."

Sue touched the cover. "Have you ever seen them in real life?"

Pepper snorted. "I didn't even really know who this guy was until I opened this book. I mean I heard about him, like his name, but I just knew it was, like, a saying. You know? A teacher said it to me in class once. 'You think you're a real *Van Gogh*.' And that was only because I was drawing a woman's tits on my desk."

"That's charming," Sue said and flared her nostrils.

Sue reached into one of her sweater pockets and took out a tiny notepad and a pen. She set them on the tabletop. Nearby, Redhead Kingpin and Still Waters had already begun working for the night. The day's newspapers were open. Both women scanned the articles.

But Sue didn't rush to join them as she might have on any other night in the past. When she looked at Pepper, she didn't want to stay quiet. She didn't mind if they spoke for a little longer.

Pepper, sensing that he'd passed some hurdle, some gate, felt a flush in his chest and arms. He said, "The thing I've been thinking about, as I'm reading these letters, is that there's actually *two* Vincent Van Goghs."

"Like clones?" Sue asked.

Pepper laughed loudly.

Behind him, Heatmiser said, "Come on, man."

Pepper leaned closer to Sue so they could speak quietly. He said, "I mean there's Van Gogh, now, whose name is used to tease a kid at P.S. 120 just because he's drawing . . ."

"Tits," Sue said dryly.

Pepper kept going. "You know they have a whole museum dedicated to Van Gogh in Amsterdam? They have a plug for it in the back of the book. A whole *building* dedicated to what he painted in his life."

"How long did he live?"

"He was dead at thirty-seven."

"Damn." Sue sat back in her seat. "I'm forty-one."

She looked at Pepper quickly, to see if the admission would sour him somehow. But Pepper didn't care. He was still on his "two Van Goghs" point. He put his hand on the armrest of her chair. He said, "But the second Van Gogh is just a guy named Vincent. *Vincent* lived for thirty-seven years. *Van Gogh* only came to life after Vincent died. Same man, two people."

Sue watched Pepper's hand there on her armrest. She tapped his arm with her notepad playfully. But he mistakenly thought she was trying to push him back. Like he was getting too close. So he pulled his arm away. Sue's disappointment passed like a breeze on the back of her neck. It made her shiver. She placed her forearm on the armrest then so if he reached out again she'd be sure to feel his touch.

But to continue the conversation, Sue said, "That reminds me of an interview I heard with Sheryl Crow once."

"Tangent!" Pepper hissed and laughed.

"Just listen. She was talking about how she made a living when she was younger. Before she became famous. She used to give music lessons in Los Angeles. And she said one day she had this guy come in for a lesson but I think he didn't come back. Or she didn't pursue it. She never saw him again.

"Then she's watching a movie, maybe it was *Thelma and Louise*, and she sees the guy who had been in her living room for music lessons. He's right there on the screen. Having sex with Geena Davis. And in the interview she said something like 'If only I'd known it was Brad Pitt!'"

Pepper watched her quietly. "And?"

"If only she'd known it was Brad Pitt? She did know it was Brad Pitt. He just wasn't *Brad Pitt* yet. Same man. Two people."

Pepper reached out and touched her wrist, there on the armrest. Nearly involuntarily, her fingers opened and her notepad fell out of her hand.

Pepper smiled. "Now we're talking."

Pepper pulled his fingers away from her skin and immediately she missed them. He leaned over to grab her notepad from where it fell. When he did, his head moved past Sue's nose, and she smelled the shampoo Pepper had used when he showered just before seeing her tonight. She had the same shampoo, of course. They all did. But when a woman likes a man, nothing about him remains common. It's *his*. Especially his. Even some no-name, half-bleachy shampoo. *Eau de Pepper*. (Available at ninety-nine-cent stores everywhere.)

Pepper handed back her notepad. She felt afraid her face had flushed, so she focused on her newspapers. Pepper returned to Vincent's letters.

They stayed at the table together until five a.m.

# 26

"Randolph Maddix, a schizophrenic who lived at a private home for the mentally ill in Brooklyn, was often left alone to suffer seizures, his body crumpling to the floor of his squalid room. The home, Seaport Manor, is responsible for 325 starkly ill people, yet many of its workers could barely qualify for fast-food jobs. So it was no surprise that Mr. Maddix, 51, was dead for more than 12 hours before an aide finally checked on him. His back, curled and stiff with rigor mortis, had to be broken to fit him into a body bag."

THE NEW YORK TIMES
*April 28, 2002*

# 27

"I'LL BE GONE in less than a week."

Sue told him this on the fourth night.

They didn't take the same table as the previous nights, close to Redhead Kingpin and Still Waters. Tonight they wanted a little privacy, which meant moving a few tables over. This one was also hidden from the view of staff members inside the nurses' station by a structural column. Considering the circumstances, this felt like running off to a private villa.

But wait! Hadn't the entire ward gone on high alert about seven weeks ago? Hadn't the aftermath of Pepper's insurrection had consequences? Well, yes: Staff members were approved for overtime pay, but that only lasted a month; Pepper, Dorry, and Loochie were checked to be sure they took their medications; legal counsel had evaluated the hospital's possible legal culpability; and the criminal matter of Kofi Acholi's death was being investigated by the New York City Police Department.

(But if the pace of Pepper's possible indictment for assaulting Huey, Dewey, and Louie weren't evidence enough of systematic sluggishness, please consider that the full extent of police activity in the likely suicide of Samantha "Sam" Forrester was that a yellow sticker had been affixed to the door of her room, sealing it shut; the yellow sticker read, in part: THIS AREA IS THE SITE OF AN ONGOING POLICE INVESTIGATION. DO NOT ENTER. The police wouldn't be back to this room for eleven more weeks. And when they came, it would only be to cut the sticker, open the room, and conclude their investigation with a few sheets of paperwork; Miss Chris would be left to scrape the remains of the sticker off the door and door frame, and halfway through, she'd pawn the job off on the nearest orderly.)

Which is to say that Pepper and Sue would be left alone at their table.

Because they sat behind the columns, Pepper felt bold. He rested his hand on her right thigh, which was slim and soft. He squeezed her leg. How long had it been since he'd been able to do that to a woman? Too long.

"You're getting discharged?" he whispered.

He knew he should only feel happy about this. Like hearing someone you care about has just had a long jail sentence commuted. But this also meant that in less than a week she'd be leaving him. When they'd only just begun. He understood that he was being selfish. He tried the same sentence again, trying to sound elated.

"You're getting discharged!"

He would walk her to the secure door. He would *watch* her walk out. And he realized that, despite his own sadness, he would be so glad she was *free*.

"I'm getting deported," Sue said.

He laughed at this. A big one. Up from the belly. Enough to make everyone else in the lounge shoosh him hatefully, as if he were a teenager texting in a movie theater. And *their* sound was so loud, so clearly hostile, that a member of the staff called out from the nurses' station.

"Everything all right down there?" she shouted.

Not just *a* nurse, but *Josephine*. Back on the job. Working an overnight shift, but wary in a way she hadn't been before. A little afraid to come down to the lounge on her own. (Especially with Pepper in there; don't think she hadn't tracked him passing by.) Then she felt resentful that this job had swiped some of her confidence, her ease.

She was no longer Josephine; now she was Nurse Washburn. She'd already started telling patients to address her that way.

In the lounge, Sue cupped her hands and shouted, "One hundred percent all right down here!"

Nurse Washburn's chair creaked as she sat back down. Then, very faintly, they all heard the clacking of computer keys.

"Come on," Pepper said quietly. "Stop playing with me."

He ran his hand down Sue's thigh, toward her knee. She clasped his wrist. She pinched her lips and softened her eyes as if Pepper were the one in need of sympathy. "I'm not playing," she whispered. "I have less than seven days."

"I don't get it," he said. "Deport you for *what*? Deport you to *where*?"

"To China."

This was the first time he really thought about the crispness of her English. "But you speak English so well," he said.

Pepper said those words before he had time to think them through. *But you speak English so well.* Just a burp produced in a fetid little chamber of his mind. The wrong thing to say. He knew it. He knew it. But that didn't mean shit to Sue.

She squinted her eyes into slits. She curled her upper lip until her teeth bucked out. "Oh, sank you velly much," she said. "Missa GI Joe Amelican!"

Pepper kissed the side of her face. Their first kiss, and it came because of this. "I'm sorry," he said. "I didn't mean it like that. I'm *sorry.*"

She pulled away from him. She crossed her arms. A fight had begun. One Pepper couldn't win with apologies. But then he noticed something new. He pointed at her mouth. "That's the first time I've ever seen your teeth."

Sue gasped as if her skirt had blown up over her head. She dropped her upper lip. She brought one hand up to her mouth and covered it.

Ah, yes, the one concern that might trump an unfortunate detour into flagrant ethnic stereotyping. Vanity! Or, more specifically, crippling insecurity. Sue kept her hand over her mouth and twisted away from Pepper.

"Come on," Pepper said. "They look nice."

Which was a lie. (Her teeth were *jacked.*)

"I like it when you smile," he said.

Which was true. And she could hear that in his voice.

She turned back to him. Her hand still hadn't moved. He reached out, pulled it down. He leaned toward her so he could whisper. "If you need me to say racist things to make you smile, I'll do it," Pepper said. "But only if you ask nice."

Sue pulled her hand from his, raised it one more time, and plunked him on his forehead. He overplayed the pain. Rearing back and stretching his mouth open, he pantomimed a howl without breaking the room's hush.

Sue grabbed Pepper's hand and put it back on her thigh now. She watched him until he returned her intense gaze. She pulled his hand higher, to the top of her thigh. He leaned forward and kissed her lightly. Not the cheek, but the lips this time. When he pulled away, her shuttered eyes seemed to have grown brighter, as if she'd drawn the blinds.

She said, "I've been held in one kind of detention or another for almost a year now."

Pepper wasn't sure what to do with this. Here they were, getting warm, and she drops a bit of information sure to cool any room. When he frowned at her and remained still, Sue said, "I'm telling you I'm horny."

He kissed her much harder the second time.

Then he slipped his hand between her thighs. He felt the mound of her pussy, warm through her nightdress. She put her hand over his and pressed him closer to her. Pepper rubbed through the fabric and she ground against his fingers. She breathed more quickly, tight and shallow little sounds. The television showed pictures of night skies from a weather forecast, showering the room in blue light.

Sue arched her back; Pepper kept rubbing.

They both wanted to kiss, but Sue had her head arched too far backward. The muscles of his right arm were already sore but he kept at it. Sue huffed, hissed really, through her clenched teeth.

Pepper closed his eyes. He didn't want to watch her, but to feel her. And he didn't want to get all *aware* of the three other people in the room; folks who couldn't help but understand what was going on ten feet from them. If Pepper started thinking of them, he couldn't keep rubbing Sue. It was just so ridiculous. Like all good public sex.

Sue had been louder in the buildup than in the finale. Maybe this is because she *had* opened her eyes. She'd seen her two friends (Rachel and Marjolein) so focused on their newspapers that they could only be listening to her and Pepper. What would they think if she really let it out, like she wanted to, at the end? This was already embarrassing enough! So when Sue came, she cut the sound off, as best she could, in her throat.

Sue had sweated across her neck and chin. The top of her nightdress showed the wetness. Pepper slipped his sore hand back into his own lap and kneaded the palm with his other hand. The top of his shoulder ached and burned, but he refused to show the pain.

Sue leaned in to him and smiled. Without self-consciousness. She was hardly there, at the table, in Northwest. She was just, momentarily, *relaxed*. It had been a looooong time since she'd been with a man. Most women appreciate busting a good nut, too (so to speak!).

Sue returned to her body. Returned to the television lounge. And this chair. Where this man sat beside her. She kissed Pepper absently. She huffed through her nose, one long breath. If she wasn't smiling, she sure felt like smiling. She tugged at Pepper's zipper.


There is *a lot* of sex going on in the nation's psychiatric units. (Not to mention the adult homes and residential units that also cater to, and care for, the mentally ill in the United States.) Adults cooped up for weeks and months and years (and sometimes decades). What do you think will result from being so tightly packed? Friction.

(We're not counting the sexual abuse that goes largely unreported, because that's *abuse* not sex. The horrible stuff happens, too: patient on patient, staff on patient, even patient on staff.)

We're focused, here, on the consensual business—a.k.a. affection;

dating; courting. Hell, even just hooking up. The *niceness*. Because, ladies and gentlemen, despite the perceived differences between them and you, the mentally ill like jooking, too!

Unfortunately, actual intercourse is about the hardest thing to achieve on the unit. The staff might huff and shout about kissing and fondling, but they'd often let the couple be. They will dole out discipline for more, though. A patient will be likely to get his butt in restraints, at the very least. There's even a chance they'll transfer him to another hospital, and how good would that be for the budding romance?

So second-tier sex becomes king. A little bit of sucking in the phone alcove, or maybe a handjob in the blind spot of the television lounge. Occasionally, very occasionally, a woman might sneak into a man's room. That's rare, though, because even if the staff doesn't catch you, there's your roommate to contend with. He isn't necessarily overjoyed that you're getting a little play and he's left cuddling his antidepressants. Some grouchy patient will snitch in record time. It's a real feat—let's go ahead and say it's a *miracle*—if two people sneak some actual lovemaking inside the psych unit's walls.

Which is why we might marvel, offer our fair share of respect to the powers of Providence. (Or *Plotting*?) The confluences of life. Because the very next night, Pepper snuck Sue into his room. She stayed with him until dawn. An actual sleepover. The kind of delight most folks take so for granted that they denigrate it with the term "one-night stand." But it's hard to dismiss a whole night when your trysts don't usually last an hour.

Pepper didn't manage this alone however. He had help.

From Loochie and Dorry.


Pepper hoped to have Sue over to his place. All their groping in front of others struck him as embarrassingly juvenile. Two people over forty should not be *wrasslin'* in ways that invite maximum humiliation unless they're in a Nancy Meyers film.

Pepper knew he had to get Sue back to his room. Not just so they could make love, but so they could be alone. As soon as she said she'd be gone in less than a week—as soon as Pepper realized she was serious—he began thinking about how he might yank her from the jaws of doom and deportation. The news had tickled that heroic nerve of his.

At six in the morning, everyone in the lounge—Pepper, Sue, Rachel, Marjolein, and Elliott—rose from their tables, collected magazines and newspapers and accordion files. The others didn't look at Pepper and Sue, still mortified by the way they'd been groping like teenagers. They all walked to the nurses' station and accepted their morning meds. Each went to his or her room to sleep.

Pepper and Sue took their meds and parted ways at the base of Northwest 3. He'd walked her as close to her door as hospital rules allowed. He watched her sashay down the hall. He felt the hot loss of her like a blush. That was the moment, right there, when he became determined to get her alone.

He'd taken his pills, seen Sue enter her room. As he wandered back to Northwest 2, the first stages of medicinal drowsiness bumped against the back of his legs like a dog, nearly tripping him. But when he reached his room, he resisted the urge to rest. Instead, he tried to drag the second bed, *Coffee's old bed*, to the middle of the room. As soon as he pulled it, the scrape of the metal feet echoed. Even though he had the door shut he felt sure the staff would hear. So he went to the bathroom and unspooled reams of toilet paper. He bunched it into balls and tucked the paper under the two legs at the head of Coffee's bed. Enough padding that the bed slid quietly once he lifted the other end. He did the same with his bed. Together they formed a cozy looking queen-sized.

He stretched the top sheets so they covered both mattresses. Tucked the sheets around them so it looked like one mattress. He fluffed the thin pillows. Got down on his hands and knees and swept the entire floor with his bare hands. (There were no new rat droppings, thank goodness.) If he could get Sue in the room tomorrow, how unsexy would it be to ask her to wait while he made all these changes? Imagine her clipping news articles on the floor while he worked up a sweat in the wrong way. Better to do this now, risk having the staff see it and make him take it apart, than to wait until his woman was with him. He knew that seduction was 96 percent preparation. (The other 4 percent was brushing your teeth.)

When Pepper finished, he actually felt reenergized, so he went out to get breakfast. He didn't eat much of it. Instead he pocketed the cereal box and palmed the milk carton. (He checked the expiration date; it was still good.) If Sue got hungry, he'd offer her a late-night dessert of Cocoa Puffs. He walked the midnight meal back to his room. He drew the room's curtains. What else to do at this point?

Get some sleep, Pepper. Tonight is going to be a motherfucker.

# 28

THAT NIGHT, PEPPER didn't drag Sue to the far table. She moved to that spot and Pepper tugged her back. She didn't like that.

"Tired of me already," she said, trying to make it sound playful, which only made her sound more wounded instead.

Pepper pulled her to one of the tables closest to the television set. Heatmiser had to hump his chair two spaces to the left so they could get around him and sit. This made the kid grumble, but neither of them noticed. Redhead Kingpin and Still Waters took notice, and Sue felt a twitch of embarrassment. This time because she'd let this man influence her in a way the other two would never allow.

That small shame is what made Sue ignore Pepper once they sat down. A different table, but she still had her materials. She perused her newspapers with an intensity she hadn't shown in days. Pepper remained fantastically unaware until he tried to take Sue's hand. She pulled away. He tried a second time, thinking she was being playful, and got more of the same. He felt a tension growing between them.

Ask her something, Pepper. About herself. Her work.

He peered under her chair. "How come that file says 'No Name'?" He pointed to the one under her desk.

Sue hadn't heard him because she was busy scolding herself. It was stupid to get close with a man when she was about to be deported! It was childish to wish the two of them might run off somewhere. And to abandon her two friends now, just because this guy started sniffing around. She ought to gather her things and leave the table, hole up in her room until the folks from Immigration came. At least there'd be diginity in that.

Three times Pepper asked Sue about her "No Name" file until, finally, Redhead Kingpin yelled at him from the next table. "I'll explain it if it'll make you shut up."

Embarrassed, Pepper stomped over to Redhead Kingpin, and stood over her with his arms crossed.

"Okay. Explain."

To her credit, Redhead Kingpin didn't return the wrath. Besides, she *wanted* to explain. Why work so hard on something and keep it to herself?

She had a manila accordion folder, just like Sue's. Written in red marker the same two words: "No Name." She stood and undid the cord that held the manila folder closed. She turned it upside down. Articles and magazine clippings fell across the tabletop. A downpour. Hundreds of clippings. They covered the table. They spilled off the side and fluttered to the floor. The sound was like the crackle of footsteps in fallen leaves.

As soon as she was done, Still Waters, at the next table, stood up. She had her own manila accordion folder. On the side, two words written with red crayon. "No Name."

Still Waters came to the redhead's table. She turned her folder over and let the clippings fall. Across the tabletop and onto the floor.

Last came Sue. Who didn't care if Pepper understood but at that moment, she was standing with her friends. No matter how wild or theatrical this seemed, she was with them. Sue turned her manila folder upside down. The clippings fell on the table, cascaded to the floor. Hundreds of them, just like the others. When it was finished, Pepper couldn't even see his feet.

All four of them were up to their ankles.

But in what?

"What you see here is the work that we've been doing here at Northwest for a total of eleven years."

To Pepper's great surprise, Still Waters was talking. She didn't look at him, didn't look up at all, but her voice resounded loudly. With confidence.

Pepper looked at the clippings. Some were yellow and brittle with age. Others showed fresh ink. Some pieces were long, accompanied by photos, but only a few. They were all, basically, death notices.

"These are just the fatalities we know about," Still Waters said. She nudged her foot through the pile. "Clipped out of newspapers we could get our hands on."

"Is Coffee's article in there?" Pepper asked. "Dr. Anand showed it to me. Did you see it?"

"It's there," Redhead Kingpin said.

Pepper stepped backward gingerly, out of the pile of papers, as if he'd been standing on a corpse.

"Coffee's got written," Still Waters said. "But people like this, people like us, usually don't even rate a paragraph. No money, sometimes no family, maybe not even a marked grave. *No names.*"

"You keep these to remember them," Pepper said.

"You've got it," the redhead said. She touched the top of Still Waters' head. "Marjolein here, she's got the biggest heart of anyone I've ever known. She's the one who started clipping. It hurt her to think of people just reading the paper, folding up these names, and throwing them away."

"So these folders are like a kind of war memorial," Pepper said.

Still Waters didn't look up but she nodded. "I like that."

Behind them Heatmiser said, "You guys are kind of making a mess, man."

Sue and Pepper and Still Waters and the Redhead Kingpin turned to look at Heatmiser. Would the women eviscerate him?

Heatmiser scratched his head absently. "Staff'll probably take all that from you if they see it like that."

A fine point. The man had saved himself a disemboweling. The women scooped articles back into their manila folders by the handful. They didn't bother to figure out which was whose. Pepper even got on one knee and passed clippings to Sue in great bunches, handfuls of epitaphs.

When they were almost done a terrific scream came down the hall. Terrific meaning *intense*. Terrific meaning *awesome* and *astounding*. Terrific meaning causing great *fear*.

A howl, coming from Northwest 3. It sounded so bad that Rachel and Marjolein dropped their folders on the table and booked it toward the ruckus. Pepper and Sue followed. Heatmiser didn't run after them. For one perfect moment he was alone in the lounge.

He climbed onto his chair. After a moment's hesitation he climbed onto the empty table. Then he sang, just loud enough for his fragile falsetto to fill the room. "You disappoint me, you people raking in on the world." His voice was beautiful and tender. He took a breath, sang louder. "The devil's script sells you the heart of a blackbird." Standing on the table he threw his arms out and took a bow. With his eyes closed he really could hear thunderous applause. He smiled so brightly that he shined.

The others tracked the screams, which continued, and grew louder. The staff leapt from their station. Nurse Washburn fumbled, trying to unlock one of the drawers. She cursed herself for her clumsiness, which only slowed her down more. The two orderlies on duty moved much faster. One bounded over the top of the desk.

The doors on Northwest 2 and 3 opened with the same quickness. Patients streamed out, most groggy, some smiling, pleased by the disturbance; it was something new.

It was Loochie Gardner.

Getting her ass kicked.

By an old woman.

When Pepper and Sue finally reached Northwest 3, they had trouble seeing clearly. There were too many spectators in the way. Pepper had to go on his toes to see over everyone else. Sue was out of luck.

"What is it?" Sue shouted. "Who is it?!"

"It's Dorry," Pepper said. "She's scalping Loochie."

The two women, young and old, were wrestling on the floor. The patients had formed a circle around them like this was a school yard fight. Dorry was on top. Loochie struggled. Her blue knit cap had already been snatched off. Everyone could see the girl's patchy scalp. Except it looked even worse now. More hair had been pulled out. The kid almost looked like a Hare Krishna, completely bald except for a little topknot. That last handful of hair was in Dorry's clutches. And Dorry seemed determined to have it out, too.

"Get off me!" Loochie cried. She sounded scared. Pepper couldn't blame her. The howls they'd heard had come from the kid.

"Get her off me!" Loochie begged. She grabbed at the last of her hair. There were small dots of blood on her scalp, where other strands had recently been yanked out.

The two orderlies cut through the crowd, but were clearly confused. They would've assumed they were coming to save Dorry from Loochie, but obviously that wasn't the case. Even though the orderlies both saw what everyone else just saw—Dorry laying the smackdown on Loochie—they still grabbed Loochie. It was like their minds had delivered a verdict long before their eyes could judge the evidence. They pulled the girl's hands away from her head, a man holding each of her wrists.

"What the fuck?!" Loochie yelled as the orderlies worked to restrain *her*. Even the other patients agreed.

"That's not right!" shouted the Redhead Kingpin.

Wally Gambino raised one hand high and whipped his extended fingers to make a snapping sound. "That shit is *cold*, yo! Y'all are *foul*."

Mr. Mack's face had a pillow crease from where he'd been sleeping just moments before. He had his sport coat on, but had only managed to get one arm through its sleeve. He pointed at Dorry and Loochie. "I am so tired of these two. Throw 'em both in lockup! It's folks like them who make life hard in here for the rest of us. They're enemies of the state! That's how I see it."

Mr. Mack slapped to his right, reaching for Frank Waverly's elbow. But Frank Waverly stepped away and Mr. Mack swatted the air. Mr. Mack looked up at his friend, but Frank Waverly didn't return his gaze, and Mr. Mack sneered, "Well fuck you, too, then."

In a moment the orderlies would realize their mistake. They'd grabbed the wrong woman. They were about to be given unambiguous proof.

Dorry leapt at Loochie, whose arms were still being held. She was defenseless. Dorry got hold of that last little knot of Loochie's hair and she wrenched it so hard Pepper swore he heard the stuff tear out of Loochie's head. It sounded like a siren wailing. Or maybe that was just the kid.

Loochie's body bucked forward so hard that Dorry knocked backward. The old woman stumbled and bumped against a wall. The orderlies let go of Loochie and she scrambled away to the opposite wall. The kid's scream cut off immediately and she just sat there, holding her now totally bald head. Loochie's mouth hung open, a terrible gasp in her throat. And a moment later she did cry. It was horrible and high-pitched, like a newborn's night cries. And every person in the hall who'd ever raised a child felt the same stab of horror and sympathy and overwhelming anxiety, and suddenly they were nearly crying, too.

The Haint slipped through the crowd. In her wrinkled purple pantsuit she got down beside Loochie and put her arms around the girl's head. Pepper thought Loochie would pull away, but she didn't. She rested her head against the older woman's shoulder. Loochie wept.

The two orderlies finally hemmed Dorry up. Each grabbed an arm and lifted the old woman who hardly seemed to notice them. Dorry hadn't been softened by Loochie's cries. She growled at Loochie even now.

"You say it one more time. One more! And I'll bite off your fucking tongue."

Loochie gulped and gasped. She kept one hand on top of her tender head. She watched Dorry for a moment. She pulled her head away from the Haint's shoulder. Despite the pain, there remained another quality to Loochie Gardner, probably the most essential. That kid was stubborn. She sniffed and swallowed, clearing her throat.

"Say it," Dorry said, grinning with loathing. "Say it. *Say it and see.*"

Loochie pulled away from the Haint. She sat straight. Met Dorry's gaze. Then, as calmly as she could, Loochie spoke the phrase she'd been repeating for six weeks now; while Pepper was off falling in love, Loochie had been tormenting Dorry with this chant—in the lounge, in the hall, when passing Dorry's room—anywhere and everywhere for a month and a half.

"*He's my son,*" Loochie chanted. "*He's my son!*"

Dorry strained forward and the orderlies holding her buckled. They gasped as they tried to keep the old woman back. They feared Dorry, just a little bit, right then.

Dorry didn't have any rage left. The orderlies held her arms up but the rest of her crumpled. "I told you I was *sorry,*" Dorry moaned. "I said it and I said it."

"And Coffee's still dead." Loochie spoke so evenly it was eerie.

Then Nurse Washburn arrived.

She waded through the patients. She'd finally unlocked the drawer. She carried a needle, full of the great immobilizer. Hearing Coffee's name made Pepper remember his roommate. Coffee's last moment. Pepper looked up. *Kofi's blood up there, on the ceiling.* The nurse injected Dorry, in front of everyone. Then one orderly escorted her back to her room.

After that, the nurse went to her knees and pulled bandages from a shirt pocket and administered to Loochie's scalp.

And at this moment, Pepper realized he had his chance.

The nurses' station sat empty; the staff were all occupied. The patients had yet to filter back toward their rooms. Pepper and Sue, at the rear of the crowd, were suddenly invisible.

But it wouldn't last.

Sue stood on her toes, one hand against Pepper's forearm for balance, taking in what she could. Pepper pulled away from her grip. He touched the small of her back. She looked at him. He nodded toward Northwest 2. She looked back at the nurses' station, at the patients clustered in the hall. She understood. Pepper put his hand out and Sue took it.

He walked her to his place.

# 29

THEY ENTERED HIS room. The lights were out. Only moonlight filtered in through the windows and clarified the space. Strange
to come from the fight in Northwest 3 and step into this quiet room.
When Pepper shut the door behind them, the distance seemed even
greater. Their heart rates were still up. Their eyes still wide with surprise. So the two of them were out of place in here, too, at least for a
moment. They stayed right at the lip of the room. They didn't step in
any farther yet. Sue raised her right hand and stuck out her pointer
finger. She spun it in a little circle.

"That was crazy," she said.

"So to speak," Pepper added.

They both laughed because what they'd just seen was terrible and
surprising, and those feelings had to come out. Then they stopped
laughing just as abruptly. They stood in silence a little while.

Finally, Sue grabbed Pepper's right thumb.

"This is nicer," she said.

They were slowing down. Their shoulders loosened. Their jaws
unclenched. They were finally ready. They walked farther into the
room.

They reached the beds, but didn't sit down. Sue let go of Pepper's
thumb, and ran her hands across the top sheet.

"It's like we're in a hotel," she whispered.

He scooped her up, swayed her in his arms, and settled her onto the mattresses. The metal frames creaked, but they weren't very loud. Pepper looked down at Sue. She shut her eyes.

"That's much better," she said.

He climbed on top of her. He kissed her on the forehead. He kissed each of her closed eyes. As his lips touched her face, he imagined a fire in his belly, growing and growing. And each time he kissed her, the heat traveled from his lips to her skin. The more the fire grew, the warmer his kisses became. He wanted to put her hand on his stomach so she could touch his hearth. When he finally kissed her lips, she rose up to meet him.

Her mouth full of embers, just like his.

They undressed each other. Not fast and wild, not tearing off stuff. All that would make too much noise. They had to be cautious. They were passionate, but could still see the chain-link fence outside his windows. They couldn't forget where they were.

So they got off the bed and she undid the zipper of his pants. Slid the slacks down. He put one hand on her shoulder as he stepped out and kicked the pants away. He slid her sweater off and undid the buttons of her nightdress. She raised her arms and he pulled it over her head. Finally both were just in their underwear. Sue wasn't wearing a bra.

Pepper pointed at her chest.

"I like those nipples," he said.

She forgot herself and jumped on him. He spun around as if he couldn't handle her weight. They fell back on the beds together. Now the frames made a powerful squeal. Much more noise than when he'd laid her on alone.

They stopped moving.

Both watched the bottom of the closed door and waited for shadows to appear. The specters of the staff. Pepper and Sue gave it a minute. An actual minute. She counted to sixty in a quiet whisper. But no one came.

Sue returned to climbing over Pepper's body until those nipples he'd admired were right over his face. He kissed one while the other tickled his shoulder. Then he traded. He nipped at them very lightly.

"Do you have gums?" she whispered. "Or teeth?"

He bit her nipples harder. She wriggled with happiness.

He slid back on the beds now, using his elbows to move. And she slid off him so they lay side by side. They turned to each other and kissed again. He reached around and squeezed her thigh. Moved his hand up and felt her butt. Oh, that butt! He smacked it. The sound seemed hellaciously loud.

Stop.

His hand hung in midair.

They watched the door again.

Counted all the way to sixty, again.

Pepper brought his hand back down, lightly resting it on her thigh.

"I think spanking's too risky," he whispered.

They both took a moment to feel unhappy about that.

"Let's get under the covers," Sue said.

They clambered around on the two mattresses, trying not to make too much noise, and trying not to separate the makeshift double bed. It took a little work. Once they were under the sheets, they'd even worked up faint sweats. Each could see perspiration on the other's forehead.

Pepper rubbed at his hairline and looked at his moist fingertips.

"This is just pathetic," he said.

Sue couldn't answer him because she was laughing. They were so ridiculous. But in the good kind of way she hadn't enjoyed in too damn long. She covered her mouth, but that didn't quite do it, so she rolled over and rested her face against a pillow and kept laughing.

Pepper touched her back firmly.

He rubbed between her shoulder blades, pressing against her spine, running his fingers down to her butt. But he didn't grab her ass. He brought his hand up and down, kneading her spine.

Sue stopped laughing and relaxed. She breathed deeply. Her body seemed to fall deeper into the bed. She raised her feet slightly and dropped them again. She groaned. So Pepper slid closer to her, and he pressed his thumb into the muscles just below her neck. When he pressed there, her feet raised slightly again, and dropped. She shimmied on her stomach, rubbing side to side, letting the good feeling of his touch pass throughout her body.

Now Pepper slid his hands under the sheets and plucked at the band of her underwear. He lifted the band and let it snap back against her skin. He then slid her panties down and lifted the sheets so he could really appreciate her posterior. He liked seeing it so much. Sue sensed this so she swayed it, side to side, while he watched. People compare that kind of movement to a clock's pendulum or a metronome, but really they must be fucking joking. To compare a woman's butt with anything man-made is to denigrate the first and elevate the second.

Pepper finally slid her panties down as far as he could. Then she kicked them off.

He rolled on his back now and she lifted her head from the pillow. Her face looked a bit darker because she was flushed. She smiled, and showed her small teeth. They were kind of gray, not even. He was so happy to see them that he smiled, too.

Sue lifted the covers so she could pull down Pepper's underwear, but right then her hand stopped moving. His underwear was already gone.

"When did you take them off?" Sue asked. "When did you have time?"

Pepper jutted out his chin and smirked as if he'd achieved some great scientific breakthrough and could not be cajoled into sharing the secret.

"Never mind," Sue whispered. She wanted to kiss that goofy look right off Pepper's face. She climbed on top of him and began.


"*That* was good," Pepper said.

The sun hadn't risen yet. It was only a little after four in the morning. They'd fucked, then dozed, and now woke together as couples all over the world like to do.

"You're right," Sue said. "You're right."

Pepper smiled at the ceiling. He looked out the window, where he could see only the tops of the trees, and a sky the color of cobwebs. It was going to be an overcast day.

"They're not really deporting you, right?"

"No," she admitted. "They're *trying* to deport me. I have to stand before a judge one more time before it's official."

He rolled onto his side toward her. "Come on," he said, sounding like a child whose older sibling is trying to scare him. "Stop playing. Tell me the truth."

Sue said, "I went to Canada, from China, when I was four. Me and my older sister, together. We were inside a shipping container with another family. I don't remember them. My sister said they weren't very nice to us. We had buckets for the bathroom. A little generator inside so we had power. I don't remember any of this. It's all what my sister told me. She was fourteen."

Sue lay on her back. She looked at the ceiling as if she could see this history playing up there, like a home movie.

"When we reached Vancouver, they took me and my sister out, and the *same day* they drove us into the U.S. I was so small they put me in a little suitcase."

Sue raised both hands and held them apart. A piece of carry-on luggage, no larger than that.

"They got us through the border and drove us down to a city called Everett. They let us out right on the street. In front of a place called the Imagine Children's Museum. Maybe they thought that was pretty funny. Our family had paid to get us to San Francisco, but we didn't make it that far. What could we do? The driver told us to get out, so we got out. We didn't know what San Francisco looked like. And we weren't with that other family anymore. There were just two of us. Two girls. Four and fourteen."

Sue pulled her covers down until her whole upper body was exposed. The small brown nipples hardened in the morning's slight chill. Pepper put his hand on one breast and touched the nipple with the tip of his thumb.

"My sister was strong. She found Chinese like us. *Hakka* Chinese. In *Everett*. They helped us contact our aunt and uncle back in China."

"What about your parents?" Pepper asked.

"They both died in a hard winter," she said matter-of-factly. "I never really knew them."

A pair of footsteps passed in the hallway. Pepper and Sue stayed quiet until they were sure the person had moved on.

"We got as far south as Portland. That's where we stopped. No more money. So that's where we found people to stay with. My sister took a job right away. I started working a couple of years later. By the time I turned sixteen, I'd been working for eight years. I went to school during the day and worked most evenings until midnight. In restaurants and markets, always with my sister. She never went to school. It was a lot, but it was okay."

She slid Pepper's big hand down from her chest to her belly and held him there.

"Once I got much older, we split up. It had to happen eventually. My sister found me a job in Florida. I was already thirty-four, but I was more scared of making that trip than the whole journey from China! Or maybe I just *remember* how scared I was because I was older. Plus, I was going alone."

"Why did you have to leave her at all?" Pepper asked. He found himself spinning, right there on the bed. What had he ever complained about? A brother who didn't get along with him? Being raised by a decent mom and dad in Queens?

"You have to go where there's work. We didn't leave China because we wanted a long boat ride!"

"Sorry," Pepper said. "So Florida. For a job."

"Yes. But that's when it all went really bad. When I had my sister around, I don't know, she could help me if I got confused. If I made some mistakes of thinking. They were nice at the job in Florida. In West Palm Beach. I was a waitress. But they had their own problems to worry about. They couldn't help me every time I got *confused*. And it kept happening to me, more and more. I basically lived alone."

Sue pressed her hand down on Pepper's. He squeezed her soft stomach. She liked the hold.

"I lived like that, four years. Five years? I worked. I sent some money to my sister, who sent more money back to my aunt and uncle in China. I talked with my sister a lot. I even dated a little bit."

Sue looked over at Pepper and pinched his chin.

"Don't be jealous."

Pepper hadn't brushed his teeth last night; they'd leapt right into bed. And he'd slept for a few hours. So by now he had a little *wolf breath* going. After she let go of his chin, he blew in Sue's face, and she waved one hand in front of her nose. "That's not attractive," she said.

He kissed her more tenderly, and she returned the kiss.

"Then what?" Pepper asked. "I still don't see how you got here."

"After five years, I had enough. Anyway, Florida had exploded. Nobody had jobs, nobody had money. On the block where I lived, four different families just abandoned their homes. Where did they go? I saw one family; they moved down the road and were living out of a motel room. It was hard times in Florida and I didn't want to stay there anymore. The restaurant was probably going to close anyway, just like everything else. I told my sister I was coming back to her in Portland.

"I spoke good English. Even you noticed that. I picked it up fast because I was so young when we came. I could find another job. I told her all this. She was my sister. She *knew* me. Maybe she could hear in my voice that I was having trouble with my thoughts. Maybe I sounded more confused than I thought. She said okay, take the bus. Cheap and you don't always need to show ID.

"I was waiting for that bus when they picked me up. Immigration cops who spend their whole day at the Greyhound station! I never knew there was such a thing. They asked to see my visa and I laughed at them."

"Why did you *laugh*?" Pepper fell back on the bed, as if she'd made such an obvious and stupid mistake.

"I thought they were kidding! Do you know how many times people said something like that to me in Florida? 'Where's your papers?' 'Show me your passport.' The white people and the black people and the Puerto Ricans. They thought it was so funny. So when these two men said it, I thought it was just another joke. Being mean. But they didn't like me laughing. They took me, just like that. I spent a year in a Florida jail. A psychiatrist saw me and prescribed medication, just like this place. But the guards weren't used to people like me. Or they just didn't care. They refused to give me the medication unless I cooperated with all their rules first. But without the medication, I was too confused to cooperate! By the time I got out, I couldn't even say my own name."

"Your lawyer got you out?"

Sue shook her head. "If I had stolen something or stabbed somebody, that would put me in criminal court. Then I would have a right to an attorney. You don't get an attorney in immigration court. That's not your right. They give you a translator. But I didn't need one of those. I understood English fine. Even the translator could see I was just having trouble with my thoughts. But she would just hold my hand and tell me how sorry she felt about it. Sometimes she cried.

"But in the courtroom, whenever I tried to answer the judge for myself, like if he asked my name or something, he would yell at me to wait for the translator. I said, 'I don't need the translator. I need my lithium.' But that only made the judge mad. When I tried to speak again, to explain, he finished with the case. I remember the words exactly: 'The respondent, after proper notice, has failed to appear.' I was right there when he said it but they put it in the record. And if I don't 'appear,' then they don't have to have a trial. The judge can just make his verdict. He ordered them to deport me back to China. That's it. The end. *I will die now.* That's what I thought when he gave the sentence. *I will die.*"

Pepper tried to imagine Sue inside that courtroom. Standing alone before that judge, who refused to see her.

"I spent another six months being held in Glades County," Sue said. "Waiting for them to throw me across the water. All this time, and my sister never knew what happened. For her, it's like I just stepped into a hole and disappeared. I'm scared for me, but I feel so bad for her. Every day she must be crying."

Pepper climbed over Sue, out of the bed, and went to the bathroom. He had a plastic cup in there and he filled it with cold water. He came back to the bed, sat on the edge and gave it to Sue. "What's this for?" she asked.

"I thought you could use a drink."

Sue sat up, the covers bunching right over her waist. She took the cup gratefully and smiled.

She sniffed it. She grimaced.

"This is water."

"Well, what did you think?"

"The way you said it, I thought you had some beer or something."

"Sorry," Pepper whispered. She shrugged. She sipped.

"So that's Florida. How'd you get to New York? How'd you get in here?"

"The police took us to church one day. Maybe for Easter. I didn't even ask to go, but they made everyone attend. It was a big church. So many people. Like *thousands*. We sat in the back. They only left two guards near us. Two men. I asked to use the bathroom. One guard came with me, but he couldn't go inside. Not at a nice church. So I went in, washed my face, and climbed out the window. Easy. I even went back to the same Greyhound station after I borrowed money from my old boss at the restaurant.

"I took a bus to New York because I thought there was enough Chinese here for me to hide. And maybe it was true. But when I came to the Port Authority, the immigration police were waiting for me! I couldn't believe it. Sometimes the world is broken and sometimes it works too well. I slipped right out of a church bathroom, no problem. I come to one of the most crowded cities on earth, and they pick me out five minutes after I get off the bus. But by then it had been a long time since I had my medication. I wasn't doing good. Laughing out loud for no reason. Shouting. Maybe the bus driver turned me in just because he was tired of me. They stuck me here until they can send me back to Florida. I'm a *fugitive*, Pepper. You just had sex with a fugitive."

Pepper took the plastic cup from Sue. "You're not a fugitive once you get caught. Then you're just a prisoner again."

Now, he wanted to go get her another cup of water, or maybe one for himself. Or to offer her the Cocoa Puffs, but that hardly seemed like enough. He wanted to do *something*. But what? Honestly. Dawn light hadn't crept into the room yet, but soon enough it would. The next day was arriving and their night together felt so brief.

*I'll be gone in less than a week.* That's what she'd said.

Pepper touched Sue's knee, the sheet so thin it hardly seemed to come between them. His throat felt warm and the back of his neck burned. "I don't want you to . . . You shouldn't have to . . ."

He couldn't finish.

Sue put her hand on top of his.

"I know," she said. "I know."

But what was she going to do? Was she supposed to comfort *him* about how he couldn't protect *her*? When she was the one actually facing extradition?

Fuck that.

Sue couldn't dredge up the patience. She also hadn't told him the straight truth. She'd told him she had less than a week before she'd be deported, but really it was happening later *today*. (Less than a week could mean six days, after all, or two.)

She couldn't dream of a better way to spend her last night. Sharing these feelings, those touches, with him. All that might've been ruined if he knew how close to the end they really were.

"Why are you so quiet now?" Sue asked.

Pepper lay with his right arm out and her head on his bicep. He closed his arm around her chest.

"I guess I was just imagining . . ."

"Tell me." .

"I was just picturing us out in the woods somewhere. And it's the middle of winter and no one else is anywhere around."

"That's nice," she whispered.

"And a tree snaps," Pepper said. "A big one. Maybe under the weight of too much snow. And the tree comes down *right on top of you*. And you're pinned underneath it. You can't get out. I have to find a way to lift it so you'll be okay."

Sue wriggled free from his forearm. "You're daydreaming about me getting killed?"

Pepper rolled over, confused. "I'm dreaming about saving you."

The first morning's light seeped into the room. Pepper saw Sue's face. She was watching him. Studying him.

"You actually think what you just told me is romantic," she said.

"It is romantic. If you think about it."

"If *you* think about it, your romantic dream includes the possibility that I will be paralyzed from the neck down."

"That's not how I meant it," he said.

Sue grabbed Pepper's arm, a mix of aggravation and affection. Her fingernails pressed into his skin.

"Your dream is about what *you* want to do, not what *I* need."

Pepper threw his hands up. "Well, what do you need? You want me to break you out of here? I'll do it. We can go on the run. I don't care."

Sue turned her back to Pepper and lay down. She reached back with one arm and pulled at him. He moved beside her, put his left arm around her chest, and pulled her closer. He squeezed Sue's ribs tight, just like she wanted. They faced the room's door. Eventually it would open but not yet. Behind them the sky had become a lighter gray. Sue said, "Did you ever finish the book about the painter?"

"Van Gogh," Pepper said. "Yes, I did."

"Okay, then, let me hear about that. We'll lie still and I'll listen to your voice. That's what I need. Tell me."

# 30

VINCENT VAN GOGH (pronounced "Van-GOCK" by the Dutch, and sundry pretentious American twits) was born in Groot-Zundert, Holland, in 1853 to Theodorus and Anna Van Gogh. The pair had three boys and three girls, and Vincent was the oldest. Their father, Theodorus, was a well liked, respected, but not terribly gifted preacher. Anna cared for the family and was also greatly loved.

In 1869, at sixteen, Vincent went to work at an art dealership, Goupil & Cie., which had ties to his uncle, and namesake, Vincent. Young Vincent was being groomed to join the trade. He worked with them in the Hague. In 1873 he moved to their offices in London. There, he roomed with a mother and daughter. He fell hard for the daughter, Ursula.

Ursula bumped him back, though. She was already engaged to another man. But Vincent was a sensitive dude and he took the news hard. Went into a depression and found solace in a deeper sense of religious faith. He also stopped rooming with Ursula and her mother. Considering the general trajectory of Vincent's adult life, this is about the most sensible thing he ever did.

He left Ursula's home but she hadn't left his heart. The man was depressed! So much so that his family worried and had him transferred to the Paris branch of the art dealership. But this only compounded his pain and Vincent worked less and less well. Instead, he spent all his free time holed up reading the Bible with a friend. And in 1876, twenty-three-year-old Vincent was fired from the art dealer's. His family had suggestions for what he should do next (they were a close bunch)—he could open his own shop, become a painter (his closest sibling and greatest friend, Theo, suggested this)—but Vincent decided to return to London to become a teacher.

Vincent got work at two different schools as a kind of curate, assisting the head of each institution. But he didn't last long there. Pretty quickly his uncle lined up a job at a bookshop. Vincent was a terrific reader his entire life, but wasn't enthusiastic about the bookstore. At twenty-four, Vincent switched gears again and decided to study theology. Some family members supported him in this plan, but others, like Uncle Vincent, were sick of his shit. The theology degree demanded *seven years* of study. There was some question as to whether Vincent had the seriousness, the fortitude, to concentrate on the subject for so long. Did he?

Nope!

Vincent stayed for only a year. He hated studying grammar and doing writing exercises. He didn't want to be an academic. He wanted to bring good cheer through the Gospels. That's it. Pretty soon his tutor agreed that Vincent was not cut out for theology school.

Instead, Vincent decided to become an evangelist in Belgium. This only required a certificate of study, no Latin or Greek, only three months of work at the School of Evangelization in Brussels. Around this time Vincent's parents wrote, in a letter, "that he deliberately chooses the most difficult path."

(We know so much about Vincent, about his family, because they were all wonderful letter writers, and many of those letters have survived. Vincent becomes famous for the letters he shared with his dear brother Theo but he wrote to many others, too.)

Back at the evangelical school it turned out that Vincent was a lousy student. He dressed strangely (meaning, he didn't pay much attention to his clothes and their care). He couldn't speak off the cuff, so he had to prepare all his remarks and read from the pages. And he didn't even do that very well. And worst of all, for the school's purposes, he wasn't "submissive." He argued with the school's leaders, didn't do exactly as told. When his three months of training were up, they refused to give him a position anywhere.

Much as he dealt with the aftermath of Ursula, Vincent took his failure at school pretty hard. He didn't eat, didn't sleep, got thin and weak. He was in a constant nervous state. This is around the first time that people close to him began to notice his "humour" and "constitution." To put it bluntly: They thought the boy was a little off. (Of course, they never came right out and stated this.)

Vincent's father came to Brussels to see him and used his influence to get Vincent a trial appointment in Wasmes, a small coal-mining town, for six months. He would get a very small salary, but he didn't get to give Bible lectures, teach children, and visit the sick—the things he actually wanted to do. He worked with the people of the mining town, but after six months his job wasn't renewed and Vincent left town. On foot, which would become a pretty standard method for him, since he never had money to spare for trains.

Time passed after the loss of the job, and Vincent lost his religious zeal. He fell into a funk and isolated himself. Theo and his parents started sending Vincent money just so he could eat, have a place to stay, that kind of stuff, but it wasn't much and wasn't regular.

Around this time, Vincent made pilgrimages to the studio of an artist he greatly admired named Jules Breton. He walked all the way to Breton's place in another town and was so intimidated and so ashamed of himself, that he just turned right back around and *walked all the way home*. Along the way, Vincent slept in haylofts or outdoors. He'd begun doing some art of his own, and he traded drawings for bread when he could, but his health deteriorated.

Finally, around 1880, Vincent declared himself a painter. He rented a room in a miner's home. (Vincent shared the room with the miner's children.) This was his first studio! He drew the miners, going to and from work. Sometimes he worked out in the garden. But in October of 1880 he moved to Brussels again to work in a small hotel. He needed the money, but he also wanted to meet other artists and Brussels offered more chances than the mining town. He wanted some camaraderie.

In 1881 Vincent moved back in with his parents. He had a good run with them but over the summer he met an older cousin, Kee. Kee was grieving over the loss of her husband and raising a four-year-old boy on her own. Vincent fell for her but she rejected him. Guess how Vincent reacted.

Yup.

This time he flipped out even harder. He didn't just go into a depression; he became irritable and unstable and pushed at this cousin, trying to win her over. It got so bad that the whole family was just embarrassed. Vincent had a really bad fight with his father over the matter and finally moved out. He returned to the Hague, and lived there for two years.

While he was there he met a new woman. She was poor, "rough," a heavy drinker, a fighter, and smallpox survivor. Also, possibly, a prostitute. In other words, Vincent hooked up with a *hoodrat*. And all the "fine" friends and family members got pissy about this. They told him this woman wasn't proper for him. And, in truth, Vincent and this woman don't sound like they were actually in love. Vincent had always wanted to do good, to help, and had failed at it again and again. This woman (admittedly only from Vincent's account) was having a hard time supporting herself and her son. If Vincent wanted to offer companionship and (nominal) financial support, why would she ever say no? So they stayed together, but it didn't last. Vincent still spent most of his money on art supplies, and not on the new family. Also, Vincent was a bit judgmental himself. He kept trying to change her ways. Eventually they parted.

In 1883 Vincent, despondent, returned to his parents' home. He lived with them for two more years. He argued with them a lot. (Folks give credit to Vincent's brother Theo, but Anna and Theodorus were *wonderful* to him, considering what a dick he could be.) In 1884 Vincent's mom suffered a fall and broke her leg, and Vincent, to everyone's great happiness, turned out to be a loving and attentive caretaker for her while she healed up. Good feeling returned to his relationship with his parents. And that's Vincent all over. Utterly selfish and magnificently selfless, all one or all the other, depending on the day.

While he was still with his parents, Vincent got one more chance at romance. This time with a neighbor's daughter. Maybe they weren't in love, but they seemed to enjoy each other's company, which is a hell of a lot of happiness sometimes. But the neighbor's family refused to accept the union. The daughter, in her despair, tried to commit suicide. (She lived.) Their relationship was over and Vincent seemed to lose hope entirely for that kind of pleasure in his life. (Pleasure meaning *love*, because he visited prostitutes plenty over the years.)

So, no love, but during this time, Vincent had been working constantly. He sketched and painted with fervor. The early stuff, like most early stuff, wasn't great but the man hoped that he *could* produce worthwhile art eventually. (From letter 106: "O Theo, Theo old boy, if only it might happen to me and that deluge of downcastness about everything which I undertook and failed at, that torrent of reproaches I've heard and felt, if it might be taken away from me and if I might be given the opportunity and the strength and the love required to develop and to persevere and to stand firm in that for which my Father and I would offer the Lord such heartfelt thanks.")

In 1885 Vincent's father died, after a long walk, right at the threshold of his home. Vincent moved out of his mother's home and went off painting people and scenes from the world around him. (During this time, he hoped to make a splash, do something great, be noticed, with a painting called *The Potato Eaters*. It's a dark, sludgy work, aping the style generally respected in the day. It didn't make him famous. It didn't sell. And for good reason. It *stinks*.)

In 1886 Vincent moved to Paris and lived with his brother Theo. Theo had joined the family business and worked as an art dealer. This time was good for Vincent. His health improved, and he even had an operation to replace almost all his teeth. (Because Vincent had lived on a diet of mostly beer and black bread—literally, bread so old it was going black, which was cheaper to buy than fresh bread—the majority of Vincent's teeth had fallen out. You know the reason he's not smiling in those self-portraits? It's not just because of his melancholy soul. It's because that poor bastard was practically toothless!) It was a good time for Vincent, but less so for Theo. As Vincent's parents learned, as nearly anyone who ever lived with Vincent learned, Vincent Van Gogh was an *asshole*. Often. Even his beloved Theo came to fight and dislike the brother he believed to be an artistic genius. (It's also worth noting that, all these years, Theo had been sending money to Vincent, wherever he was living, so he could spend as much time as possible painting and not holding a job. Despite this,Vincent treated Theo much the same as everyone. He was messy, argumentative, and bossy. During all the years they wrote to each other, there was one request Vincent made more than any other: Send more money! And Theo did.)

In 1888 Vincent left Theo. He now hit the creative high point of his life. It would last only two years. During that time he produced *thousands* of paintings and sketches. Theo worked his butt off to try to sell the stuff. He failed. Vincent produced, Theo believed, the world was blind.

This period, from 1888 on, was the time when Vincent did the stuff he became famous for. The romantic round. This was when he roomed with Paul Gauguin. (That didn't last.) Cut off a part of his ear in an absolute frenzy and presented it as a gift to a local prostitute. (She fainted.)

This was also the time when Vincent began his commitments to mental institutions. In 1889 Vincent's neighbors became tired of him and his antics, and they signed a petition to have him put away. Involuntary commitment, nineteenth-century style.

Vincent got out but soon after he commited himself to an asylum in Saint-Rémy. He stayed there for a year. While the paintings from 1888 show the style that would make him legendary—rich with color, sensory and explosive—the ones he made in 1889 began to show another side. The colors became duller here and there. A deep and lasting sadness seemed almost visible on the canvas.

In 1890 Vincent returned to Paris where he visited Theo, who had married a woman named Johanna. (The woman who would, really, take up the mantle of her husband and expose Vincent's genius to the world.) There he also met Theo and Johanna's first child, a son, named Vincent.

In May of 1890 Vincent left Paris. He went to Auvers to paint again.

On July 27, 1890, Vincent walked out into a field alone and shot himself in the chest with a revolver. (There have been rumors Vincent was shot by someone else and Vincent didn't name names, allowed everyone to think his death was pure suicide. Is it true? The evidence is sketchy at best. But the bullet wound is no rumor, nor is its effect.) The bullet didn't kill Vincent out in the field, so he *dragged himself* back to his home. A watch was kept as he lay in agonizing pain. Theo made it to town in time to see his brother still alive. On the morning of July 29, Vincent died of his wounds.

Of course now, over a century later, this end (and the death of Theo, from a complete breakdown six months later) is cast as some epic denouement. But imagine the article that might've run then. Or now. One that might've been creased and clipped by three (soon to be two) women late at night in the television lounge of Northwest. Maybe the headline would read this way: "Drifter Commits Suicide."

But, really, something like that wouldn't even be considered news.

# 31

PEPPER AND SUE fell asleep holding each other and stayed that way for another hour. Pepper woke first. To a familiar sound over his head. The faint *creaking*. Directly above their makeshift double bed. Over them.

Sue stretched next to him as she woke up. Even in the gray morning light she looked lovely to him. Who would've called either Pepper or Sue beautiful? Maybe his mother; her sister. Besides them? Just each other. Which was plenty right then.

"How long have you been awake?" Sue asked him.

"You hear that?" He pointed at the ceiling with his left hand.

She lay quietly. "I don't know what I'm listening for."

"Like a creaking sound. You don't hear it?"

Sue shut her eyes. She pursed her lips tight so she wouldn't breathe too loudly.

"I know that sound," she said quietly.

As soon as she said that, the creaking stopped.

She opened her eyes. Pepper scanned the ceiling and she joined him. They lay there, vigilant, for quite a while. But the creaking didn't return. Finally Pepper felt less fear and he remembered their talk from only hours ago. Pepper said, "What do you need, then?"

Sue looked at him, her mouth open with confusion.

"I was listening," Pepper said. "What do you need now?"

Before she could even answer him, she just flushed with happiness that he'd asked the question. He'd heard her. She kissed him for that.

But, of course, that didn't mean he could actually do anything. She wasn't going to take him up on the offer of a prison break. Look how well the fugitive plan had worked out for her before. Anyway, she didn't want to do that to Pepper. He'd come in to New Hyde with a local case, no need to leave with something federal. Besides, she didn't really like being an outlaw. It was exhausting.

"I need my sister," Sue said.

"So let's get in touch with her."

Sue said, "I've tried that. I called the number I had for her in Portland. Then I tried every number I could with my last name in the whole city. Do you know how many Hongs there are in Portland? Too many. But I never reached her. I think she must have left. And I don't know where she might have moved to now."

"Why would she leave?" Pepper asked. "Wasn't she expecting you?"

"A year and a half ago. That's when she expected me. She probably thinks I'm dead. Maybe she left Portland so she could forget me. If she did, I don't blame her."

And Sue really wouldn't blame her sister. Sometimes hope just fades out. But that generosity, that pragmatism, didn't make the next steps of Sue's life any less frightening. The United States government would send her back to China, and maybe she'd find her aunt and uncle waiting at the airport. They'd see her, deep in a depression (compounded by great *confusion* if they didn't supply her with her meds during the trip), and what would her aunt and uncle do for her? Think the United States has a bad way with the mentally ill? Holy shit, you better check out the rest of the world. Here's what Sue could look forward to in China: arrive at the airport, likely be thrown into some kind of detention center, and someday she could look forward to dying. Any wonder the lady had turned tense?

Pepper was still focused on a solution. He said, "If she left Portland, where do you think she might go?"

"How would I know?"

"You know her. Think about her. Would she move east?"

She wanted to tear the lips off Pepper's face right then, but she knew that anxiety, the anger, wasn't about him. He was just talking things through. Why not humor him? "I think she'd stay out west. She liked it out there, except for the weather."

"Okay. So she stays on the West Coast, but she wants to be somewhere warm. Los Angeles?"

"There's a lot of Chinese, which she would like, but I don't think she'd go that far. Maybe San Francisco. Or somewhere near there. That's where we were supposed to end up at first, anyway. But what does it matter? God, Pepper, you're doing it again! Stop trying to fix things! Just *shut up*. It's like even *you're* trying to kill me."

"You make me sound like a monster," Pepper muttered.

She took a breath and when she came back, she put her head on his chest. She listened to the thick thumping sound of his heart.

"I'm sorry, Pepper. I am. Hard times make people scared. And scared people see monsters everywhere."

Pepper nodded, he wasn't offended, but before he could explain he caught himself. He lifted his head.

"Isn't Oakland right next to San Francisco?"

Which is the moment when the room's door *blasted* open. Pepper wouldn't be blamed for having flashbacks to when the NYPD's tactical unit had powered through the front door. Both Pepper and Sue recoiled like they'd been sprayed.

Miss Chris stood in the doorway.

Sue grabbed the sheets and pulled them up to her neck. Pepper stammered, just repeating the word *we* until it didn't even sound like itself. Just a stream of noise.

"We, we, we, uh, we . . ."

But Miss Chris wasn't even looking at them. She'd opened the door and reached in to flick the lights on. (Didn't even have to turn her head to find the switch, that's how well she knew the rooms.) Miss Chris shouted, "Wake-up hour! Come for breakfast!"

Then she walked to the door across the hall and did the same.

Door banged open, light flicked on. "Wake-up hour! Come for breakfast!"

Then Miss Chris moved ten feet down the hall to rooms 8 and 9.

Pepper and Sue still shivered there where they were. Sue took another moment before she let go of the sheets and Pepper still hadn't stopped blabbering.

"We, we, uhhh, we, uh . . ."

Sue touched the side of his face and that calmed him down.

"Stop talking," she said.

They looked at each other quietly. From down the hall they heard the routine.

Door banging, the click of the light switch being flicked.

"Wake-up hour! Come for breakfast!"

Which is when Pepper and Sue *laughed*. All that fear turned to its happy opposite. They clutched each other as Miss Chris awakened the patients in room 10. And rather than getting up, getting dressed, Pepper and Sue settled down again. Just enjoy the last minute, fuck it. They spooned one last time. "Whose room is that?" Sue asked, pointing to the one across from his.

"Room six. That's . . . Japanese Freddie Mercury."

Sue lay quiet a moment. Down the hall, they heard Miss Chris, at room 11.

Sue said, "You mean *Glenn*?"

"Is that his name? How would I know? The guy never speaks."

Sue laughed quietly. "That's not right, Pepper."

Pepper raised himself on his right elbow, so he could lean over and see her face. "You don't think he looks like a Japanese Freddie Mercury?"

"Because of the teeth?"

"Well, it's not because he's a great singer."

They watched the open door of the room across the hall now. Pepper and Sue wanted to see him, since they'd just been talking about him. Pepper even wanted to call him out by name. *Hey, Glenn!* If Sue knew his name he must be able to talk, the man just hadn't spoken to him. Then he thought maybe Glenn only spoke to other Asian people like Sue. Which seemed kind of racist to him. Then Pepper just had to admit he'd never introduced himself to the guy, probably he was just shy and maybe that—the simple, clear explanation, as Dr. Anand would stress—was the truth.

They watched Glenn's room, but could see little more than the floor and a pair of blue footies that Glenn had probably kicked off before going to sleep. They saw the same double windows as in Pepper's room but Glenn's faced the New Hyde parking lot, a sight much worse than Pepper's lawn and trees. Then one of the ceiling panels in room six shook.

"What?" Sue whispered.

The wood-fiber ceiling tile buckled. There was a weight, on the other side, pressing down.

"No," Pepper said.

Miss Chris reached room 12 (there were sixteen rooms in each hall). The door slammed open. From this far off, they couldn't hear the light switch flip up. Miss Chris gave the same call as before.

"Wake-up hour! Come for breakfast!" Her breakfast call camouflaged the sound of the ceiling tile when it snapped. The two pieces of the panel dangled for a moment before tumbling to the ground.

Sue and Pepper watched but couldn't speak now. They couldn't move. They forgot about Miss Chris. What could her wrath compare to the sky falling in?

Just a moment later, they watched as something plopped out from the darkness overhead. It landed on the tiled floor.

A rat.

It was as long as Pepper's forearm if you included the tail. Its fur was gray. It fell and stayed there on the floor, on its side, stunned from the impact. Its paws were curled close to its body. The long whiskers on the right side of its face stood up slightly. Every few seconds, they quivered.

"That thing must weigh twenty pounds," Pepper said. "To break through the ceiling like that."

And yet, despite his disgust, Pepper felt such relief. It was a rat, yes, but only a rat. At New Hyde that almost seemed like a happy ending. "People say there's thousands of them living up there," Sue said.

"Rats in the *walls*?"

"On the second floor," Sue clarified.

The rat's whole body shook once now. Its paws clawed the air.

Slowly at first, but then more frantically. Until it worked up enough momentum to rock itself upright.

Miss Chris reached room 14 now, and Pepper wondered if there were even any patients in all these rooms. Maybe it didn't matter. Do every room quickly and you'll get everyone. Stop and check, room to room, and you'll waste more time.

"Wake-up hour! Breakfast!"

Now that it was up, the rat scurried right out of Glenn's room. It crossed into the hall, hustled into Pepper's room, shot under the bed, came out the other side, and went right for the box of Cocoa Puffs Pepper had brought to the room the night before. It had been close enough that he could've reached for it if Sue had been hungry. Now the rat had sniffed it out.

The rat reached the box of sugared cereal. Pepper and Sue watched, absolutely gobsmacked. It bumped the box so the box fell flat. Then in one swift motion, the rat clamped its teeth into the nutritional-information chart. Prey captured, the rat plowed right back under the bed. It came out the other side, wobbling a bit. It kept its head up so the box didn't drag on the floor. Imagine a man carrying a *sofa* in his arms on his own. Better yet, imagine a man carrying *your* sofa off like that. That little rat gangster shuffled through the open doorway and into the hall.

"Vermin!" They heard Miss Chris shouting from down the hall. The rat didn't return to room six, it fled down the hall, away from Miss Chris, headed for the nurses' station. In a moment, Miss Chris, moving with more agility than Pepper had seen her employ in more than two months, came shuttling past the open doorway.

"Vermin!" she shouted to the staff members at the far end of the hall. "Get the broom!"

Who would win? The staff or the rat?

Hard to say which side Pepper was rooting for.

Sue and Pepper lay there in shocked silence.

Sue finally looked at Pepper. "Why do you keep cereal on the floor?"

Pepper laughed and thought about how to explain, but any response was interrupted when he looked over Sue's shoulder into Glenn's room and saw a pair of feet dangle down from that hole in the ceiling.

Pepper opened his mouth but nothing escaped.

Sue turned in time to see the legs appear. Thin and pallid. The skin mottled and loose. They swayed, forward and back, floating in Glenn's room. The soles of the feet looked gray and hard.

Then the figure dropped. They saw the lean, cadaverous body. The impossible, monstrous head.

The Devil stood in room six. It gazed at them. "Do you see that?" Pepper whispered.

"Yes," Sue said.

Even from across the hall they heard it breathing, heaving.

And if Miss Chris, the rest of the staff, the rest of the *world* was making any noise, they sure couldn't hear it now.

Pepper held Sue's left arm and she grabbed his hand tightly.

The last time he'd seen the Devil it had been bleating with panic; Loochie's hands had wrestled its horns back and Pepper had been draped across the backs of those skeletal legs. It had seemed so weak for a moment. Spent. All the vigor knocked out of it. Maybe Coffee could've blinded it with those two needles.

If only Dorry hadn't been there!

Then maybe it wouldn't be here now.

But there it was.

The Devil pulled its lips back, exposing teeth the color of oyster shells. The tangles of fur below its chin were clumped and wet; they swung like curtains of moss. Pepper heard a muffled sniff. But it wasn't the monster this time. Sue was crying.

"It's okay," he whispered. He kissed her cheek.

"I heard *you* cry once," Pepper said loudly. "You were *scared.*" He wasn't talking to Sue.

The Devil turned its enormous head sideways, as if to see Pepper more clearly. One gray-white eye fixed on him. It inhaled deeply. It took two steps toward them.

It grabbed room six's doorknob for balance.

"You're not getting her," Pepper gloated. "At least she's leaving."

Sue sniffled. When she spoke, she whispered.

"There's a Devil waiting for me in China, too. If this one doesn't get me, that one will."

The Devil's head tipped forward, then lifted again. It seemed to be nodding, agreeing with Sue. But if that was the case, if Sue was meant to be taken, why not just come into this room and try? *Just fucking try it!* Pepper's arms and legs got stiffer, his chest filled with hot air, his face felt like it was vibrating. He was getting *amped*. It was going to come in here for Sue. Win or lose, he was going to fight. He was ready.

But Pepper wasn't prepared for what happened next. The Devil didn't come out for them. It stayed over there.

The Devil slammed Glenn's door shut.

When that happened, Pepper and Sue had the same thought: *We're safe*.

Pepper and Sue watched Glenn's door. They didn't move. They didn't touch each other. Each was too shocked, too ashamed, by how relieved they felt.

"Vermin!" Miss Chris shouted again from the end of the hall. The squeaking sound beneath her cry might've been the rat getting bashed or the soles of Miss Chris's old Crocs.

"Maybe Glenn's not even in there," Pepper offered.

"Maybe," Sue agreed, though neither of them was convinced.

Pepper hopped out of bed and was in the hallway before he remembered he was naked. No time to turn around for a costume change! Pepper went through the door. What did he find?

Glenn's body being pulled up into the ceiling.

The man's head and neck and shoulders had already gone through the open hole. The rest of him dangled, four limbs flailing as they rose. Picture a large fish being yanked into a boat.

Pepper rushed toward the man, a guy he hardly knew, and threw his arms around the thighs. Pepper bear-hugged them and pulled.

Glenn's body slipped down. Everything from the shoulders up reappeared. A bedsheet had been tied around Glenn's shoulders, pinning the arms against his sides. The sheet ran into the crawl space, into the dark. The tension on the sheet fell slack. Pepper still held him up, arms around the thighs. Glenn's eyes fluttered and opened. He saw Pepper there. He grinned, showing all those fucked-up teeth, and the overwhelming beauty—the spark of *life* in that grateful smile—made Pepper's breath catch in his throat.

Pepper heard a gruff snort from the crawl space. Then the sheet went taut and Glenn's body rose toward the shadows again.

But Pepper squared off. He tightened his hold on Glenn's legs. He spread his feet and planted himself. One time, in a fourth-floor walkup, an upright piano had slipped loose from Pepper's partner on a flight of stairs and Pepper had steadied himself like this. That day he'd stopped a piano that should, by all rights, have crushed him.

The Devil wanted Glenn?

Well, it couldn't fucking have him.

Pepper held on tight and leaned backward. That brought Glenn's body back down again. But this time, the sheet stayed tense, and the grunting in the crawl space was followed by a scratching sound, like the Devil was bearing down, and the sheet slipped from around Glenn's shoulders. But it caught around his throat. It had become a noose.

Glenn opened his mouth to shout but only spit came out. The man's cries were being choked off. Pepper didn't have enough weight to win this tussle alone.

But he wasn't alone. Now Sue was with Pepper. She clambered around him until she'd grabbed Glenn's ankles. She squeezed them in her arms just like Pepper did with Glenn's thighs. And in the darkness of the crawl space they heard another snort, but this time it sounded weaker.

And in a moment, Glenn's body fell toward them. Pepper and Sue tried to hold him up but he slipped and his back slapped *hard* against the tiled floor. At least it wasn't his head. The sheet came spooling down after him. It gathered over Glenn, cloaking his face. Sue let go of his ankles and Pepper set his legs down. Sue pulled the sheets from Glenn's face. His mouth lay open, his tongue fat. His eyes were closed and his skin as purple as a plum. Sue put her fingers under his nose and held them there. She whispered, "He's breathing."

Sue and Pepper were on their knees like attendants preparing

Glenn's body for mummification. The sheet remained tied around Glenn's neck. Sue touched it, but wasn't sure if she should untie it. Would that hurt Glenn more?

"Now how you like *this*?"

Pepper and Sue found Miss Chris there in the doorway. The red plastic key chain was around her wrist, and the keys dangled near her knee. They swung loosely and clinked against the door frame.

Pepper and Sue hopped to their feet. Naked, they looked like John Lennon and Yoko Ono on the cover of *Two Virgins*. But less attractive. Pepper said, "We found him like this."

Miss Chris looked at Glenn, who looked dead. Miss Chris's face betrayed no emotion. She alerted the rest of the staff by calling out the code for a suicide attempt.

"Red Jack! Red Jack! Red Jack!" she yelled. "Northwest Two! Room six!"

Miss Chris waved Pepper and Sue out of the room. "Move now!" she said. "They coming with the cart."

Pepper and Sue did as told. Miss Chris grabbed Sue's arm as they passed her.

"You get dressed and you come back to me, hear?"

Sue dropped her head and nodded.

Miss Chris now ran into Glenn's room. She kneeled, she looked into his eyes, and grabbed his wrist. Pepper didn't keep watching. He went back into his room with Sue. He pushed the door shut.

"You think he'll live?" Pepper asked as they dressed. His eyes were bright and wide. He still felt charged.

"I guess he's got a chance," Sue said. She almost sounded jealous.

Pepper held her. He slouched so his chin rested on the top of her head. She pressed her face into his chest so she could smell him.

Miss Chris walked into the room without knocking.

"Let's go now. Let's go." She had one hand on her hip but her voice hardly sounded angry. Just tired, like an aunt who's been put in charge of her fast little niece.

"I have an idea about your sister," Pepper said. "It's kind of wild, but *Coffee*—"

Sue kissed Pepper. Even while Miss Chris watched. Pepper laughed and returned the kiss. He squeezed her with the kind of hug that nearly every human being loves. An embrace.

When she pulled away, he said, "Coffee had this number. It was in Oakland."

Miss Chris grabbed Sue's wrist and led her away.

He said, "Wouldn't it be crazy if . . ."

But now Pepper spoke to an empty room.

It didn't matter. He figured he'd get in some trouble for sneaking her in—maybe they'd throw him in irons for a bit—but they'd probably let him up for dinner. And he'd have Coffee's binder with him, the one Coffee left behind. He'd pull Sue into the phone alcove and show her the last phone number Coffee had scrawled on a sheet of paper: 5102821833. It *would* be Sue's sister. Pepper believed it. And Pepper would help Sue with the conversation, just in case she got confused. He'd put the two sisters back in touch and the older sister would come through. How would that save Sue? He couldn't guess yet. Not exactly. But he'd listened to Sue. Heard what she needed. She needed her sister. Good enough. He'd get her that much. And let the sister do something he couldn't manage from in here.

Pepper didn't realize he would never see Sue again.

Actually, that wasn't quite true.

He would see her one more time.

In an article, clipped from a newspaper.

# 32

PEPPER WAS WRONG about his punishment, too. They didn't snap him into restraints, lash him to the bed. Miss Chris had enough to do with inputting her notes about Glenn's "episode" into the computer. The inappropriate program, Equator, had been swapped out for the proper record-keeping program, Equator Zero. Instead of "charting," the staff would now spend much of their shifts "logging." Even Miss Chris, the stalwart, had been trained well enough that she could log in, find "Incident Report" on the main menu, and type out, however slowly, the facts about Glenn. She left out the part about Pepper and Sue. As for the Devil's role in this, she made no mention. She hadn't seen it, after all.

The staff put all the patients on lockdown. Keeping them in their rooms for as long as it took to move Glenn to the ICU. Pepper spent the time clutching Coffee's binder as if it contained ICBM launch codes. Inside he found the pages and pages of meticulously kept records. Coffee had done some formidable charting of his own. He'd reached out to government representatives at every level: neighborhood council members, community reps, borough presidents, citywide officeholders, state and federal representatives. No success with any of them.

Coffee had reached members of the press as well. And had better luck teasing them with the catnip of exposé and scandal. Since New Hyde was a New York City hospital, he'd had particular interest from a reporter from *The New York Times*. A woman who, even from Coffee's notes, clearly worked hard to use Coffee as a source. But inevitably, the ties were severed. Relationships with reporters lost. In his notes Coffee entertained the paranoid fear that all these journalists had been visited by thugs from "Coffin Industries." Told to button up or, even worse, killed. What were the chances he'd come up with that company's name randomly? Dorry probably spun the same tales to every new admit. The tour, the stampeding buffalo, the cliff, and Coffin Industries. Like a speech given to incoming freshman by a college president. The ward's common myths.

But all that really mattered now was scrawled on the last page in the binder. Ten digits in blue ink. The last number Coffee ever dialed. Pepper could even *hear* Coffee just now.

*Washington, D.C.! The nation's capital. No that's not where I am. That's where you are! What do you mean "Oakland"? The President doesn't live in Oakland.*

Pepper spent the morning in the makeshift bed he'd shared with Sue. Every wrinkle in the sheets, each indentation in the pillows seemed to hold a trace of her. Pepper lay in the bed, dressed in his street clothes. The binder held tight in the crook of his right arm. When staff let all the patients out of their rooms for lunch and midday meds, Pepper was the first in line. He swiped his little white cup out of Scotch Tape's hand. He swallowed the pills so eagerly that Scotch Tape and Nurse Washburn suspected a trick. After he slugged the pills, Nurse Washburn put her hand out. "I'll throw out your cup."

When Pepper handed it back to her, she peeked inside.

But Pepper felt too good to take insult. Today he was going to help Sue, and nothing could break his great mood. "You don't trust me?" Pepper asked.

Nurse Washburn, the former Josephine, looked at Pepper coolly. She closed her fingers around the empty white cup, crushed it into a ball, looked over Pepper's shoulder and said, "Next."

Pepper went on his way, almost *dancing* toward the television lounge. Where he found a new orderly manning the lunch rack. Pepper accepted his lunch tray and took the far table. Where he'd first kissed Sue, first touched her. Pepper practically bounced in his chair. He didn't even eat.

The regulars rolled through for their food. Wally Gambino bopped along and Heatmiser shuffled. The Haint appeared, somehow looking as spiffy as ever even though she wore the same purple pantsuit and matching hat every day. Yuckmouth showed up, too, took his lunch and sat alone. He might've been bereft at the damage done to his friend but who could say? His expression was as impassive as always. Mr. Mack and Frank Waverly arrived together. No one had claimed the television, so Mr. Mack flipped to the station, and the show, he loved most. Mr. Mack clapped when that stone idol, Steve Sands, filled the screen. Frank Waverly huffed like an agitated mutt.

Mr. Mack glared at his roommate. "Oh, *hush*."

And there were the two new admits. The older women Pepper had seen on the night Dorry attacked Loochie. They weren't Sam and Sammy, he could see that clearly. Older and a bit more professional-looking in their air. Former Supreme Court Justice Sandra Day O'Connor and Doris Roberts from *Everybody Loves Raymond*. That's who they looked like. Sandra Day O'Connor and Doris Roberts.

They sat down one table over from Mr. Mack and Frank Waverly.

"Now everybody listen to this man," Mr. Mack announced. He raised the volume on the set. "He grew up right here in Queens!"

"Yo," Wally Gambino said, with a mouthful of macaroni. "How's this motherfucker's show *always* on?!"

"Language," the new orderly said, but it came out weakly, like he was still practicing giving commands. Everyone ignored him.

"He's popular," Mr. Mack said to Wally. "That's why they air his show three times a day."

"When does this dude sleep?!" Wally pressed.

"The truth don't need a rest," Mr. Mack said.

Frank Waverly huffed again but Mr. Mack didn't notice.

Steve Sands, as per usual, looked as though he'd just been thawed. Not soft enough to melt yet, but starting to bead.

"Welcome back to *News Roll*. And I'm Steve Sands. You might remember a month ago when I brought you the story of a mental patient who had to be put down by New York City Police when he tried to harm another patient. There was some outcry about the case. Some felt the police went too far, but I wondered if people wanted the police to wait until the man hurt or killed some innocent person before they stopped him. But we won't get back into that debate."

The picture of Coffee from the news piece appeared over Steve Sands's right shoulder. It hadn't become any more pleasant since the last time Pepper had seen it. If anything, it looked worse because now, projected on that flat television screen, the image was about the size of a magazine page.

"Well, I'd also mentioned in that piece that this man, Kofi Acholi, was an illegal. He overstayed his time in this country by abusing our work-visa program. And today, we've found out that his body will be shipped back to his home country. The nation of Ooganda. Am I pronouncing that right, Beth? You-ganda? Thank you. He'll be shipped back to Uganda where he'll be buried, or whatever they do over there."

Pepper remembered sitting in his room with Coffee, each man on his bed, lunch tray in his lap. He looked down at the tray in front of him now. He peeled the small orange they'd given him. He'd traded a few orange wedges for a can of Sprite. Such a stupid, insignificant way to remember a man. And yet as Pepper ate the orange, his face softened. He looked at his lap and, very quietly, he cried.

When he looked up to the screen, the picture behind Steve Sands had changed from Coffee's face to a giant green dollar sign.

"But here's my question," Steve continued. "Who's paying to send Mr. Acholi back? You know the answer. The same people who paid for Mr. Acholi's stay in the hospital. Where he enjoyed the *finest* health care services in the world. For free. Well, it was free for him. But for you and me? We picked up the bill for this man to spend a year getting medical care in one of our nation's hospitals. So what should we call this plane ride back home? The *tip*? This system carries some of us, but it's on the backs of the rest of us. That's the ugly truth. Well, we've been used for too long, my friends. We can't afford it. *Every man for himself.* Make sure *your* butt is covered."

Doris Roberts and Sandra Day O'Connor frowned at each other as the show went to commercial. Doris Roberts said, "Well, I don't like that."

Mr. Mack sniffed at her. "I suppose you'd like it if we all go bankrupt taking care of deadbeats? Well, I'm about *through* with kicking back while our enemies prey on us." Mr. Mack waved a finger at the ceiling. "Steve Sands is on my wavelength."

Sandra Day O'Conner forced down a few bites of her tuna-fish sandwich, then she unwrapped her cookie. She bit into it and almost immediately spat it out. "That man makes more money in one year than you've made in your whole lifetime," she said.

Mr. Mack nodded. "Yes. He's very successful."

Sandra Day O'Connor looked at Mr. Mack, bewildered, and he smiled back. Pepper couldn't take the glee on Mr. Mack's face. He shouted at the old man. "You know Steve Sands would deport *you*, too."

Mr. Mack, three tables away, narrowed his eyes at Pepper. "I'm an American citizen."

Pepper pointed at the television. "Not his America."

Mr. Mack glowered. Next to him, Frank Waverly grinned.

Pepper stomped out of the lounge and to the nurses' station, where Nurse Washburn sat alone, *logging*, now that Miss Chris had finished Glenn's incident report. There were four stacks of paperwork on the desk. All of it had to do with Coffee or Glenn. Nurse Washburn had been told to hurry and get all this information into the computer. The faster they updated the records, the faster they could move on to the next step, the whole point of Equator Zero.

But none of that mattered to Pepper.

"I'm looking for Sue," Pepper said. "I thought she'd be at lunch since we didn't get breakfast."

Nurse Washburn looked up from the computer and stood up. "Repeat yourself," she commanded.

"Xiu." He tried her Chinese name but did no better with the pronunciation than before. "The Chinese Lady."

Nurse Washburn looked toward Northwest 1.

"Oh, her. Yes. They took her this morning. She's gone."

Did Nurse Washburn take a certain pleasure in telling Pepper the news? Best to stop thinking about it before she had to admit the truth. Get back to the paperwork, converting paperwork into electronic files. Ignore the big man, who was leaning against the nurses' station and moaning like an abandoned child

*She's gone.*

Pepper stumbled into the phone alcove and found it empty. He took out his wallet, tried to use his credit card to make a call, but when he punched in his card number, an automated voice told him the card had been declined. He'd forgotten it was maxed out.

Then the phone rang.

Pepper picked it up so enthusiastically it nearly fell. He bobbled it like a football, but the pass remained complete. He held the receiver to his ear. Who would be on the other side? Sue? Her sister? (Somehow?) Maybe his brother, Ralph? The moment felt primed for magic.

"Hello," Pepper said hopefully.

"Hey, there." A woman's voice. Cheerful. Bouncy.

"This is Pepper."

"This is Sammy," the woman said. "You remember me?"

"Sammy?"

"I was in there, too. Been gone about a month, though it feels like a lifetime!" She laughed into the line.

Pepper's hand felt cold. He felt like he was hearing from a ghost.

"Listen," she said. "I'm trying to reach Sam, but every time I call, people just get quiet and—"

He hung up on her.

Sammy was alive.

As soon as Pepper set the phone down in the cradle, he wanted to pick it back up again. He wanted to explain to Sammy. That everyone knew Sam had killed herself because she thought the Devil had taken her friend. And now, to hear Sammy's happy laughter on the line, to think Sam took her own life simply because her best friend had been a little preoccupied? It was too much. It was absurd. Pepper almost couldn't register the enormity of such a cosmic joke.

But he couldn't explain any of that to Sammy because Sammy wasn't on the line. Only a dial tone. How many times would Sammy have to call before someone had the presence of mind to explain?

Pepper set the receiver back into the cradle. Remember Sue. It was too late to explain anything to Sammy. (And much too late for poor Sam.) But for Sue there was still time.

Pepper left the alcove and knew what he had to do. Regardless of pride. (And irony.) Nurse Washburn and Scotch Tape stood inside the nurses' station now. After Nurse Washburn finished inputting a file, Scotch Tape took each one and tossed it into a blue plastic bag. There were two bags at his feet, already full. Paperwork that had been logged into the computer, and now would be sent out for shredding.

This sort of hurt Scotch Tape. Right in the wrists. Him and Miss Chris and all the staff who'd been working at New Hyde for a while. How many *years* had they committed to charting. Now it would all be turned into shavings. The same information saved with the press of a button. Progress, yes, but he wished it had come long before he'd developed some kind of early-onset arthritis.

Pepper shlumped up to the nurses' station, giving Scotch Tape and Nurse Washburn a start. He leaned his elbows on the counter. He bowed his head before he met Scotch Tape's gaze.

"Let me borrow a quarter?" Pepper said.


Panhandling is *hard work.*

Pepper sure found out.

Neither Scotch Tape nor Nurse Washburn was inclined to give him any coins. And Mr. Mack cackled when Pepper asked. Frank Waverly at least looked pained when he reached into his pockets and came out with nothing. Nothing from Heatmiser or Yuckmouth. Wally Gambino shouted, "Hells-fuckin'-no!" The Haint didn't even seem to hear him, she shuffled past and didn't look up from the floor. Redhead Kingpin and Still Waters weren't up and about during mid-day. Doris Roberts told him she'd write him an IOU and give him something when her family came for visiting hours later in the week. And Sandra Day O'Connor scowled and told him to "get a job." ("What job can I get inside a mental hospital?" he asked. Her response? "Get a job!"—only louder.)

He met Loochie as she was leaving the television lounge. She had a white towel inelegantly draped over her head. The rest of her remained as polished as ever, baby-blue Nikes, clean jeans and a sporty little sweatshirt, but her head was hidden. It made her seem like a ghoul. He wouldn't have recognized her if not for the sneakers. She almost walked right past him, lost in a daze. But he touched her arm.

"Loochie," he said.

The shrouded figure stopped. It looked down at his hand, still touching her elbow. Pepper pulled his hand away. Then Loochie looked up at him. He could make out her eyes under the towel, but little else.

"How are you?" he asked quietly.

She stared at him.

"I'm sorry. . . ." He put his hand on the top of his head.

"My mother hasn't seen it yet," Loochie said.

Pepper couldn't see her lips move when she said this. It was disconcerting. As if she hadn't said it, only thought it, and he'd read her mind. "Did you tell her?" he asked.

"You think I should?"

"Call her," Pepper said. "It's going to be worse if she just shows up and sees you like . . . this."

"It looks bad?" She patted the towel with one hand, as if she'd only just realized how absolutely bizarre she must look.

"You've looked better," Pepper said. He didn't mean that harshly, but that's how Loochie took it.

"Well, your girlfriend is gone," Loochie snapped back.

Pepper smiled. At least Loochie hadn't lost her fighting spirit. He admired her very much for holding on to it. But there was still the important business at hand. The reason he'd been roaming the halls, accosting everyone.

Pepper said, "Can I borrow a quarter?"

Loochie's surprised laugh made the sides of the towel shake. "You know who you sounded like just then?"

Then she lost her smile, as if she was embarrassed by it. "I don't have a quarter," she said. "Why don't you ask *her*?"

Loochie pointed into the television lounge. Where Dorry sat alone. Not just by herself, but in an empty room.

Pepper looked at Dorry, then back at Loochie. But Loochie had already walked off.

Pepper walked into the lounge and looked up at the screen. The Weather Channel gave the five-day forecast.

Pepper approached Dorry.

"What you watching?" he asked.

She lifted the remote, turned the volume down. "I'll give you a quarter," Dorry said. "But you have to sit with me."

Pepper rested one hand on the tabletop. He didn't want to sit, but he did want that money.

"You've been avoiding me," Dorry said. She peered at the empty lounge. "Everyone has."

Her white hair was brushed back, fully exposing her face. She looked thinner. Her eyes were red and dry. "Notice something different?" she asked.

"No more glasses," Pepper said, still standing.

"Loochie broke them in our fight. Staff won't replace them. That's one of my punishments, I guess."

Pepper pulled a chair back and sat down.

"I thought I could do it," she said quietly. "I *really* did. I'm so tired, you see? I thought maybe we could work something out. Like a truce. I don't know. I was kidding myself. Maybe I wanted you to stop him. But then I saw Coffee with those needles and . . ."

She stopped and looked out the lounge's windows. She tapped the remote against her forehead a little too hard. Instinctively, Pepper reached out and pulled her hand down.

"I feel so bad about it, Pepper, you have to know I do. But I couldn't see him hurt any more than I could see any one of you hurt."

Pepper pulled his hand back. His mouth went dry. "But one of us did get hurt, Dorry."

"I know! *I know.* You're *all* like my children. Doesn't matter how old or young. My sons and daughters. And I try to be good to *all* of you. Don't you know that's why I'm the first person who comes to the door? The first face a patient sees should be a friendly one. I show each of you around. Get you a little more food if you need it. Dorry does that. For everyone. Even him."

Pepper strained forward in his seat. Suddenly he wanted to shake her.

"But why do you have to be that way? Can't you just use a little common fucking sense! Take a look at that *thing* and figure out it doesn't deserve to be treated like . . . one of us?"

Dorry slid the remote control toward him as if she was passing him a baton.

"Should I have done that when you came in?" she asked. "You weren't one of us. You said it yourself."

Pepper stood up and pushed his chair back so hard it fell over.

"All your best intentions," he said. "And we're still stuck in this hell. So what's the point?"

Was he scolding Dorry, or himself?

Dorry gave Pepper a tight-lipped smile. "You help," she said. "That's the point."

Pepper crowded over her. From a distance, it must've looked like he was about to crush the old woman. And he was. "You haven't helped anyone. You've made every life you've touched—me, Loochie, *Coffee*—worse."

Dorry's eyes fluttered. He thought she might actually faint. But he couldn't stop himself now. The anxiety he'd been feeling for Sue, the grief for Coffee, the pity for himself, it all became rage. He wanted to trample Dorry just then.

"So what good are you really?" he asked. "What good are you to anyone?" Dorry pursed her lips and blew out quietly. She looked down at her hands.

"Yes," she whispered. "I guess I see what you mean."

She reached into her bra and took out her "coin purse." It was really just a length of paper towel folded and wrapped around some change. She put the whole thing on the table.

"I said I'd give this to you if you sat with me," she told him.

Pepper grabbed it right away. He felt no remorse for what he'd just said to her. He was too busy unwrapping the paper towel and counting the money.

Dorry looked toward the window again but could hardly see anything beyond blurs. She sighed deeply.

"Maybe this *is* the world. Northwest, I mean. If you think about it, what's so different? Wake up in the morning, eat some breakfast, take a few pills to start the day. Go to a conference room and waste time. Go to lunch, take a few more pills. Bullshit the afternoon away. Eat dinner while you watch TV. Take a few more pills and go to bed. Isn't that how most people are living? It's been awhile since I was outside, but that's what the news is always saying. Maybe out there is a lot like in here. The United States of New Hyde."

Pepper felt dejected when he finished counting. Only eighty-five cents. Enough to reach Oakland? Maybe the initial three-minute call. He'd have to pack all the important information into that window. No greetings. No explanations. Just Sue—immigration jail—New Hyde Hospital—extradition.

"One big asylum," Dorry muttered.

The old woman walked away from Pepper. She pushed a chair up to the windows as Pepper left the lounge. She sat and stared at the broad, cloudless sky, watching afternoon turn to evening.

# 33

BY DINNERTIME DORRY still remained in that chair.

She didn't get up to eat dinner. Didn't notice when other patients filtered back into the lounge. They turned on their shows, ate their meals, enjoyed some conversation, and Dorry hardly noticed any of it. One of the nurses on the night shift appeared with her evening meds. She took them without incident.

Meanwhile Pepper felt terrible.

You know what eighty-five cents got him? A recorded message that still demanded sixty-five cents more to connect the call. And where would he get that? He'd tried all the other patients, and the staff members on the night shift rebuffed him.

Now what? Pepper had been asking himself that question for a few hours by the time Dorry took her evening meds. The only solution he could see was to get behind that nurses' station again and use their phone. Once again, he'd be mimicking Coffee! (And, of course, he had to wonder if that last step—gunshots—would follow.)

This plan had no chance of success, though. New Hyde's phone protocol had been changed. The staff's phone had been removed. Poof. Vamoose.

Son of a bitch!

THE DEVIL IN SILVER 293

Staff members had been approved for cell-phone use. Simple. No more need for a machine on the desk. Especially if it was going to incite a riot. Pepper entertained the idea of pickpocketing one of the staff members, but he knew he could never pull it off. Pepper was as subtle as a sonic boom.

When he reentered the television lounge that evening, the man was just salty. He wore a grimace that would've struck fear into the hearts of a well-armed militia. More than a few of the patients went on alert when Pepper entered the lounge. Think of the great white shark roaming the shores of Amity.

Mr. Mack watched Pepper wander the lounge for a full thirty seconds, feeling the agitation flying off him like hot sparks. Finally Mr. Mack said, "*Sit* your ass down or move on."

But Pepper felt like a failure right then, not a thug. His grimace was just a sign that the contents had spoiled. Pepper spun toward Mr. Mack but he didn't argue or even glower. He sat his ass down, across the table from Heatmiser. Heatmiser looked at Pepper quickly, and turned his chair away ninety degrees.

"It's my half hour," Mr. Mack announced.

Nearly everyone in the room groaned.

"Like it or not, we got a system," Mr. Mack said. "And that means it's *my* time."

The remote was passed to him, and Mr. Mack flipped the channels until he reached his favorite station. Pepper wondered if Mr. Mack truly loved this show so much, or just loved forcing everyone else to sit through it.

"Hello, and welcome to *News Roll.* I'm—"

That's all they heard because Frank Waverly, right next to Mr. Mack as always, snatched the remote out of his friend's hand. Frank Waverly pointed the remote at the screen and turned it *off.* First time that had been done in over five years.

Mr. Mack looked at his friend, too shocked to be cruel. He almost whined when he said, "Well, now what are we supposed to do?"

Frank Waverly tucked the remote in his lap, under the table, and picked at his dinner quietly.

Doris Roberts grinned at Mr. Mack. "It's actually Frank Waverly's half hour."

Mr. Mack's mouth dropped open like he'd been gutted. "Oh, that's fine," Mr. Mack said, now picking at his dinner with a plastic fork. He looked across the table. "That you, Frank? I don't even recognize you right now."

Frank Waverly chewed his substandard food and did not look up.

The rest of the room stayed quiet, too. As if they were all getting used to the lack of the television's sounds and sights. Soon people began speaking with one another. When other patients' television times arrived, they chose to keep the set off. The conversations continued and many of the people lingered. For so long that when Redhead Kingpin and Still Waters arrived, they had to share one table. The lounge had gone all Old World, where the point of dinner was to talk with people, not just to clear your plate.

It was nice. Only Dorry was left out of the pleasure. No one tried to make conversation with her. They just left her there in her chair at the window.

Even Pepper let himself rest. A momentary reprieve. What else could he do, at this very moment, for anyone? Tomorrow, he would ask any visiting family members for change. They couldn't get Sue down to Florida, process her deportation order, and shove her on a plane in just one night. No system on earth worked that well.

One of the night nurses entered the lounge. She was accompanied by an orderly. He walked behind her and scanned the room, paying particular attention to Pepper.

The nurse reached the glass door in the television lounge and said, "Smoke break. Everyone who wants one, line up."

Here and there people pushed back their chairs. For the first time in hours.

Dorry moved, too. As a line formed, Dorry walked to Pepper's table. She held a white envelope. She'd had it curled in her palm for so long that it had rolled into a tube when she set it down in front of Pepper.

He looked at it but didn't speak. It had been hours since he'd said those cruel things to her, and guilt finally crept across his scalp like a chill.

Dorry pointed at the envelope.

"When they brought you in, I knew you were here to find your purpose," she said. "But I can't force you to be what I hoped you would be. I should've learned that from raising my children."

The line of patients going on smoke break continued to grow. The room, without television, was quiet enough that nearly every patient in the room could hear what Dorry said.

"There is a way out," she told Pepper. "I've seen it." She tapped the curled envelope with two fingers. "This will show you how to get there."

The room seemed to get quieter, conversations dying down. The only people making as much noise as ever were the oblivious staff members. The nurse and orderly were flirting with each other.

"You think you're cute," the nurse teased.

The orderly laughed quietly. "You think so, too."

Dorry swept one hand, indicating the patients in the room. "You can take them all, or just save yourself. I leave that choice to you."

Pepper put his hand over the envelope after Dorry pulled hers away. She joined the smokers line. The nurse finally looked away from the orderly and noticed the patients waiting there. She unlocked the door while the orderly stood beside her, ready to bodycheck anyone who might get unruly.

The patients filed outside.

Mr. Mack stood up, hands on his hips like a cartoon villain. He said, "I have been waiting for a while just so I could say this." He stuck his hand out toward Frank Waverly, who still had the remote in his lap. "It's my turn now, according to the schedule."

"Why don't you just leave it off?" Sandra Day O'Connor asked.

"Why don't you wipe the gravy off your chin," Mr. Mack replied.

Sandra Day O'Connor looked at her friend, Doris Roberts, who hadn't had the heart to point out the small brown smudge. Doris Roberts pointed to the spot and Sandra Day O'Connor daubed at it with her napkin.

Frank Waverly, meanwhile, had not given up the remote. So Mr. Mack reached across the table and slapped Frank Waverly's tray. The empty juice carton flew to the floor.

The orderly at the glass door saw this and said, "You can't use your hands like that, Mr. Mack."

Mr. Mack looked over his shoulder and scowled. "When I want to hear from *you,* I'll tell you what to say."

The nurse joined in. "You don't speak to Rudy like that."

"Big girls shouldn't have big mouths," Mr. Mack spat back.

Rudy, the orderly, stomped over to his table, the nurse right beside him. But the nurse caught herself. She remembered Pepper was nearby and went back to the glass door leading out to the court. She locked it, then returned to Rudy's side. The patients out on the court didn't notice this, they were trying to smoke down three or four ciga-rettes before being called back in.

"You going to apologize to Clio, my man." The orderly loomed over Mr. Mack. Frank Waverly, at the same table, hadn't looked up yet. He ate even more slowly. The remote remained in his lap.

The nurse, Clio, said, "Please give me the remote, Mr. Waverly."

Frank Waverly handed it to her.

"Now this is a reasonable man," Rudy said, pointing at Frank Wa-verly.

"He's a turncoat," Mr. Mack growled. "I got a Judas as my room-mate."

Rudy, a new employee at Northwest, tried to be reasonable. "There's no need for this fuss . . ." he began.

Clio touched Rudy's shoulder lightly, appreciatively, but also try-ing to call him off. They weren't going to get an apology out of Mr. Mack.

This was turning into an entertaining little dessert course for all the other patients. At the very least they might see Mr. Mack disci-plined, and Lord knew everyone wanted to see that. A little theater before bedtime. Well worth watching. Except. Except.

Except Dorry had just taken off her nightdress in the courtyard.

Dorry pulled it right over her head and stood there exposed.

Then, naked, she finished smoking her cigarette.

Rudy and Clio were focused on Mr. Mack, who grabbed at the remote control even though it was in the nurse's hand. Those three
were busy.

Which is why only the patients noticed what Dorry had done.
Stripped down to her altogether. The ones inside stopped talking
with one another quickly. They gathered at the windows of the
lounge. The ones outside continued to smoke and watched Dorry
coolly. What were they going to do? Best to let her have her freak-out.
Soon enough, the staff would escort Dorry back to her room and
sedate her. Nobody found this moment unfathomable. If you haven't
caused a scene in a psych unit, it's just because you haven't been inside long enough.

Dorry held the nightdress in one hand. It hung there like a line of
rope. She pulled the cigarette from her lips with her free hand, blew
out a small wisp of smoke. Then she looked into the lounge, saw the
other patients, seemed surprised by their attention. Not embarrassed
but almost amused.

She threw her nightdress over one shoulder. She looked like a nude
bather. She waved at them, as if she was about to go for a swim.

Dorry turned her back to them. She walked toward the fence. Her
flesh quavered with each step. Her skin sagged. The backs of her
knees, her calves, were mottled blue.

Dorry reached the chain-link fence. She tossed her nightdress over
the top so it covered the barbed wire. The white nightdress rested on
the top like snow covering a hedge.

Pepper watched her, like all the others, absolutely smacked.

He'd been so surprised by her actions that he left Dorry's envelope
behind when he walked up to the windows with everyone else. It lay
curled into a tube on the tabletop.

*She's making a jailbreak,* Pepper thought. Then he felt slightly
angry. *She stole my fucking idea!*

Clio finally noticed the atmosphere in the lounge. She turned away
from the intractable Mr. Mack, the impassive Frank Waverly, and saw
all the patients gathered at the windows. When she joined them, she
saw Dorry climbing the chain-link fence.

Actually, Dorry was already at the top.

A rush and a push and she'd be on the other side.

"Oh, my good Jesus," Clio muttered.

"Code two! Northwest Five!" Rudy shouted seeing Dorry. Loud enough that Dr. Anand almost heard him, and Dr. Anand was four miles away, at home. "Code two! Northwest Five!"

The rest of the night staff, an orderly and another nurse, scrambled from the station. Clio pushed her way through the crowd of patients, trying to reach the door that would get her outside. But the patients? They didn't part for her. Their loyalties were split. They'd been trained, and medicated, for maximum docility, but despite all this, they remained willful human beings. If Dorry wanted out and had the fire to make the climb, then let her go.

But when Dorry reached the top of the fence, she didn't hop over. Instead, she perched herself up there, in a crouch, like a gargoyle at the top of a building. Despite the nightdress the barbed wire was digging into her soles, but her face showed no pain. No exhaustion. No worry. Dorry had balanced herself in that crouched position and then, even more remarkable, she stood.

Because it was night, the dull silver fence was practically invisible, so the old woman seemed to be floating eight feet above the concrete court.

Dorry *levitated.*

More than a few of the witnesses would remember the moment that way.

The other staff members reached the lounge. They pulled patients aside. Rudy fussed with his keys, trying to find the right one for the door. But he had fallen into a panic, and his fingers wouldn't work. Even when he found the right key, it didn't help. Each time Rudy tried to slide the key in the lock, he lost his aim. He was just stabbing at it, grunting with frustration. Clio, try as she might, couldn't get Rudy to step aside and let her open it.

Dorry scanned the lounge until she found Pepper's flabbergasted face. She smiled, as tenderly as when she'd given him the tour of New Hyde.

Dorry mouthed one word to him.

*Rest.*

She took a step forward, as if she was just walking down the sidewalk. One foot out and she plunged. It wasn't that far to fall. About eight feet.

Dorry landed on the side of her head. Her neck bent so hard, so fast, that for a moment her ear touched her elbow.

Then her body smacked flat on the concrete. She shivered once.

Rudy finally got the door open.

Three staff members ran out to Dorry's body while Clio stayed in the lounge and used her cell phone to call the trauma unit.

The patients could not be ushered back to their rooms, no matter what the staff threatened. They wouldn't stop staring at the old woman's body. Her head had come to rest in a cluster of old stubbed cigarettes.

Before the crash cart arrived, Doris Walczak bled to death.

VOLUME 3

—

# STARRY NIGHT

# 34

"WHAT THE FUCK is *wrong* with you people?"

Pepper and Loochie sat quietly. They didn't give an answer. And with good reason. This wasn't meant as a question.

"You look like the rest of us, you were born just like the rest of us, but spend a few hours around you and it becomes obvious. *You are not like the rest of us.*"

Still, Pepper and Loochie stayed silent.

"I'm not even going to play games anymore. Pretend you're just 'different.' We're all *special* and *wonderful* in our *special wonderful goddamn* way. It's a *different* ability not a *disability*. You don't suffer from an *illness,* just an *otherness.* I mean, what does that even mean?! Well, forget it. I'm just going to say this because I need to say this. Out loud. To your faces. There *is* something wrong with you. You people are fucking crazy."

Pepper and Loochie shifted in their chairs, not sure if they were supposed to laugh.

"I know that seems like a joke, since we're here in a mental hospital. But it's not a joke. You are terrible people. And honestly. Truly. Sometimes I want to kill you."

Now everyone in the room, three bodies sat quietly. The last sentence filled the space like poison gas.

"Yes. Good. Fine. I said it. There are times when I go to bed and pray, please, God, just let me wake up to find out that every mental patient in the world has died. And I don't even believe in God! Every day I look at your fat, ugly faces and I wish I could slap each one of you. I know it's supposed to be the medication that makes you obese or slow or dazed or incoherent, but I don't blame the medication. Look what it has to work with! Brains so warped, so poorly wired, that *nothing* will ever fix you."

Pepper and Loochie were wondering when this would end. How long were they expected to just sit here and listen.

"People who have never been around you can talk and talk. I can't think how many times I've been at a dinner with my wife and someone will start telling me about the evils of the mental-health profession. And when they're done lecturing me, I ask them what *the hell* they know about it, and they tell me they read some damn *book*! Or they listened to a story on goddamn *NPR*! Well *fuck* them and *fuck* you!"

And with that, Dr. Anand ran out of breath.

He sat behind his desk, in his office, heaving. His brown face had gone red. (Which made it look sort of chestnut, really.) He'd risen from his chair as he ranted. Now he plopped back down and the cushion of his chair let out a sigh, as if even the furniture was fed up.

It was late morning, April 16. Dorry had killed herself the night before.

Dr. Anand's "office" was another repurposed room on Northwest 1. The trio sat there, listening to the clock on the wall. The second hand clucked as it spun, and now it was the loudest thing in the room.

Doris Walczak's body had finally been wheeled out of Northwest only hours ago. Off to the Rose Cottage. Dr. Anand had been called after she was pronounced dead. He'd come to the unit at four a.m. He'd been in this office for the last seven hours, interviewing patients.

The man wore a different pair of glasses than usual. These frames were metal and old and lopsided. The rubber guards on the ends of both arms (called temple tips) were worn down. Dr. Anand had a habit of using the ends to dig into his ears when they itched. Over the years they'd gone white-ish. These were not Dr. Anand's professional pair, but he'd been so tired when he was called that he put on the wrong ones. It was as if he'd forgotten to put on his professional face. So he'd shown up as Samuel Anand, husband and father, who owned a two-family house in Rego Park. That's the man who sat down with Pepper and Loochie in his office. And because he was tired he'd said way too much.

Dr. Anand leaned forward in his knockoff Aeron office chair, until his head touched the desktop. It looked like the man had fallen asleep. Pepper and Loochie looked at each other. Loochie still wore that damn towel on her head, which had been the last straw for Dr. Anand when he saw them walk in.

Pepper raised one hand to jostle the doctor, but then Dr. Anand's shoulders trembled. They watched him a moment longer and that's when they realized the man was crying.

Weeping.

Well, now what?

Pepper brought his raised hand back down to his lap and looked behind him at the room door, wishing some other staff member—a trained therapist perhaps—would come in here and take over. But that didn't happen.

So Loochie reached across the desk. She patted the top of the man's bushy head.

"Don't cry, Dr. Sam."

Pepper was surprised to hear Loochie's charitable tone. But Loochie's touch, Loochie's tenor, only wrecked the man even more.

"Don't *cry*, Dr. Sam."

This time, Loochie *mushed* the doctor's scalp. And her voice lost some of its kindness. The first time, it was like Loochie wanted to make him feel a little better but by the second, it was like she couldn't believe that he, of all people in this building, was the one most in need of support. Dorry and Coffee (and Sam) were *dead*. Glenn's larynx had been crushed. Loochie's hair had been torn out. Pepper had spent weeks in manacles, with Dr. Anand's tacit approval. So who ought to be in tears right then? Dr. Sam? Really?

While Loochie might've had a reason for her righteous indignation, Pepper's perspective differed. He was forty-two to Loochie's nineteen. At nineteen, the world seems so simple. This is because nineteen-year-olds have it almost completely wrong. Pepper knew differently. Who had a right to a few tears just then? How about every single one of them? Dr. Sam, too.

Dr. Anand pulled his head up. His eyes were wide and wild.

"I'm sorry," he whispered. "I can't believe I just said all that."

Dr. Anand took off his glasses, almost slipped one temple tip into his itchy ear. But he stopped and laughed at himself when he realized which glasses he'd worn to work. He spoke to Pepper and Loochie more evenly now.

"You know how many of us started out together at New Hyde?" he asked. "I'm a forensic psychiatrist. There were three of us when I first arrived. I'm the only one left. I had friends who worked in other departments, not just the psychiatric unit, and do you know where ninety-five percent of them are now? They're in private practice, or they work for a private hospital, or they went into research. They're almost all gone, and I stayed. I don't want to be applauded for that, but I don't want to be punished, either."

Pepper cleared his throat. "We're not . . ."

Dr. Anand had regained his professional authority. He raised his hand to quiet Pepper.

"I've spent years lobbying my superiors for more funds. More staff. Better oversight. I've spoken with politicians. I've tried the press. I've gone to the community-board meetings. No one could ever tell me why the funding never materialized. I mean never. Do you know what Govenor Pataki did to our services when he was governor? The man butchered us."

Dr. Anand sat back in his chair. He looked at the ceiling.

"One day the truth came to me. A wise man once said that every system is designed to give you the results you actually get. If you understand that, you'll see that this system is *working*."

"For some people," Pepper said.

Dr. Anand shook his head emphatically. "No. Wrong. The system is working *exactly* right for those it was *intended* for. That's why it hasn't been fixed. Because it isn't broken!

"Can you imagine anything more terrible? Doesn't it *hurt*? I love being an American and I know it hurts me. I mean, New Hyde's board knows we've got trouble with patients in Northwest. People hurting themselves, even dying. And what's their solution? *Equator Zero!* Do you know what that program actually does?!"

Dr. Anand clapped his hands and glared at them, but they didn't have any idea what Equator Zero was. Dr. Anand said, "The system is working and it hates us." He shook his head and looked at his empty, open hands. "Sometimes I can see why people believe in the Devil."

Dr. Anand's cheeks drooped, his mustache sagged.

"But it can't just be terrible and that's that," Pepper said. "Even on a sinking ship people still want to try to get out, to survive."

"And you'll be the one to save them, is that right?" Dr. Anand asked sarcastically. "You want to know your diagnosis? I finally figured it out."

"I don't want to hear that."

Dr. Anand jabbed his finger in the air after each word. "Narcissistic. Personality. Disorder."

He grinned at Pepper, but it wasn't pleasant. "You're going to get a lot of people hurt with your delusions of grandeur, Pepper." He dropped his hand onto the table. "Maybe you already have."

Behind them, the office door opened. Scotch Tape peeked in. "Dr. Anand?"

"What is it, Clarence?"

Scotch Tape jerked his head backward. "Cops is here."

Dr. Anand pushed his glasses up with the knuckle of his pointer finger. "Okay," he said. "Tell them to give me two minutes. I'm not done here."

Behind Scotch Tape, the *squawk* of a police radio made everyone in the room jump. Scotch Tape's head pulled back and the door opened wider. A cop stood there now, bulky and short. If he'd been out of uniform, you might've taken him for a funny guy; he had the build of a neighborhood comedian. The kind who taunts people and causes fights. In uniform, the same dimensions made the man seem petty and easily offended.

"Why don't you talk to me right now?" the cop said. He had his hand on his police radio as if that were the handle of his gun.

Dr. Anand stood right up. Much to the surprise of Loochie and Pepper.

Dr. Anand walked over to the officer, and the officer said, "We can talk in the hall. I don't care."

The doctor looked back at Pepper and Loochie, narrowing his eyes. He tried to guess which would result in greater humiliation: ushering Pepper and Loochie out of the room, perhaps having to fuss with them about it (in front of this bossy cop), or just stepping into the hall as if following a command, here on his own unit. Which promised to wound his pride more? Dr. Anand stepped out into the hall and pulled the door three-quarters closed behind him, but held on to the doorknob. The doctor and cop had their conversation out there. Pepper heard their voices but couldn't make out their words.

He looked at Loochie.

"Narcissist," she teased.

He looked away from her. Could already imagine the time (how much time?) on the unit and all the days and weeks and years (decades?) when she'd whisper that word to him and it would be part of their secret language, a joke between lifers, and he despaired.

He scanned Dr. Anand's desk. He heard the officer raise his voice, shouting to another cop there in the hall. Dr. Anand had been speaking with patients for hours, saving Pepper and Loochie for last. Was he trying to get the others to pin the blame for Dorry on them? On him? (*Narcissist.*) Pepper might've continued thinking this way if his eye hadn't spied one particular device there on Dr. Anand's desk.

Dr. Anand's office phone.

They'd removed the device from the nurses' station because patients regularly gathered there. But who would've thought to do the same in here, the doctor's inner sanctum? Pepper didn't hesitate.

"Loochie," he said. "Will you do me a favor?"

She turned in her chair. "Why should I do anything for you?"

"It'll piss off Dr. Anand."

A grin tugged at Loochie's lips, there under her towel. "Tell me." She listened.

Pepper whispered, "Will you shut the door and keep them out?"

"That's going to get us in some shit," she said.

"Probably."

Loochie grabbed the towel and pulled it tight around her scalp, tying it up as if she'd just stepped out of the shower. It was a surprise for Pepper to see her face again, unobstructed. To be reminded that he had just talked a child into committing another infraction.

Loochie stood up and jiggled her head from side to side. Limbering up. Then she picked up her chair with one easy motion and walked right up to the three-quarters closed office door. She kicked that bad boy closed.

Dr. Anand still had his hand on the knob, so when it slammed, he yelped with surprise. The cop next to him watched this in dumb paralysis. The door shut and they heard something jostling on the other side.

"They're locking you out?" the cop chided.

Dr. Anand reached into his coat pocket. He pulled out his set of keys. "The door only locks with one of these."

But Loochie hadn't tried to lock it. She'd wedged her chair under the handle and braced her shoulder against the door. A makeshift barricade.

Pepper didn't waste the opportunity. He jumped from a seated position and onto Dr. Anand's desk. It didn't even seem like he rose to his feet. One moment he sat and the next he flew. Landing on top of Dr. Anand's paperwork with his big boots.

"That was pretty good," Loochie said, admiringly.

"Lucretia!" Dr. Anand shouted from the other side. "*Open* this door!"

The cop's police radio frazzled and bleeped. The cop said, "This is a violation, miss. Miss, you can't do this."

"A violation of what law?" Loochie said through the door. "You name the law I'm breaking."

The cop said, "Unlawful trespass."

"Dr. Sam invited me into his office!"

The cop was quiet a moment. "Just open the *goddamn* door, miss."

One of them rattled the doorknob. Not with any force. Just testing.

Loochie had her right shoulder against the door. She grabbed the knob with her left and held it tight.

Pepper picked up the phone. He held the receiver to his ear.

Loochie said, "You have to dial pound-nine-three first."

Pepper was surprised that Loochie remembered what Dorry told Coffee on that Saturday night, but, of course, she'd been there, too.

Pepper dialed the code first and then the ten-digit number Coffee had written on the last page of his binder. By now Pepper had memorized it.

Someone in the hall heaved against the door. The sound was loud enough, the force heavy enough, that it had to be the cop or maybe Scotch Tape. Loochie didn't believe Dr. Anand had that much gunpowder in his shell.

No more begging. It was time for battering.

But Loochie held steady.

"You better hurry," Loochie said.

Pepper crouched on the desk, holding the receiver to one ear. He cupped his free ear with his other hand to drown out the banging at the door.

A dial tone.

Ringing.

A woman's voice answered.

"Hello?" the woman said.

"Do you have a sister named *Xiu*?"

This time, Pepper pronounced her name perfectly.

A long pause, then, "Yes."

"Would you like to save her?" he asked.


Xiu's sister, Yun, cried on the phone. At first, it sounded like she was sneezing. Pepper didn't interrupt right way, even though he was in a hurry. She asked him to explain so he did—quickly—and Yun was relieved. At first she'd assumed Pepper had kidnapped her sister. (It happens.) Pepper told her about the judge in Florida, Sue's stay in immigration jail and the denial of her medication, her escape, her recapture in New York, her stay at New Hyde Hospital, and then being pulled out of Northwest yesterday. Every few seconds, Yun muttered to herself quietly, using her little sister's pet name, saying, *"My girl, oh, my poor A-Xiu."* When Pepper had told Yun everything, she said she must hurry and she hung up immediately. Didn't even say good-bye. Pepper understood.

He set the receiver back down in its cradle.

Sure, one could wonder if Yun would be able to find help for her sister in time. First step would be to find a lawyer. A lawyer in California? (Where Yun lived.) One in Florida? (Where Sue had been sentenced.) Or one in New York? (Where she had most recently been held.)

And this would have to be a lawyer who was willing to work for *nothing* because Yun was a cashier at an Albertsons supermarket in Oakland.

Then that lawyer would have to contact the courts in time.

File the proper paperwork to delay the extradition.

Head down to Florida and petition the court for Xiu's release. (Or would it be handled in a New York court?)

The lawyer might propose that Xiu be released into Yun's custody so the two could return to Oakland. But what if they had to appear before the same petty dictator who'd sentenced Xiu to deportation? How likely was it that such an unreasonable prick would be reasonable now? (Although bullies like that usually act a whole lot nicer when the bullied person has retained counsel. Probably just a coincidence.) But even with a (free) lawyer, that judge would still have to turn over his original order. Or another judge would have to contest the Florida ruling.

There were so many steps to Xiu's rescue. Even with Pepper's phone call, there were a dozen more chances for it to fail.

But if two mental patients at New Hyde Hospital could commandeer a doctor's office and dial out while police tried battering down the door and if they actually reached the right person using a phone number that a third mental patient pulled out of his ass (or from the vast Internet computer cloud with his brain), if all those steps worked out, well, shit, maybe the others would, too. It could happen. They'd just have to practice patience now. Take the long view. Success is airmail, not email.

Loochie looked back at Pepper when he hung up. Though her body rattled as she held the door, her face burned with pyrotechnic brightness.

Pepper looked as luminous as Loochie just then. Maybe it was the sunlight streaming through the office windows, but for a moment, the man's aura glowed a triumphal red.

Pepper hung up the phone and told Loochie she could let them in. She kept her shoulder to the door for a minute more. She hadn't barred the way just for Pepper's sake.

Loochie didn't know the Chinese Lady, so it wasn't for her, either. She'd be the last to admit it, but this whole time she'd been picturing her mother and brother on the other side of that door. Loochie held it closed for that last minute.

Then she stepped back and pulled the chair away.

Loochie felt disappointed when the door opened and the cop and Dr. Anand didn't fall into the room. She'd been hoping they'd spill across the floor, a little slapstick for the midday show. Instead, the door banged open and the two men stood there, huffing and glaring. Behind them stood two more officers in plain clothes, concerned but confused.

Funniest part? The pair in the second row were two of the three officers who'd brought Pepper to New Hyde. Huey and Louie. Pepper felt a shock because he hadn't really expected them to come back for him. Yet here they were. Was it finally time for him to go before a judge? Receive his sentence? Huey and Pepper locked eyes and Pepper waited for some reaction.

Zero recognition.

Louie looked at Pepper and his demeanor was the same. Blank. Nothing.

"Where's Dewey?" Pepper asked. He didn't mean to say it, the words just came out. Of course, he regretted it—it was like he was trying to remind them who he was.

The question sounded completely random, nutty, so they ignored

Pepper. (Dewey was actually back in the parking lot, waiting in the Dodge Charger. He'd refused to come inside the building, no matter what.)

"We done here?" Huey asked the cop in the uniform. It clearly galled the detective to have to ask the patrolman anything.

"Sorry," said the pudgy one. He barked the same question to Dr. Anand. "We done?"

Dr. Anand stormed inside. He found Pepper sitting again, but remained suspicious. He checked his desk, every drawer. He checked the file cabinets in the corner. What had they been doing in here? What had been taken? What had been defiled? To Pepper's great satisfaction Dr. Anand never even peeked at the telephone.

Dr. Anand surveyed his desk a second time. He noticed Pepper's big boot print on the papers. But what did that prove? That Pepper had been stomping on his desktop? In a way, this actually calmed the doctor. They'd just been acting out, venting. A pair of monkeys who'd gotten loose. And, in a way, it had been the doctor's fault. Samuel Anand chastised himself. He never should've left them alone. He'd spoken much too freely, feeling frazzled and forgetting himself, and that had led him to be lax. He must always be wary. He looked at Pepper, and then at Loochie, who had taken her seat again, too. The four cops crowded the doorway.

"You did *something*," Dr. Anand said to them.

Loochie said, "We washed the floors for you, Dr. Sam."

And do you know the four cops actually peeked at the tiles? All four. (Oh, if only Loochie had seen them do it. She would've grinned for a week.)

Huey nudged the patrolman.

"We got this other thing here," the doughy cop said. Then jerked his head down the hallway. Meaning the reason they'd been called in. Because Dorry's neck had snapped. Over in the smokers' court. Where the old woman's blood soaked the concrete.

Dr. Anand gave Loochie and Pepper the once-over. "You can go back to your rooms," he said. "We'll decide what to do with you later."

"After the cops are gone," Loochie said quietly.

"Yes," Dr. Anand said. "Once we have you to ourselves again."

Pepper and Loochie looked at the pudgy cop.

"You heard that?" Pepper asked. "He's threatening us."

The cop rubbed his shirtsleeve across his sweaty forehead and said, "Probably." Then he and the other officers left the room.

Dr. Anand stooped forward, resting his knuckles on the desk. "Was it worth it?" he asked. "Are you going to keep causing me trouble?"

Pepper felt himself flush with honesty. He couldn't lie.

And, "Yes," he said, "yes. I will. Yes."

# 35

AFTER PEPPER AND Loochie left Dr. Anand's office, the doctor made a phone call to a member of New Hyde Hospital's board of directors. He'd been dreading this moment since he got the call about Dorry. He stood while he talked. He wondered if they would finally fire him. He didn't think he'd mind.

Pepper and Loochie entered the hall and walked toward the nurses' station. As they entered the oval room, they saw patients scuttling all over. The unit was abuzz.

The sounds of running showers could be heard from Northwest 2 and 3. The rumbling of dresser drawers in people's rooms sounded like bowling balls rolling down multiple lanes. Then the drawers slammed shut and it sounded as if every patient had just hit a strike.

Loochie and Pepper reached the nurses' station. Miss Chris sat in front of the computer; only a very short stack of paper files on the desk. Miss Chris wore a pair of glasses down near the tip of her nose, and she tilted her head backward to see through them. Pepper and Loochie leaned against the high counter of the station.

"What's going on?" Pepper asked.

"Is someone else dead?" Loochie asked.

Miss Chris sucked her teeth to dismiss Loochie's question. She looked up at them, over the top of her glasses. "You're leaving," she said.

Pepper gestured to him and Loochie. "The two of us?"

The nurse frowned. "All of you."

"Leaving where?" Loochie asked.

"We're taking you out. So the police can work without any nonsense."

Loochie and Pepper recoiled at the suggestion. It was the sound of that sentence: *You're leaving*. It's what Pepper and Loochie wanted, of course, but they both realized they were a little scared by the idea. They'd been to the courtyard but now they were being promised the mountaintop. Outside. Pepper had only been here for three months, Loochie for ten, but already both had kind of forgotten what *outside* really meant. Right now it sounded like sudden peace at the end of a long and delirious war. The thing everyone had been hoping for even as they stopped believing the day would ever come.

Loochie's mouth went dry. "Where are we going?"

Pepper leaned almost over the nurses' station counter, as if pulled by some magnetic force. His lips parted with muted surprise.

Miss Chris took some pleasure in keeping the answer to herself. "You'll see," she said. "Soon, soon."


So many of the patients were showering that there wasn't even any hot water by the time Loochie and Pepper reached their rooms. That didn't stop either of them. It didn't matter how frigid the water temperature, the thrill of stepping outside had started a fire inside. Curiosity fed the furnace. They each had a core temperature of 180 just then. If those showers were cold, they barely noticed.

Those patients who hadn't worn their outside clothes in years, yes *years*, pulled them on no matter how tight or semi-tattered or out of style. Women and men brushed or combed or picked their hair. Pepper even tried to get the crinkles out of his shirt by rubbing it back and forth against the edge of his door, working the wood like he held a saw.

He must've really been putting some energy into smoothing his shirt. The door vibrated, causing some of the ceiling tiles to bump and shake. The tile with the stain, which had never been changed, even sprinkled a handful of flakes to the floor. The sight of the ceiling cracking caused such a visceral panic in Pepper that he dropped his shirt and jumped into the hallway shirtless and shaking. He stood there watching the ceiling, expecting a monster to come crashing down.

Pepper was shaken out of his trance when Mr. Mack stuck his head out of his room, saw Pepper, and shouted, "Nobody wants to see your pasty chest!"

Pepper ignored the insult (after all, Sue had liked it) and walked back into the room, to the ceiling tile. There were dozens of tiny cracks running from the stain, in the middle now. Pepper doubted this part of the ceiling was strong enough to hold much of anything anymore. A weak spot. Still Pepper found himself crouching slightly as he put on his shirt and left the room.

Scotch Tape stood at the secure door and tried to temper the patients' enthusiasm. *"Relax, everybody,"* he told them more than once as they lined up in front of him. *"It's just, like, six blocks."* As if they would be disappointed. But he couldn't understand. Scotch Tape walked eight blocks at the end of each shift and waited for the Q46. That bus took him to the Q30 and then he transferred one more time for the Q9. All this so he could get to Jamaica, Queens, where he then got on the J train and traveled home to Brooklyn. A ninety-minute commute. Sometimes longer with transit-system delays. He'd been working at New Hyde for three years. Making that commute five, and sometimes six, days a week. So this little trip of six blocks . . . to him, meant hardly anything.

The patients gathered at the door and Scotch Tape waited. He kept peeking out the plastic windowpane as if he were expecting company to appear on the other side, an armed escort maybe. That's how some of the patients read his gesture, but of course some of them were clinically paranoid. Really Scotch Tape kept looking out the front door as an excuse to avoid the patients' gazes, their conversations.

The ones who got there first looked to him like dogs do to their masters. *Let us out! Open up!* He was already exhausted by their undisguised need. But finally they had all arrived. "Ready?" he asked.

"We've been ready!" Doris Roberts shouted playfully. She had even done her hair after borrowing Sandra Day O'Connor's brush.

The other patients stared at the door. *Let us out. Open up!* Pepper and Loochie were the last patients on line. Loochie had decided against wearing the towel wrapped around her noggin. Instead she'd returned to the blue knit cap. She'd removed the strings that once held the pom-poms. Nurse Washburn and a second nurse were behind them. The patients stood in pairs, like schoolchildren.

Scotch Tape unlocked the secure door. That click barely audible over the twelve patients' heartbeats. He held the door open.

"Come on now," he said to Mr. Mack and Frank Waverly, the first two in line. Their old sport coats were so crisp they looked steamed. (An easy trick if you run a hot shower and hang the coat inside the bathroom.)

"Don't rush me," Mr. Mack told him.

Scotch Tape nodded and waited, exasperated and respectful. Mr. Mack reached up and tried to close the buttons of his coat before moving. But his fingers were trembling so fast they damn near blurred. He had trouble getting the first button through its hole so Frank Waverly tried to help by reaching for Mr. Mack's coat. But the littler man slapped Frank Waverly's help away. Leaving Mr. Mack to wrestle with the fabric a little more. Frank Waverly got bored and walked out of the unit without him. The rest filed around him, too.

Mr. Mack was the last patient to go. His sport coat still unbuttoned.


The group passed through the secure ward door and into the hallway. The fluorescent lights above them cast the same old sickly yellow glow, but the lavender walls were a welcome change.

They walked through the empty lobby with its cheap chairs and sofas. These didn't look any better just because they were on this side.

But then the group reached the double doors that led to the parking lot. Scotch Tape opened one door and the sunlight came in. Somehow this sunlight seemed different from the stuff that reached the smokers' court. There, the light looked like melted margarine. But out here? You know.

Like butter.

Twelve patients stepped outside and proceeded to act the fool. They squinted up at the sun and covered their eyes with their hands. They sniffed the air theatrically. Some hummed. One yipped at such a high pitch it sounded like a birdcall. They wiped their hands over their faces as if they'd just lifted their heads out of a pool. It was the middle of April, and a wonderfully pleasant day. A strong wind played among the trees and some folks shut their eyes, just listening to the quivering leaves.

*Shhhhhhh*

*Shhhhhhh*

*Shhhhhhh*

"That's nice," Loochie said.

Pepper gazed at her and wondered if he looked as happy as she did. He hoped so.

Loochie opened one eye. "I *thought* someone was watching me."

"You're just being paranoid," Pepper said.

She shut her eye, breathed deep once more. "That's what the doctors tell me."

"They have pills for that," Pepper said.

Loochie laughed with him. The other patients seemed to be having their own reveries. Even Mr. Mack was feeling better out here. With his eyes shut, he found the top button of his sport coat. With steady hands he slipped it through the corresponding hole in one try.

"Everybody ready to walk?" Nurse Washburn asked.

Scotch Tape raised one hand at the front of the group. "Let's go."

They took the six blocks slowly. Some of them, like Pepper and Loochie, could probably have done with a faster pace but others, like Mr. Mack and Frank Waverly, the Haint, and Sandra Day O'Connor, had more gingerly strides. This wasn't just the fault of old age or medication. The sidewalks around here were also a mess. On every block, there were a few trees whose roots had finally cracked through the

concrete surface, causing the sidewalk panels to buckle and occasionally shatter. Neighborhood joggers didn't bother running on
those sidewalks because it was double hell on the knees. Joggers, bike
riders, even folks out walking their dogs tended to move in the street.
The only people limber enough to risk the sidewalks were neighborhood children, who found all the dips and rises kind of fun. The staff
wouldn't let the patients walk in the road, even though everyone
could tell it was the commonsense choice. What if one of them got
smashed by a passing van? All three staff members would lose their
jobs for that one. Not to mention the tragedy of someone getting
smashed by a van. (But really, the fear of losing a decent-paying job
in 2011 could not be overstated.) So if the older patients, or the dazed
patients, or the morbidly obese patients took their time to move six
blocks, well, no one felt too angry with them.

People from the neighborhood watched the group go by. An old
woman dragging her garbage bin out from the side of her house or a
middle-aged couple returning home from the grocery store. They
didn't throw eggs or stones. No pitchforks and torches.

Mostly, the neighbors just watched them, as you would any time a
parade made its way down your street. The neighbors watched intently but refused to admit it. They did this strange move where they
ducked their heads as the patients passed, looking at the sidewalk or
their front lawns or their garbage bins, always toward the ground.
But anyone could clearly see the eyes shifting up to gawk.

"Hey, Pepper," Loochie asked. "How come white people do that?"

She mimicked the move; head down but eyes surreptitiously on
alert.

Pepper frowned. "Why you asking me?"

"You're about the only white guy I know," Loochie said.

Pepper blushed red. "That's not true."

"What other white guys you think I come across?" she asked. "I
live in Laurelton."

Now he caught himself looking at the folks in the neighborhood.
All the people in front of these homes *were* white. He hadn't even
been thinking about it. But now he watched the neighbors like he was
actually going to explain some behavioral trait to his naïve friend.

And once Loochie had mentioned it, he had to admit it seemed kind of true. *Looking without looking.* As soon as the group of patients reached them, the locals dropped their heads, but Pepper could see their eyes shifting warily. Was this really something white people did? *Only* white people? Did he do it, too?

At first, Pepper wanted to tell Loochie it was a way to pretend the patients weren't there. A trick for making others invisible. That made a simple kind of sense to him. But as Pepper watched it happen again and again, he changed his diagnosis. It began to seem like these people thought that by dipping their heads they were actually making *themselves* invisible. As if you couldn't see them if they didn't look directly at you. Talk about insane!

That's where things got uncomfortable for Pepper. After all, he was a white guy. So wasn't Loochie criticizing him? Assuming he knew why white people played this eye-contact game meant that he, too, had probably done it. And had he? Probably! Pepper, who never really thought of himself as some great defender of the white way of life, felt the impulse to fight back.

"Let me ask *you* something," Pepper said. "How come black guys are so loud on the subway? Like when they start yelling out rap lyrics? Or they just play music through those little speakers on their phones instead of using the goddamn earphones like normal people do?"

Loochie raised her eyebrows and let them drop. She sighed with disappointment.

"That's easy," Loochie said. "Those loud black guys on the subway? They're being assholes, *too.*"

Then Loochie broke ranks and walked ahead of him.

Something strange happened after the patients left the hospital. Inside, they were patients, but the farther they walked, the less this seemed true. Pepper turned into a white guy from Elmhurst. Loochie, a black teenager from Laurelton. It's not like this hadn't been true (or obvious!) before, but inside Northwest it hadn't really counted as much of a difference. Not when you considered their enemies: the pills, the restraints, the Devil. But out here, there were no restraints and no pills. Maybe even the Devil had been left behind for now. So something had to rise in the order.

And it wasn't just the two of them. Suddenly Doris Roberts drifted away from Sandra Day O'Connor and gravitated toward Still Waters, two generations of Jewish women. Sandra Day suddenly found herself pulled toward the Redhead Kingpin. Wally Gambino and Loochie, kids from Queens, slid into step. Only Mr. Mack and Frank Waverly didn't break off for new friends. Each man walked alone.

Pepper watched these allegiances shift. He did a little quick math. If everybody paired off with the people who looked most like them, he'd be spending this whole field trip with Heatmiser. What was he going to do, listen to that bastard mumble for the next hour because they happened to share skin color and genitalia? He picked up his pace and found Loochie, who was walking side by side with Wally Gambino. Pepper had to balance on the curbside, dodging trees and fire hydrants, if he wanted to keep pace. Wally was in the middle of a sentence when Pepper caught up.

". . . and that's why I'm saying," Wally purred. "I *been* had my eye on you girl. I like that bald look. You lookin' like a sexy mannequin."

Loochie walked with her head down, not looking at Wally. She tugged her knit cap down lower, so it almost covered her eyes. She watched her feet as they walked, but she cut her eyes to the right, watching Wally warily.

"You're doing the same thing right now!" Pepper laughed and pointed.

Wally glared at Pepper. "Big man! You got to back up. Me and shorty is having a *parlay.*"

Loochie jabbed her thumb toward Wally. "*This* is why *women* do it. I just didn't know why white people do."

Wally was in between them. They talked across him.

"Maybe it's the same thing," Pepper offered. "We just don't want to be bothered."

Wally leaned closer to Loochie and deepened his voice.

"I'm saying. You need to spend a little time with me." He looked back at her butt. "You got a *bubble* I want to *pop.*"

Pepper couldn't help himself. He laughed.

"I'm a virgin," Loochie said with comical sincerity.

But Wally hadn't heard her. Instead, he looked at Pepper. "Big man, you don't want to be laughing at me. You know what they call me back home? They call me *Bloody Loco*! Make sure you recognize that name. ASAP!"

"I thought they call you Wally Gambino," Pepper said.

"You don't put no fucking fear in my heart," Wally shouted. He was smaller than Pepper and much thinner. "You or *no* fucking man put no fear in my heart!"

Behind them, Nurse Washburn said, "We can take you back to New Hyde, Wilfredo. Turn you right around. *ASAP.*"

Wally sneered at Pepper. "We ain't done," he said.

Then he walked forward until he stomped alongside Scotch Tape. Now Scotch Tape had to listen to Wally grumble.

Pepper looked at Loochie. "Are we cool?"

Loochie nodded. She pointed at Wally Gambino, up ahead. "That's why I keep my head down," she said. "Sometimes I don't even realize I'm doing it. It's just easier to protect myself from guys like him."

"Yeah," Pepper said. "I see."

"But here's what I still don't understand," Loochie continued. "White people do it to *everyone*. Even each other."

Pepper sighed. "So?"

"So how much of the world are you all scared of?"

# 36

THE CREW REACHED Union Turnpike, and Scotch Tape pointed at the sign on the awning of their destination: Sal's Restaurant & Bar Incorporated.

"Cheese on bread," Mr. Mack muttered. "This is it?"

Scotch Tape pointed at the green awning, its white lettering. "Yessir!" he said. He tried to sound enthusiastic though he understood the look of disappointment creeping across each patient's face.

A dozen patients shuffled and mumbled. They looked to the nurses who also nodded to show that indeed they'd reached the destination. *Sal's Restaurant & Bar.* The staff tensed, a decision was being made by the group's mind. Both nurses and the orderly calculated. Twelve patients and three staff. Imagine the debacle if even five or six of them decided to bolt, underwhelmed by this field trip. Half a dozen mental patients scrambling across Union Turnpike, that four-lane roadway with buses and big trucks speeding in both directions, perfect for splattering fleeing patients. There was a bus stop two stores down from the restaurant. Scotch Tape waited there after each shift as he began his ninety-minute journey home. *Don't run, don't run, don't run.* That's what the staff members were chanting in their heads.

"Who's paying?" Loochie asked.

"New Hyde Hospital." Nurse Washburn patted a sweater pocket where she carried the department's debit card.

A little more murmuring. A few looks back and forth.

"So let's get in there!" Scotch Tape said, grinning much too widely. He bounced from one foot to the other. He was getting himself ready to tackle the first person who tried to make a run. Young or old, man or woman. The first one to bolt was going to get *whomped*. A lesson for the others.

The second nurse said, "They make good pizza. I ate here before."

"Can we get beer?" Pepper asked.

Nurse Washburn rolled her eyes. "No beer."

"But you're paying for the slices," Loochie clarified.

"Two each." She patted her pocket again. "That's right."

No declarations were made by the patients. No one shook hands or signed a treaty. But the potential rebellion had been quelled. Heat-miser walked to the door of Sal's Restaurant & Bar Incorporated. He held it open.


Sal's Restaurant & Bar was bigger than your average pizza place because it really had been a fine establishment once. (It had also once been owned by a guy named Sal. Now it was actually owned and operated by a man named Joseph Angeli, but who was going to pay to fabricate a whole new awning? You?)

The bar had been removed (Sal took his liquor license with him) and replaced with the traditional bank of ovens for cooking up slices. But the dining area remained the same. Seating for fifty, and each table had a maroon tablecloth. The back wall had a faded trompe l'oeil painting of an Italian city under a blue sky. When the patients entered the restaurant, a few of them cooed.

"This is *nice*," Redhead Kingpin said.

The patients crowded the nearby counter. One old man stood behind it, looking bemused. He had his hands in a gray plastic bin of shredded parmesan cheese. His full head of wavy white hair sat flat on his scalp from working near the heat of the ovens. His eyebrows were thinning and his face clean-shaved. His cheeks and forehead were red, and his nose had a high arch, like an Art Deco eagle, which made the man look angry all the time. Another person could be heard behind a swinging door, clattering pans. The patients jammed themselves against the counter, and the old man looked at them. He nodded once, and said, "So what's all this?"

They called out orders.

"Lemme get two pepperoni!"

"Lemme get one anchovy!"

"Lemme get three with sausage!"

But the guy didn't even take his hands out of the cheese. He just scanned. Finally Scotch Tape entered the restaurant. "Everybody go take a seat," he shouted. "Take a seat!"

The patients glumly moved away from the counter.

The old man smiled and pointed at Scotch Tape.

"*That's* my guy."

A teenage couple occupied one table in the restaurant, a single half-eaten slice between them. The girl leafed through a newspaper, and the boy ticked away on his cell phone. But as the patients moved past the pair, they looked up. Were they shocked to see so many mental patients cresting over them like a wave? No, it wasn't that. These two kids were just amazed to see so many customers. Normally, Sal (they didn't know his real name was Joseph Angeli) wouldn't serve this many people in a week.

The patients took their seats. There were plenty of tables, but they clustered near each other, as if afraid to drift too far apart. While the others were discussing their orders, Redhead Kingpin and Still Waters paid attention to that newspaper at the teenagers' table. The girl flipped the pages loudly out of boredom, and those two watched her enviously.

Both nurses took a table together and pushed out a third chair for Scotch Tape. Scotch Tape remained at the counter, jabbering with the owner. Sal looked at the group as Scotch Tape pointed at them. He nodded his head faintly.

Scotch Tape returned to the group. He clapped his hands at the start of his announcement. "I told Sal that everyone is getting two slices apiece."

Loochie raised her hand, "I want mushrooms on mine."

Scotch Tape waved one hand. "We're not getting into all that. Everyone gets two cheese slices and a soda."

Sal came from behind the counter carrying a plastic tray crammed with Coke cans, all perspiring chilled droplets. He went from table to table plopping down cans. Three people demanded different drinks. Sal didn't argue. He took the Cokes and returned with two ginger ales and one Diet Coke. Once that was done, he stood before the patients and rubbed his big hands, making a swishing sound.

"I'm happy to have you all here today," he said. "Call me Sal. I'll be making your pizza."

He smiled at them, much too widely. He really waggled his eyebrows. Cartoonish gestures. The kind of thing you might do when first meeting a group of kindergartners.

Pepper leaned toward Loochie. "Why's he talking to us like that?"

"Have any of *you* made pizza before?" Sal asked. "It's not that diffi— hard. But it's hard to make it *right*."

Loochie sighed. "He knows we're mental patients."

"Scotch Tape must've told him," Pepper said. Sal was about to explain what dough and cheese were. After that, maybe he'd give a lesson on the oven and the transformative power of heat! Pepper didn't feel like humoring the guy as he tried to "communicate" with them. They were out for a trip, a kind of vacation. He wanted a reprieve from the unit, not a reminder.

"Hey, Sal," Pepper called out. "Can you make my slice with Haldol?"

That made Loochie grin. "I'll take lithium on mine," she added.

"I want a little Depacot on mine," Doris Roberts shouted. *"A dank!"*

Even the silent patients enjoyed themselves. Heatmiser and Yuckmouth and the Haint grinned. Laughter rippled through the group.

Sal wasn't stupid, he understood he was being ridiculed. But he couldn't understand why they were doing it. He was being nice! But okay, fine, Sal (Joseph) had his own worries in life. (Like a daughter, an addict, working in the back, who made a habit of lifting money from the register when left to work the shop alone; which is why the man never got a day off; which is why the man was tired; which is why he lost his patience.)

"Ahhh, you can *choke* on the slices," Sal said.

Which made even the staff members laugh.

Sal stomped behind the counter to cook.

The teenage boy set down his phone and ate the rest of the slice in two bites. He gave the crust to the girl. She chomped it while getting up, and the pair left.

The girl forgot her newspaper. Didn't even look back for it as she went. What did she care? It was *am New York,* a freebie handed out weekday mornings at subway stations and bus stops. If she'd returned, even just a minute later, she wouldn't have found it anyway, it was already at another table. Still Waters flipped through the pages and now thoroughly ignored Doris Roberts. Each time a page turned, Redhead Kingpin, at the next table, faintly whimpered.

Soon enough, the slices arrived.

Sal didn't bring them over himself like he had the soda cans. The serving duties fell to Sal's daughter, a woman in her forties who never introduced herself. A woman who didn't seem put off by or scared of the patients, didn't act friendly or solicitous, either. She seemed so utterly indifferent to the patients that they immediately felt quite fond of her. This woman had served that teenage couple in exactly the same way. Equal-opportunity disinterest.

Before their meals began in earnest, Mr. Mack picked up a napkin dispenser and clanged it against the tabletop like a gavel.

"I think we should say a little prayer for Dorry," Mr. Mack said.

There were many differences about the patients on the outside, but none more so than with Mr. Mack. If inside he was as irritable as a weasel, outside he'd found a new kind of steadiness. Not calm, but more commanding. Less weasel, more badger. Maybe this is how he'd been before he entered New Hyde. Or how he might've been had he never been committed. He was at his table alone. He stood up to lead.

Those who were in the practice shut their eyes and whispered the proper words from memory. Even Frank Waverly, at his own table, mouthed the phrases. Those who weren't the praying types still clasped their hands.

"We wish you the best, Dorry," Mr. Mack said. "You're probably talking God's ear off right now!"

There was a long silence, people squirmed, unsure if the caustic old man was mocking the dead.

"But unlike us," Mr. Mack added. "The good Lord will *appreciate* the sound. Amen."

"Amen," Loochie whispered.

Pepper found himself unable to speak. He'd been so cruel to that woman with his last words. And, if he thought about it, hadn't she helped him yet again, even in death? It was because of her suicide that he'd been brought to Dr. Anand's office. Once in there he was finally able to call Sue's sister. Even now, sitting in Sal's pizza shop—the entire patient population getting *out* so the cops could work on Dorry's crime scene without interruption—even that was kind of her doing, too. Maybe Dorry really had been like a mother. He'd treated her so badly but still, in her way, she'd taken care of him. How could he thank her for that? How could he ever repay it?

And in this moment, Sal came from around the counter again. The dining area had turned so quiet that he wanted to make sure they hadn't all somehow dined and dashed. He found the patients and the staff with lowered heads.

Sal watched quietly for a little while.

"That's good," he finally said. "I like to see that."

Pepper and Loochie and all the rest opened their eyes. They looked at Joseph Angeli, who was leaning forward, both hands flat on an empty table. His head dropped, and when he lifted it again, his eyes were moist. He pointed to the painting on the back wall, the Italian city. "That's Florence," he said quietly. "The birthplace of *Dante*." He shook his head. "Dante knew the truth."

The thunder of crashing pots came from the kitchen. It shook everyone but Joe, who was used to it. The clatter nearly drowned out his last words.

"The Devil is *real*," he said.

The pizza was fine. But the setting made it scrumptious. And the staff didn't rush the meal. Scotch Tape tried to play like he was being magnanimous. When one patient or the other asked him how much time they had left before they must return to New Hyde, Scotch Tape just waved one arm to let them know there was time. And he was giving it.

So they ate slowly, but eventually Nurse Washburn rose and walked a circuit around the tables.

"All done?" she asked loudly. Not for the patients but for Scotch Tape. She didn't much care for his benevolent-king routine, especially since she and the other nurse (Nurse Washburn hadn't learned the woman's name yet) outranked him. She wandered among the tables twice, as if taking a count, then she stopped alongside Scotch Tape. She stood next to him but didn't face him. (She didn't want it to appear like she was reporting to him.) He stayed seated. Nurse Washburn said, "If we're all done, then we can line up."

Scotch Tape pointed at his plate, the crusts of his two slices. He hadn't been meaning to eat them until Nurse Washburn spoke up. "I'm not finished," he said.

"Can't you can take them with you?"

Scotch Tape stayed silent. The patients watched both of them. Everywhere you go, someone is vying for power! Nurse Washburn, a white woman who wanted to assert the hard-won dignity of her position. Scotch Tape, a black man who loathed public disrespect. Somehow leaving a pizza parlor had turned into a war of the oppressed.

The stalemate was broken by Sal. He walked into the dining area, waving a slip of paper.

"Who's going to take the check?" he asked.

That worked like a bell signaling the end of a round. Nurse Washburn walked off to pay the bill, shoulders pulled back proudly as she was the one entrusted with the hospital's card. Scotch Tape wolfed down his crusts (which he hated), then sprang up and clapped for all the patients to get in line as if that had been *his* idea. Everyone was happy.

Pepper and Loochie stood side by side. Mr. Mack was in front of them, alone. He turned back and looked at the pair, up and down.

"You two sure got close," he said, leering at them.

"Close?" Pepper asked, sounding thrown. To him it was like Mr. Mack had suggested he was sleeping with his niece.

Loochie grabbed Pepper's arm. "Close like Bethlehem and Nazareth."

Mr. Mack leaned back, surprised. Loochie batted her eyelashes at Pepper and smiled. "Isn't that right?"

"Most definitely," Pepper said.

He knew she was just fucking with Mr. Mack, but Loochie had also spoken the truth. To his great surprise, and hers, Loochie was now his closest friend.

They expected this would be enough to shoo Mr. Mack away, but like a fruit fly, the man kept hovering. "Put out your hand," he said.

Pepper did. If Mr. Mack spat into his palm, he realized, he was going to crack the guy in the chest.

As Nurse Washburn returned from paying the bill, Mr. Mack dropped a white envelope into Pepper's open hand. As soon as it landed, it curled into a tube.

"Dorry gave that to you," Mr. Mack said. "But you left it on a table."

Pepper had totally forgotten about it. Loochie went on her toes then so she could see it better.

"You opened it," Pepper said. The top of the envelope showed the tear.

"You left it there, so I picked it up," Mr. Mack said. "Caveat emptor. Let the buyer beware."

Pepper sighed. "That's not what that means."

"Carpe diem," he tried.

"That's better," Pepper said.

"What was in it?" Loochie asked.

At the front of the line, Nurse Washburn and Scotch Tape were both trying to assert their place of leadership. Until they made peace, the group couldn't even walk out of Sal's, let alone march back to the hospital.

Mr. Mack cut his eyes at Loochie. "A map and a . . ."

"Come on now!" Sal shouted from behind the counter. "You're blocking my door!"

Food served, prayers shared, bill paid. Now get the fuck outta here.

So Scotch Tape and Nurse Washburn tried to walk through the doorway simultaneously. They crunched each other. Then Scotch Tape held the door and Nurse Washburn waved the patients through. The group moved.

"A map of what?" Pepper asked.

Mr. Mack didn't answer until they were outside. "The whole building," he said. "First floor and second floor. Including the *exit*."

"An escape?" Loochie asked.

Mr. Mack tapped his temple. "That's the idea."

Pepper grabbed at Mr. Mack's small shoulder. It was like seeing a teenager maul a toddler. But Mr. Mack had more vinegar than a one-year-old. Pepper grabbed him and Mr. Mack smacked the big man's hand off. And it hurt.

"Let me see it," Pepper said.

Mr. Mack broke formation and walked alongside Loochie, the three of them in a row. "That idea is void," Mr. Mack said. "Everything stays with me."

"Dorry gave it to me."

Mr. Mack looked ahead of him and behind.

"You think I'm going to let you run the show," Mr. Mack whispered. "And get myself killed like Coffee did? No. That's *void*."

"Stop saying that," Loochie told him.

"We're going for the change-up this time," Mr. Mack continued in full voice, so the nearest patients would hear him. "*You* don't lead, you follow. I've already studied Dorry's map. There's a way to get from our rooms up to that second floor. From the second floor we can slip out without notice."

"Fine," Pepper huffed, wishing he'd been smart enough to just grab the envelope when Dorry offered it. "Who's going?"

"Mr. Mack!" Nurse Washburn pointed at him as they reached the corner. "Lines of two."

The old man nodded and waved at her. He slipped in front of Pepper, marching next to Yuckmouth. "All of us are going, because all of us are at risk if we stay. But first, we'll find that *thing*," Mr. Mack promised. "Instead of being trampled, we're going to do some trampling."

"And what about when we're out?" Pepper asked. "Have you thought that far?"

Mr. Mack sighed. "We get out and we're *free*. Every man and woman can do whatever the hell they want to. First thing I'm going to do is sneak back into the parking lot and piss on the doctor's car. I know which one it is."

They walked, and Pepper let Mr. Mack gloat over his imagined victory to come. A piss-stained tire. Dream big! Pepper had a feeling that Mr. Mack's plans didn't go any further than that. He finally had a little power and what did he want to do with it? Ruin shit. Nothing more.

Pepper could still see the sign for the bus stop two stores down from Sal's. Even if the bus was slow, it would, eventually, come. A six-block sprint. If they ran in the street instead of the sidewalk, they could avoid doing something stupid like tripping and spraining an ankle, a bad scene from a horror movie. If they really could slip out unnoticed by the staff, he and Loochie could wait for that bus as calmly as they pleased. They'd be off long before any alerts were raised. The other patients, if they wanted to, could spend their time relieving themselves all over New Hyde's parking lot. He'd be gone. And he was taking Loochie with him.

"When?" Pepper asked.

Mr. Mack spoke without turning back, so Pepper and Loochie had to lean forward to hear him. From a distance, you would've mistaken them for subjects bowing to an emperor.

"When I'm ready," Mr. Mack said. "Until then, you just sit tight."

Loochie opened her mouth to protest, but Pepper touched her arm and shook his head. "You see this path we're taking? Back to New Hyde?" he whispered. "I want you to memorize it."

It might seem unnecessary to commit a six-block walk to memory. Compare that with stories of people who marched from one country to another to escape the ravages of some hellacious war. (Like the Von Trapps.) But imagine it's nighttime and you're *zonked* on pharmaceutical drugs. A walk to the damn bathroom might turn you around. Both Pepper and Loochie knew this personally, so they whispered the street names to themselves. Noted little landmarks.

"What's the signal going to be?" Pepper asked.

"Keep your mouth shut," Mr. Mack said. "That's the signal."

Loochie noted the enormous tree that actually tilted so far over that some of its leaves caressed the roof of a one-family house. You'd remember something like that, night or day.

"You got cut off before," Loochie said to Mr. Mack. "There were two things in that envelope, right? The map and what else?"

But Mr. Mack didn't turn his head, didn't break his stride, and he sure as hell didn't deign to answer her.

# 37

SO THEY WAITED.

Pepper thought this might mean hanging back until dinnertime. When he reached the television lounge that evening, he felt a charge seeing Mr. Mack going from table to table, whispering in the ear of each patient gathered there. Pepper had taken his meds but was expert enough by now to know his drowsiness would pass in about twenty minutes. He went to the orderly and took his tray. When he scanned the tables he realized all the patients sat with their backs to the courtyard.

The police had set out a tarp right over the patch of concrete where Dorry had bled out. The crime scene. The tarp was weighed down with fist-sized stones so it wouldn't blow away. But when the wind slipped underneath, the plastic tarp rose and fell, rose and fell. In the dark it looked like Dorry's body might still be under there breathing.

Pepper sat with his back to the smokers' court, just like everybody else. He took a seat with Redhead Kingpin and Still Waters. Back inside the unit, they were a team again. He was surprised to see them. It was only seven p.m.

"You all are up early," Pepper said.

Redhead Kingpin poked at her macaroni salad with her spoon. "Haven't gone to sleep since Xiu left."

Pepper looked to Still Waters, who could barely lift her head, but this time it wasn't out of shyness.

"You look like you've been crying," Pepper told her, trying to be playful.

She stared at her tray. "I'm all cried out."

Then Mr. Mack came to their table. He stood across from Pepper. He didn't even have to lean down to look Pepper in the eye. He held Pepper's gaze. "Tonight . . ." Mr. Mack began.

He looked over his shoulder at the orderly who had his now-hospital-approved cell phone out and was texting away.

Mr. Mack looked back at Pepper, who was nodding so enthusiastically that he felt like a mutt.

". . . is *not* the night," Mr. Mack finished.

Then he bowed slightly and turned away. He walked to the edge of the television lounge and raised one arm. They all looked to him. Mr. Mack twirled his hand, haughty as an aristocrat. After that, he left the lounge.

"He's enjoying himself," Redhead Kingpin said.

Pepper scooped up his dollop of macaroni salad in three bites. It felt terrible to have to wait on a man like that. Even worse to imagine Dorry really was still out there in the courtyard, lying under the plastic, suffocating. He could almost hear the flapping of that tarp as it rose and fell.

Redhead Kingpin pushed her chair back and said, "Wait here."

Still Waters left with her.

On the television they were playing a whole lot of nothing, which was pleasing just now. People talk badly about mindless television, but the shit has its purposes. For instance, it stopped Pepper from tearing the keys off the orderly's wrist and opening the glass door out to the courtyard and pulling back the tarp so poor Dorry could *get some air*.

Redhead Kingpin returned to the lounge, Still Waters trailing only inches behind her. Each of them carried an accordion folder. They took their seats again. One folder blue, the other manila.

"Those are Sue's," Pepper said.

Still Waters turned the manila folder, so Pepper could see the two words: "No Name." Still Waters curled her left arm around the bottom of the folder like a boa constrictor.

"We're keeping that one," Redhead Kingpin said. She slid the blue folder between him and his dinner tray. "But she wanted you to have this."

Pepper looked down at the blue folder. He saw two words written in black ink on the side: "Nice Dream."

"Have you heard anything from her?" he asked. "About her?"

Both women pinched their mouths and shut their reddened eyes. That was their only answer.

He undid the elastic string that held the blue cover down. He opened the folder and saw all those pages from all those magazines. Reykjavik, Accra, Fiji, Wichita, Holland.

"She'll never get to visit those places," Redhead Kingpin said. "But it would make her happy if you ever saw even one of them."

Pepper leafed through the pages. There were hundreds of them.

"How's that ever going to happen?" Pepper whispered. "I'm stuck in here like everyone else."

Still Waters leaned forward, pulling Sue's No Name folder even closer to her chest. She concentrated on the tabletop when she spoke. "You be patient," she whispered. "Let Mr. Mack enjoy his little games."

"Then you *escape*," Redhead Kingpin added. "Just like the rest of us."

A nice dream, but Sue's file had a nightmarish effect on Pepper. Holding the glossy pages, knowing she'd left without them, only made him grim. Why not hold on to these beautiful photos at least? Unless Sue had left New Hyde in the deepest pit of despair imaginable. A place where even fantasies must be abandoned. And because Pepper loved her, this thought filled him with anguish.

By the time he returned to his room after dinner, he'd decided to wait up for the Devil.

He didn't know if it would come tonight, but let it come tonight.

He sat on the windowsill, his back to the two giant panes. He held the blue folder in his lap. He watched the ceiling. Let it come.

But the Devil didn't show up.

Both it and Mr. Mack were going to make him wait.

Three more days and nothing going. Mr. Mack made the rounds each night, letting people know he'd decided to push the date back. He claimed he was giving people a chance to get their houses in order, but what did that mean exactly? Who fucking knew?

And over these three days Pepper disintegrated. He spent his mornings and afternoons sorting Sue's magazine clippings by continent or climate or even just by how far away they were. And at night he sat in the windowsill and waited for the Devil. Three nights like that and the man wasn't doing well. He hadn't showered. He'd hardly eaten.

On the fourth morning, April 20, Scotch Tape visited Pepper's room. The big man had been tardy for his morning meds. Scotch Tape found him lying on his double bed, clutching at a blue accordion folder.

"You got to get up," Scotch Tape said. "Come on, Pepper."

It was the first time Scotch Tape had said the name without a little salt in it.

"And you're going to have to take these beds apart."

Pepper sat up. He'd been sleeping on Sue's side.

"You're getting a new roommate," Scotch Tape said.

"Today?"

"Soon."

Scotch Tape watched as Pepper got out of bed. Pepper wore the blue pajama top and bottom. He had a little trouble getting out of bed because he wouldn't put the folder down. Scotch Tape had believed this man was fine, mentally, only sixty-two days ago. But now?

"Let's go," Scotch Tape said brusquely, just to stop thinking.

Pepper walked with Scotch Tape to the nurses' station. He took his meds. As he swallowed, he heard all this conversation coming from the television lounge.

"What's going on?" Pepper asked, pointing to Northwest 5.

Scotch Tape was back inside the nurses' station already. A stack of files sat next to the computer. Pepper could read the name on the tabs. "Doris Walczak." There were fifty-two different files. The records of Doris Walczak's entire stay at New Hyde. Ready to be logged.

Pepper decided he had no questions about what her files were doing there. He decided to forget them. Instead, he pointed at the lounge and asked again. "What's going on?"

Scotch Tape sat down in front of the computer. "It's visiting day," he said. "And it looks like everybody's family decided to come."

Pepper nodded. He didn't say, *Not everyone's.*

He went to the lounge anyway. If only because it spared him a little time before he'd have to pull apart his double bed. Before another body filled the mattress that had carried Sue's.

Every table was full, and there were still so many folks that many had to stand around. The lounge looked like a cocktail party thrown on a New York City subway train.

Doris Roberts and her extended family. Mr. Mack and his. Heatmiser had a sister there *and* a fucking girlfriend! Yuckmouth and his peoples. Wally Gambino had a whole damn crew. (How did that happen? Each patient was only allowed two visitors at a time but Wally had ten; they'd probably just bum rushed the door.) The Haint sat with two members of her church. Sandra Day O'Connor sat with an old man, her husband. Redhead Kingpin and Still Waters had pulled two tables together and were introducing their family members to one another. Frank Waverly stood outside in the courtyard, alone, smoking.

"Well, shit," Pepper said to himself. He was practically caressing the blue accordion folder just to have contact with something.

"Pepper."

He heard his name but he ignored it. You know the only person he wanted to speak with right then. Not Sue. Not Mari. It's almost too embarrassing to share.

His mother.

He wanted to hear his mom's voice.

"Pepper!"

But of course that wasn't his mother.

It was Loochie.

At a table with her mother and brother.

The same mother and brother he'd sworn he'd apologize to.

Loochie waved Pepper over. If there's one person who wouldn't forget her promise, it was definitely Loochie.

Pepper lumbered to the table. His feet slapped on the cool floor.

There were three white cartons of Chinese food set out at the Gardners' table and a game that all three were playing. The game was called That's So Raven Girl Talk Game. There was a small circular board, and in the middle was a little electronic device meant to look like a purple crystal ball sitting on a golden stand. Cards and little round chips were spread all around the table. A note on the side of the box recommended the game for children eight and up.

"Come say hi to my mom," Loochie said.

He got close and pointed at Loochie's head. There was something quite different about it. No more knit cap, no more towel. Loochie wore a wig.

"You've got a new look," Pepper said.

Loochie touched the wig tentatively. "I told my mother what happened. She brought me one of her wigs until my hair grows back."

Pepper could tell it was her mother's. A fifty-year-old woman's style. Jet-black and shaped into a poof that screamed "legal secretary!" No doubt it suited Loochie's mother at her job, but it had a different effect on the daughter. Not entirely negative. A fifty-year-old woman's wig on a nineteen-year-old, it served to age Loochie by about ten years. That might sound flattering—and Pepper certainly wouldn't say that to the kid—but it matured Loochie in a way that seemed fitting. All she'd experienced, just in the time Pepper had known her, she sure as hell wasn't your average American nineteen. Better this way. She looked like a woman. Herself, but wiser.

"It looks good," Pepper said.

Loochie smiled. "I wish I could argue with you."

Pepper laughed as he grabbed the free seat. "Can I sit?" he asked Loochie.

Loochie's mother huffed. "You ask her, but you're the grown-up."

"She looks like an adult to me," Pepper said.

The brother leaned forward to introduce himself, but didn't offer his hand.

"I'm Louis," he said.

Pepper looked from mother to daughter to son. Funny when you see family members together like this and begin that job of detecting the traits that have been passed down. The tangible and the intangible. Both Loochie and Louis had their mother's slim neck. Their mother's narrow head and even the same shape to their eyes. Their mother had to be in her fifties but looked ten years younger. A little heavy but her face retained its beauty. Large brown eyes that were only more striking on the mother because the mother was black (dark brown, actually). Loochie and Louis were lighter-skinned so Pepper figured the dad was white or maybe a Latin guy. Mom wore a faint red lipstick and her eyes were done, but her black wig sat slightly too low on one side. The slanted wig made her look like she'd gotten dressed a little too fast. Like she hadn't planned to come visit today. Maybe Mr. Mack's suggestion, about getting one's house in order, made Loochie push or plead. And now her mother and brother were here.

"I owe you an apology," Pepper said to Loochie's mother. "About a month ago, I bumped into you. And your son. By mistake."

Loochie's mother looked at her daughter.

"This is the guy who knocked you down," Loochie said. "And Louis."

Now her mother stared at Pepper again. "That was *you*?"

He smiled because he liked the idea that she'd forgotten. Something so ridiculous on his part being hardly a blip in her life. But then he saw her scan down his unwashed hair and his tired face, the blue folder still clutched in one arm. His pajamas and bare feet. She didn't recognize him. Had he really changed so much since then? Inside, he didn't feel so different but the woman across from him showed otherwise. Pepper felt so embarrassed that his stomach clutched up and his thighs tensed and he wanted to get up, walk away. But he stayed.

The brother, Louis, opened his carton of Chinese food, steamed vegetables, and picked up a piece of broccoli with his fork.

"Well, I want to thank you for saving us from this game," he said, motioning at That's So Raven. "We've been playing it for six years."

Their mother laughed quietly and looked at Pepper with slight embarrassment. "Not *that* long," she said.

"Loochie was thirteen when we got this," Louis said. "We took it to her when she was at Long Island Jewish."

"And why did you do that to her?" Pepper asked Loochie's mother. Even he was surprised by his bluntness.

All three members of the Gardner family snapped their eyes at Pepper. Louis stopped chewing his broccoli. Mom set the goofy game's little chips down on the table.

Loochie's eyes narrowed. "Watch yourself now, Pepper."

He ignored her. "I'm really curious. What could she have been doing at *thirteen* that made you give her up like that?"

Loochie's mother looked at Loochie, then at Pepper. She sat up in her chair as tension ran through her back and into her shoulders. "Do you have children?" she asked.

"Are you going to tell me that if I don't have children I can't understand?"

Louis finished chewing his food. "I used to have a plant," he offered.

Loochie, surprisingly, had dropped her head and sat back in her seat. As if she was getting out of the way of Pepper and her mother. As if she actually wanted to hear her mother's answer to Pepper's question, too, but never could've mustered the courage to ask.

"I ask you that," Loochie's mother said, "because I want to know if there's anyone you ever really cared for. Not just loved, but looked after."

"I've tried to be there for people," Pepper said. "If that's what you mean."

"Okay. And what happened?"

"What do you mean?"

"How are they doing?" she asked.

Pepper pulled the blue folder against his belly.

"I don't know."

Loochie's mother nodded. "That's the worst part, isn't it? You try, you really mean well, but you still don't know what's going to come of it."

She placed her hand on the top of Loochie's wigged head, very lightly, then pulled it away. "I tried to get help for my daughter. But the help she needed was more than I could give. So I searched *everywhere*, I asked *everyone*. What do I do? I don't want to embarrass my daughter, so I'm not going to say how she was acting. But we checked her health. Blood tests. Scans. The best that Medicaid could provide!" She laughed bitterly. "And finally we ended up at Long Island Jewish. They spoke to me about her *mental* health. And I didn't want to hear that." She was quiet a moment. "But eventually I had to."

Pepper said, "But she's just locked away in here. A kid her age. All she knows about the world is these five hallways and what she sees on that television. That's her whole life!"

Loochie's mother reached for the little round game chips and squeezed a few of them in one hand. She opened and closed that hand, feeling the faint pain of the shape against her palm and squeezing harder so she felt the pain even more. She didn't speak.

"You asked me if I ever cared for someone," Pepper said. "There's a woman I met here that I really cared for. If I'd had to, I would've *died* for her. That's how much I wanted her to be safe."

Loochie's mother looked at Pepper. Her eyes were dry. She wasn't going to cry because of what Pepper said. Think she hadn't said much worse to herself already? But it was Pepper's last words that made her speak.

"That's the funny thing," she said. "Men always want to *die* for something. For someone. I can see the appeal. You do it *once* and it's done. No more worrying, not knowing, about tomorrow and tomorrow and tomorrow. I know you all think it sounds brave, but I'll tell you something even braver. To struggle and fight for the ones you love today. And then do it all over again the next day. Every day. For your whole life. It's not as romantic, I admit. But it takes a lot of courage to live for someone, too."

Loochie's mother had reached out for Loochie's arm. Her fingers were held tight around her daughter's wrist. Loochie was crying quietly.

"Once Lucretia asked me why I didn't just let her die. Can you imagine it? She was *fourteen years old*. 'Why don't you just let me die?' I told her that my life without her wasn't worth living. As long as she lives, I live. Those words are written on every good mother's heart."

She pressed her forehead to the side of her daughter's face. "As long as you live, I live," she whispered to Loochie.

The brother had watched all this quietly. Now Louis sat up in his chair and grinned at Pepper. His face looked tight, faintly gray, like he felt sick. Do you know that this grown man, twenty-nine years old, was *jealous*? Not in a way he could name, or explain, but it was real. So Louis wanted to change the atmosphere. Otherwise he imagined his sister and mother doing a lot more hugging and loving while he sat there poking at a carton of steamed vegetables.

"My sister tells me that you all think there's a monster in the hospital," Louis said.

"The Devil," Loochie said, pulling her arm away from her mother's hand. "That's what I said. And I told *Mom*."

But Louis didn't look at his sister. He kept his gaze trained on Pepper.

"*You* believe that?" Louis asked.

Loochie's mother lost her pensive air and looked at her son with a frown. "All right," she said. "Don't start something."

"I'm asking the man a question," Louis said.

Pepper assessed this guy. He was short-ish and fat-ish and wore thick glasses in stylish frames. His hairline was receding and he already had a fair amount of ear hair. And yet this guy was obviously so pleased with himself. Pepper always marveled at this kind of man. Who calculated his value based on some mystery math. Simple addition would assess this man a dud but Louis was using calculus plus.

Loochie's mother picked up a card from the game deck and waved it over the purple crystal ball twice. An electric *whoosh* played, a sound like water crashing on rocks or a hundred plates smashing against a floor.

A moment later Raven Symoné's voice played loudly.

"I don't *think* so, girlfriend!" Raven shouted.

Mom was trying to distract the table from the line of conversation, but it wasn't enough to stop her bullheaded boy.

"Come on," Louis pressed. "Do you believe that, too?"

"There's something going on behind that silver door," Pepper said.

"Yeah," Loochie said, looking at Pepper with mild disgust because he wouldn't just come out and say its name. "The Devil."

Now Louis slumped back in his chair, his mouth hanging open slightly. He looked incredulous.

"What do you know about the history of silver mining in this country?" Louis asked.

Aha. Now Pepper understood the source of this man's massive overconfidence. He thought he was brilliant. Pepper remembered a quote he'd read once, it was attributed to James Hetfield, the lead singer of Metallica. Hetfield was asked the difference between him-self and Sting. (Why *that* comparison? Who can say?) Hetfield said the difference between him and Sting was that he read a lot of books, too, but he didn't need you to know that. Now, whatever Louis might say next, Pepper couldn't help but hear dreadful late-era Sting music being strummed (on a fucking lute, no doubt) in the distance.

"Silver mining in the United States didn't start, like hard-core, until the mid-1850s," Louis said. "And only really got big when the Comstock Lode was discovered in 1859 in California."

"Okay," Pepper said. He kind of hoped that was it.

"My brother thinks he should have been a scientist," Loochie said.

Louis grinned. "Everyone at my job does call me the Professor."

"Not behind your back," Loochie said.

Their mother waved another card over the purple crystal ball. It was her only defense, really, when her grown-ass children reverted like this. Would it work?

"*Not* gonna happen!" Raven Symoné shouted.

"I'm a manager at Hertz at JFK Airport," Louis explained. "And when I have downtime I *read*. Unlike everybody else there."

That lute playing got a little louder.

"Anyway," Louis continued, "the silver deposits found at the Com-stock Lode only caused people to go digging around for it every-where. Silver mines popped up in Nevada, Colorado, Idaho, Montana.

People thought they were going to find more and more silver, so whole towns were built to accommodate them. And not some little wooden shacks. Luxury homes and fine businesses. People were sure the good times would only get better."

"But they didn't," Pepper offered, trying to beat him to the point.

Louis grabbed his mother's hand and pulled it away from the purple crystal ball when she moved toward it with a card for the third time.

"No, you're right," Louis agreed. "It didn't. Lots of people went bust. But I'm really trying to tell you about what happened to the *miners* during the silver rush.

"It was bad work. Dangerous. Like any mining. But silver also lets out fumes when it's mined. Even Pliny the Elder wrote about how harmful the fumes were, especially to animals. You know Pliny the Elder?"

Pepper nodded. "Moroccan guy who ran the bodega around the corner from my apartment?"

Neither Loochie nor her mother laughed because, hell, they thought that might be who this person was.

Louis smiled without mirth.

"The problem with the silver fumes," Louis continued, "is that, over time, they gave the miners *delusions*. Bad enough that they had to stop mining. Their health deteriorated. And a bunch of them even died."

Hard to make fun of something like that, so Pepper didn't.

"Do you know what people would say, in these mining towns, when they saw one of these miners falling apart? Walking through town muttering and swinging at phantoms? They said the Devil in Silver got them. It became shorthand. Like someone might say, 'What happened to Mike?' And the answer was always the same. 'The Devil in Silver got him.'"

Louis sat straight and crossed his arms and surveyed the table. "Do you understand what I'm trying to tell you?"

"You're saying we're just making this thing up," Pepper said quietly.

Louis seemed disappointed. He dropped his hands into his lap and folded them there. He looked at his sister and Pepper. He turned his head to take in the other patients gathered with their family members there in the hospital.

"I'm saying they *were* dying," Louis said. "They definitely weren't making that up. But it wasn't a monster that was killing them. It was the mine."

Visiting hours continued and Pepper stayed at the table with Loochie and her family. They didn't keep talking about the Devil in Silver, about slow death and delusions, because that shit is *grim*. Instead, they spent the last half hour of visiting playing Raven Symoné's game. If it never became fun, it did pass the time. (Pepper also learned that someone *liked liked* him, which is always nice to hear.)

At the end of the visit, Loochie's mother gave her a handful of change as per custom. Then she took Pepper's hand, and dropped two dollars' worth of quarters into his palm.

"Call your mother," she said. "I'm sure she'd like to hear from you."

"I don't know about that," Pepper said, laughing.

"I do," Loochie's mother said.

"I don't even have her number," Pepper told her.

Loochie's mother pointed at Louis. "You're always bragging about your little phone, aren't you?" she asked. "Show me what it can do."

Louis probably hadn't looked more pleased at any point that afternoon. He made his mother and sister watch while he used his Smartphone. A quick search, not more than two minues, and he had Pepper's brother's number. He beamed at his mother. "See?"

"Very nice," she said, patting her son's back. Then she looked at Pepper. "Well?"

Rather than dithering, he walked straight into the phone alcove. It sat empty. He didn't hesitate.

He dialed the Maryland number, and Ralph picked up on the second ring. It seemed so simple, so normal, that it almost couldn't be real. After all his time, his younger brother was on the line.

As soon as Pepper heard his brother's voice, he wanted to hang up.

He was so scared. But he remembered Loochie's mother and that he wanted to speak with his own. He couldn't just stand there breathing heavily and expect to be put on with her.

"Ralph S. Mouse!" he said, a bit too loud.

The line stayed quiet.

"Peter Rabbit," Ralph finally answered.

"Did my friend Mari ever call you?" Pepper asked. Instantly, he wished he hadn't said it; two sentences into the conversation and he sounded critical.

"I think she spoke to Maureen," Ralph said. "But that was awhile ago. I'm sorry I didn't call; we've just had so much going on here. Denny got sick so we all got sick. He had to stay out of school."

He wondered what Mari might've told Ralph's wife. Maybe just that Pepper was in some trouble, since Ralph didn't mention the hospital. Was there any point in telling him now?

"How's Mom?" Pepper asked.

Pepper realized he still had the blue folder under his arm and he was choking the poor thing just now. He balanced it on top of the pay phone.

"Mom's going to outlive both of us," Ralph said, sounding lighter for the first time.

Pepper rested his forehead against the cool wall. He'd been a little afraid that Ralph would tell him their mother had died while he'd been in here. Something irreversible.

"Is she there?"

"Yeah," Ralph said, sounding relieved to hand off the baton. "Let me bring the phone to her."

Then a little jostling as Ralph walked from his bedroom, off to find their mother. Pepper heard the creak of different doors being opened, Ralph calling their mother's name in room after room. *So much space,* Pepper thought. Then Ralph's voice on the line again. "Listen, man," he said. "I just want to say . . ."

Then quiet again.

Pepper spoke instead. "Ralph," he said. "Thanks for taking care of Mom, yeah?"

Ralph sighed and Pepper could almost see his kid brother, six or seven years old, actually blushing because his big brother had, in some way, acknowledged him. "It's okay," Ralph said quietly. "You take care of yourself."

And then his mother's voice on the line.

"Is that Peter?"

"*Ma.*"

"Peter Rabbit," she said serenely.

The automated voice on the phone piped in telling him to add more coins or the call would be cut off. He did. First, the quick little bleeps and bloops, then he was permitted to speak with his mother again.

She asked how he was doing. Pepper didn't tell his mother where he was. He asked how she liked Maryland. She told him that everyone in the family had his or her own room with a few more rooms left over.

"I know I'm supposed to like it," his mother said. "But all I do is worry if they can afford it. With the economy and the housing market. It's always on the news. You know. Where are you living now? Still in the same apartment?"

"Still in Queens," he said. This was true.

"Still moving furniture?"

"I gave that up for a little while."

"Trying something else?"

He pulled away from the wall. Soon enough it would be time to take his evening meds. He didn't want his mother to hear them calling him for that.

"You sound tired, Peter."

"Maybe I'm a little tired," he admitted.

His mother breathed on the line, in and out, and the next voice he heard was the damn electronic drone telling him to give more coins, but he was out.

"Mom," he said so quietly it sounded weaker than a whisper. "I'm going to have to go."

"Do you want to go?" she asked.

"No, but I'm out of money."

"Are you at this new job now? Why don't you give me the number and I'll call you back? Ralph gets long-distance free."

The number was right there under the phone's cradle. He read it to her. A moment later they were disconnected.

Pepper set the receiver back down and waited. He counted to himself and hoped his mother had written the digits down correctly. When the phone rang he snatched it up.

"Anyway," his mother said, as if they hadn't been cut off, as if her son weren't keeping all the particulars in his life mysterious. "I want to tell you a little story."

Pepper leaned to the right, the receiver still to his ear, and saw the patients forming a line in front of the nurses' station. As soon as those folks had been dosed, one of the staff would come looking for him. He'd rather hang up on his mother, in the middle of a sentence, than to let her get some clue about the state he was in.

"When your father and I still had the video store," his mother began, "we used to take inventory of the tapes at the end of each week. You remember?"

"Siesta Sundays," Pepper said, smiling faintly. Pepper and Ralph would have twenty dollars to spend on whatever dinner they pleased. Did Nehi orange soda and Rolos count as dinner? They did on Siesta Sundays.

"Raymond and I would close up at nine and spend three hours checking to make sure all our videos were accounted for. We were meticulous about keeping track. On the week I'm thinking about, you must've been about fourteen or fifteen, we discovered two tapes missing." She made a faint humming noise as she tried to remember the titles.

Pepper leaned back again, the line of patients was moving forward. Half as long as it had been only a minute ago.

"*Tales from the Buttside,*" his mother said. "And . . . *Chesty Murphy, Double-D Detective.*"

"Ma!"

She laughed on the line. "*You* remember."

He felt suddenly exposed. As if his mother and father were in the alcove with him and he had no pants on.

"Your father wanted to turn your room upside down to find them," his mother said. "Do you know how much the adult tapes were worth to us? This is before the Internet. Nothing made bigger profits for us."

"I can't believe you're telling me this," Pepper said. But he *could* believe it. His mother, bless her, had always enjoyed giving her sons a little hell.

Outside the alcove, he heard a staff member call out. "Who's left?"

His mother, meanwhile, just kept raconteuring. "Raymond would've torn your and Ralphie's room apart, *and* taken you to small claims court. But I told him to wait a week."

"Where's Loochie?" Scotch Tape called out.

"I'm here!" Loochie shouted. "I'm coming."

"A week later *Tales from the Buttside* and . . ."

"Stop saying the titles, Ma, *please.*"

His mother chuckled again. "A week later those two films were right back where they were supposed to be."

He brought one hand over his eyes. "Why are you telling me this?"

She cleared her throat. "I don't know what you might be going through right now, Peter. I wish you'd tell me, but I can't make you. So I told you that story because there's something I want you to always remember. You took those tapes, but you put them back."

"Come on," Pepper said. "What does that prove?"

"It told me something about your *character*, Peter. It might sound silly to you, but even those small indiscretions reveal so much."

"We got one more missing!" Scotch Tape called out. "Don't make me come looking for you."

Pepper spoke softly into the receiver, looking over his shoulder for an orderly or nurse. "I had to return those tapes, Ma. I wasn't being noble. I stole them from you and Dad. Anyone would've put them back."

"Really?" His mother laughed quietly. "Because Ralph never did."

# 38

PEPPER LEFT THE alcove feeling like gold bullion. So good that he didn't mind taking the meds. As soon as he was done, Redhead Kingpin and Still Waters crowded around him. Standing so close they could've picked his pockets. (If his pajamas had pockets, that is.)

"What's this?" he asked.

Redhead Kingpin looked at Still Waters. "Show him," she said.

Still Waters carried her manila folder, "No Name" on the flap. She opened it.

"I don't want to know," Pepper said. They were carrying the terrible folder that only housed the terrible news. Whatever they were going to pull out from there would only wreck his mood. He moved around them and started toward Northwest 2. If he made it to the threshold of the men's hall, the pair, and their news, would be left behind.

But the pair double-teamed him. Redhead Kingpin squaring off in front of him, while Still Waters dug through the crowded folder. Before he could bob and weave around the redhead, Still Waters had found the article in question.

"Read," she said.

Pepper scanned the top of the page. This one had been torn out of the newspaper quickly. One edge uneven and ragged. It was from *The*

*New York Times.* The byline read "Nina Bernstein." It was accompanied by a picture of two women sitting in a train car.

Reluctantly, Pepper read aloud.

" 'Holding tight to her sister's hand in the bustling streets of Oakland's Chinatown, Xiu Quan Hong looked a little dazed, like someone who has stepped from a dark, windowless place into a sunny afternoon.'

" 'In a sense, she has. For a year and a half, Ms. Hong, a waitress with no criminal record and a history of attempted suicide' "—Pepper stopped there a moment, then began again—" 'was locked away in an immigration jail in Florida and then held in a psychiatric unit in Queens, New York.'

" 'With no lawyer to plead for asylum on her behalf, she had been ordered to be deported to her native China, which her family had fled when she was only four years old. She was trapped in an immigration limbo: a fate that detainee advocates say is common in a system that has no rules for determining mental competency and no obligation to provide anyone with legal representation.' "

Pepper found his hand was shaking, but he read on.

" 'Then, through a fluke, her sister discovered her whereabouts in New York only three days before her deportation order was to be executed. Her sister, Yun Hong, a cashier at a supermarket in Oakland, found Theodore Cox, a New York immigration lawyer, through an Internet search and convinced him to take her sister's case for free.'

" 'Now Ms. Hong, 41, is free on bail and living with her sister in Oakland.' "

That's where he stopped.

He looked up at the picture again. Two women sitting in a train car. He didn't know the woman on the right. He knew, but didn't recognize, the one on the left. "That's Sue?" he whispered.

Her hair had been cut short and now framed her face, where before, her face had been hidden. She didn't look at the camera but her head was held up. She seemed to be looking out the window behind the photographer. She wore a pink short-sleeved T-shirt and black slacks. In her lap sat a big stylish yellow purse. The woman on her right, her sister, was caught in profile because she looked at Sue. In the snapshot she had one hand up and was gently fixing Sue's hair.

Still Waters pulled the paper away from Pepper's face.

At least that's what seemed to happen next.

In reality Pepper had staggered backward and came to a stop only when his back touched the wall behind him. And his legs trembled, they were about to give out, so he slid down the wall until he smacked the floor.

*Now Ms. Hong, 41, is free on bail and living with her sister in Oakland.*

Pepper spread his legs and lifted his knees and leaned forward so his head faced the floor. His shoulders trembled, and, to his great surprise, he sobbed openly. It sounded like he was choking. He felt Redhead Kingpin and Still Waters come down to the floor and surround him. Still Waters actually put one hand on his back and patted him there.

"We knew you'd be happy to see that," Redhead Kingpin said.

He looked up into their faces and could see that, if they weren't crying now, they had been very recently.

"It's really true?" Pepper asked.

They stayed there with him as other patients passed through the room, as staff members logged in files at the computer. If anyone noticed the trio there on the floor, it was only to walk around them.

"You can keep the article if you want it," Redhead Kingpin said.

Pepper looked at Redhead Kingpin, who grinned tightly and nodded. Then at Still Waters who clutched the paper and kept her head down.

"But you need it for your files, don't you?" he asked.

Still Waters looked up at him with a broad smile of relief.

The women stood up when Pepper clambered to his feet.

In the article he'd been downgraded to a "fluke." But Pepper didn't even notice. Pepper's part wasn't the bulletin. Nor Sue's sister's efforts. The kindness of the lawyer. The diligence of the reporter. All incredible, but secondary. Sue was safe. That was the lead. Sue was safe.

Is there ever any good news in this world?

Yes.

Then Mr. Mack had to go and change the subject.

He entered the oval room and walked right up to Pepper, Redhead Kingpin, and Still Waters. He moved around them, on his way into the phone alcove.

But just before he passed them, he hissed, "Tonight."

"How will we know when?" Pepper asked.

Mr. Mack had one foot in the alcove already.

"I'll come knocking on your door," he said.

# 39

AND THE OLD man wasn't lying. Pepper had just finished separating the beds in his room. (What did that matter now?) He put on the street clothes Dr. Anand gave him. He pulled his boots on. Then a faint rapping began. Rapping, tapping at his door. But when Pepper opened the door to his room?

No one was there.

He peeked into the hallway and saw that every other door to every other room in Northwest 2 was shut. Down at the nurses' station, Miss Chris and Nurse Washburn and Scotch Tape were on night duty. All three sitting or standing in there, looking serene. Probably a first for them on the unit. Everyone seemed to have gone to sleep. Not even the late-night crew of Heatmiser, Redhead Kingpin, and Still Waters were up. Quiet rooms were good. Logging files into the computer was all they had to do now. The clacks of the keyboard were audible. Pepper ducked his head back into his room.

But before he could shut the door, he heard the faint knocking again. It was coming from the wall, where his dresser had once been. From the door that had been painted over, sealed shut.

For the third time he heard the knocking.

Pepper brought his face to the wall. (Door?) "Mr. Mack?"

From the other side, a harsh whisper. *"Hush!"*

Then came this chipping and chopping sound from the other side of the wall. It seemed to go on so long, though really it was only minutes. That rust-colored ceiling tile, the site of the leak, quivered each time the door in the wall was hit. More small cracks appeared up there. Pepper thought it would almost be funny if all Mr. Mack's work caused the ceiling to cave in.

Then a few bits of paint fell from the wall on his side. A small hole, no bigger than a dime, appeared at waist height. A moment after that, a piece of metal poked through. The business end of a flathead screwdriver.

The screwdriver blade stayed still in the hole for a moment, but then, slowly, it *turned*.

"Push," Mr. Mack whispered from the other side of the door.

Pepper pressed at it. Mr. Mack had chipped away at the paint around the door frame on his side, but on Pepper's side it remained intact.

"Put your weight behind it," Mr. Mack commanded.

Pepper shouldered the door hard. When the paint separated, it sounded like ice cracking, a frozen lake splitting under someone's weight, and Pepper felt his face go cold, as if he'd been dunked. It was the fear that he might've been heard by Miss Chris, Scotch Tape, and Nurse Washburn. Pepper stopped pushing and watched the other door.

When he turned back, Mr. Mack had pulled the former wall door open.

Now Pepper could move freely from this room to the next. No need to walk out into the hallway and risk the wrath of the staff. Thank you, Repurposing. In order to cut costs, the hospital had inadvertently provided them with a secret path.

Mr. Mack held the screwdriver like a scepter. He used it to wave Pepper through. Into room seven. The floor here was littered with off-white paint chips. They looked like pencil shavings. Pepper stepped into the doorway, but didn't enter the other room yet. Being right here, where a threshold had suddenly just appeared, made the moment seem so *magical* that he expected to step through and be transported to some fantasy kingdom.

(*The Lion, the Witch, and the Psych Unit.*)

But that didn't happen, of course. This moment was fantastic enough as it was. Pepper entered room 7 and saw, in the far wall, that another doorway, exactly like this one, had been pried open. It led to room 9, and past that, another doorway that led to room 11. Room after room, all the way to the last in line. The door in room fifteen, down there, was still sealed. A white wall. What was behind that? The sidewalk?

What if this was the last time he'd be in this place? He stepped back into room 5. What should he take? His wallet, yes. And Sue's blue accordion folder? It seemed cumbersome to carry the whole thing. He'd probably drop it. How bad would he feel if somehow that was the thing that got him caught, the staff following the trail of magazine pages like bread crumbs? Instead, he opened the folder and stuffed as many pages as possible into the front pockets of his pants. He hoped he was taking enough of Sue's dreams with him. Then he went back into room 7 and followed Mr. Mack.

"Where'd you get a screwdriver?" Pepper asked as they walked to the next room.

"When I said get your houses in order, what did you think I meant?" Mr. Mack asked. "Share a few kisses with your family? Shit. I asked a little bit more of mine."

Pepper entered room 9. It looked just like his, generally. Two beds, two dressers. But this room hadn't been occupied in a long time, so there weren't any personal effects. It felt like the showroom version of a mental hospital's bedroom. Pepper almost expected to find a mannequin in the bed, but that would've been hellaciously weird.

"This isn't prison!" Mr. Mack squawked on, lifting the screwdriver like a prize. "They might check your visitor's purse or bag, but they're not sniffing anyone's booty cheeks for contraband."

"You had someone put a screwdriver up their ass?" Pepper asked.

Mr. Mack sniffed with disdain at Pepper. "It was up my nephew's coat sleeve, if you really want to know."

They entered room 11. This one had been occupied. Pages from magazines had been taped up to the wall over one bed. Lots of shots of black and Latino and a few white teenagers either squinting at the camera with a sneer or posing with cars, girls, and guns. Wally Gambino's little acre.

"Rooms one and three are empty, so we don't need to pop them open," Mr. Mack said. "That's better anyway, we don't have to get too close to the nurses' station."

Finally, they reached the last room in this lane. Room 15. The one shared by Mr. Mack and Frank Waverly. They'd been there for many years. Relatively speaking, the place was quite nicely appointed. The same beds and dressers, but there was a low bookshelf near one of the beds. And these guys had even set up a kind of garment rack. They'd run a cheap tension bar across the windowsill so they could hang up their sport coats, shirts, and slacks.

Frank Waverly waited in the room. He sat on his bed, reading a book. Wally Gambino walked out of the bathroom, wiping his hands against his jeans.

Wally saw Pepper. "This motherfucker?" he said.

"Don't start with that," Mr. Mack told him.

Wally squinted at the old man (a lot like the dudes in the magazine pages taped to his wall), but he acquiesced.

Mr. Mack walked to Frank Waverly's bed and held out the screwdriver.

"Your turn," he said.

Frank Waverly sat there, still reading. Mr. Mack repeated himself. Reluctantly, Frank Waverly set his book facedown on his bed, leaving it open as if he expected to return to it quite soon. Pepper couldn't help himself, he peeked at the cover. *Emma*. By Jane Austen.

"Is it good?" Pepper asked Frank Waverly, pointing at the book.

Frank Waverly gave the thumbs-up.

"You two want tea and goddamn biscuits?" Mr. Mack snapped. "Or can we get to work?"

Frank Waverly touched at the outline of the door in this wall. He found the groove between door and frame and stabbed the screwdriver into the layers of paint. Once he cracked through, he dragged the screwdriver blade along the top edge, slowly chipping off more.

"What if we pop this door," Wally asked. "And get outside and some alarm goes off?"

"That's not going to happen," Mr. Mack said.

Pepper had moved to the jerry-rigged clothing rack, eyeing the changes of clothes with envy. "How do you know that?" Pepper asked.

"Because this door doesn't lead outside," Mr. Mack said matter-of-factly.

Frank Waverly had already chipped away the paint at the top of the doorway and moved on to the right side. Though he'd seemed hesitant, though he was at least as old as Mr. Mack, he moved quickly and with vigor.

"Best I can tell from Dorry's map"—Mr. Mack patted the breast pocket of his sport coat—"the space on the other side of this wall used to be the *front* of the building. Maybe from when it was an eye clinic. The front of Northwest faced the sidewalk. People could just pull up out front and drop off the patient who would walk right in. But when it became our Northwest, for mental patients, they sealed that entrance off. It was like the building turned its back to the neighbors."

"Like it was ashamed," Wally said.

Frank Waverly worked hard but remained as quiet as ever. He didn't even grunt as he chopped at the doorway. The only sound was the sawing of the screwdriver against old paint. The way the chips flew, you would've thought Frank Waverly was using an electric saw.

"Now Dorry has this map all laid out," Mr. Mack continued. "She drew it by hand but it's detailed. She was in fifteen on Northwest 3, last in her row. She didn't have a roommate. So who knows how many times she was back there. Plenty, I'm guessing."

"Why would she?" Pepper asked.

"Maybe she's been leaving the building whenever she wants," Wally said.

Mr. Mack said, "I don't think so, Mr. Gambino."

An address that made Wally smile.

"That wasn't Dorry's way. Each one of us got the greeting and the tour from that woman. She never just thought of herself. She could be a trial sometimes, but she was never selfish."

*You should see a friendly face first.* That was one of the first things she'd said to Pepper. And so he had. So had all of them.

Frank Waverly moved to the other side of the doorway and got to chopping. They watched him quietly for a moment. As hard as Frank Waverly was working, each man willed him to go even faster.

"But because Dorry was a soft touch," Mr. Mack continued, "I'm going to tell you what I think she was really doing back there all these years. The map shows a way to get out of this building. Through an air duct on the second floor. But the map also shows a back path that leads to one room in particular. One that's off-limits to patients, normally."

"The silver door," Pepper whispered.

Mr. Mack reached into the breast pocket of his jacket, but instead of pulling out that map, he revealed something else.

A key.

Mr. Mack said, "I think she took care of that thing like she took care of all of us."

Wally slapped his own leg. "She took care of a fucking *monster*?! Nah, that ain't right."

Pepper looked at the ceiling. "She always said it was just a man."

"She even wrote his name down," Mr. Mack said.

Frank Waverly continued to chip and Wally Gambino laughed.

"That old bitch was double crazy!"

Mr. Mack pulled out the map. The sheet of paper had been folded into a small square. He handed it to Pepper.

"Why are you giving this up?"

"I got it memorized already."

Pepper unfolded it. Wally couldn't help himself, he went up on his toes and tried to see the map, too. They looked like two boys who'd just found a page ripped out of a porn magazine.

"Now what we're going to do," Mr. Mack announced, "is break through this door and then move over to the other side of the men's hall and get the two fellas there. Then we go to the women's hall and we do the same. Everyone's expecting us. It's going to take us awhile, I know, but *everyone* needs to be involved."

"Involved with what?" Pepper asked.

Mr. Mack pointed at the door, slowly being revealed. "We're going to teach that thing a lesson or three."

Pepper scanned the map. Dorry was so good that she'd even detailed the number of steps they would find on the staircase that led from the first floor to the second. (Dorry had a bit of that OCD going strong.) The route to the air duct looked simple enough. As did the path to the Devil. She'd also scribbled a note. Funnily enough, the note wasn't addressed to Pepper. Not to anyone specifically. Which made Pepper wonder how long Dorry had been planning to pass on this knowledge. How long she'd been hoping to take her rest.

> *Hello, my friend,*
>
> *I've been in here a <u>very</u> long time, and I don't want to be here anymore. I've stayed this long not for myself, but for everybody else. How much longer can I give until there's nothing left? If you're reading this, then I guess you have the answer.*
>
> *This is the last thing I'm going to do. Giving you this map and this key. If you want to leave, there is a way. I've marked it. But let me ask you this: Where will you run? I'll tell you one thing I've learned over my long life. This <u>is</u> the world, my friend. As much as anyplace else. Our trials don't change, only the court.*
>
> *This key opens a second silver door. I hope I've passed this on to the right person. Please don't hurt Mr. Visserplein. If you look into his face, truly see his face, you'll understand.*
>
> *Please forgive me for my weaknesses.*
>
> *Doris*

Mr. Mack made each of them chip and crack a doorway open. The men and the women. All in a spirit of fair play. Everyone's hands getting dirty. The group learning to act as one. The only doorway they didn't have to crack open was the one that led into Dorry's room. She'd opened that one many, many years ago. The doorway was so well trod that the doorjamb dipped in the middle.

By the time every patient had been gathered, it was three in the morning. All of them were *sweaty*. All of them were out of their rooms and standing in the darkened chamber once known as the New Hyde Hospital Ophthalmology Welcome Pavilion.

(Though nobody had ever really called it that. This was Queens; people just said "the eye clinic.")

The pavilion had been stripped down decades ago, so now it was like being in the shell of a structure waiting to be finished or torn down. The skeleton intact, but no organs. The only nice touch that remained was the gray granite floors.

The windows along the far wall had all been removed (once there'd been a bank of them, each twenty feet tall). Now it was all dry wall. The center of the ceiling, two stories above, showed an enormous oval pane of glass. It looked vaguely like a single almond-shaped eye. That had been intentional. Moonlight drifted down through the glass and caught the speckles in the granite tiles. This made the floor seem to glow, as if a layer of low fog filled the room.

"So here we are," Mr. Mack said.

Twelve patients. Pepper and Loochie, Mr. Mack and Frank Waverly, Redhead Kingpin and Still Waters, The Haint, Heatmiser, Wally Gambino and Yuckmouth. Even the two newer admits, Doris Roberts and Sandra Day O'Connor. They gathered in a tight circle directly beneath the great glass eye in the ceiling.

Pepper couldn't help but imagine Dorry in this cavernous space—how many times?—alone at night. Back here on a mission much too batty to believe. To comfort the Devil. (What the fuck was a Mr. Visserplein?!)

They stood in the large empty space, in the circle of direct moonlight, and none of them dared to step out of the circle alone. There used to be two sets of double doors not fifty feet in front of them, the front entrance to the clinic, but the doors had been sealed over just as surely as the windows. The moonlight lit the room, but only so much. There were shadows on all sides. Mr. Mack was the first one to step out of the moonlight alone. All of them, even Pepper, held their breath.

Once he was out, he spread his arms wide. "I'm fine," he said. "You'll be fine."

With that, more of them moved. Just a few steps. Fanning out. Until only Frank Waverly remained under the moonlight.

"There's a staircase over here," Doris Roberts called out.

"Here, too," mumbled Heatmiser.

Two sets of staircases, at either end of the lobby. Leading up to a second-floor landing. Everyone followed Doris Roberts's voice and used her stairs.

Only Heatmiser went his own way. His low, affectless voice could be heard in the dim hall.

"That's fucked up," he muttered as the others moved off.

Then the lonesome yelp of his sneakers, alone, on his set of stairs.

The patients gathered all together again on the landing and looked down at the first floor. Because the room was so dark, the hall so stark, the granite tiles looked much farther below them. Fifty feet instead of only ten. A railing ran at about waist height on the landing. The braver patients leaned over it to give themselves the thrill of faux vertigo. They were having a little fun, playing tag in the graveyard.

Finally, Mr. Mack called them to order.

"We've got things to do and there's no point in waiting," he said.

Their eyes had adjusted enough to understand the layout here. It was exactly like on the first floor. They stood before the doors that would lead to the second-floor version of Northwest 2 and Northwest 3. The rooms above their rooms. They'd all known this second floor was up here, of course, but the idea had remained academic. Now, standing on this landing, looking at the actual doors, it was like coming across an alternate universe and being shocked because, all along, it had been this close.

Mr. Mack walked farther along the landing. They followed him. And right there in front of them, they saw it, another silver door. Mr. Mack slapped it. The sight of him actually *touching* the door caused every patient to tense up, recoil. They expected staff members to appear and tackle the old man.

But that didn't happen.

Mr. Mack left his hand on the silver door because he, too, couldn't quite believe Miss Chris wasn't running toward him with a needle. Now the others wanted a touch. They didn't take turns. They *mobbed* the door. Each one placing a hand where he or she could. When Pepper did it, up near the top, he expected the silver door to feel cold or hot. Maybe that smell again, of piss and filth. Something. But a different surprise awaited them.

Wally Gambino shouted, "Yo!"

Even though they were as far from the nurses' station as they could be, Wally's voice still sounded too damn loud there in the pavilion. Everyone flinched or curled up expecting some kind of attack. But Wally remained oblivious, too excited by his realization to feel afraid.

"It's a fucking *exit* door!" he said.

"Keep your voice down!" Mr. Mack snapped.

Wally looked around, as if he'd just stepped into traffic and someone had called out that a truck was bearing down.

"Oh, yeah," he said more quietly. "My bad."

But now that Wally said it, all the others could *see* the door more clearly. As he'd just described it. Before it had been repurposed. The stainless steel door of a stairwell exit. Only silver from a distance.

"They've got it living in a stairwell?" Redhead Kingpin asked.

She almost sounded sympathetic. Even in the dimness Mr. Mack saw the spark of pity burnishing her face.

"I want to remind you what's on the other side of this door," Mr. Mack said. "I don't care if it has a lazy eye and a wooden leg. That damn *Devil* has been feeding on us like we were the sheep! And it *is* the wolf at the door."

He knocked on the door to make his point. The sound echoed across the landing and the patients drew closer to one another.

"Before you get all weepy about where this beast makes its bed," Mr. Mack continued, "please remember a few names. Dennis Drayton, who we all called Fogey. Miss Grace. And Sam. Coffee. Dorry. Maybe Glenn, too, if he ends up dying in the ICU. Remember them before you go feeling sorry for their predator."

Mr. Mack reached back and knocked on the silver door lightly. Then he reached into the breast pocket of his sport coat. He pulled out a small gold key.

"I'm not going to tell you what to do," he said. "I'm going to ask you a question. How long have you been scared?"

They watched Mr. Mack silently, but each seemed to lean toward him, his voice so full of gravity.

"How old is that fear we all been feeling?" he asked. "Sometimes I think I've been afraid my whole life. Like I got born with it and didn't realize it was with me all along."

The moonlight streaming through the great glass eye in the ceiling couldn't reach them on the landing. Standing in the dark, they appeared nearly like phantoms, even to one another.

"Well, I'm tired of that feeling," Mr. Mack admitted. "And more than that, I'm angry. I find myself wanting to send a message. *You're not going to abuse me no more.* I don't care what is on the other side of this door, I only know it is my enemy. And I want to finally *fight* what's out to kill me.

"I vote for taking a stand." Mr. Mack raised one hand. "Who's with me?"

When Pepper looked at Loochie he was surprised to find she'd already raised her hand. And she looked just as startled, because his big paw was in the air. He hadn't even realized he'd done it. Other hands rose as well. Seemed like everyone's went up.

Then Frank Waverly reached out from the crowd. He plucked the little key right out of Mr. Mack's fingers.

Frank Waverly put his body between the crowd and the silver door. When he turned to the crowd, what did he see? So many angry faces. Stupified with rage. Not shouting or cursing but seething silently. They weren't really looking at him. Their eyes locked on his right hand, the small gold key.

"Don't be dumb," Mr. Mack barked. "You can't save nobody."

Frank Waverly's mouth opened, the lips hung open for just a moment. "But you can help," Frank Waverly finally said.

It was the first time any of them—even Mr. Mack—had heard old Frank say a word. His voice sounded raspy from disuse, it wavered and showed he was scared. But everybody heard him. Surprise kept them rooted as Frank Waverly lifted the key to his lips. And then, do you know what he did?

He swallowed it.

Suddenly, it was like Mr. Mack's spell had been broken. At least for Pepper. He didn't wait a beat. He grabbed Loochie by the arm. He yanked her sideways, hard.

She stumbled into Pepper, looked up at him with confusion.

"Let's go," Pepper said. "This is about to get ugly."

Consider Loochie and Pepper the breakaway vote. Loochie went with Pepper when he pulled her. Who else did she trust as much? Only herself. And even she wasn't sure what to do just then.

They ran along the landing. Leaving the others behind. They reached the door to the room that sat right above Mr. Mack and Frank Waverly's room.

Pepper pushed at it, but couldn't open the door all the way. Just wide enough to fit his head and shoulders through, but no more. Pepper peeked inside but couldn't make out what might be blocking the doorway because the windows had been boarded over. His eyes had adjusted to the level of darkness on the landing, but in here he found darker shadows.

Pepper reached inside, too keyed-up to be cautious. His hand caused a *clang* when it connected with some enormous piece of metal. Pepper strained and finally slipped into the room. Then Pepper reached out of the doorway and clapped a hand around Loochie's wrist.

"Stay with me," he told her.

Pepper's plan was simple: Enter this room, then slip back into the hallway that ran right above Northwest 2. Book it until they reached the hallway directly above Northwest 1. Find the air duct marked on Dorry's map. The one mentioned by Mr. Mack. Climb up, climb out, escape.

Now that she was inside the room, too, Loochie's eyes adjusted. She could see that the big metal thing blocking the doorway was just a filing cabinet. An old-school model. Back when they made everything out of lead or something. When even forks and knives weighed five pounds each. Loochie pulled her hand from Pepper's grip so she could feel around the dark room and get her bearings.

There were four of those enormous filing cabinets in here. Two desks that had been stacked in front of the boarded windows. How many typewriters on the floor. Ten? Twenty? All this in one room.

The second floor had been turned into a warehouse. Storing the office equipment of decades past. It occurred to Loochie that all this stuff might be valuable in an *Antiques Roadshow* sort of way. She even tried to lift one of the typewriters, like some brave knight from a fairy tale, trying to take just one piece of treasure out of a dragon's cave. But that machine seemed to weigh fifty pounds, and Loochie couldn't see how she could haul it easily. She set it back down, and when she turned, Pepper had crouched down right beside her.

"I thought of doing the same thing," Pepper whispered, patting her shoulder consolingly.

But now, down that close to the floor, another thought occurred to both Loochie and Pepper. In a space like this, so dark and full of nooks, there should've been pests everywhere. Pepper had seen one giant rat, so why wouldn't there be thousands more? Wasn't that how rats rolled? In great numbers?

But there were none.

Nothing scurrying underfoot. No roaches moving along the walls. No spiders spinning webs in the corners. No flies. No mosquitos. The room was cluttered and chaotic, but lifeless.

Then a howl came, from the landing. A man.

"What if they're hurting Frank Waverly?" Loochie asked.

Pepper rose to his feet. "They're definitely hurting Frank Waverly," he said. He patted his surroundings, feeling for the nearest wall.

"What should we do?" Loochie asked, still crouched.

Pepper had found the door he wanted. Not the one they'd just come through, the one that led back onto the landing. The other one. The one that would take them farther away. It led out into a hallway. Pepper opened it.

"This is what we should do," he said.

He held it open for her, and Loochie, after a moment's hesitation, followed Pepper's lead. Once they both stepped through, Pepper shut the door behind him. Now the two stood right above Northwest 2. The staff, on the first floor, could they even imagine what was going on above their heads?

The lights worked here. At least a little. One bulb lighting the hallway. Maybe it was left lit as a basic safety precaution. Maybe some idiot had just forgotten to unscrew it.

Loochie and Pepper walked down the hall now, following the same floor plan as the level below. They left Mr. Mack and Frank Waverly's room. They passed Wally Gambino's. Then the empty room. All these doors were closed. And finally they reached room 5. Pepper's room. This door sat half open. As if someone (something?) had recently been inside. Had been stalking across the floor right above Pepper's head.

Pepper couldn't help it. He had to look in. Unlike the last room, this one was almost empty. Only one piece of equipment, but it was a beast. A reclining chair, like you find in a dentist's office. This one had a small crane attached at the top. The crane hung over the seat and had five metal attachments hanging down. The crane was like a wrist, the attachments enormous fingers. Pepper imagined a patient strapped into this device. Someone on his back, looking up at that rusted hand. The digits reaching down to do what? He pictured the giant, inorganic hand slowly, methodically plucking out the patient's eyes. One at a time. Say you're having trouble with your eyes? Bet you won't have that trouble now.

Pepper moved around the chair, circling it, as Loochie watched from the doorway. Whatever this machine used to do, it had once been the height of modern medicine. Ophthalmologists probably heard about it and drooled. The chance to use a PX-1000! And now it was entombed in a dark room. He doubted anyone even knew it was there anymore. *I will decay*, Pepper thought touching the abandoned machine. *I will be buried. I will be forgotten. What was my life worth?*

Pepper moved around to the spot in the ceiling that had leaked into his room. Here the floor trembled from his weight. He knelt and felt the residue of rainwater. He traced it back to one of the boarded-up windows. A piece of the board had rotted through. He thrust two fingers through the hole and felt a night breeze on his skin. It felt cool and comfortable outside. "Let's go," Pepper said.

Loochie was still in the hallway. "I'm waiting on you," she whispered.

They followed the hallway all the way to the oval room. This corresponded with the first floor, too. Right below their feet sat the nurses' station. The staff members logging files onto the computer. Talking with one another. Checking email on their phones. Living normally. Up here, in place of a nurses' station, they found only a chair on the second floor. One office chair, very old, three wheels instead of four. It tipped forward slightly, forlorn in the dim light.

When Pepper and Loochie trod across this room, they hardly lifted their feet. They moved like cross-country skiers to quiet their footfalls as they passed over the staff's heads.

They reached the hallway above Northwest 1. They walked even slower, more quietly just because they were so close.

And finally they found the air duct.

It was exactly where Dorry had drawn it on her map. It corresponded to the place right above the secure ward door.

The grill over the air duct had been lost long ago. The hole, that crawl space, sat open. The faint light from the hallway illuminated the mouth of the duct. It wasn't even that high up. Pepper would give Loochie a boost, but with a little effort she could've pulled herself up.

"Okay," Loochie said, looking at the air duct. "This is it, right? We're really here?"

Pepper took out the map as if he didn't know. He triple-checked. He shook the sheet of paper. "No question."

Loochie pulled her wig down so it was tighter on her scalp. She knelt and retied the laces of her baby-blue Nikes. When she rose again, Pepper said, "Why didn't Dorry leave?"

He wasn't really speaking to Loochie, just out loud. But she answered him anyway. "She probably couldn't climb up by herself."

"Did you see her scale that fence?" Pepper asked.

"I don't know why she didn't," Loochie told him. "But I know we can."

Loochie patted her face, opened and closed her fists. Getting her courage up. The air duct looked relatively big to her. It might be a little tight around Pepper, but she'd have a little more room to breathe.

*Why didn't Dorry leave?* Pepper couldn't let the question rest.

"Gimme a boost," Loochie said.

*Why didn't she?*

He knew why.

"I've got something I want you to do for me," Pepper said quietly.

Loochie was already at the air duct. Reaching up, she grazed the opening with her fingertips. She turned around. "What are you waiting for?"

Pepper reached into his pants. He pulled out a single glossy magazine page. It was crumpled up. He handed it to her.

"Open it," he said.

He didn't know what she would find any more than she did.

She scanned the headline. "The penguins of Antarctica," she read.

Pepper shook his head. "That's a little ambitious."

He reached into his pocket again. Pulled out another page.

"Borneo's best beaches," she said after scanning.

"Well, fuck," Pepper muttered.

He pulled a handful of magazine sheets out of one pocket. He held them up to his face so he could read each one. He snapped through them until finally he found one that seemed right.

Loochie held the paper close. "Van Gogh's Amsterdam."

"That's the one," Pepper said.

She dropped her hand. "What is this?"

"I got interested in this guy," Pepper said. "He's a painter. But they only had black-and-white versions of his stuff in the book I read. This article says they have a whole museum devoted to his stuff. I want you to go there. See his paintings. For me."

And what he didn't say, but could've added: *and for Sue.*

Loochie crumpled the article in her fist.

"See it for yourself, Pepper."

He nodded, but didn't respond to what she'd said. "You'll have to apply for a passport first," Pepper instructed. "You can do that at the post office. Then you buy a plane ticket. Then you go."

Loochie almost laughed. "Okay, fine, let's play this game. You know a passport costs money, right? And the plane ticket? You think they'll let me fly free if I ask nicely?"

Now Pepper went into his back pocket. He took out his wallet and removed a blue card. "This is my ATM card," he said. "Go to any branch. You can't take out more than a thousand a day. But take it out. It's yours." He told her the code.

She looked down at the ATM card. Why was her face feeling so warm?

"Should be four thousand dollars left," Pepper said. "But take it all out before the end of the month or else Time Warner and a few other assholes are going to take their cut. I'd be happier if you had it."

Loochie shook her head and thrust the card back at him. "I'm not . . ." she began, but couldn't finish. She raised her free hand, balled into a fist, and hit him in the chest, but there wasn't any power in it. She hit him again.

"Come on now," Pepper said.

She looked up at him. "I'm *scared* to go alone."

Pepper went down on one knee. He looped his fingers so she could put one foot in them. "You put that card and that article in your pocket," he said clearly and loudly. She was so stunned that, probably for the first time since grade school, she just did what an adult told her to do.

"Now give me your foot."

Loochie did that, too. And next thing, she was climbing into the air duct. Scrambling really. She had enough space that, if she curled herself tight, she could turn herself around. She did that, and looked down at Pepper.

Being inside the air duct, hearing the tinny echo of her movements, caused a panic to rise in Loochie. It felt like bile climbing up her throat. She shook. She almost felt angry. "Why are you doing this!" she shouted. She didn't concern herself with whether or not the staff on the first floor might hear her. "Just come on. We can both make it. Why won't you leave?!"

Far behind them there was a second howl. Even louder and, somehow, wetter. Like someone was screaming underwater. Pepper looked over his shoulder, then back to Loochie.

"I gotta go help," he said.

Loochie looked past Pepper, down the long hallway.

"You let me know that you got there," Pepper said. He waved one hand in front of her face to get her attention back. "That's how you repay me."

Loochie couldn't speak. She only nodded.

Pepper saw that, with the wig on, Loochie really looked like a new version of herself. If she walked right past him in another context, he doubted he'd even recognize her. In a way, Loochie's mother had supplied her daughter with a great disguise.

"Turn around now," he said.

Loochie focused on his face. Her eyes became less cloudy, her lips firm. "Don't tell me what to do," she whispered.

Pepper grinned. "That's the Loochie I know."

She slowly turned herself around in the air duct again. She crept forward on her belly.

Pepper watched her go. It took less than a minute before he couldn't see her in there. He listened to the squeak of her sneakers as she inched ahead. Finally Pepper turned away.

He retraced his steps.

He went back in.

# 40

PEPPER AND LOOCHIE had been right earlier, that the second floor of the unit was surprisingly critter-free. No water bugs. No gnats. No rats. (Plural.)

There was *one* rat in the entire two-story. Pepper had seen it come tumbling from the ceiling in Glenn's room. A single common rat roamed. His name was LeClair.

LeClair the Rat.

And he was old.

That point is less about his age than his inflexibility. LeClair had been at Northwest his entire life, four years. Now that might not sound so amazing, but the average rat life span is two to three years. So roughly speaking, LeClair had lived the equivalent of 120 human years.

He hadn't seen another rat, though, in over a year. (That's thirty human years.) Long ago, they'd bred on the second floor like, yes, rats. The females, called *does,* matured like rats everywhere do, reaching puberty at only six to eight weeks old. They went into heat every four to five days, for about twenty-four hours at a time. The average litter size was twelve. So you want to talk about a population explosion? If you're talking about rats, it's not even an explosion, it's an expectation.

And yet the back spaces of Northwest were barren. Why? There were three reasons: 1) New Hyde Hospital didn't make a habit of spending its money, as staff salaries and the profoundly wack-ass computer at the nurses' station should attest; but there was one expenditure that did enjoy New Hyde's enthusiastic financial support. Besides administrative salaries, which were astronomical at the very top, New Hyde paid for pest control. Nothing shuts down a hospital faster than vermin, so New Hyde paid for exterminators without hesitation. Practically had the trucks on standby. Northwest's second floor got bombarded with nerve toxin–type poisons at least twice a year. (Don't mention that to the patients on the first floor.) That's reason number one for why the second floor was so lifeless.

2) Human beings weren't the only living things the Devil stalked. It fed on warm bodies and fostered fear; rats would do just as well as humans. The Devil had been wandering these halls for years—longer than LeClair had been alive. Dropping down into a patient's room was the main course, but a passing rat might serve as an aperitif. The rats even had their own name for the beast. Not the Devil. What do rats know of such things? They called him "With Teeth." Named for the way he killed their kind. He became a kind of legend among the rats, a tale told to make children cower in the dark. But eventually, the rats grew tired of such haunted grounds. They decided to leave Northwest. To flee from With Teeth. A mass exodus.

(Spiders and roaches and all other small life following not far behind.)

So that explains why the rats fled, but not why LeClair the Rat remained behind. That's because he—LeClair the Rat—was the third reason the other rats all left, en masse. To put it bluntly, nobody liked the guy.

LeClair the Rat was profoundly intelligent. Unfortunately, he felt it was terribly important that every other rat in the world *know* this about him. He was a real bore and a pedant, but worst of all he was just a weenie. But so what, right? Why not just ignore a rat like that? Why abandon him? The problem was that LeClair was also a good scavenger. He foraged food, rummaged nesting materials—but when he returned with the goods, he wouldn't share them freely. Instead, he'd force the other rats to sit around and listen to him—all his *brilliant* thoughts—before handing over the precious materials. You say you just want to know if those kernels of corn LeClair discovered were edible? Plebeian. You'd just hoped to use these bits of shredded newspaper to line a nest? Troglodyte. Didn't you want to hear what LeClair thought about newspapers? And the dangers of how humans artificially increased the size of their corn? And, while he was at it, let him weave in the history of . . .

The point here wasn't that LeClair the Rat was hated because all the other rats were dull-witted, anti-intellectuals. (Though, of course, some were.) The point was that LeClair the Rat had *ideas,* and he divided the entire rat population into two groups: those whose ideas agreed with his and those who had none. He couldn't fathom that other rats might simply value different ideas and methods from his own. (That possibility was void, as Mr. Mack would say.)

As time passed, the other rats grew tired of their lives in Northwest: dodging the exterminators and their arsenal of poisons, cowering as With Teeth plagued the second floor, avoiding the increasingly sanctimonious LeClair. Some of the elder rats told stories of another world, someplace beyond Northwest. *Outside.* Where they might procreate and forage and procreate and die. What more could a rat ask for?

And eventually the rats did leave. Some lived in the wilds of New Hyde's poorly maintained grounds; others found their way to the main buildings of the hospital; and others reached human homes beyond the fence line and their descendants still live there now. (Sorry, but it's true.) But none of the rats ever told LeClair that they were going. He'd heard them talk about that place, *Outside,* but dismissed it as a myth. (If it was real, he would've been the one to think of it.) And one day LeClair the Rat found himself living alone on Northwest's second floor. Nearly alone. Him and With Teeth. LeClair at least knew enough to keep his distance from that one. (In fact, the day he'd come crashing through Glenn's ceiling was because With Teeth had been chasing him, trying to take a bite.)

He tried to stay brave in the face of his isolation. He didn't admit to missing his fellow rats; instead, he cultivated a growing disdain for them. And that helped him make it through the year of solitude. But today, LeClair the Rat had to finally admit the truth.

He was lonely.

He'd tried, one last time, to find purpose in his work. He'd boldly leapt out, in plain view of the humans, and *annexed* a box of sugared corn. He almost got clocked, one of the humans chopping at him with a broom, but he escaped. And returned to the second floor. He'd felt pride in his daring, but could share the story, and the cereal, with no one. That's when he came to realize that it can be honorable to stand alone, arguing for a righteous cause. But sometimes "taking a stance" becomes confused with "just being an asshole." It had taken quite awhile, but on this late night LeClair the Rat finally accepted that, long ago, he'd turned into a prick.

But today LeClair the Rat was going to change.

Could he really, though? Hard to say. At least he might try.

So that night he'd passed through every room on Northwest's second floor. Surveying the discarded furniture where he'd made his nests, the wiring he'd chewed through, it was surprisingly difficult for him to give up the grounds he'd cultivated, no matter how barren and lifeless now. He might not have gone through with it, but then he heard the humans nearby. They'd found their way into his realm. Sure, there'd been the old woman, who sometimes sprinkled bits of food on the floor for him, but this night there were a dozen humans crashing around. Howling and battling and encroaching on his territory. This, finally, was what convinced LeClair to go. He thought he might make his way to that place—*Outside*—where the other rats had gone. Maybe he would find some of them. Or maybe he would die. But at least he wouldn't be stuck in here, bereft, adrift, alone.

This is how LeClair the Rat came to be in a section of the air duct when Loochie appeared. She found that big old rat directly ahead of her.

Wow! She could *scream*. The only thing that shut her up was when the rat turned toward her. She thought LeClair the Rat might charge and bite off her nose. This threw her into a dazed silence.

She tried to turn around, or scoot backward, but pushing back only seemed to wedge her in tight. She imagined getting stuck here, unable to wriggle free, dying in a fucking pipe. She didn't know what to do. She could slide her hands up in front of her, one at a time. At the very least she could try to guard her face. Bat the big rat back if it came at her.

But what did LeClair the Rat know about this human in front of him? Zip. As far as he was concerned, this body in the air duct might be kin to With Teeth. It hadn't been able to catch LeClair, so it sent this smaller one. It wasn't only Loochie who was smacked with a sudden case of *fright*.

Loochie watched the rat.

And LeClair watched her.

Finally, the rat turned away from Loochie. It moved again.

Loochie thought she'd wait long enough to let the rat disappear. That was what her revulsion suggested she do. But she had to admit that she felt lost. The air duct hadn't just run a straight line out of the building. The air duct twisted here and there like bends in a road. She wasn't entirely sure if, at the end of her journey, she'd be looking out on a night sky or just back into the second-floor hallway, where she'd started. Pepper hadn't given her Dorry's map after all. In here, she was on her own.

In her mind, she'd already retraced her path to the bus stop in front of Sal's Famous Pizzeria. (Or whatever it had been called.) She was already looking for the tree that leaned so far over that its leaves touched the roof of one home. She was already planning on the face she'd pull when she pretended she left her MetroCard at home and could the bus driver *please* just let her ride to the depot. She imagined the letter she would write to her mother, explaining why this, as wild as it seemed, was the sanest choice she'd made for herself in many years. For all her hesitation, her fear of hurting her mother, Loochie was already determined to leave.

Then Loochie thought about that rat. *Like rats fleeing from a sinking ship.* That's the cliché, right? But the point of the line, really, is this: Life wants to live. She didn't know her way around an air duct, but she bet that rat did. If she followed it, where would it lead? Right back into the building, maybe. But in that case she wouldn't be doing any worse than she already was. But the rat might also make its way outside. And she would come tumbling after it.

Loochie followed the rat, at a distance. She could barely make it out ahead, its claws *scritching* on the air-duct metal as it moved. But she managed. And in this way, for once in his life, LeClair the Rat helped someone without being a prick about it.

Loochie reached the end of the air duct. The panel here had been knocked off by hordes of fleeing rats long ago. She saw the big gray rat slip right out. She saw the starry night ahead. She peeked out. A Dumpster sat directly below the duct, lid closed. A one-story drop. Dangerous but manageable. Even if she would have to go out hands-(and head) first.

Loochie watched the rat where it lay on the Dumpster. It surveyed the open parking lot. She shifted in the duct, making noise. The rat looked up at her. Then it shot off the Dumpster and ran into the parking lot. She watched it dart between parked cars and off into the distance. As silly as it sounds, she wished that big old rat well.

She slipped partway out of the duct. She inhaled the air, hoping it would be fresh, but nothing so poetic awaited her. She was right over a Dumpster. She smelled garbage. She hadn't reached the last step, but the next step. She looked down at the drop. She tried to breathe slowly.

She would curl into a ball, protect her head with her arms. She imagined that was the best way to do it, but she'd never tried anything like this before. Unbidden, she saw herself falling at the wrong angle. Flailing. Her head smacking the Dumpster. Her body crumpled on the ground. Bleeding out, alone. Just some trash. She couldn't stop imagining it now. She talked to herself, trying to calm down. But there is only so much that talking can do. She had to move. Right now. Right *now.*

Lucretia Gardner went out.

# 41

PEPPER LEFT THE air duct and tracked his way back down the hall. He passed the single off-kilter chair in the oval room. He reached the hall right above Northwest 2. He passed the room right above his own, the one with the machine inside. The half-open door made him scurry past, as if the big machine inside might reach out to snatch him. Then he entered the room with all the old equipment. As he felt his way through the filing cabinets, stepping over errant typewriters, he hoped Loochie was safe. Then he reached the other door. He stepped back out to the second-floor landing. Moonlight still filtered down in a beam cast through the glass eye in the pavilion's ceiling. Pepper felt as if he'd been gone from here for quite awhile. That was because Pepper didn't hear anything. Meaning that the screaming, those howls, had ceased. Just a heavy silence now.

His valiant urge had already ebbed. He should have gone with Loochie. She was probably getting on a bus right now. Already a guest of the MTA. They were shuttling her to safety. Meanwhile he was here. *You volunteered to return to this?* he asked himself. *You must be fucking crazy after all.*

Pepper walked with hunched shoulders, his head swiveling left and right. He didn't see the others until he was practically on top of them. Their backs were to him. He counted six standing together.

And farther back, in another clump were three more. He couldn't say who was who. They were all so still, so quiet, he felt like he'd stumbled across a crew of sleepwalkers.

"It's Pepper," he said, just to avoid startling them.

They didn't answer. The six people with their backs to him stood adjacent to the silver door. When Pepper got closer, he could finally hear something. This group breathed hard, grunting and panting. Their shoulders rose and fell.

Pepper walked around the group. He stood between the cluster of six people and the clump of three others. He wasn't sure who he should be wary of. From his new position he could make out the trio: Redhead Kingpin, the Haint, and Wally Gambino. Proton, neutron, electron, that's how tightly packed they were. They didn't even seem to notice Pepper. Their gazes trained intently, guardedly on the six: Doris Roberts, Heatmiser, Still Waters, Sandra Day O'Connor, Yuck-mouth, and Mr. Mack.

Pepper moved toward the larger group. His boots *squelched*, like he'd stepped in jelly. The floor between him and them was slick.

Pepper's eyes followed the trail of slickness, more like oil really. To their feet. All six of them were standing in it. There were blotches of it, like dark paint, on the fronts of their clothes. Their hands were so wet they dripped.

Of those Pepper had accounted for, Loochie and he made eleven.

"Where's Frank Waverly?" Pepper demanded.

No one answered. No one moved.

Pepper padded to the edge of the landing and looked over the railing, but Frank Waverly wasn't down there. The moonlight brightened Pepper's boots here at the edge of the landing. The soles, the toes, they were almost a reddish brown. The stuff he'd just stepped in almost looked like mud. Pepper returned to the others. Stood in front of Mr. Mack directly.

"*Where* is Frank Waverly?"

Mr. Mack raised a fist slowly. It looked like it had been dipped in balsamic vinegar.

The fingers opened. A small gold key sat on Mr. Mack's palm.

"They just . . ." Redhead Kingpin whispered.

Pepper looked back at her.

"They just . . . opened him," she said blankly.

It wasn't possible. Pepper couldn't move.

"They just . . ." Redhead Kingpin began again.

Where was Frank Waverly's body? Tossed aside, in some dark corner, like a torn candy wrapper? If breathing wasn't an involuntary function, Pepper would've choked.

Mr. Mack walked to the silver door. Triumphant. Not only did the man have numbers on his side, he also had insanity. Not mental illness, but true madness now. Mr. Mack slipped the key in the lock. The other five members crowded closer to Mr. Mack. Imagine trying to talk them down at this moment, to bring them back to the rational, even if ill, human beings they'd very recently been. Pepper doubted that even a volley of tranquilizer darts could stop those six now.

The silver door unlocked with a click as loud as a grandfather clock.

Mr. Mack waved the others back so he could open the door.

The doorway was as dark as an elevator shaft.

Pepper hadn't realized he'd stepped backward until he was beside Redhead Kingpin, and the Haint, and Wally Gambino. Those three were holding hands. Pepper joined in.

"Don't hide now," Mr. Mack taunted the darkness. "Don't run."

No movements inside the doorway. No sounds. This made Mr. Mack feel bolder. He took a step toward the open doorway, the darkened room.

"Wait." One of Mr. Mack's group called out to him. Hard to tell which one. That one seemed to be speaking for all of them. And even for the other four, watching from farther back.

Another step.

*Wait.*

But the caution of the others only fueled Mr. Mack's brashness. One more step and his foot passed through the doorway.

Then Mr. Mack lost his balance. He fell, headfirst, into the shadows. He didn't even yelp when he fell.

Mr. Mack was there and then he wasn't.

Everyone, all nine of them, just stood there, dumbstruck.

Wally Gambino was the first to break the silence.

He *laughed*.

And not a little laugh, either. A real gut-buster. He had to let go of the Haint's hand. He leaned forward with his hands on his thighs for balance. And he kept on laughing.

"Old boy took a *lump*," Wally shouted.

And that was that. The cloud that had been hanging over all of them parted. The others didn't laugh, not at all, but they'd all been teetering over a precipice just then. Wally Gambino's utterly inappropriate reaction bonked them from that edge.

"Be quiet," Pepper said, after a moment. "Listen."

They heard this low, insistent huffing coming from the darkened doorway. As a group they moved closer. The ones at the front had the good sense to brace their hands against the door frame to keep from falling in, too.

"Mr. Mack?" Pepper called.

The huffing sound rose again. Its pace quickened but then slowed. A deep breath taken. "I landed hard," a weak voice said. "On my leg."

The huffing again. Then a crinkling noise, hard to place.

"What's that other sound?" Pepper asked.

The same thing—huffing speeding up, then slowing down. A deep breath.

"I landed in a pile of plastic," Mr. Mack said.

"Plastic?" Doris Roberts asked.

"Wrappers," Mr. Mack grunted. "From those goddamn cookies they're always giving us. Got to be thousands in here."

"That's probably what broke your fall," Pepper said.

Pepper remembered Dorry tucking those cookies into her lap at every meal. She must've been bringing them to the Devil for *years*. Of course the Devil would like them, they were as vile as he was.

"How far down are you?" Doris Roberts asked.

"About ten feet, I think."

Mr. Mack had fallen to the first floor.

New Hyde Hospital, in its relentless penny-pinching, had indeed repurposed a stairwell and made it into a room. When they'd closed off the second floor, they'd seen that this stairwell would essentially go to waste. (There was a main stairwell already, on the other side of the secure door.) And they needed a room where a violent patient could be kept. Now contrary to most news reports—and the storylines of commercial television and movies—the vast majority of mentally ill people weren't remotely violent. If they hurt anyone it was usually themselves. But it was true that a very small number of mentally ill patients did cause others harm. For those patients, it was necessary to have a room where they could be sequestered. In the case of Northwest, that would've meant constructing a reinforced room. And do you know what that costs? Much more than New Hyde Hospital was willing to spend. But they were already repurposing so much of the building for its transition into a psychiatric unit, so why not be *creative*. Someone who worked with the board (it was actually that legal rep guy who'd used an iPad at Pepper's meeting after Coffee's death), suggested that a concrete stairwell could serve their needs as a holding room for any violent patient. The space already had a stainless-steel door, much more resilient than wood, and the walls were reinforced as per the fire code. All New Hyde had to do was remove the stairs. As simple as pulling teeth. Then they'd have one secure room, as legal standards demanded.

"Do you want us to try and get you out?" Pepper asked.

They listened to the huffing and let it play out its natural rise and fall. But after the inhalation of breath, there was no response.

"Mr. Mack?" Doris Roberts called.

"I'm not down here alone," he finally said.

They heard shuffling. Then a hard clopping on the concrete floor. Then a deep inhalation followed by a short puff of air, like a bodybuilder lifting a great weight up over his head. A moment after that, a heavy *whomp*, like a fully packed suitcase being slammed to the floor.

A moment after that, Mr. Mack whimpered softly.

Then in the dark, the Devil inhaled deeply again, lifted the old man up with a short puff of air. And again, the heavy *whomp* of Mr. Mack's body hitting the floor. Mr. Mack whimpered once more.

"Stop it!" one of them up on the second floor landing shouted.

"*Please,*" another said.

"Why won't you leave us alone?"

The same routine again, ending with the *whomp* of Mr. Mack's body against the floor for a third time. Every patient strained to listen, but Mr. Mack didn't even whimper this time.

They waited. What to do? Forget rescuing the old man. What about them? Each of them wanted to run, in their minds they were already sprinting, but they couldn't make their bodies move.

They heard the sounds of some new exertion from down below, in the dark room. Puffing and straining. Who else could it be but the Devil? One quality of the noise had changed, though. It was much closer now.

They all saw a shape moving down there, in the darkness. It seemed to be floating. Up from the depths. Down by their feet a pair of mottled hands appeared, gripping at the very bottom of the doorway.

It wasn't flying. It climbed.

Yuckmouth lifted his foot, as best he could in the crowded space, and stamped down on one of the hands. He landed hard with his heel. He might've done it again, but already the Devil was emerging from the open doorway. It seemed to catapult out, headfirst out of the shadows. It rammed right into Yuckmouth's guts and that was it. Yuckmouth soared backward, right over the people behind him. He landed on his side and wasn't even stunned. His survival instinct took over. Yuckmouth scrambled away on hands and knees.

And now the Devil was among them.

It moved so fast. Bashed right into Sandra Day O'Connor's back. The poor woman went facedown, hard, and the Devil trampled over her. His hooves did the most damage. One came down—*clop*—on her hand.

Doris Roberts turned back when her friend cried out in pain. That's when Doris Roberts got clipped. Not full-on impact, more like she got grazed. But one of the Devil's horns tore her exposed forearm, a gash that ran from elbow to wrist.

Now the patients were all hollering. The Devil seemed to be coughing loudly, or was it laughter? Moonlight had turned to the first rays of dawn. That new light burned the first floor orange.

Heatmiser, poor Heatmiser, he ran along the landing toward the far staircase. He took the first step down and the Devil reached him. It had built up speed. When its head connected with the small of Heatmiser's back, that mumbling kid got *clobbered*. His body went into the air and hit the wall, then he bounced off the wall and skipped down the stairs like a stone expertly tossed across a pond. Five hops and Heatmiser lay motionless on the first floor.

Still on the second floor, Pepper stood alone.

Unlike the others, he hadn't tried to flee down one of the staircases. He'd held close to the shadows along the landing.

Pepper watched as the Devil descended the far staircase. It stood over Heatmiser and snorted at him. It bumped the body with the side of its head, rolling Heatmiser onto his back. Heatmiser shivered and sputtered. The Devil looked down into its victim's face, almost daring the body to move again.

*It's just a man.*

Pepper said this to himself. He tried to play Dorry's voice in his head. She'd been so sure when she said it.

*It's just a man.*

But Pepper's eyes just wouldn't agree. Here in the pavilion, the chaos like a toxin in the air, the fear a hallucinogenic, he couldn't say what, exactly, he saw. Reality, or the reality they'd all agreed upon?

Heatmiser remained still. This disappointed the Devil. It bumped his body one more time, then abandoned it. It rushed back up the staircase to the second floor. When it did, Redhead Kingpin and Still Waters moved to Heatmiser and tried to help him up.

The Devil returned to the landing. Come to see who else it could hurt. He found the Haint, too shocked to move, too old to run. She stood there in her purple pantsuit. Her matching hat had been lost. Her hands were crossed in front of her, daintily, as if she were waiting for a streetlight to change from red to green. The Devil didn't even charge her. It didn't have to. He could lean on her and she'd snap in two. It stalked toward the old woman slowly.

But someone stepped in between the Devil and the Haint.

It was Wally Gambino.

"Nah!" he shouted at the Devil. "That's *out*. You ain't fucking with this old bird. Not while I'm around. You wanna fuck with *me*? When I was twelve I went to hell for snuffin' Jesus!"

The Haint hardly seemed to notice Wally's chivalry. She kept the same pose, hands crossed in front of her, patiently waiting. But the Devil's stance switched. Lowering its head so the horns could gore the brave kid's flesh.

*It's just a man,* Pepper repeated in his head. *It's just a man.*

Wally Gambino worked himself up. A little chemical change to the mind and body before entering combat. A mechanism as old as battling. "You know what they call me back home?" he yelled. And then silence. He'd forgotten the answer to his own question. The kid was brave, but also terrified. In that frozen moment, Pepper ran up behind the Devil and clutched it around the throat with one meaty arm. Pepper's eyes were shut. He whispered to himself, "It's only a man."

The Devil thrashed in Pepper's grip. A trapped animal, a hemmed-up human being, the same beast at that point. It hissed and flailed. It bucked. Pepper kept his eyes closed and repeated those four words—*It's only a man*—as he dragged the Devil backward. Away from all the others. Back toward the door he and Loochie had used minutes ago.

"I don't *need* you protecting me!" Wally Gambino said.

But his voice, it wavered. He sounded so relieved. He turned to the Haint. He took her by the arm and quickly led her down.

Pepper slammed into the door with his back, using his momentum and the combined weight of two bodies to force it open. The filing cabinet on the other side groaned as it fell. When it landed it sounded thunderous in Pepper's ears, like a skyscraper had been tipped over. Pepper pulled the Devil into the darkened room.

In here, alone, Pepper looked down at the figure in his arms. What did he see in the lightless gloom?

The same grand bison's head. The gray-white eyes rolling in their sockets. The long, fat pink tongue shooting out of its mouth.

"I know what you are," Pepper said. He moved backward with the Devil. Where was he taking it? (Him.) Pepper wasn't sure. Maybe he'd stuff the thing (man) inside that air duct. Let it (him) stay there, stuck, until it (he) rotted away.

Pepper pulled the Devil out into the same hallway he and Loochie had just been in. Here and there he could still see Loochie's small footprints in the dust. The bulb here cast new light on Pepper and the Devil. And when Pepper looked down, he finally saw it. Him.

No bison's head. An old man.

Pepper grunted, triumphant. He looked down into the wild eyes of an old man. The old man had a head covered with graying hair that fell as low as his shoulders. The tips of his ears peeked through his hair. He had a full graying beard, the hair knotty and unkempt. The old man's eyes were waxy and dry and red all over, with veins the color of bloodworms.

"Mr. Visserplein," Pepper said.

The old man shook his head, but it wasn't clear if he was refusing the name or trying to break free.

"You've got problems," Pepper said. "I guess that's why you're here. But you're hurting people. You're hurting us."

The old man puckered his lips. His eyes grew wet and weak tears ran down his cheeks. They dotted Pepper's forearms. Pepper didn't understand what the old man was trying to tell him. Finally, the man raised one hand and patted at Pepper's arm faintly, the one around his throat. Pepper loosened his grip and the old man *breathed*.

The old man craned his head backward so that he looked up into Pepper's face. And Pepper looked down into his.

Years ago, Pepper had dated a woman who had kid, a girl eleven months old at the time. Sometimes Pepper would hold that little girl just like this. She'd peer into his face, upside down, just like Mr. Visserplein did now. She'd seem confused by the angle at first, almost dazed, but sometimes she'd break into this smile, showing her handful of tiny teeth. And in those moments Pepper experienced such uncomplicated love for that child. She wasn't his daughter but it didn't matter at all. Her joy was a universal language. The memory of those times could make Pepper feel tender even years after he and the mother had stopped dating.

So maybe that's why Pepper experienced a jarring swelling in his throat as Mr. Visserplein stared up at him. Because Pepper realized that even this man had probably shared that same kind of smile with *his* parents. He had been a baby in someone's arms. That's all he was once. Not yet this man. And had those parents ever dreamed their baby would be dumped in a place like this? How could they? And yet here he was. Here they all were. And who would ever have guessed?

"Now that's sweet," a woman said.

Pepper looked up to find the other patients hadn't skedaddled back to their rooms. They'd regrouped. They'd followed Pepper's tracks. They were all there in the second-floor hallway. Still Waters, Redhead Kingpin. Heatmiser. The Haint. Wally Gambino. Yuckmouth, Doris Roberts, and Sandra Day O'Connor. They crowded together. They stood around Pepper and the old man.

"Now that you've got him," Redhead Kingpin said. "What are we going to do with him?"

Mr. Visserplein howled. And Pepper, without thinking, tightened his grip around the throat again.

"That's it," Heatmiser mumbled.

"Just choke him right here," Sandra Day O'Connor said plainly.

The group crowded closer, all as one. Were they grinning or was that just a trick of the dark?

"Choke him and let us listen," Redhead Kingpin said.

Pepper inched himself and the old man backward down the hall.

Wally Gambino moved to the front of the group. He landed a damn powerful kick right into Mr. Visserplein's thigh. Yuckmouth followed Wally's example, kicking Mr. Visserplein in the ribs.

Pepper tried to get up off the floor. while keeping hold of the old man and pushing backward. The other patients followed. They didn't speak but only made sounds. When Pepper looked down at the figure in his arms, he got confused. One moment, he looked down and saw the same gaunt, bearded man. But in the next, he saw the bison's head again. And the more confused he became, the more scared he felt. Mr. Visserplein was becoming the Devil again.

Heatmiser and Doris Roberts landed punches against Mr. Visserplein's chest, his spindly arms. At this point, Pepper realized he was holding the old man still so the others could pummel him. It was an old-school *beatdown*. Eight on one. They meant to kill the old man. They'd open him up, just like Frank Waverly. But what was the last thing, the only thing, Frank Waverly had said?

Pepper rose to his feet and dragged Mr. Visserplein backward, yoking the old man off his feet. He turned so the others couldn't land any more blows on Mr. Visserplein. So instead they hit him. They didn't care now. They probably didn't even notice. Pepper got to room 5. Because he'd left the door half open it was easy to slip inside. And just as quickly, he slammed the door shut with his butt. The rest were on the other side instantly, their grunts and cries muffled. Hands slammed against the door and feet kicked. The wood rattled.

"You're safe," Pepper said to the old man. "You're okay."

But Mr. Visserplein had recovered. Pepper tried to calm him, but the old man only hissed through his clenched teeth. Then, of all things, he laughed, as if this was the most fun he'd had in decades.

That was when Pepper grasped just how far gone this old man must've been. So detached from this reality that maybe all of them seemed like figments of some grand dream. As Mr. Visserplein's laughter grew louder, Pepper understood why Dorry must've snuck out of her room every night. Why she brought nourishment, even, to him. Because Dorry saw that this man wasn't monstrous, he was tragic.

The pressure on the other side of the door only increased. There were eight people over there determined to get through.

The door didn't splinter, it bent.

Pepper couldn't wait. Whatever he was going to do must be done now. But what? He guessed it had to be five or six a.m. (Six thirty-three, actually.) The morning shift and the overnight shift might all be in the building. He needed to introduce a new element. He needed to get them all—including Mr. Visserplein—away from this floor, this room. Suppose the others did kill this old man. How soon before they turned on him for helping the Devil? Then on one another?

Pepper lifted Mr. Visserplein. He carried the old man in front of him, like a baby being cradled. He ran toward the great old chair sitting in the middle of the room. The door finally gave up. The upper half cracked from the attack on the other side. The patients crowded, climbing over one another to get through the broken door.

Pepper moved around the far side of the chair. When he reached the proper spot, weak from leaked rainwater, he jumped up and down just once, as if he and Mr. Visserplein were playing on a trampoline. The floor couldn't hold their combined weight.

The floor caved in. The two of them fell through. Down to the first floor.

They landed back in Pepper's room. Mr. Visserplein provided Pepper with a bit of cushion because the old man hit the floor first. He cried out like he'd been struck by the Holy Spirit, but it was just Pepper's elbow. Considering the circumstance, Pepper didn't feel too bad about bashing the guy once in the nose.

The other patients reached the hole but had the good sense not to drop. They looked down at Pepper and the Devil and, for that moment, in the light coming through the windows of Pepper's room, even *they* saw an old man, lying on his back, blood running from his nose and across his cheeks and chin so profusely that it looked like he wore a red kerchief.

The door to Pepper's room opened. The morning shift hadn't clocked in yet, but the night shift was still there. Miss Chris, Nurse Washburn, and Scotch Tape entered the room. They saw Pepper and Mr. Visserplein from Northwest 4 on the floor. They saw a hole in the ceiling the size of a washing machine. They walked closer, looked up through the hole and saw eight other patients peering down.

"I gonna quit," Miss Chris said.

And she might. But not just then. Order must be restored and she was still on duty. The three staff members had to corral those upstairs, see to Mr. Visserplein's bloody face injuries, and call Dr. Anand to report all this wildness. Eventually they would discover the bodies of Frank Waverly and Mr. Mack, both men dead from brutal injuries. Both, somehow, would be written up as suicides.

Because of all this, no one paid attention to the enormous smile on Pepper's face for the rest of the morning. He did his best to hide it while helping the others down once Scotch Tape retrieved a service ladder. Pepper kept his face near his armpit as he reached up to steady patients on the ladder. He looked out the window, at the sunlight crossing the tops of the trees, rather than at anyone in particular. But he couldn't stop grinning.

It had taken a while, he'd certainly failed and fumbled along the way, but right now Loochie at least *might* have escaped, Mr. Visserplein—that malevolent nut—was going to live, and the other eight patients had all survived this terrible ordeal. He'd done more right than wrong tonight. He'd helped as much as he could and many had come through.

# VOLUME 4

—

# INTAKE

# 42

EVERYBODY FELT WELL rested.

This was mostly because Dr. Anand had the staff replace every patient's blood with an equal amount of tranquilizer. Or nearly that much. What else was he going to do? The fallout of the rebellion was a storm cloud of scrutiny. You're not going to lose two patients (Frank Waverly and Mr. Mack), have another five suffer serious injuries, and experience property damage that totaled $82,000 and not draw some attention.

The harm done to the building caused the most uproar. The board of New Hyde Hospital wasn't pleased to see such trouble coming out of a department that, frankly, didn't generate enough in profits. The slapdash security room for Mr. Visserplein was of particular concern. Who had allowed such a thing? It was time to appear concerned. Someone would have to be punished. That person was the legal rep who'd sat in on Pepper's meeting with Dr. Anand. Mr. iPad. He became a martyr to the cause. The *cause* being protecting New Hyde Hospital from myriad lawsuits. The man was, metaphorically, burned and buried in an unmarked grave. Only a day after he'd left New Hyde, no one at the hospital could remember the dude's name. (His name is Robert Paulson. His name is Robert Paulson.)

Dr. Anand quickly figured out that if that guy could be let go so easily, then maybe he could, too. The doctor figured he needed to prove he could get the unit back to full compliance, not running but coasting. Release the sedatives! With the patients sufficiently stupefied, he shuffled them. He turned the conference rooms in Northwest 1 into the women's bedrooms. And the long-unused rooms of Northwest 4 were aired out and turned into the men's hall. Repurposing like a motherfucker. He transferred Mr. Visserplein to New Hyde's geriatric unit, far off in the main building; pawning his troubles off on those staff members (and patients!) without a word of warning. He even oversaw the construction crews who were brought in to permanently seal off the painted-over doors and patch up the ceiling in Pepper's old room.

There was still the question of how Mr. Visserplein had been able to climb up to the second-story door. An old man doing something like that, how had he managed this? It wasn't magic. The stairs in the stairwell had been removed, yes, but not the handrails. (*You son-of-a-bitch you left the bodies and you only moved the headstones! You only moved the headstones!* That kind of thing.) (Anyway, why would they have taken the handrails out? Who, in all sanity, would imagine a patient having the determination—and the Crazy Strength—to pull himself up to the second floor that way? *Nobody*, that's who.) In the aftermath they finally removed the railing from the former stairwell, too. They cleared out the thousands of cookie wrappers. They scrubbed out lines from a song the old man had scrawled on the wall beside his bed (Welcome to where time stands still, no one leaves and no one will). In other words, Dr. Anand did some heroic reshuffling at Northwest, and he hoped this would let him keep his job. (For all his despondency earlier, he needed the salary.)

When the patients finally awoke from their medicinal slumber, became truly *aware* again, they didn't realize how much had happened while they were out.


Pepper lay in his new bed in his new room. He missed his old room. The view from this window offered little but the single tower of New

Hyde Hospital's off-white main building in the distance. It looked like a giant vanilla wafer. Pepper missed seeing the tops of the trees.

He got out of bed. He wore pajamas, top and bottom, and slipped on his light blue slipper-socks. He looked at the ceiling and listened for the creaking sound. Pepper heard nothing but the low buzz of the lights.

He went to his dresser. Had he brought all his things with him when he transferred rooms? He'd been so medicated, he could hardly remember. One set of outdoor clothes? Check. Coffee's binder? Check. Sue's blue accordion folder? The folder was there, but nothing sat inside. The two words were still there. "Nice Dream." He'd have to fill it with something new.

His boots stood beside the dresser, upright and at attention. He left them there for now.

Pepper stepped out into the hallway, and instinctively, turned left instead of right, thinking he was still on Northwest 2, but he was on Northwest 4 now. The silver door was at the end of the hall, propped open.

Pepper flinched and held his breath as he braced for the Devil (*Mr. Visserplein*) to come bounding out of the room. But that didn't happen. Pepper caught his breath again. He stared at the open door.

A light glowed inside. He walked toward the room cautiously but nobody came to stop him. He looked over his shoulder but no one paid attention. He reached the silver door. He touched the stainless steel.

He looked inside.

Imagine a concrete stairwell without stairs (and now without railings). Twenty feet up, in the ceiling, a single strong bulb cast light that filled the room. No shadows. No bed. No evidence at all that anyone had ever lived in here. Been kept here.

Pepper looked at the concrete floor, almost expecting to see Mr. Mack's small crumpled body. Or at least a bloody stain. But the floor was clean. Power-washed. All the surfaces were so bright because they'd all been repainted.

He left the room and paced back down Northwest 4 slowly. His feet hurt. So did his knees and hips. How long had he been underwater? That's how he felt. Like a man walking out of the ocean. All but drowned. His nose and eyes even stung. When he reached the nurses' station, it looked a little different. Another change courtesy of Dr. Anand. The lower half of the nurses' station was the same split-level rectangular desk but the upper half was no longer open. Shatterproof plastic panes had been installed. The nurses' station now looked *exactly* like a ghetto Chinese-food counter.

Pepper walked up to the station. Nurse Washburn sat inside.

Pepper knocked on the plastic with a little force. He wanted to believe this new partition had been put up as a joke. He'd tap it and it would tumble down harmlessly. But that didn't happen. He knocked and the plastic rattled but stayed firm. Nurse Washburn looked so small inside that clear cage.

"I'll take the General Tso's chicken," Pepper said. "Gimme an extra-spicy mustard."

Nurse Washburn, to his great surprise, grinned at him.

"You haven't seen all this yet."

"How long has it been since . . ."

He gestured toward Northwest 2, his old room, with his chin.

"Two months," she said, and looked embarrassed to tell him.

He felt a little shocked, but only a little. He remembered the passing of days. Meals eaten. Television watched. Showers taken. Smoke breaks under the maple tree. He might even have had a few conversations. Two months. Was it June?

Nurse Washburn tilted her head to the right, a look of real sympathy.

"It's no surprise," she said. "The doctor just lowered everyone's meds back to normal."

"How is Dr. Sam?"

She shook her head. "Not him. He's gone."

None of the *improvements* had helped Dr. Samuel Anand. The board of New Hyde Hospital voted to terminate his contract. He was replaced. The Devil had vanquished the doctor, too.

Aside from the new plastic shielding, the inside of the nurses' station looked largely the same. The desk phone had been returned.

Nurse Washburn sat in front of the same outdated computer screen. On either side of it were more stacks of patient records.

Pepper leaned forward. He read the names on the tabs. Gerald Mack. Frank Waverly.

"What are you doing with those?" Pepper said. "Those men are dead and gone."

Nurse Washburn, Josephine, looked down at the paperwork and back up at Pepper. "Dead, yes," she said. "But not gone, not with Equator Zero."

"Dr. Anand talked about that," Pepper said. "But he didn't explain what it meant."

Josephine rolled backward in her chair. She gestured at the computer screen. "Equator Zero is a program for filing patient records."

Pepper nodded. "What's wrong with that?"

"Not just for *keeping* records. But for *filing* them."

Pepper raised both hands, like a scale. "You like Clamato and I like Clamahto."

"New Hyde is a public hospital," Nurse Washburn said. "That means it gets city, state, and federal money to take care of its poorest patients. Which is just about all of you. No offense."

Pepper doffed an invisible cap. "Thanks."

"All these agencies pay different fees for different treatments," she continued. "And one of the reasons we *charted* so much was because we were basically writing up receipts. In the past, we would send copies of those receipts in, and the different agencies would pay the hospital."

Nurse Washburn opened one folder and waved the sheets of paper under her chin like a fan.

"But now everything is computerized. That means we don't have to send copies of anything. We just send electronic files from our computer to their computer. Then their computer authorizes money to be deposited in New Hyde's accounts. But Equator Zero is kind of like automatic billing. Once the patient is in our system, New Hyde Hospital will bill for that patient's care until the end of time."

"At least you all won't have to keep doing it yourselves every month."

Nurse Washburn put the papers back into their folder, closed it, and set it neatly at the top of a stack. "No, Pepper. You don't understand. Equator Zero will continue to charge for the care of a patient even after that patient is gone."

"Discharged?" Pepper asked.

She put her hands on the paperwork again. One on Frank Waverly's pile. One on Mr. Mack's. *"Deceased,"* she said.

"But what about when they get caught?"

*"If* they ever get caught, they'll call it a computer error. They'll repay some portion of what they made in a settlement. But the amount they take in before they're ever called out will be *ten thousand times* what they have to pay. Equator Zero makes patients profitable in perpetuity. That's how Dr. Anand put it once. You all are worth more to them missing than present. More lucrative dead than alive."

Pepper nodded appreciatively.

"Wow," he said. "That's devilish."

"Dead souls," Josephine sighed. "Good business."

And quickly, instantly, Pepper saw himself trying to tell someone about Equator Zero. Nurse Washburn, Josephine, had just offered him quite a lot. He had the name of the program, he had the names of at least four dead patients (Kofi Acholi, Doris Walczak, Frank Waverly, Gerald Mack), and if he thought back a bit, he could probably list the exact dates when they died. Compare that to the dates on the bills recently submitted in their names and you had a report—verifiable, credible, simple, clear—that could force someone else outside the walls of New Hyde to take a goddamn interest. Pepper even saw himself using Coffee's blue binder and trolling through the list of names and numbers of public officials that his friend spent so long amassing. And if those channels failed, maybe he could even try the reporter who'd written about Sue. Pepper wouldn't change Coffee's plan, just complete it.

Josephine tapped at the plastic pane, as if she was about to hand him his food order. She scanned the nurses' station.

"I've got something here for you."

Now one of the lines on the newly returned staff phone lit up. A bright red beacon on the cheap tan plastic phone. Josephine stopped searching for Pepper's item and picked it up, didn't even listen for a voice. "Be right there," she said, then hung up again.

She walked to the formerly open end of the nurses' station. There was a shatterproof plastic door there, running from ceiling to floor. Josephine slipped the red plastic key chain from a pants pocket.

Pepper walked toward the door of the nurses' station, almost like he was the nurse's escort.

"Stay where you are, Pepper." Josephine didn't sound scared like she might have a couple of months ago. She locked eyes with Pepper when she spoke, held his gaze until he nodded and backed away. She unlocked the door and stepped through, shut it again and locked it.

"That's new regulations," she told him. "I wasn't trying to snap at you."

Pepper put his hands up. "I didn't take it that way."

She nodded and, as proof of her comfort, she let him walk alongside her freely. He followed her. She began down Northwest 1, toward the front door. This was the only item on the unit that cost too much to move. Pepper passed the threshold of the hall, and Josephine put her hand out, just a millimeter away from his belly.

"No men on the women's hall," she said. "You know that."

Pepper looked at the doors of the former conference rooms.

"But then how do you get male patients in and out of the unit?"

He pointed at the front door as proof of his clear logic. And Josephine didn't fight him. She just shrugged and waved him toward her.

"That was easier than I thought," he said.

"Maybe I don't care because I'm leaving."

"You got another job?"

As she walked, she looked from side to side, from one room door to the next. The swivel of a seasoned staff member. She was leaving just as she got good at the job. "I found something a little less . . . unpredictable," she said.

"Bomb squad?" Pepper asked.

"Close!" Josephine laughed. "I joined the Army."

"Get out of here!"

"Better pay," she said. "Sad as that is. And I already feel like I've had some war training."

"That's kind of insulting," Pepper said. "But I see your point."

They reached the secure door. Josephine looked through the plastic and spoke loudly to someone on the other side. "Got to wait for the doctor to let you in!" she shouted. She shrugged as if to say, *Regulations.*

"Hey!" Pepper said. "What was it you had for me? A going-away present?"

"You're not leaving yet."

Josephine heard how harsh that sounded. "I mean that's got to be settled by the new unit head," she added. "But I don't think it'll be too long. Really. You know who's been telling the new doc that you're not ill? Miss Chris!"

"She just doesn't like me," Pepper said.

"That's true, but she wouldn't lie. She means it."

Pepper waved her off. He didn't want to start *expecting* good news. Nothing made waiting worse. At the very least, he hadn't been removed from the unit and taken to a lockup, so the original case of assaulting the officers probably had not been brought before a judge yet. Josephine walked back toward the nurses' station. Before Pepper joined her, he pressed his face to the door's window. On the other side he saw two paramedics, one man and one woman. They looked at him for a moment, standing straighter and widening their eyes. He realized they hoped he was the doctor and was about to let them in.

Pepper didn't bother trying to explain. Instead he stared at the third person out there. A big man. Not tall but wide. The polite term is heavyset. (The clinical term is *hyperobese.*) A black guy. Maybe. Or a Latin guy? Pepper couldn't say for sure. Late twenties or early thirties, his hair was kind of a wild puff and his head was down. The EMTs watched Pepper, but this heavyset guy was more interested in his own toes. He had his arms crossed. He looked thoughtful, morose, like that presidential painting of JFK. Almost identical except this guy wore a bright blue windbreaker and weighed about three hundred pounds. Pepper knocked on the little window hard enough to shake this big guy from his daze.

He looked up at Pepper. Pepper returned the stare.

Then someone tapped his back.

Pepper turned and found Dr. Barger. The man didn't smile now like he often had in Book Group. And his shirt, once open down to the chest, was buttoned to the top. He wore a tie and a frown.

"Dr. Anand had a lighter touch with patients," Dr. Barger said. "But I'm going to expect more from you."

Pepper waited to be recognized.

"Now, I want you *out* of this hallway," Dr. Barger said. "It's for the female patients only." The doctor looked at him blankly. He didn't recognize Pepper at all.

Pepper decided not to try to remind the man of the good old days in Book Group. What would be the point?

"Go," Dr. Barger commanded.

Pepper saluted.

"Yes, Captain!" Pepper said.

He returned to the nurses' station where Josephine had already let herself back in. When Pepper appeared, she was already moving charts and peeking into drawers.

"Go over there," Josephine pointed. At the end of the station, opposite the long door, was a window the size of a dinner tray. Josephine opened one last drawer, pulled something out, and came toward him. Inside the nurses' station there was a small plastic knob that she used to slide the plastic window open.

"Don't see much mail coming through here," Josephine said. "But you got a postcard last week."

"Why didn't you give it to me when it first came?"

"I couldn't have a conversation with you," Josephine explained. "You were just, *out*, you know, from the meds."

Pepper nodded and opened his hand to her, right outside the window.

"Plus, I liked looking at the picture on the front," she said. Josephine handed the postcard through. "It's by a man named Vincent

Van Gogh. Have you ever heard of him? He was a painter. A real genius."

Pepper let the postcard lie in his large palm with the image facing
him. It was in color. Bright yellow and orange. Van Gogh's *Vase with
Twelve Sunflowers.* The image so vibrant that Pepper felt the warmth
of the sun that fed those flowers. Pepper traced a finger over each
one. He lifted the card now and turned it over.

The postmark read: Amsterdam, the Netherlands.

In the space for a message he found two words, in large print (and
a punctuation mark):

"LOOCHIE LIVES!"

Pepper's heart leapt so hard, he almost didn't survive.


It's fair to say Pepper haunted the oval room. He didn't know where
else to go. His room seemed sort of lonely, but the lounge—and that
big, blaring television—just seemed to promise a different kind of
isolation.

Instead he stayed in the oval room, right by the phone alcove,
while Josephine returned to logging the paperwork that New Hyde
Hospital hoped to flip into fraudulent profits. She continued, rather
than walking off the job in protest because she needed the paychecks
that would come for another week. Frankly, she was more concerned
with how she'd pay for the elder-care home she'd found for her
mother. (She couldn't leave Mom in the house alone, after all, while
the Army deployed her to the other side of the world.)

Pepper didn't bother her again. He hovered near the phone alcove,
and every few minutes he slipped Loochie's postcard out of the breast
pocket of his pajama top and looked at it. Van Gogh's painting and
Loochie's note, which was more beautiful? (Okay, the painting, but
not by much.) Loochie was out there in the world. He felt so happy it
almost made him nauseous. He wondered where she was. Still in
Amsterdam? Back in the United States? Maybe even somewhere else
by now.

But really, it didn't matter where Loochie had gone. Didn't matter
if she'd ever face hard times again. (Of course she would, like any-

one.) For now Loochie was something she hadn't been through six years of on-and-off institutionalization. Loochie was *alive*.

Beside the phone alcove, he watched some of the other patients emerge from their rooms. He watched Northwest 1, the new women's hallway, and the female patients who turned in the wrong direction, too. Disoriented by the rearrangements. Facing the front door rather than the nurses' station and getting totally rattled until they saw Pepper, eyes so bright he shined like a lighthouse. He waved and they set course toward him.

He greeted each one, then sent him or her to the lounge. As those men and women ate breakfast—those who'd survived the terrible night—the food on their trays tasted damn near gourmet.

And finally the new admit finished his intake meeting. Dr. Barger and his team had kept the first room, right next to the secure door, as a meeting space. But since the new patient was a man, Dr. Barger escorted him all the way down Northwest 1 to the nurses' station. Dr. Barger told the new admit to wait there for Josephine, who had run to the bathroom. (Though the doctor remembered her name as *Karen*.) Then Dr. Barger returned to his team in the intake room.

The new admit hadn't responded to Dr. Barger, or anyone else during the meeting. He waited at the nurses' station now in the same pose as Pepper had seen before. Head down, arms crossed, he didn't take in the surroundings at all.

Pepper knew what he was going to do even before he began. He slipped Loochie's postcard into the breast pocket of his pajama top. There, it fortified him, like any good talisman.

Pepper approached the new guy slowly. What to say now? How to break the ice, one dude to another? Pepper didn't want to look stupid. Suppose he spoke and this guy only glared at him, or tried to bite off his nose, or laughed at him. It seemed so ridiculous to be nervous about saying hello to a stranger after what he'd been through at New Hyde. But there it was, even here, just some mundane social anxiety. Pepper rested one hand on Loochie's postcard. This made it look like he was about to recite the Pledge of Allegiance. He felt himself calm.

Now Pepper walked closer and extended his hand. "What's your name?"

The new admit left Pepper's hand hanging there. Kept his arms crossed.

"Anthony," he finally said.

"People call me Pepper." He lowered his hand.

Anthony grinned to himself. He kept his head down, but spoke loud enough to be heard.

"Is that because you give everybody the squirts?"

Pepper laughed. Anthony grinned, then returned his gaze to the floor.

At the Vincent Van Gogh Museum in Amsterdam, there's a bit of text printed on the wall of the second-floor landing. It explains Van Gogh's ambition as a painter; that Van Gogh viewed his work as a kind of "love letter" to humanity. He hoped to be a great artist, but not simply to bring praise upon himself, his talent. (Though that would've been nice, dammit.) He hoped to reflect the world's own glory, with love. An artistic impulse, but one not exclusive to artists. For instance, Coffee. For instance, Dorry. And now, Pepper. The aspiration is so rarely rewarded, or even understood, that most people don't even try. But wherever it's found, whenever it's displayed, it's an act of genius.

Soon enough Pepper would be released, but until then what would he do? Sit in his room and *wait*, or might there be more he could offer? Like now, with this new guy, so overwhelmed, so clearly scared, helpless. Pepper touched Anthony's arm lightly.

"I like to greet the new admits," he said. "You should see a friendly face first."

Pepper raised his free hand and waved as if to take in the entire world. He smiled at Anthony.

"Let me give you the tour."

# AUTHOR'S NOTE

MY WIFE GAVE birth to our first child, a son, in May 2011. We were overjoyed and exhausted. We're both writers and each of us had books due to our publishers by the end of the summer. That gave us about three months to complete our manuscripts. We were scared shitless and figured it was impossible. But with a new kid we needed money more than ever. My wife and I made a deal. We'd give each other two hours out of the apartment every day, seven days a week until September arrived and we had to return to our teaching gigs. (We ain't making a living on the writing alone!) We stuck to the schedule religiously and the pages piled up. Did we make the deadline?

Hell, no.

But we created decent routines. Leaving home for only two hours meant that I couldn't travel far. I ended up working at the Twin Donut on Broadway and 180th Street. Nine tables, no elbow room. If it was packed I'd go down to the Dunkin' Donuts on Broadway and 178th. Between my two offices sat the Port Authority, George Washington Bridge branch. When the coffee ran through me I used its wretched but reliable public bathroom. I wrote this novel in those donut shops out of necessity, not design. But this book wouldn't be what it is if I'd written it anywhere else.

Each day I had the privilege to hear, see, (and sometimes smell), a cast of characters as broad and beguiling as anything out of Dickens or *Days of Our Lives*. I'm talking about the old women trying to hand out Spanish-language editions of *The Watchtower* inside the Port Authority, the fruit and vegetable sellers lining the sidewalks between 179th and 180th, the bus drivers on their coffee breaks, the mothers rationing donuts out to their already amped-up kids, the Chinese women selling bootleg DVDs out of their handbags, the addicts panhandling cars coming off the George Washington Bridge, the twitchy men lined up for far too long at the urinals inside the Port Authority bathroom, the old Dominican men who spoke in shouts so loud that my iPod could never drown them out, the cops and the high-school kids, the tourists and the meter maids, the dude in his fifties who just came through the Twin Donut carrying a handful of knit caps and chanting, "Good hats, good hats, five dollars." All of them, and more, are in this book. A few even inspired some secondary characters at New Hyde Hospital. If I'd worked on *The Devil in Silver* someplace secluded and serene, I might've forgotten how bonkers and beautiful people can be. So thank you, Twin Donut, Dunkin' Donuts, Port Authority, and all the folks I watched file through. You people nearly wore my reclusive ass out! Also, I love you.

The same can be said (the love I mean) of my wonder-editor, Chris Jackson. This is our third book together, and by now I really can't imagine how I'd write a good book without him.

Thanks also to Julia Masnik for being so bright, warm, and really damn funny when I called in to my agent's office.

Thanks to the John Guggenheim Memorial Foundation and the MacDowell Colony for their support.

While I had personal experience visiting psychiatric units around New York City, this book demanded research to learn how the units run, and what kinds of systems keep them operable (if not always working). Dr. Monique Upton and Dr. Jennifer Mathur were kind enough to answer my many questions. Thanks also to Nina Bernstein, whose insightful reporting on the story of Xiu Ping Jiang inspired portions of Sue's story. I'm in their debt. Any mistakes or simplifications about how the mental-health system runs are mine.

My wonderful wife and closest ally, Emily Raboteau, gave me great help with this book. She also gave me our son, Geronimo, who is a badass. Little man, I knew you were dope ever since you were semen!

Being a kid from Queens means I grew up with people of every color, nationality, and faith. Among those were plenty of working-class white guys. They were my friends. But when I saw guys like them in books, movies, or television, they were usually depicted as: 1) drunks, 2) abusers, or 3) drunk abusers. The guys I'd known deserved better than those portrayals. They were as capable of goodness as anyone else. I wanted Pepper, flaws and all, to be complex and surprising, like real human beings. I'm thankful for the friends who inspired him.

The name Kofi Acholi is not a Ugandan name. This was a purposeful choice. I have a large extended family on my Ugandan side and I didn't want any of them thinking I based Kofi on them. So I used a name one would never find in real life simply to spare myself any hell at the next Ugandan picnic.

I'd like to send a heartfelt *fuck you* to St. Luke's-Roosevelt Hospital's psychiatric unit. No doubt they've long forgotten why I loathe them, but I will never forget.

Okay, I got that out of my system. But I don't want to end on a poisonous note.

While Emily was pregnant we lived in Amsterdam thanks to the Dutch Foundation for Literature. While there, we got to visit the Van Gogh Museum. The museum does a great job of drawing a visitor deeper into the story of Van Gogh's life. His work is displayed in a sort of timeline, floor by floor, until by the time you've reached one of his last paintings, *Wheat Field with Crows,* it feels as if you've really come to know the man. Those visits inspired me to pick up Van Gogh's letters. I practically devoured them and, soon enough, his spirit possessed this novel. I have to thank the Van Gogh Museum for being curated so damn well.

Finally, I thank Vincent Van Gogh aka Big Vince aka the Red Tornado. If there is an afterlife, I hope you finally got to see how much you've meant to so many.

VLV

*March 15, 2012*

# ABOUT THE AUTHOR

VICTOR LAVALLE is the author of *Slapboxing with Jesus,*
*The Ecstatic,* and *Big Machine.* He's been the recipient of
numerous awards, including the Shirley Jackson Award,
the Ernest J. Gaines Award for Literary Excellence, and
a Guggenheim Foundation Fellowship. He teaches at
Columbia University. He lives in New York with his wife
and son.

# ABOUT THE TYPE

This book was set in Minion, a 1990 Adobe Originals typeface by Robert Slimbach. Minion is inspired by classical, old-style typefaces of the late Renaissance, a period of elegant, beautiful, and highly readable type designs. Created primarily for text setting, Minion combines the aesthetic and functional qualities that make text type highly readable with the versatility of digital technology.